THE

THIEF

VINTAGE RUSSIAN LIBRARY

THE
THIEF

BY

LEONID LEONOV, *1899-*

TRANSLATED BY *Hubert Butler*

VINTAGE BOOKS : NEW YORK

1 9 6 0

Introduction

TO THE VINTAGE EDITION

LEONID LEONOV has compared the Soviet world to a new star recently launched into space. When its harsh, scorching surface cools, flowers will take root and grow—the flowers, presumably, of a humane, gracious, and literate civilization. We find in all Leonov's writing a sense of the manifold discrepancies between the remote dream (which he shares) and the far-from-perfect present, which he explores with ruthless candor. And the blast furnaces of the future, glowing below an ever-receding horizon, will not easily redeem the human deformation and moral disorder: wasted lives in his novels always measure the cost of forced progress. The way to Leonov's future is not marked by technological achievements, but by the cultivation of a new breed of man, dignified, alive, intelligent, and humane, who bears a closer resemblance to Marx's "whole man" equipped with a full range of appetites, senses, emotions, than to the conformist technicians and arid bureaucrats who are called heroes and men of the future in the USSR today.

Leonov has not waited for the earth to cool under his own feet. He has written and published steadily since the earliest days of the Soviet regime. His career is one of the longest, most prolific, and least troubled in Soviet letters. He has turned out novels, plays, and novellas, as if on order, which "cover" every important stage of Soviet development: the Civil War (*The Badgers*, 1924), the New Economic Policy (*The Thief*, 1927), the first Five-Year Plan (*Soviet River*, 1930, and *Skutarevsky*, 1932), the thirties (*Road to the Ocean*, 1935, and the play *Orchards of Polovchansk*, 1936), World War II (two plays, *Invasion*, 1942, and *Lyonushka*, 1943, and a novella, *The Taking of Velikoshumsk*, 1944), and the postwar era (*Russian Forest*, 1953).

Through these turbulent and dangerous years Leonov has avoided arrest, disgrace, and the inner disintegration that has silenced so many Soviet writers. Though his imaginative designs are often flawed by "compromise" in the resolution of dramatic issues, or by a maddening narrative indirectness and obliquity of statement, he has managed to stay within the limits of the permitted without surrendering to the stupefying orthodoxy that has governed the Soviet imagination during much of its life. He has steadily applied a genuine writer's intelligence—cultivated, critical, and ironic—to the rapidly changing world he inhabits, and out of the tension between what he sees and what he wants men to want he has fashioned the world of his fiction.

In common with other members of the small group of Soviet writers who speak to us above the clamor of ideology—Babel, Olesha, Sholokhov, and Pasternak—Leonov has established a moral center outside the politically generated values that are the standard fare of his compatriots. Leonov's extra-political mooring is in a solid sense of the continuity of human history through the shocks of political and social discontinuity. Different realms of being are in question: men's efforts to analyze, understand, and manipulate the institutional facts of their existence are separate from the needs, appetites, and aspirations of every human life and of all human lives taken together. Leonov would differ from most Western opinion in his clear belief that in his society the two will eventually coincide, that the achievements of Soviet planning will contribute ultimately to the enlargement and enrichment of human capacities. But in insisting on the separate identities of the human and of the political, Leonov betrays his dependence on the classical writers in his own tradition. Tolstoy, Dostoevsky, Turgenev, and Chekhov all defended a diffuse but immense and unyielding thing they called "life" (each would define it differently) against the categorizers and reducers of human complexity and against the men who would manipulate other men for their own good.

Leonov's second major novel, *The Thief*, appeared in 1927. It was written during and about the New Economic Policy, the officially decreed breathing spell that fell between the holocaust of Civil War and the frenzied resumption of the revolution with the first Five-Year Plan in 1929. It was a time of rest, of stocktaking, and of disillusionment. Leonov characterized the period he was writing about in *The Thief*: "Life flows on as before: the drunkard drinks, the priest prays, the beggar begs, the diplomat's wife manicures her nails, and nothing's upset. . . . The organism's growing a new skin, for it's terribly cold without one." For many the new skin looked distressingly like the old one. The resumption of private trading had spawned a new class of vulgar speculators who dismayed many early believers in the revolution. But this also meant that the Party had not yet acquired the power or the techniques to supervise and manipulate the lives of all its citizens. Nor did it aspire to. The limited freedom permitted economic enterprise extended to many areas of Soviet life. In the arts the Party made explicit, in a decree issued in 1925, its tolerance of a variety of literary approaches.

The conflicts between competing schools of literary thought during these years tended to cancel the claims of each to full hegemony over the literary imagination. The Party's neutrality and the impotence of the orthodox critics permitted a group of independent writers to seek the meaning of their country's tumultuous experience quite freely through literary forms. Leonov was foremost among them, and *The Thief* foremost among the novels produced at this time. Even then its indifference to Communist pieties came close to the limits of official tolerance. Orthodox critics reviewed the novel with harsh words at the time, and it has never been republished. But for the modern non-Soviet reader the efforts to measure its ideological fitness are of little interest. It is the sense of the complexity of human beings entirely transcending the schematic view of life held by the political revolutionary that brings the novel to our attention now as a serious and original product of the Russian humanist tradition.

The translation of experience and ideas into elaborate metaphor is central to Leonov's method. Early in the novel he may be said to have announced his major theme through the image of a blighted birch tree, one of a clump that he compares to "a band of wild girls." One of the trees has had the motto "Down with Authority" carved in its bark by a wandering revolutionary agitator before the revolution. The fate of the tree is described:

> From those fatal words, scored deep into its pith, the old birch tree sickened. The misery and suffering of men borne here upon the wind found a nightly shelter in its long and drooping branches. Through the tiny window of this inscription a terrible canker had forced its way into the birch; the wound swelled, and black and curling growths festered around its lips. The ulcer ate in deeper, destroyed the wood, and, relentlessly advancing, killed the tree. It turned this way and that, piteously rustling its leaves; it struggled against death, and, in the frenzy of the spring, shed its bark, hoping that it might slough off the accursed scar as well. A hurricane put an end to its agony, for one morning the old birch lay on the ground, its mighty trunk stretching across the whole length of the meadow; it lay in the dust, exposing its secret to the sky, and the torment of its roots. In a single night the maidens had grown old and stiff, and their leaves had lost their virgin freshness. The old tree rotted and covered the whole meadow with debris; the death-dealing words met death themselves, and fell away like a scab. Yet even in death the old tree did not surrender, for from its roots in the spring a slim and fragrant shoot sprang up.

The image of the birch is meant to apply directly to the life of Mitka Vekshin, the novel's hero, who has also been infected by the stranger's words, but the amplitude of its comment on the novel's action is much greater. It should not be read as an explicit political comment (this is where the commissar-critics go astray), but rather as a symbolic representation of the disastrous encounter between the forces of revolutionary destruction and the body of human Russia. The shock of uprooting, the disorder of the debris-strewn meadow, and the hope expressed in the new shoot of green life apply in one way or another to most of the inhabitants of Blagusha, the backwater sub-

urb of Moscow. Manyukin, the last Russian nobleman
(*barin*), is doomed beyond hope of regeneration by the
blow struck at his class roots, and acts out his disintegration before our eyes in the rule of the liar-buffoon made
familiar by Gogol and Dostoevsky. He tells lies for his
meals, or, as it sometimes seems, for the pure joy of creation, but his flow of language is also directed into the
strange testament-prophecy that is meant to outlive him.

The figure of Chikelyov bears witness to the bleak survival into the new era of the Czarist *chinovnik* (civil
servant), harsh to his inferiors and servile to his betters,
ruthlessly authoritarian in his attitudes toward society and
pathetically inadequate in his human relations. Zinka, not
so easily cast as a social type, enacts for us one humble
instance of organic adaptation, through personal tragedy
and social dislocation, to the new forms of life. Puchov,
who is finally revealed to us as a believing Christian, is
protected against the fate of the birch tree by his faith,
but his prescription for survival is not for others and is
pointedly rejected by Mitka Vekshin at the turning point
in his own life.

It is Mitka's fate that gives the novel its design. He
represents a special quality of life—strong, rebellious, gallant, intense—which must be reclaimed for the new order.
His self-recovery is complex, and has been aptly compared
to Raskolnikov's moral journey in *Crime and Punishment*.
The revolution has disoriented Mitka in more than one
way. Steeped in its delirious climate of violence, he has
killed in cold blood the captive White officer who caused
the death of his horse. Unlike the ferocious Agey who has
killed so often that he has forfeited his moral sense, Mitka
is never able to remove the act from his conscience. The
quest for expiation is one of the deepest motives in his
cryptic, erratic behavior. He has also been intoxicated by
the revolution's heady sense of dedicated purpose and its
intense battle-front comradeship. When the fighting ends
and peace seems to restore some of the worst excrescences
of the past, Mitka cannot accustom himself to the stagnant, unheroic atmosphere of the N.E.P. He is driven
underground by a hopeless need to recapture the past.

Still responsive to the motto with which he was scarred
in his youth—"Down with Authority"—Mitka pursues his

multiple quest in the role of a daring and resourceful thief. The ground movement of the novel, then, is in Mitka's effort to recover his moral identity, to discharge the burden of guilt, and to release himself from the past. As we are never permitted the interior view we have of Raskolnikov, we must follow Mitka through a series of external experiences, encounters, and interviews, each of which contributes a small but vital element to his reclamation. Thus, his visit to the country cuts him off from his peasant past and his childhood, but restores in him the capacity to live harmoniously in the world of nature. His final encounter with Masha Dolomanova makes it clear that there is no resolution of the implacable conflict of prides which their love has become. Most important is his final encounter with his wartime orderly, Sanka the Bicycle. When he discovers that Sanka is betraying him and his gang to the police he loses forever the living symbol of his nostalgia for Civil War heroics and discovers at the same time that in his arrogance he has become a far more destructive kind of thief—a plunderer and despoiler of human souls. Plunged finally into a delirious fever by the painful sequence of shocks and discoveries, he emerges from it purged of his guilts and illusions with the way to a new life open before him. He has also begun to formulate in the later stages of his underground journey—and this might be missed by the modern American reader—the terms of his personal accommodation to the revolution. Thus, to name but one instance, he discovers during his visit to his native village that the revolution can mean the direct application of intelligence and authority to the hitherto meaningless stream of human history. The new life toward which he moves takes place beyond the limits of the novel, we are told in close paraphrase of Dostoevsky's final paragraph in *Crime and Punishment*, and will include presumably the full application of Mitka's fund of heroic energy to the support of the new order.

Leonov has complicated and enriched his narrative by including the device of a novel within a novel. Firsov, the novelist-character, serves as a recording sensibility close to the center of events, and as a philosophizing voice that comments on the action as none of the other characters can. But it must not be thought that Firsov is simply a spokesman for Leonov. The "novel" that Firsov "writes" seriously distorts "real" events at important moments, and Leonov is able to deepen the reader's understanding by pointing to Firsov's misinterpretations and falsifications. By writing a novel about how a novel is written at that time, Leonov has provided himself with a unique vantage from which to comment on the literary scene in the Soviet Union. Firsov's novel is criticized by Leonov as typical of a school that embellishes and sentimentalizes reality to gain cheap literary effects. By "publishing" and "reviewing" Firsov's work before his own is finished, Leonov is able to give an acid summary of clichéd critical attitudes, to anticipate criticism of his own work, and to tell us something of his own literary values.

In one of the literary digressions in *The Thief*, a principle is enunciated that accounts in part for Leonov's achievement in a world where the prosperity of art was never certain: "an artistically honest work can scarcely ever be ideologically false." Leonov's hopeful formulation, shared by a number of other independent writers at that time, was to have no lasting currency in the Soviet Union. But the order of values implicit in it suggests that in *The Thief* Leonov was exercising his right to write freely and well and independently of the claims of total politics. Leonov is certainly not anti-Communist, nor is he anti-political, as Pasternak is. The revolution is present in the novel as a remote and inarticulate force. It causes terrible human damage in the pursuit of its aims, but requires neither justification nor apology. The point is that Leonov holds his focus steadily on the human creatures in the foreground, on the riddle of life as it is lived, which has always been the subject matter, after all, of good Russian novels.

RUFUS W. MATHEWSON, JR.

Columbia University
1960

Contents

P R O L O G U E

A CITIZEN in a checked ulster stepped out of the empty tram car, and, lighting a cigarette, peered thoughtfully over the rim of his big spectacles. He was wondering where tramline 14 and his erratic profession had landed him, but even the sharp-eyed traffic policeman could detect nothing suspicious about his loitering. His round glasses and ulster made him look like a learned foreigner, and his whole appearance was bizarre. On closer examination, however, he proved to be unshaven, and lumbered along uneasily in his hobnail boots, while his "foreign" ulster was the homeliest of articles, drolly suggestive of an ancient carriage rug.

It was a desolate, God-forsaken corner of Moscow, and the two dilapidated old posts of the Semyonovsky turnpike, mottled with green mold, looked as if they had been soused in cabbage soup.

The citizen made a bee-line for the policeman, and cautiously touched his rough serge sleeve.

"Tell me, Comrade," he began politely, glancing as he spoke at the low dwellings that nestled along the Ismailovsky Avenue, "is this Blagusha?"

"What street are you looking for? There are twenty-two here and three Hapilov Streets. Moscow's the limit!" The policeman smiled, encouraged by the citizen's tactful surprise. "Why, there are seventeen cemeteries here, not to speak of forty-nine police stations!"

The man in the ulster thought for a moment. "Yes, and . . . and how many thieves' dens on your beat?" he asked, cautiously clearing his throat.

The policeman frowned and took a step back, but at the same instant a huge truck, full of empty barrels, stuck on the tramline, and in a moment the barrels were rumbling gaily through the dirt of the autumn streets.

As the citizen did not have the courage to insist on an answer to his question, he stepped onto the pavement and walked off like any other pedestrian along the interminable street. The whole way not a single flicker of curiosity crossed his face, nor does everyday life in Blagusha offer much that is noteworthy. In summer, at least, everything here is covered with green, and the eye is gladdened by a pockmarked poplar struggling upward in every garden, or a barren, battered currant bush, whose dusty leaves will one day brew schnapps for the tipsy stocking weavers of Blagusha. At this time of the year, though, geese pasture here in the frosted grass, and there is nobody to scare them with his step. Workmen's dwellings jostle each other familiarly on either side of the road. The eye rests on a gaily painted inn sign, and then on the fading greenery with its thin coat of frost, but can find nothing to betray the hidden soul of Blagusha.

In a small, almost empty side street the wanderer caught sight of a respectable-looking person in a canvas cap and green gaiters, who sat on the steps of a grocery store, and looked drowsily at the checked apparition across the road. There was nothing to do but take a seat beside him.

"Have you come out for a breather?" asked the man in the ulster, his sharp eyes masked by the impersonal twinkle of his spectacles, dropping down beside Green Gaiters. "There's nothing like watching the grass grow after the daily grind."

"I was promised some vodka, and now I'm waiting for it," the other replied tersely in a husky voice.

"Your quarter's got a nice, lazy name, Bla-gu-sha. There's a real old Russian sound about it. I bet they'll change it now," said the Ulster thoughtfully, and offered his companion a cigarette, which he took without the smallest glimmer of surprise or gratitude. "It's awfully quiet here."

"They've been taking their dead along this way—that's why it's so quiet. The Reds and the Whites, both. Anyway it's a poor life here."

There was to be no easy flow of conversation, it was evident, and the wanderer shivered, for the cold could creep without difficulty through the great, worn cheeks of his ulster. All the same he made an heroic attempt to rouse his surly neighbor.

"I wonder if you've heard of me—my name's Firsov."

"Ah?" said the workman without enthusiasm. "I had an uncle, but no"—he stopped—"no, my uncle's name was Fomin . . . yes, Fomin."

In front of them wound a shallow ditch and behind it lay market gardens and behind the market gardens rustled the forest. On the threshold stood November with its piercing cold. The sun turned away from the earth. The rivers clothed themselves in mail. In the bare trees the stream of sap slowed down, and the earth grew hard as a nut that shelters its kernel from the foul weather. Who was Firsov? Perhaps he was a contractor who jerrybuilt on vacated sites, or a clever police spy, or perhaps he was an observer of life. Perhaps, with that careful scrutiny of his, he was even now selecting a plot on which to build his imaginary houses? His unsociable neighbor had long ago departed, despairing of getting drunk today, but Firsov sat on alone with himself. Somewhere in him there flowed a gentle stream of thought that gladdened and enriched his soul.

"Out there lie wide stretches of land that no one has built on, amply large enough for a man to come into the world, to endure his appointed lot of suffering, and to pass away. Up above in space the stars rush in all directions along their thousand times repeated tracks. Below is man —is life. And without life—how meaningless and empty would everything be! In filling the world with himself and his unhappiness, man creates it anew. . . .

"Houses and trees rise here, a dog runs by, a man goes past. Leaves, frozen till they are brittle and tinkling, drive down, and pile themselves in rustling heaps. Everything is bound in a whole by a knot that cannot be loosed. If the leaves did not fall from the trees, the cutting wind would not blow, for what could it do alone in an empty field?"

The first snowflake danced down from the sky, whirling through the air. Firsov caught it in his palm and observed it attentively. As it thawed, it had a wistful, timid look like a tear. Suddenly a breath of cold and darkness struck him sharp in the face. Birds black as soot, which had hidden themselves among the frosty skeletons of the market gardens, flew up noisily, and their cry proclaimed the approach of winter. And then Firsov saw things as they really were.

BOOK

1

EVERYTHING was clear and intelligible to Nikolka Zavari-hin. The life of the capital stood in bold relief before his eyes, and although the densely falling snow was thickening into a veritable storm, Nikolka saw it all as if under a magnifying glass.

This city, raised by piling insensible stone on stone, in-carnated a sort of relative eternity. Engines of steel rolled backward and forward on the stone, wearing it away and wearing themselves in turn to dust, and, as if imitating these, men themselves went through a ceaseless round of movement. Nikolka hated the city for this convulsive haste, and viewed it with a countryman's instinctive dis-trust. Although this was not his first visit to the city, yet, as before, his soul was captivated by its inexhaustible, cor-rupting loveliness. It was in vain that ear and eye and nose called to him in rivalry: "She is your enemy—she will be-tray you—and torment you to death—do not trust her!" It was with his instinct, more than with his mind, that Nikolka apprehended the forms of life; it was the instinct of the animal that sniffs out cold and danger, the length of the road and the welcome smell of the prey.

Nikolka had slept through the arrival of the train, and did not waken until the rhythmic swayings of the carriage, which had soothed his healthy slumbers through the night, abruptly ceased. He sneezed in the tobacco-laden air and looked down from the upper bunk; the carriage was empty, and through the window peeped an unappetizing view of Moscow. Still under the balmy spell of his dream phan-toms, Nikolka left the carriage, yawning. A little lump of snow slid over his sleep-flushed cheeks, and he found its thawing extraordinarily agreeable. Then he took a few steps and stopped dead—the sight that met his eyes was as startling as a vision.

He saw her sitting in the middle of the empty platform, in the wan snowy light of early dawn—the woman he had seen so often in his dreams—she was sitting and crying; and Nikolka felt that he was still dreaming. A woolly scarf lay round her shoulders, and her dark, untidy hair had a sprinkling of fine snow; her fur coat was flung back as if with a gesture of despair. Her tears could not disfigure the beauty of her face, but made her adorable and familiar to Zavarihin, who had seen so many tears in his short life. After the night in the railway carriage, in which desires that were senseless in the light of day had taken solid shape, his body cried out for love. . . . His instinctive distrust of women, from whom he had jealously guarded his strength, gave place to a mad tenderness. He was stunned by the beauty of the unknown woman, and he could offer no resistance to this sudden enchantment. His face clouded, his breath failed, and his heart opened like the abyss that swallows a falling stone.

He would not have dared to speak to her had she not turned and overwhelmed him with impatient entreaties. She waved her hand toward the melting snow drifts, and her pink, manicured nails excited his imagination—it would be nice, he thought, even to be scratched by them. At last, when he grasped that some thief had snatched her bag from her, he lost his head, and with a generous gesture threw his basket at her feet. He shouted to her to look after it (he felt as if it were himself he had thrown down before her), and then bolted across the scrunching snow after her bag.

To his heated fancy it seemed that someone was running between the carriages as if to escape. Rage lent wings to his feet, and it was not till he recognized the man, whom he soon overhauled, as the guard of the shift that had just been relieved, that he stopped and noisily drew breath. He felt certain now that he had behaved like a fool —the old hatred of his fathers for the city overwhelmed him again, and he looked with the cold eyes of reason on the woman, who had been touched neither by his impul-

siveness nor by his poverty. He had some trouble in finding again the scene of his misplaced sympathy. The snow
was falling thicker, and blurred yet more the faint, confused traces on the platform.

"It's all nonsense!" he said aloud, and the broad cleft
of his mouth narrowed down till a knife blade could
scarcely have passed between his tight-pressed lips. His
rage sank, and gave place to scorn. From his short fur coat
he drew the half of a home-made cake, and, chewing it
sulkily, took stock of everything. On his face, which his
jauntily twirled mustaches made more redoubtable, there
was an expression of haughty distrust. Just so does a spy
look at the treacherous gate of a foreign city—"All nonsense!" he repeated, smiling.

"What is made by man cannot last." Nikolka remembered his dead father's words, as he looked at the masses
of iron and stone that had been shattered to fragments,
and then piled up again in massive and wonderful shapes
to suit the taste and the needs of those town dwellers.

The dead man had frowned, and, stroking his beard,
had gone on: "We don't see the real world, but only the
world that men's hands have made, and men's hands are
the awfullest things in the world. There are sticky hands
and long hands, and hairy and crooked ones, and bestial
and tyrannical ones, and hands with every sort of filth
on them." For Nikolka his father embodied the stillness
of the virgin forests and the untrodden snowfields that to
this day slept around his home.

The shunting engines, snorting and clanking with me-
chanical fury, rushed up and down the lines; tirelessly
steel rubbed against steel. One of them, with swelling
breast bathed in oily sweat, glided by Nikolka as he stood
chewing, but he barely flinched. Somewhere not far off
a bell pealed shrilly, forlorn and despairing like a caged
bird. Dully he strove to recapture the details of his meeting with the woman, but all that his memory could
recover was the scornful yet melancholy expression that
played around her eyes. There was something strange in
his sudden capitulation, but everything about him was
strange . . . the quiet gleam in his cruel gray eyes, the
leather edging on his elegant felt boots, the orange color
of his fur-lined coat, the rainbow colors of his gloves,

which were bright, as if their maker had sung as he made them.

A change was to come over Nikolka's feelings as he grew. At first, while he was still young, he kept thinking of the woman with a jealous longing; he thirsted to possess her. Later on, when in his prime he shaved off his patriarchal beard, and, leaving his village forever, trafficked in hemp and flax, finally bringing honor and fame, even in foreign lands, to his obscure peasant stock, then it was with quiet grief that he remembered the vision of his youth. That ecstasy that had warmed and enriched his soul was never again to return. Overlaid with experience and knowledge, he had long squandered the heat of his passion on things of no account. In such moments the head of the firm, the lord of flax and hemp, would shut his eyes, stretch himself in his armchair, and sit motionless as a corpse, jealously guarding his bitter silence.

And though in later days lovely Manka "the Snowstorm" lived and loved and wasted away near him, in all that time he only met her once again. Even as an old man Nikolka Zavarihin hid sternly, even from himself, his one tenderness, and never searched for her.

IN AN old dilapidated house in Shishov Street in Blagusha lived Nikolka Zavarihin's uncle, Yemelyan Puchov, a master locksmith and an honest man. The signboard that hung askew over the small door of his workshop did not advertise his qualities, for on the left side of it an ochre-colored Turk was smoking a pipe, and on the right smoked an inextinguishable primus stove; it was impossible to say which of the two smoked the most. In the middle of all this smoke there stood, defaced by sun and rain, the single ridiculous word—"Pnchov."* Yemelyan, who six years before had painted this signboard with his own hands, had suddenly forgotten which way up the loop of the letter "u" should go. Master Puchov was a simple fellow, who went his own straight course in life. His acquaintances had no preciser knowledge of him, and perhaps this was the better for them, for it is unwise to peer too closely at one's neighbors.

All the same there was a great deal of tittle-tattle circulating about him, based on the whimsical snubs he dealt the busybodies. They said that a little maggot lived in Puchov's ear; it had crept in there many, many years before, when Puchov was still fond of drink. In bad weather it began to creep around (that was when his back ached so much), and kept on creeping till the first rays of the sun. People might exchange winks over this strange tale, but they could get no nearer to solving the riddle of Puchov's mysterious existence; and that was well

* The joke involved here is untranslatable, being a play on the Russian word for the sound of a sneeze. (Editor's note.)

for them, for it is best to know no more of a man than he shows you himself. Even his closest friend, Mitka, did not know much more of Puchov; he knew that he had been living a long time alone with his metals, and had taken on their reticence and reserve; he knew that after his military service Puchov had tried to wear the cowl— but it had not been to his taste, and so he had escaped limping from the sacred precincts, for he had injured his foot in the monastery. Then, he knew, Puchov had earned his living in a stamp factory, but there too he had not been happy. He had given it up, and gone away. An interval of a few dark years, and then the hand-painted Turk had begun to smoke on the signboard, to the amusement of toil-worn Blagusha and to the delight of the author with his notebook.

As he was always busy, Puchov was none the worse for his loneliness. He was not a learned man, yet he had learned some things, and could master the most complicated technical drawing. His mind, like his hands, was endowed with an amazing gift for tackling anything. He knew how to solder a samovar, to draw a tooth, to plate a church candlestick, to cure pimples or habitual drunkenness. He had no sooner displayed his many attainments in Blagusha than the neighborhood expressed its deepest astonishment and gratitude, and looked on Puchov as a great master. There could have been no Blagusha without Puchov, and without Blagusha what would Moscow have been?

In the eternal twilight of Puchov's house, under the cracked ceiling, the primus stove hissed interminably, warming a teapot or heating the melting pot. Everything in the room, even he himself with his bushy brows, his squat figure, and his black hair (peasants, who stand nearest to Nature, keep the color of their hair longest), everything was steeped in the foul smell of sulphur, which produced an almost nauseating stench when it came in contact with old tin. In the corners piles of scrap iron rusted: it was difficult to keep from sneezing. A samovar with a dent in its side appealed for one's sympathy, and amongst the other clutter was a waterpipe shaped like a knee with incredible twists in it. There was a machine on wheels, of which it was hard to say whether it was a part of something, or the whole. Over all those monstrosities Master Puchov now presided, and not far from him sat his nephew fiddling with the anvil.

"I had some presents for you in the basket." Nikolka was still grumbling over the morning's misfortune, but he omitted to give any more intimate details of his misadventure. The windows were covered with snow, and fresh snow was still falling, buffeted by gusts of wind. "Look at the storm!"

"Did your mother have a peaceful end?" asked Puchov, slamming an iron stove door.

"She was ill from Easter till autumn—that's what kept me back in the village. I want to start a small business. . . . Will you give me your blessing?"

Puchov was silent. In spite of their relationship through Nikolka's mother, there was little sympathy between them because of their contrasting characters. The congenital greed of the Zavarihins was alien to Puchov's generous heart. The Zavarihins strove to wrest what they could from each day as though they had stolen it from someone. They lived long, for they treated themselves seriously, and their neighbors coldly. Grandfather, father, son—the three of them stood in Puchov's mind as solid as a row of tarred oak posts. Fate might treat them badly, but they never complained; they would face up to it again without a murmur, or any need for Puchov's sympathy. In any case, Nikolka, intoxicated with his own power, never noticed his uncle's antipathy: he made straight for his goal, which beckoned to him from afar, took little interest in the men he might meet on his way, and strove to keep all useless rubbish out of the roomy cupboard of his soul.

"Can't you chuck away some of this lumber you have cluttering up the place? Lord, what a life! . . . Aren't you fed up?"

He began to button up his short skin jacket, but at the same moment the door opened, and in stepped a huge man in a long cloak and a hood thickly covered with snow. The face that looked from under the hood had sharp, almost ascetic features, and a beard so black that it was hard to believe it was real. The man smacked and sucked his lips, and his blinking eyes explored every cor-

ner of the room. When, with icy indifference, his glance
fell on Nikolka, the young man felt a strange embarrassment rising up in him.

"Hallo!" said the newcomer gruffly, and cleared his
throat. "Still tinkering away? Puchov, I don't believe you
care a hang for any of us!"

But Puchov worked away at his bench without stopping. He looked his visitor in the face, but ignored his
greeting, and replied to Nikolka: "You say I ought to
chuck all that out," he pointed at the heap of rusty iron.
"Well, it's only a small job I have here, but I can't shirk
it because of that—a piece of tin's a piece of tin. Don't
turn up your nose at my work, my boy! Every knock
means a kopek, and a kopek's not to be sneezed at nowadays. . . . One can just keep body and soul together,"
he added, and Nikolka cast a side glance at the old man
blinking at the other side of the room.

"Who've you got here?" the newcomer inquired
abruptly, pointing at Nikolka. "He seems to be making
himself at home all right. . . ."

"He's one of my folk," Puchov answered hoarsely.
"He's my nephew. He's come in from the country today."

"Oh, a new chap!" cried the guest, and gave a quick
poke with his finger at Nikolka's embroidered shirt front.
"A beefy lad!" He laughed, and in his laugh there was a
husky rattle of catarrh. He walked up to where Nikolka
sat, and his gigantic body towered over him. . . . "If
you're in difficulties, come along to me—there's room
enough for all up at Artemy's." Suddenly from under his
soaking cloak he drew out the thin worm of a schnapps
condenser and passed it to Puchov. . . . "Mend it, will
you? . . ."

"Do you still make schnapps, Artemy?" Puchov gave
a wry smile. He took the pipe, and in a moment a volley
of tools resounded; they rasped and screeched in Puchov's
black hands, and soon the pipe was ready again to squeeze
out its gay poison.

"Mitka's been let out. He's grown terribly thin. He
was asking if the primus man was still alive," Artemy announced, and waited for Puchov to ask a question, but
none came. "Well, well . . . there's a terrible gale.
You'd better keep an eye on your Turk."

"Maybe," answered Puchov dryly as he shredded to pieces a wick he had accidentally come upon.

Artemy was preparing to leave when the doorbell rang, and a new visitor appeared. Covered from head to foot in snow, and as grotesque as a scarecrow, the man in the checked ulster stood on the doorstep and fidgeted with his spectacles, from which he was trying to wipe the mist. He screwed up his eyes shortsightedly, and looked at the machine on the wheels. He felt hostility in the sudden silence, so his voice sounded affected and faltering.

"Er . . ." he said, and coughed to maintain his dignity. "Could you mend my primus for me? It has always burned well, you know, but today it's leaking and won't burn."

"I must see the primus first," Puchov explained stiffly, and stepped out from behind his workbench.

"I'll bring it round tomorrow. My name's Firsov. . . . I live not far from here," the new arrival explained in suspicious haste. "I've a child's bath, too, to be mended. . . . I'll bring it along at the same time—no—perhaps I won't bother with the bath, I'll just bring you the primus! I just happened to be passing your way, so I thought I'd come in and inquire. . . . Yes, the snow's frightful!" Saying this, he opened the door wide, and left Puchov's workshop almost at a run.

Artemy stepped quickly to the window, but could not follow the checked ulster even to the other side of the street, for the window was shrouded by the glittering snow.

"That's a queer fish!" said Nikolka, shaking his head after a moment's silence.

"Poking his nose in where he's not wanted. My head was fit to burst with the cold, so I got myself this hood, you see," Artemy grumbled discontentedly, and concealed his head in it. "Take care, Puchov!"

"Take care about what? I've no secrets," murmured Puchov, and took off his tarred apron.

Midday approached, and Puchov's dinner hour, when he left his iron alone for a bit. Artemy had gone some time before, and Nikolka sat on, yawning as usual, without insisting on an answer to his searching questions about Artemy. Puchov put out the primus, and the workshop became unusually quiet. He stood there a moment and gazed at the four damp, dirty walls as if he wished to estimate how much noise was still to be extracted from all the iron that lay piled up against them. He seemed to be listening intently.

"How's the maggot?" inquired Nikolka facetiously, and got up from the log of wood on which he was sitting.

"A bit frisky!" answered Puchov jestingly, and thought of Firsov. His eyes, as keen as a hawk's, had easily pierced through the stranger's outer shell and reached the man that lay behind. . . . Yet Puchov could not find any harm either in the shabby ulster or the soaking boots, and he grew ashamed of his intentional rudeness.

"Master Puchov, the man from Blagusha"—that was how Firsov enthusiastically described him later in his story. "The world would have been a worse place without his sharp, scornful glance from under his black Tartar brows. To him came restless ne'er-do-wells, and men whose hearts had been hardened by undeserved misfortune, men who had been driven to shamelessness, and men who had lost all trust in themselves. Often Puchov laughed at them, but he loved even when he disbelieved, and this gave him the right to smile at the whole world. He did not turn away Mitka when he came to him empty and a pariah. He cherished no grudge against Agey, though often he wished his death, as a mother wishes it for her misbegotten child. He gave shelter to Pugel when he had sunk to the depths, and kept him with the work of his hands. And many other creatures, inarticulate and unblessed, got from Puchov a friendly word that never left a sting.

"In his soul he was tranquil, as men are tranquil who see far. From his youth up, Master Puchov had felt this urge toward composure and tranquillity, and had given his heart to the joiner's trade—he loved the shavings that curled up with their gay fragrance beneath his chisel. In secret, though, he believed in the existence of a country where there grow golden trees, and birds trill all day long from silver throats. Perhaps it was only to realize more richly the mighty meaning of Peace that he had sentenced himself to the locksmith's craft and the companionship of violent men.

"And when, finally, he attained the peace he longed for, and lay stretched and stiff like a soldier at an imperial parade, there was no one there to disturb him; no one came to escort him to the graveyard. Only Pugel followed the coffin, driven wild and desperate by his burden of bereavements. Not even Mitka Vekshim, the friend of his heart, accompanied him."

EXCEPT for a few samples of hemp and embroidery and felt boots, the products for which Nikolka's home was famed, there had been nothing in the stolen basket. It was not because of the theft that Nikolka had had to abandon all the high hopes with which he had come to the city. He had called on country folk from his own parts and had been told by them that the ready money he had at his disposal, though it might seem wealth untold in the village, was not sufficient for setting up in business; so Nikolka had begun to drink.

After leaving his uncle in the evening, he wandered off, as chance led him, into the farthest quarters of the city, and kept to the dark streets, where he would not have to blush so much for the artless gaiety of his short skin coat. Lured by shafts of light that fell across the darkness of the dirty pavement, he turned the corner and realized suddenly where he was going. A bright lantern swayed in the wind in front of a green signboard, and through the misted windowpanes there shone a promise of warmth and fellowship. He drew his coat closer around him and smoothed out the creases, so that suddenly he seemed taller and slimmer. Drops of melting snow fell down from the roof and splashed on his skin coat as he hesitated. Finally they drove him inside.

The small, narrow room was filled to the door with smells and sounds and men and lights. On the platform a comedian in a striped costume was singing comic songs about love, and stamping the boards with his patent-leather boots. It was only in the back room, where there was less light and the faces of the customers looked consequently more mysterious, that Nikolka could find a small table for himself. This room looked like Sodom without its merriment. Tipsy men called to each other from the corners; they jeered and quarreled and bragged, but for the time being their squabbling had not taken a serious turn. Thick clouds of smoke shrouded the foliage of an artificial palm, and a few bad pictures were hung upon the walls with artistic negligence. This evening orgy looked as if it were being held at the bottom of a deep well from which there was no way out; and the customers, who were used to it, no longer looked upward. They were all of them casual pleasure-seekers, blown here by the wind, as the waiter Alexey, a fellow with well-greased hair and a face as spotty as his napkin, explained to Nikolka with a tired laugh.

"So you're from Saratov, then?" Nikolka asked him excitedly as he munched some soaked peas. "I hear the chaps there have swapped a church for a harmonium. . . . Were you in that? They're a tough crowd there, but they know which side their bread's buttered, all right."

"My folk never had any land because they were all waiters. My family's gone the round of the restaurants up and down . . . proper wanderers!" Alexey said bitterly, and made to rush away, but Zavarihin held him back by the sleeve.

"Mate," he whispered with a glance around him, "what sort of fellows are these . . . are they thieves?"

"Thieves!" replied the waiter in a loud voice. "That's a good 'un! Today's Saturday, and everyone's out for a bit of fun—life's hard, you know." Alexey expressed his sympathy with a slight roll of the eye. "And we've got a cabaret here, too, you know, and girls. A very decent crowd comes here. We've got a writer over there sitting in the corner. Do you hear his pen scratching? He writes all kinds of things down from life."

"Where?" Nikolka craned forward, for he could see nothing except the checked ulster; but the boy escaped and ran off.

Nikolka knew country alehouses where one could quench one's thirst with tea or strong cabbage soup, and if one got drunk occasionally it was in noisy good fellowship and there was nothing vicious about it. But here men's eyes looked dull, as if they saw everything through a cloud of smoke, behind which they hid themselves from the truth of the coming day. This truth promised them no good, none whatever, indeed, but all the same it attracted them as a magnet draws a tiny piece of iron filing to itself. In the tumult of their unbridled excesses they clutched at the flying moment, for they felt, with sinking hearts, that a single pause in their headlong rush to the abyss would break them into tiny fragments. It was impossible for a stranger to look without secret panic on these ravaged faces; Nikolka was perplexed, and when a shy, quiet, insignificant girl offered him a pinch of snuff, he pushed away her hand with an angry glance and leaned back against the wall in disgust and bewilderment. The girl slipped past him like a mouse, with the traces of her foul disease in her hollow eyes. Nikolka, who had to go out, got up, and not till then did he notice with astonishment that he was drunk.

When he returned again, more visitors had arrived, and in the thickening atmosphere the din grew greater. In a moment, one felt, the sharp stench of food must congeal and fall down in gray flakes like snow. Zavarihin shifted his chair so that he could see the stage. A conjurer with a dirty face had some time ago taken the place of the striped clown, and after him came a strapping female in wide trousers and a sleeveless blouse. . . . She was almost beautiful, she was so huge and well-proportioned and had such red cheeks. In a deep, vibrating voice she sang songs about convict labor; she crossed her arms over her deep bosom, or wrung her hands in feigned despair, or opened them wide, as if she were giving herself to the two low-browed harmonica players who sat on either side. She was well known here, Zinka of the sweet voice, and it was no wonder that the bull-necked fellow in the smart skin coat twirled his mustache complacently, and in a cheerful, tipsy voice kept on asking for more beer and songs. In a deep silence, modulating the tremolo of the harmonica players with her hand, and with one plain gold brooch sparkling on her breast, she sang the famous song: "I have given myself to sin—I, your bright queen." The eyes of her audience, which swayed in time to her song, glowed with enthusiasm. A drunken rough hidden in a corner started to cry and stared with lusterless, protruding eyes at Zinka's buxom charms. Nikolka sat on by his unfinished beer, spellbound by the song and unwilling to exchange the cozy stuffiness of the café for the wet and dirty streets and the company of his unsociable uncle. Finally he gave up the struggle (for when he was drunk he lost all restraint), and ordered another bottle of beer. Then a new patron stepped into the café, who instantly drew on himself the attention of all the customers.

No one vouchsafed the singer any further notice; they no longer clapped their hands or followed her with tears in their eyes. She hastily put an end to her song and hurried down the rickety steps, which sagged under her weight. The habitués looked at the new arrival with wide-open eyes, and astonishment and excitement were written on their faces. The man in the short skin coat cast a quick glance around the room, and his dashing mustaches seemed to droop disgustedly. Somebody whispered "Mitka!" but this conveyed nothing to Zavarihin. Actually the young man, who wore a hat and a racoon coat twinkling with hoar frost, deserved the attention he excited. His short mutton-chop whiskers were brushed carelessly across his cheeks, and over his high forehead there ran a curious deep furrow like a scar. Zinka had had good cause for stopping in the middle of her song, for Mitka's calm, clear glance had utterly disconcerted her. Zavarihin felt as if he were under a spell and did not protest when the newcomer, without asking his permission, seated himself at his table. He gently pushed Nikolka's bottle to one side and ordered tea and lemon. "He wears a coat like that and only drinks tea and lemon." Zavarihin's inclination to feel offended grew, and Mitka's contemptuous indifference to his array of bottles exasperated him. . . . He became angry.

"You don't take much care of your coat, old man," said Zavarihin with a patronizing nod, and pulled at a frayed tatter that hung from one sleeve.

"I've had that since prison," the other replied simply, and continued to brood over his slice of lemon.

Zavarihin filled his glass with beer and pushed the foaming drink over to his companion, right up against the tea and lemon. The tea glass tottered, and the slice of lemon all but fell on the table.

"Drink!" he called out pugnaciously, looking into Mitka's raised eyes. He saw in them the light of a clear, cold autumn day; they asked nothing, but there was a warning in their glance, and Nikolka felt that this man must be either one's friend or one's enemy. "Drink, or I'll drink it up myself. Drink! You'll not have to pay! Drink it up, man! This one's on me." Mitka looked silently at Zavarihin, stared silently at the root of his nose, where the bushy eyebrows met. Gradually Nikolka felt his anger ebbing out of him . . . but with his native truculence, which later on was to build for him his success in trade and industry, he flung discretion to the winds. He stood up against the wall in all his bulk, and though he was very hard up, he offered to treat all this shady company of topers to a free drink at his table. "Drink, you devils!" he shouted. His face flushed scarlet, a vein in his forehead darkened like a storm cloud, and his orange jacket flashed aggressively. Nikolka's grandfather had been a coach driver on the great country roads, and rumors of his deeds of daring still circulated among the peasants. The spirit of his grandfather's hands seemed to have passed today into Nikolka's. They longed to lash and tame; they needed a rebellious *troika* to dominate and force to submission.

The customers listened to him with mistrustful attention and glanced across at Mitka, as if to ask his permission. Meanwhile the exit had been blocked with tables so that Nikolka might not escape without paying. A strapping fellow, obviously a thief, though he was dressed as a workman, sat down at an adjacent table, coughed, and called to the others to join him. Many had already withdrawn, foreseeing a disagreeable ending to the evening; but those who remained seemed to have multiplied in a second. Spotty Alexey had barely time to open the first dozen bottles with the help of a volunteer, before the guests were sitting down at the tables, which had been pushed together, and tactfully awaiting their host's instructions. Nikolka passed the first glass with an inquiring glance to Mitka, but Mitka refused it with a shake of the head, and in a temper Nikolka poured its contents into a palm pot. Some of the customers were angry, others laughed. The traces of anger had completely disappeared from Nikolka's face.

"Drink . . . why don't you drink, damn you!" said he contemptuously through his teeth. "Alyosha, call the writer here! Zavarihin must stand him a drink!" His voice sounded tired, but again he squared his shoulders and his breast swelled. "Drink!" he roared, rolling his eyes— "drink, you devils!"

That was what they were all waiting for; greedily the guests' lips were pressed to the thick rims of the tankards. These had already twice been emptied and refilled, and Spotty Alexey was sweating over the third dozen when someone called to him from behind:

"The *barin* . . . the fat *barin's* coming! Wait!" The crowd fell back and allowed a man to walk with small, fussy, hurried steps up to Nikolka. The newcomer was fat and had that look of spongy impotence which comes with old age and misfortune. He swayed now to the right, now to the left, as he walked. His cheeks wobbled against his dirty collar, and one shoe creaked louder than the other. Once in the distant past he had been the embodiment of earthly well-being; now he was a mere symbol of disappointment and embitterment.

He ran up to Zavarihin, fanning his face with a piece of embroidery somewhat like a lady's handkerchief, scraped his feet, and smiled a smile in which uneasy courtesy was blended with the terror of the down-trodden.

"Pardon me. My heart plays me tricks," he explained, biting the tip of his tongue in his hurry. "Dear, dear! it plays me tricks," he repeated, waving his hand languidly, as if he were too feeble even to joke. "I'd kill myself for fifty kopeks."

"What?" called out Nikolka with interest, unguardedly fingering the wallet sewn in his breast.

"Give him fifty kopeks! He can tell stories, very amusing stories," an unknown young man, whose face looked as if it had been bashed in, whispered to him. "That's Manyukin, Manyukin—a *barin*—fifty kopeks won't beggar you, you devil!" he added in a tone which was more threatening than persuasive.

An awkward silence reigned again. At one moment

Manyukin drummed with his fingers on the table, at another he tried to give a foppish tweak to his collar, which looked as if it was covered with freckles. Nikolka wrinkled his forehead and waited: he could not make up his mind to this piece of extravagance.

"Sit down and have a drink," he growled sourly, trying to avoid the *barin's* eyes.

"I can't drink—be so good as to forgive me. I've got to work," Manyukin declared. "I must eat and pay my rent, and then the taxes . . . only fifty kopeks, what?" He put his head on one side to express his willingness to do any service whatever.

"That's his job! can't you understand?" voices shouted rudely behind Nikolka's back, and somebody swore.

Nikolka drew out a piece of gold silently and flung it on the table. It would have rolled off if a dozen hands had not held it fast on the very edge. Suddenly Nikolka became aware of his utter isolation, and buttoned up his coat, ready for a brawl if it should come to that.

"What shall I tell you about?" asked Manyukin with a grateful bow, fiddling in his pocket with the money he had received.

"He's waiting," threatened a citizen with a bandage on his cheek, who was brooding over his beer mug with deadly gravity.

"Don't disturb yourself on my account . . . I can wait!" said Manyukin, stretching out his hands beseechingly.

"Tell me something about a horse, you *barin*," said Nikolka, looking with disgust at the gray, unshaven cheeks, the obsequious gestures, and the worn breeches of the *barin*. ("Horse" had, as a matter of fact, been the first word that had come into his fuddled brain.)

"I can tell you something about horses. . . . Ah, yes, you bet!" murmured Manyukin, sitting down in the middle of the room and sinking his head between his shoulders. He cast an impatient glance at some guests who were chattering in a corner; it silenced them immediately. He refused with a gesture a cigarette that was reached out to him. "Don't write it down! I forbid you to write it down!" he called out affectedly to the writer, and a flush of shame mantled his cheeks, which were pale with excitement. He ran his hand across his bald scalp with the gesture of one who throws back a mane of luxuriant hair, and began in a hesitating voice, while he stroked his patched knee, first with his left hand, then with his right. "Well . . . I remember once a funny thing happened to me. . . ."

THE *barin* Manyukin earned the black bread of his random existence by telling stories about adventures that never took place, and with this object he appeared here, as regularly as clockwork, in quest of unconsidered half-roubles. His audience was usually a tipsy government clerk who was drinking away the government money or some foreman on the booze, or a carousing thief. Although on most of them the choicest pearls of his invention were lavished in vain, yet all the same they guessed that behind his laughter there lay some great and profound sorrow. When some rogue tried to show his wit at Manyukin's expense and to humiliate him too far, the whole band would raise an outcry and rally to the defense of the facetious *barin*.

He lied with the desperation of one with his back to the wall, but often, too, with the quiet ardor of innocent enthusiasm. He was like a soft wind that blows over the snow fields without knowing the goal of its gathering frenzy. He believed in the truth of the stories he invented, for certain things in them had actually taken place in his useless existence. The wheel of the revolution that had broken him had flung him living, but a wreck, on the farther shore. His stories consisted chiefly of what, standing on the hither bank, he could remember of the old one he had left so long ago. They always won him applause, even if they did not always bring him material gain; Alexey, of course, maintained that a couple of years before, Manyukin's stories had been much spicier and neater and naughtier.

"One day I came to Balamut Pototzky. There was a storm in the air . . . it was summer." Manyukin sighed, and his listeners gathered around him, for they wished, not only with ear and eye, but even by occasionally touching him with their hands, to convince themselves of his magical gifts. "I went into the house and found my dear friend at home on his terrace playing patience, the kind called 'The Expulsion of the Moabite.' He was eating preserved fruit jelly, while round him cohorts of flies hummed and buzzed. He would have won a prize at a fat-stock show. The war finished him off, for, as there wasn't enough room for him in the trenches, he had to stay on top, and they picked him off there."

"With one shot?" called out voices from the audience.

"Into fragments," squeaked Manyukin, and the chair under him squeaked, too. "We kissed each other, and my face was smeared with the jelly. 'Well, your serene highness,' said I, 'why have you got such a grim expression on your countenance?' 'I've had a piece of bad luck,' he answered. 'I bought a mare at the stud farm Koributt-Daskevich. It was perfection itself, chestnut brown with perfectly formed hoofs—one hundred and thirteen versts an hour.' 'What's her name?' I asked impatiently. 'Gribundi,' he cried, and tears streamed down his cheeks. He soaked himself with them and me too. 'She was sired by the celebrated Bukeya, who took part in the races at the London World Exhibition, as you remember. King Edward, of blessed memory, gave him a memorial portrait for his speed . . . an enamel portrait with nineteen blue rubies. . . .' 'Well, what happened in the end?' I cried. 'Well, you see,' he answered, 'for six weeks we've been trying to tame the mare, and she's eaten through three bridles already. She's ripped up Andokut the Korean's belly, and she's served Vasska Yefetov—you remember that monster, don't you, the trainer?—in the same way—the belly, too.' Then I just told him" (here Manyukin assumed a haughty pose), "I just laughed and patted his cheek and told him: 'You're an old woman, count,' said I. 'You're nothing but an old woman! Yesterday I lost the whole of South America and all its cactuses at the tables, yet am I crying?' "

"Come off it!" said Zavarihin incredulously, wiping

away the sweat from his face and looking doubtfully at the tittering audience. "Well, and how?"

"We played Polish Bank," Manyukin retorted, rapidly resuming his tale. "Trump . . . trump . . . Ace! 'There you have your America,' I said. 'A whole month it took me to play away the damned thing—a great country, and you're such an old blubberer that you go all to pieces on account of a mare. Stop whining! Aren't you a member of the State Council? and yet you sit there and leak like a water butt. I can tell you that from the time I was eleven I never left the race course while the races were on. The jockeys and horse dealers and gypsies were the friends of my youth. I idolize beautiful horses and elegant women. I've got *élan* and verve, my boy. Oh, the old days in Paris, what pranks we played! Once I harnessed forty naked *mouzhiks* to my landau, and in the landau I put a coffin draped in Scottish tartan, and in the coffin I put myself with a shiny top hat and a cockade. I drove around the city like that for four days. A squad of the devil's own blared before me on tubaphones, and eight striped Negroes sat behind me on the footboard. The President of the Republic was furious, of course.' "

"Are there really striped Negroes?" asked Alexey, grinning.

"I had them specially brought from the Congo. Two of them conked out on the voyage with meningitis ninety-six degrees. Well, the President was furious. 'You're insulting public decency, Seryozhka,' said he, 'so I'll have you extirpated off the face of the earth.' But I merely twirled my mustache. 'And I'll put three or four billion pood of melanite under your mangy old Mont Blanc and bang it off to the glory of the Russian empire.' The Pope of Rome had to make it up between us. It might easily have come to war."

"Well, and what happened to the mare?" asked Nikolka, greedily licking his lips, excited by the thrilling narrative.

"Oh, yes. 'Well,' I hallooed out, 'I won't break my fast till I've tamed this wild mare. Lead her up here, your Bucephalus! I'll ginger her up properly for you, the quadruped!' " Manyukin rolled his eyes wildly and pulled up his right sleeve. "Pototzky barely believed his ears. He called out his wife. 'Masha,' he whispered to her, 'look at this idiot . . . he wants to break in Gribundi.' Then his wife tried to talk me over—she was the cleverest woman in Europe, though she was no paragon of beauty."

"That's like my grandmother, she . . ." began Firsov, winking at Manyukin to whip up the zest of the story-teller.

"Died of a pregnancy outside the womb, too?" Man-yukin caught him up like a whirlwind in the middle of a sentence—"for that's the way this woman died. . . . Well, she wanted to talk me over. But I got into a blaz-ing temper and cried out: 'Give me the saddle, and I'll show you the eighth wonder of the world!' Then they took me into the yard, where a positive assembly of people was collected, and Gribundi was led out with an iron yoke and a sack tied over her eyes. All the same the beast smelled me out, and neighed. 'Put her with her nose to me!' I screamed in a wild frenzy. 'Tear off the sack!' They tore it off. Then I crossed myself, with my face toward Andokut. He stood there with his belly bandaged up, grinning, the rascal! I crossed myself and flung myself on the mare. I dug in my knees—it hadn't the slightest ef-fect: the horse quivered like an old donkey. Andokutya laughed and so did I. And sud–denly"—Manyukin hunched up into a small ball—"the mare leaped into the air and turned seven somersaults. The saddle slid down onto her belly, she gushed foam like a siphon, and kept on jerking up her spine. 'God Almighty!' thought I, 'she'll send me to my grave without issue. . . .' I flogged her with the whip—no result! I pulled at the bridle till her slobber ran over my kid gloves—no good! Then she took the bit between her teeth, set back her ears, and, with her eyes starting out of her head, galloped madly toward a precipice . . . a precipice forty-three yards high! A cold breath blew up from below, and at the bottom men and trees looked like black beetles crawling around. . . . It was horrible! When she flung me down there"—Man-yukin clutched at the seat he sat on with closed eyes, and moaned—"I struck on a small stone. . . . One eye and half my skull was bashed in . . . and green sparks re-volved in front of my remaining eye. Meanwhile the Pototzkys let themselves down on a rope to me. 'Are you alive, Seryozhka?' they called out. 'I'm alive,' I answered. 'That mare of yours is a first-class galloper!' Well, and then they douched me with collodion so that my skull should grow together again." He felt himself over convulsively, as if to assure himself at once that his limbs were still intact. Then he arranged his tie, which had come loose, and wiped his face: it was no easy job to earn himself his black bread. His gaze wandered indifferently over the crowd of men, who sat there petrified with enthusiasm and sympathy. Zavarihin, who believed implicitly in the terrible skull wounds of the unskillful horse trainer, rewarded the story with a hearty laugh.

"The brute! but you should have given her a blow with the fist between the eyes. I had one on my hands like that once. I gave her a welt as hard as I could, and she sank down on her forelegs immediately. Do you say she took away half your skull?" he stammered, and pressed into the *barin's* flabby hands all his coppers, which he drew out of his pocket together with a lot of filth. "Take that for tobacco. . . . There, it's from Zavarihin. What a brute! to think of her treating you like that!" He reached out his hand to feel the *barin's* skull, but, disconcerted by the general silence, suddenly stopped speaking.

No one was drinking the free beer now—except Firsov, who held his mug to his pinched lips and studied the twitching face of the storyteller. He felt himself done out of his right to laugh. Nikolka was angered, and flourishing a three-rouble piece under the nose of the *barin*, ordered him to go around the beer hall on all fours. Only in the noisome air of this seething, sweltering pit of humanity could such a vile desire have taken shape.

For a moment an empty stillness reigned like that in the fields before a storm wind blows over the rustling grass. If the crowd did not rush at Nikolka after this insolent request, it was only because Manyukin himself spoke first.

"Why do you speak like that, citizen?" he asked, putting his hands to his twitching lips. "I haven't sold myself to you, body and soul. Take back your fifty kopeks!" The coins gleamed on his open palm. "I didn't insult you, I merely told you about a horse." He withdrew, leaving the money on the edge of the table.

He went slowly, as if he knew that they would stop

him. And so it was, for with a couple of strides Firsov had caught him up and, seizing him by the shoulder, forced him back with a rough push.

"Take the money!" he whispered furiously. "You earned it with the sweat of your brow. Why do you behave like a calf in front of that lout?"

Manyukin grabbed the money like a thief from the table; he was agitated and terrified, and ran to the exit. Firsov followed him. Instantly from all sides there rose shouts and angry growls.

"Hitting a fellow when he's down!" a tipsy stalwart cried out, and his gold teeth, which he hadn't managed to drink away yet, gleamed.

"He wants to make himself important here, he and his copper coins, the swine!" said Alexey, fluttering his napkin spitefully.

The mention of the insignificant price he had paid to humiliate the *barin* infuriated Nikolka. He stood face to face now with his eternal foe. His eyes wandered around involuntarily, looking for something, and when under his feet he saw a trampled piece of black bread, he fixed this incident firmly in his consciousness by the phrase: "The black sacrament of peasant labor is being trampled underfoot."

"You!" bawled Nikolka, and his face, which was pale with pent fury, flushed scarlet again. "How many are there of you against me, you spouters? You sneer at my fifty-kopek piece, do you? Look at me! I'm speaking to you!" His rage sobered him. "Don't you sneer at my fifty kopeks! It was honestly come by. Yes, you've got a tooth in your head that shines like the sun . . . but it takes more than that to burn me up." He made a gesture as though to draw the stalwart nearer to him, closer to the hail of his words.

"Do you know how much bread costs today? And what it means to char coal, sixty cubic meters for fifteen roubles, or to tramp earth for thirteen days on end without sleep? Have you ever worked in a saw mill or a rolling works or a railway workshop? Have you ever earned a single kopek a shift? Go away and play, you!—go, and earn my fifty kopeks, and then you can sing away, you canting swine!"

He had barely uttered a tenth of the venom in his

soul, but already there was an ominous stillness around
him that threatened at any moment to burst into a storm.
He felt hot, and with an offensive smile he flung open
his short coat. The only reason why, at that moment, a
knife was not flung at Nikolka was because Mitka himself
now took part in the brawl. He touched Nikolka's shoulder lightly and drew all the company's attention on himself. He stuck his face into Nikolka's, but his expression
was worried rather than angry.

"Why did you insult the *barin?*" he asked with an involuntary glance at Nikolka's gay shirt. "You come to a
place like this and start a row."

"Oh, it's easy to blame the wrong fellow for rows,"
Nikolka snorted back impertinently, yet he still felt respect for his enemy because of his coat.

"Do you think just because you're big, one couldn't
put you in one's pocket, you fool!" Mitka went on, and
his right eyebrow twitched.

"Take care! If it comes to blows, you might get hurt. I
let myself be tickled four times, but the fifth time I start
tickling myself, and you bet I'll . . ."

Nikolka smiled warningly as he spoke, and shrugged his
shoulders. They stood opposite each other, flesh against
iron, Nikolka against Mitka, ready, if words failed, for action.

Perhaps Puchov would never have seen his tipsy
nephew again that night if a new arrival, the last of this
evening, had not appeared on the scene. She came like a
cooling draft in the sweltering gloom of a pit shaft. With
the amazement of a wild animal who sees a miracle,
Zavarihin stared over Mitka's head at the woman who had
suddenly materialized there. Mitka had evidently been
waiting for her the whole evening.

A girl whose sober, almost colorless clothes were relieved only by a gray scarf across her shoulders, now stood
behind Mitka. Even at close quarters her face looked
sweet and charming, although in profile her slightly prom-
inent chin gave her a startlingly childish expression. Her
pensive eyes with their blue radiance added greatly to the
quiet loveliness of her face. She greeted Mitka in a clear,
firm voice—she told him she had just finished her work
at the circus and Stassik had escorted her here.

She took Mitka by the arm and accompanied him to the exit. She did this purposely, as though she wished to emphasize that she had nothing to be ashamed of. They were about the same height, and from behind they resembled each other. Those who remained behind followed their departure with a respectful murmur. Nikolka hastily paid his bill and hurried after them. His flurried exit raised a laugh, and he made off none the worse for his folly. Enthralled by this new vision, he turned his back on his drinking companions and dashed out. For a drunken man there are no obstacles; when Nikolka had almost reached the couple, who were standing under a street lamp, he reeled and stopped.

"Nikolka Zavarihin!" he shouted out suddenly, and, striking his chest, took off his hat.

"You're drunk, boy . . . but there's nothing marvellous about that," said Mitka seriously, and laid his hand on his shoulder. "But now go off to bed!"

They went on, but Nikolka stood rooted to the spot, overwhelmed with perplexity. The lantern outside the beer hall was put out, and Nikolka went on his way. His heart was harrowed with pain and heavy as a mill wheel, to whose monotonous thudding the last clouds of drunkenness dispersed. A hateful winter shower began, and from the high roof drops splashed down. Through the filth and the puddles on the roadway Nikolka hastened back with long strides to his uncle in Blagusha, his felt boots splashing drearily in the melting snow. Two women rose before his mind: she who had set her seal upon the previous morning struggled in his fancy with the woman of the evening. She of the morning had endeared herself because she cried, she of the evening because she smiled, and alternately they held sway over him. To the end of his life he was to love them both without betraying either of them. They fused together into one whole, like two halves of a sliced apple; they held him fast with strong, unbreakable bonds. At this moment Nikolka would thankfully have gone back home to his gray village and faced again the dreariness of a new start.

MANYUKIN's den was in the third story above the beer hall, so there was no need to put on an overcoat to go from one door to the other. Besides, Manyukin had not a coat, only a kind of woman's cape, which, he used to say facetiously, was lined with flea skin. In any case the flea skin suited his way of life perfectly. The lantern over the door was not burning, so Firsov, in spite of all his efforts, did not succeed in reading Manyukin's mood in his face.

"One moment," he pleaded in a whisper. Manyukin stopped and, turning around, waited with his head buried in his collar. "I won't keep you long. My name is Firsov, if I may introduce myself." He bowed and looked over the top of his glasses, but this made no impression on the other. "So you live in number eight? Don't in Heaven's name suppose that I . . ." and he delivered himself of a host of reassurances that he was a respectable man, who never abused a stranger's confidences.

Manyukin shivered and, answering "It's very windy," hunched up politely and covered his neck with his hand. "And I don't want to get a sore throat. Would you mind telling me quickly what you want?"

"Oh . . . that isn't so easy to say all at once. Look, wouldn't it be better if we went up to your room?" Firsov pointed toward the pitch-dark staircase, down which a breath of icy cold was blowing. "We could sit together a bit and share a bottle: I've got one in my pocket. Please don't suppose I'm a . . ." (He reassured himself secretly that the bottle was still intact.)

"I've got a roommate . . ." confided Manyukin in a whisper. "The sort of chap who spits on everything just out of spite." The *barin* laughed pointedly, but Firsov remained silent, tactlessly persisting in his idea regardless of hints. "He isn't a bad fellow, but, well—he's apt to turn nasty, to put it mildly," Manyukin blurted out. Suddenly he bowed his head submissively. "Let's go! but mind you don't break the bottle."

So, in the deep silence of the night, while all around them unknown people slept, they climbed the cold, dark staircase. It smelled of lime and dogs. Through the broken staircase window an icy draft blew in, and from outside a star seemed to twinkle and disappear. And although there was no star at all, yet Firsov held it fast in his memory and clenched his fist on it, for in his unfinished story there was room even for the star.

"If you'll excuse me, I'll just stop a moment to get back my breath." Manyukin stopped and leaned against the banister. "I hate this black staircase. It attracts you so. I'd sooner live on the ground floor, where there's nowhere to fall to." The darkness disposed him to confidences.

"You live a long way up," Firsov agreed sympathetically.

"Another story still," said Manyukin, and his irregular steps began to scrape again on the stairs.

Firsov wiped his spectacles in the dark passage and listened to his companion's cautious movements.

"I'm taking off my boots. . . . I promised my roommate," Manyukin explained, for Firsov was watching him in dumb amazement.

"Ought I, too?" his visitor inquired.

"No, no, of course not! You've got on galoshes."

Manyukin led his visitor into an empty room beyond his own, and dragged in chairs and a small lamp. The stinking paraffin light that filtered tipsily and drowsily through a sooty globe revealed that Manyukin had even succeeded in mustering some cups for the promised carouse.

"I couldn't resist your wine," he admitted candidly, and, sitting down on the edge of his chair, pointed to a second seat. "What is it we're going to talk about?"

Firsov examined the room. It seemed to be a two-windowed, freshly whitewashed cubicle. There were still traces of lime on the floor. Through the ventilator a damp, unwholesome vapor forced its way in. On the walls hovered a pair of bandy-legged shadows; the little lamp stood on the floor. Firsov closed his cigarette case with a snap and leaned over the little lamp to light his cigarette. Manyukin stole a glance at his visitor. Firsov's head reminded him of an iron cannon ball, it had such a stubborn look. His forehead was as broad as a shovel, his gray eyes protruded slightly, and a curly beard grew on his chin. Firsov puffed out a cloud of smoke.

"As you may have guessed already, I describe men, their characters and ways of life, and everything about them worth describing. Excuse me, might I close the ventilator?" He went to the window and exclaimed: "It's too high, I can't reach it! And the blasted thing's got no glass!" He cursed again and resumed his seat. "You see, I'm a writer, though actually only the author of a single book. No one will print my stuff. The day before yesterday an important personage said to me: 'If they were printed, they would give offense to the whole world. Why don't you describe people who matter instead of burrowing about in nonentities? Besides, you ought to write something useful, of course, and of general interest.' But, you see, it's just the hidden roots of people that fascinate me. For me every man has an individual birthmark, and birthmarks are what I'm interested in."

"What sort of a man are you looking for now?" asked Manyukin gloomily.

Firsov's silence was eloquent. "I am interested in men in their nakedness, my dear . . . my dear . . ."

"Sergey Ammonich," completed Manyukin. He fidgeted uneasily on his chair, and stopped pouring his visitor's wine into the teacups. He could barely hold himself upright for fatigue; the light of the small lamp threw all his wrinkles into sharp relief—the faithful record of his passions and pleasures and privations. But Firsov only marked a single furrow: it ran from the root of his nose to his lips, cutting across everything else; it was the line of utter human disillusionment.

"You never see a man per se but always, so to speak, in his"—he searched urgently for the right word—"trappings. The trappings can take any form you like—the make of a tie, the way of holding a cigarette, the cut of his thought, family traditions, culture level, standards of morality, and everything else of the kind. A man without them is a naked man. The point about our revolution was that it stripped man of his trappings. In any case, perhaps men had grown to hate the smell of them! . . . What?"

"No, I wasn't going to say anything"—Manyukin shrank back—"at least I only wanted to ask you to speak more softly: my roommate is asleep." He nodded his head toward the wooden partition behind him.

"But now everything is settling down again," said Firsov, lowering his voice and looking into the deep, turbid wine. "Life flows on as before: the drunkard drinks, the priest prays, the beggar begs, the diplomat's wife manicures her nails, and nothing's upset. . . . The organism's growing a new skin, for it's terribly cold without one. The naked man is disappearing, and one has to go down into the depths to find him. I'm sorry, I've let some ashes drop on your knee."

"It doesn't matter." Manyukin shrank back as if he had been burned, and some of his wine splashed over the edge of his cup. "I'm sorry, I haven't quite understood you—do you want to describe me? Well, I'm naked enough anyway, stark naked, so you won't find it hard. Yet you know I'm a graduate of Heidelberg University—I've even given some lectures on slavery," he confessed in a faltering voice, "but I've forgotten everything, it might all never have happened. Yet it did once, it did! At the time of the revolution my grandfather's books were carried away on seven lorries. Yes, it did . . . it really did once! But am I crying? . . . Why are you smiling?"

"When you were telling about Gribundi just now in the beer hall you had the same expression as you have now . . . but it's nothing, really—I wasn't thinking of you. Tell me, does Vekshin live in this building, too? I want *him*. Will you allow me to come and see you now and then? I want, as an experiment, to depict something straight from life. A naked man needs rather unusual circumstances—but what is more unusual than life? If you'll let me, I'll bring the whole house into my story."

"Oh, of course!" said Manyukin expansively. He drank up his cup and stepped to the window. Firsov followed him after he had turned down the dying lamp.

The dawn crept in, and the light breeze of sunrise blew the smoke clouds from both their cigarettes out of the ventilator. The cool gray-blue air outside the window shimmered with rainbow colors in the swirling snowflakes. The tottering old wooden houses of the suburbs are twice as marvellous in a snowstorm. A thin film of snow lay on the puddles below.

"Don't you want to sleep?" asked Firsov.

"I've given up wanting, but anyway I don't complain. I've got used to cold and insults. I don't complain that the grass goes on growing out there, whatever it's good for"—he nodded at the space framed by the window—"while I, a man, lie here breathless and useless. Life is its own justification, I suppose—everything points to that nowadays, my dear friend. I have learned to understand all this ridiculous farce."

"It's snowing," said Firsov pensively. "The city looks marvellous in the snow." He paused again. "The city is the greatest load that man has ever laid upon his neck."

"I see everything now, but I don't run away. One can't run away from one's own eyes!" Manyukin exclaimed with a queer laugh. "One only need run away if one has something to preserve. But I've nothing left." He showed Firsov the empty cup. "Drunk up and licked clean! and how many tongues have licked at it!"

Steps resounded through the stillness. Someone was approaching who evidently had no wish to conceal his coming, and was not frightened of disturbing Manyukin's excitable roommate. Sergey Ammonich had barely time to open the door to prevent any needless noise when the man of whom Firsov had been thinking the whole time with a teasing persistency stepped into the room. Firsov's heart almost stopped beating for excitement.

Mitka was pale, and perhaps drunk, but this was not apparent either in his speech or his walk. He held himself straight, and except in the hard lines of his forehead his face betrayed no trace of his sleepless nights. The snow on his coat had not yet thawed. He stood in the doorway with his hat in his hand and looked satirically from one to the other; obviously he was in no mood for a quiet, friendly chat.

"Learning secrets?" he inquired with cheerful impudence, coming close up to Firsov. "Who are you, anyway?"

"My name's Firsov," answered the other without any embarrassment, and he seemed to be pleased at something.

"Do you rummage in papers in an office and enter up goods that don't exist?" jeered Mitka, and it was patent now that he was sober.

"No, I write about men," answered Firsov softly, without taking his eyes off him.

"Ah!" replied Mitka patronizingly. "And my trade's hairdressing, I shave heads. I've shaved a good few now, you see, but so far I've never had a single real, round head under my hands: they've all been long, bottle-shaped ones. . . ." They studied each other. "You're drinking," Mitka remarked reproachfully, and struck his foot against the empty bottle.

He spoke with deliberate loudness, as if he were drunk, and this terrified Manyukin.

"For God's sake, be quiet!" he implored. "He'll be the

death of me yet. He's sleeping— Pyotr Gorbidonich, I mean."

"Sleeping, is he?" cried Mitka, still more loudly and tipsily. "Who has the cheek to sleep when I come? No one must sleep when Dmitri Vekshin is awake." He stepped up to the locked door that joined the two rooms and kicked it several times. "Hullo, Pyotr!" he roared, to the utter consternation of Manyukin. "You Chinese samovar, you crafty old schemer, get up!"

And instantly behind the door something vast and momentous and menacing began to move and curse. Manyukin was still tearing around the room in a panic, with the telltale bottle in his hand, when the door opened and the tenant of the room next door stepped in, greeted by jeers from Mitka and a little squeak of alarm from Sergey Ammonich. This personage was an undersized creature with a red conspirator's beard, and he was draped in a blanket that trailed along behind him and permitted a glimpse of two hairy, shaking legs. His oddly colored eyes rolled peculiarly, searching for the spot he should let fly at first.

"Ah-ha!" he contented himself with saying, but it was enough to paralyze Manyukin, and the bottle he was hiding behind his back rolled clattering over the floor. At the same instant his roommate dived to the right and then to the left and, drawing out his hand from under his blanket, pointed it at Manyukin. "You sit there drinking, but you'd never think, of course, of paying your taxes as a citizen with an independent profession, oh, no! You not only break all the regulations that should be the guiding principle of your life, but you abandon yourself to luxury and debauchery as well."

The bottle lay with its label upward, and twinkled treacherously in the light of dawn. "As clerk of finances I refuse to tolerate this. I'll take proceedings against you through the house committee and the police." He shouted out a lot more . . . about the financial situation and the country going to the dogs and finally about his broken sleep.

Manyukin stood petrified by the window and made no attempt to defend himself, which merely increased the fury of his roommate. Finally Mitka felt it necessary to turn the matter aside with a joke, and this no doubt was proof of his sobriety.

"You'd give any woman the creeps, you old schemer, and for all that you're thinking of marrying. Take a look at your face, just! Just buy a looking glass, and look at yourself in it an hour every day. That'll take the nonsense out of you."

"Doesn't matter . . . the ladies don't find me repulsive," answered Pyotr Gorbidonich quick as lightning, edging closer to Manyukin. "Let me alone, citizen," he cried, and thrust at Mitka's chest with his fists.

"Where are you off to, my fighting cock?" asked Mitka, delighted with himself.

"Will you let me go?" snarled Chikelyov, screwing up his eyes.

"No!" laughed Mitka.

"You thief!" yelled Chikelyov, who now lost all control of himself. "You're a thief. We all know it." He pointed to the crowd of house tenants, who had been awakened and were peering in at the door. "Just wait, though! I'll be even with you yet!"

"Thi-ef?" said Mitka, tottering back. His expression had changed, and he was smiling peculiarly. "Say that again!"

"Thief," repeated Pyotr Gorbidonich in a feeble, wooden voice.

Mitka seized Chikelyov by the shoulders and looked for a full half-minute into his suffused face. The force of his hatred gave Chikelyov the strength to bear Mitka's terrifying stare . . . and Mitka suddenly left the room as if beaten. Manyukin gave a feeble groan, and Firsov could hardly contain his amazement. Mitka had been publicly put to shame; but he withdrew in ominous silence (if it had not already been too late Pyotr Gorbidonich would even now have run after him with apologies), and when Mitka dropped his cap, someone hurriedly picked it up for him.

The extinguished lamp stood in Mitka's way. Firsov waited impatiently for him to kick it away with his foot, for that was what the episode in his unfinished story demanded. But Mitka passed the crucial spot without any accident, and almost immediately afterward Zinka Balduyeva, whose songs had so much delighted Firsov a few hours before, stalked into the room.

"Thief?" she asked Chikelyov scornfully. "And do you know what Mitka runs the risk of if he's caught? How many waiting bullets are aimed at his forehead? . . ." She gloried in Mitka's crimes, and Firsov divined the love that underlay her exaggerations. "Yes, he takes other people's property, but you steal without running any risks! Where did you get all the drawing pins for sticking up the regulations in the closet? You wouldn't even dare to take a bribe, you coward! You chicken snout, you! Why don't you put boots on your hands and run around on all fours to denounce Mitka? Ah, Pyotr Gorbidonich, what a skunk you are!" She turned from him with a withering glance, and looked for the checked ulster she had observed with astonishment a moment before.

But Firsov was no longer in the room; he had begun his first assault on the treasure house of Mitka's enigmatic existence. He paced in torment up and down outside Mitka's door and coughed to test the ring of his voice. Then he smoothed his ruffled hair and opened the door. At the same moment another door opened and someone called out Manyukin's name, but Firsov heard nothing, for his whole attention was strained on Mitka. A bad beginning might have capsized his carefully premeditated plan.

Mitka lay in bed, his eyes turned to the ceiling. His coat, which he had torn from his back in a rage, lay on the floor with the fur uppermost—the sleeve lay pitiably in a small puddle that had dripped from the window. There was nothing in this room, which was bare and roomy as a prison cell, to give a hint of his profession. On the table there lay a few of yesterday's newspapers and some paltry objects of daily use. Everything showed that this room was only his temporary home.

"I've come without asking your permission," began Firsov, closing the door behind him and shutting out the reverberations of the fracas in the other room. "I'll sit down, if I may." He made an easy, unconstrained gesture, but cautiously refrained from sitting down, as he did not yet know how to interpret Mitka's silence. "A poisonous chap, that Chikelyov." Mitka remained silent. "One's glasses get frightfully dirty here."

"Well, then, wipe your glasses," said Mitka expressionlessly.

"Thanks, I will." Fortune seemed to smile on Firsov's endeavors.

"I've been trying to meet you for a whole month. I've heard a lot about you, a Russian Rocambault, I understand. In my profession we have to . . . how shall I put it?" He shrank into himself, and it was obviously a torture to him to bring out an appropriate explanation. "I regard you, I frankly admit, from the philosophical standpoint, for you are a great idea . . . yes, an idea! Why are you staring at me like an owl?"

"A wri-ter?" said Mitka, syllable by syllable, making a lazy movement with his boot. "The way you go on, one would think you were a spy, but judging by your mug you're just a damned skunk."

Firsov scratched his temples, though they didn't need scratching, and twitched his eyebrows comically.

"I'm sorry, Comrade," he said huffily, and moved backward to the door, with a wave of his hat. His glasses had only been half polished.

There was nothing to keep him here and soon the feltcovered door closed behind him. On his way downstairs Firsov drew out his notebook: it was accustomed to sudden emergencies, so opened of its own accord at the right place.

Sternly, with eyes half closed, Firsov listened to the unforeseen conflict of his thoughts, while his pencil idly drew a nonsensical drawing. Suddenly everything went of its own accord into the notebook.

"Manyukin is a worn-out screw from a wrecked machine. Can one judge the whole from the individual parts? Our fathers robbed their posterity. Peasants are numbered by the head and books measured by the square yard. I must introduce a daughter, of course (and perhaps, though not necessarily, a son), and there must be a 'clever' conversation. The old culture must adapt itself to the post-revolutionary new, or else—crash! We, the people, are the immediate heirs of the great victories of the past. We too with the hands of our forefathers have plowed those mighty fields—and eagerly, too. But where are we to begin: 862 or 1917?

"Mitka's brow is honest, rebellious. The earth, indifferent to their differences, bore Mitka and Zavarihin in the same hour One sinks, the other climbs. Where their ways meet, there is catastrophe, battle and hatred. The first will die a cruel, splendid death, the second will thrice give death the slip. Both of them are right: the first on account of his honor and his will, the second on account of his strength. Both are emissaries of the wakened millions. Life begins again from the beginning. . . .

"Chikelyov is a degenerate epigone with a wound instead of a face. He is the trusted president of the house committee, and has held his post as finance clerk for fifteen years already. He works honestly and willingly, obeying the standing regulations, but the law can be pretty vampirish. My pencil revolts at writing more about him."

In any case, the pencil broke at this point and Firsov looked around. Through the rectangle of the main door he saw light, nimble snowflakes falling. The dawn was breaking, and a vague sound issued from the houses and filled the stairway; at the foot of it a homeless, yellow cur sat in a corner shivering with cold.

"Hullo, dog!" said Firsov, and stroked the dog's wet back. "Are you still running around? I run and sniff at everything I meet, too . . . and nobody wants either of us. But we know life better than anyone else all the same, know its smell. It smells good, it's pleasant and sweet; one eats it, and dies, and nobody notices. Good-by, doggie!"

He reflected a moment irresolutely whether he should hail a passing cab or not. His hand felt two cold coins in his pocket—only two—so he did not call to the driver, but hurried home on foot with undamped ardor.

THE WRITER Firsov, who was sadly familiar with the hidden reefs of existence, was not particularly chagrined by his ill success. In any case he already knew a good deal about Mitka, for in his wanderings around the disreputable quarters of the city he had constantly been falling in with friends of Mitka, who supplied information about his past. Like a tireless bee Firsov stuck together all the tiny morsels he had collected, and lo! the comb was there —only the honey was wanting. . . . Then one day he met Sanka "the Bicycle," an undersized thief, but assuredly the most innocuous of all Moscow's rogues.

Firsov treated Sanka liberally, and in return Sanka told him that Dmitri Vekshin had been a great Bolshevik and had done his bit valiantly in the great October revolution. When the counterrevolution began to gain ground on all sides, he was made Commissar of a cavalry regiment and won the devoted loyalty of his comrades. He led his regiment as though he had a dozen lives, and indeed fought like a dozen Vekshins. Sometimes he had been hard-pressed, but his horse, a nag with a broad chest and a dappled coat, always pulled him through. His orderly, Sanka Babkin (nicknamed "the Bicycle"), used to say of Sulim that he had a "humanitary" soul and went as smoothly as water.

Firsov wrote: "In those years they fought for the good of mankind, but had little care for human beings. Their great love, distributed to all equally, had about as much warmth as a single candle. Loving the whole world with the love of a plow that cleaves the soft, submissive earth,

Vekshin cherished Sulim alone with a tender, almost womanly love. And when in a close fight a bullet struck Sulim fatally between the eyes, Vekshin cried as though they had killed the half of himself. He was very young then, and neither success nor wine nor good fellowship could console him.

"By night he abducted Sulim's murderer from headquarters, where he had been brought for examination, and led him out behind a thin, straggling birch copse. Sanka Babkin, whose heart had been turned to stone by his sympathy for his master's grief, assisted him. Above the barbed-wire fence the brazen moon rose against the dark background of the sky. In the silence not even the leaves rustled.

" 'Do you know what you have killed?' asked Commissar Vekshin in a deep, slow voice, gazing at the torn tunic of the youth, who had reached the rank of captain in the first six months of the civil war. The boy was silent, for he had killed so many men that day that he did not know whom they were talking about. 'You have killed Sulim,' Vekshin went on, and his lean, tense brows bent and straightened again like a bow that has shot its arrow. 'Now salute me.'

"The other obeyed: he was terrified by the moonlight and the misty blue distances of the night, the silence of the frozen grove and the piercing, black pupils of the Commissar. But when he lifted his hesitating arm, the arm that killed Sulim, Vekshin raised his sword and hacked it off. Sanka Babkin, who had the weakest nerves of the three, groaned and sank upon the cold, wet turf. Vekshin dragged the half-dead man back to headquarters and flung him into a ditch by the road close to the main entrance.

"He received a severe reprimand from the division, and he seemed to take it to heart He and his regiment scoured the front more madly than ever, and perhaps there may have been some truth in the story that he had been seen in four places at once But he fell more and more into a morbid lethargy and brooding, which robbed him of his sleep and his vigor. And then he fell ill.

"The secretary of the Party unit, a Georgian who had fought in the same regiment as Vekshin, came to visit his sick friend. Unaffectedly glad at his friend's good fortune, he brought the news that Mitka had been recommended for the Order of the Revolution. Sanka Babkin, who was standing on the doorstep of Vekshin's hut, for a long time refused to admit him. Sanka's face was scratched and bleeding, and he was without his belt: with his eyes starting out of his head he began some rigmarole about the infectiousness of his master's illness. But the secretary pushed Sanka aside and went in. He almost cried when he saw Vekshin's pitiable condition.

"The floor of the hut was covered with bottles, about a dozen of them. They stood or lay in an exact circle, and Vekshin was crawling around in the middle like the hand of a clock, dead drunk and blue in the face, his wrists bound with a strap (he was always a solitary drinker). The secretary sat on the edge of the bed, and with his hand on his hip silently observed Vekshin's antics.

" 'How have you come to this, Mitka?' he asked in the tone more of a doctor than of a judge. 'Is it a commemorative feast for Sulim? Take my horse, Kambala. She's Sulim's wife, and his match in a race.'

"Three days of heavy drinking had loosened Vekshin's tongue. At the door, Sanka Babkin could hear his feverish, reckless words—the same words which later on he weakly sold to Firsov for beer, and Firsov thereupon published for all the world to read.

"The gist of Vekshin's ravings was that the revolution was really a national movement, that it was the wild unrest of the Russian blood before its fabulous blossoming.

" 'It's a lie!' screamed Vekshin drunkenly, embracing the immaculate boots of his friend. 'My blood isn't cooled yet: it's flowing still and throbbing hot in my veins.' At every word he struck his chest violently, as he might strike something that did not belong to him.

"The secretary of the unit did not interrupt the torrent of wild, heretical words that fell from Vekshin's lips; he listened to everything, and went away without saying good-by. When he sat in his room again he took a piece of paper and made four rough copies before his report to the political department of the division seemed to him forcible enough. He summoned all his will, and stifled the rising impulses of friendship: these were hard days, and the two-headed eagles that flew across from Siberia were successfully rending the Red armies." So it was that Firsov concluded this very significant episode.

Two days afterward, Vekshin read aloud before the assembled regiment the divisional orders signifying that he was relieved of his command: he had himself been acquainted with the decision of the Party unit the evening before. An excited murmur ran through the ranks; it was a dull, misty morning that left a pale reflection of itself forever afterward on Mitka's face. It would have been easier for him to give for the last time the order "Fire!" to rifles leveled at himself. When he had read the paper to the end, he joined the other soldiers in the ranks, resigned to any humiliation. After a short rest the regiment reassembled and went into battle.

Even now he still fought with unabated fury, as if there were ten men inside him driving him to some distant, longed-for goal. Sanka alone guessed that this was not Vekshin, but only Vekshin's shadow clothed with his image and girded with his indomitable will. He fought valiantly while the life of the Republic was at stake; but the days went on inexorably. The war came to an end, and its fires were dimmed by the humdrum routine of every day. Then Vekshin returned to the city.

It was that stage in the second half of the revolution when the fight had assumed a more insidious form, and numbers took the place of armaments. Now the front was at every corner, in every brain, in every house. The shops were being rapidly repaired in the squares, the lights of pleasure resorts flared up, and laughter was heard more often. The demobilized soldiers of the revolution watched with sullen contempt shopwindows that only yesterday had been riddled with bullets, rising up more glittering and luxurious than ever. But today these shopwindows only aroused feelings of hunger, or terror, or amazement. Vekshin regarded all this closely and contemptuously, comforting himself with the secret thought: "I wished this—and it was so; I shall wish again—and it will be no more." But he refused to realize that beside him another Vekshin was pacing: Life. And the days went by inexorably—the hot days of summer.

On one such day he stood before a grocery store with

Sanka Babkin. It was hot, and in the shopwindow the fat was dripping from a headless sturgeon: Vekshin was hungry. An elegantly dressed woman wanted to go into the shop, and he politely reached out his hand to open the door for her; but she misunderstood him. She struck him with her glove on the hand grasping the latch, and would have struck again if he had not awkwardly withdrawn. Sanka Babkin, who had witnessed his former glory and now was to see his humiliation, was overwhelmed by the look of horror on Mitka's face. The woman, an official's wife, had in the meantime passed into the shop.

That evening Mitka got drunk. In one of the remoter quarters of the city, in a thieves' den, he drank in gulps a bitter, poisonously intoxicating drink from which there streamed a stench of corruption. Sanka stared indifferently at a spot on the damp wall. The acquaintances he formed that evening had a far-reaching effect on his life. When his master had no more money for drink, Sanka stole for him, and next day Vekshin repaid the service, merely from stupid loyalty toward his friend. He and Sanka were caught red-handed in their amateur thefts, which, from the professional point of view, had been sadly bungled. In prison, where his cup of bitterness and shame was filled to the brim, Vekshin became simply "Mitka," and Sanka got his nickname. Two others joined them: Lyonka Zhivotik and Donka Lyubov, two incompetent crooks, whose only claim to fame was to be their association with Mitka.

Mitka's strength had not yet been all spent, nor had his mind yet been utterly poisoned by excess. For they had been steeled in desperate ventures, and now they were to do him good service. He became the leader of the band, simply because he was the moving spirit. He distinguished himself by his audacity and resourcefulness, and for a whole year he eluded all pursuit. It was upon him that the eyes of the whole thief world were turned: he was their pattern and their hero. Money slipped through his fingers with incredible speed; but there was always something about his expensive clothing that excited ridicule, and the room he rented under the name of Korolyov, the barber, was as empty as a beast's cage.

Even the great ones like Vassily Vassilyevich Panama

the Fat, the cheerful cheat, who sold copper as gold and was an expert in railway robberies, or Fyodor Shchekutin, the supreme craftsman, the inspired rogue, who had both of them in the old days been on foreign tours—even potentates such as these valued Mitka's advice and often listened to it.

Mitka himself never became close friends with them, yet never avoided them either; and only for one of them, Agey, did he feel a profound loathing. For Agey's eyes, which closed slowly and heavily like prison doors, seemed almost to touch one's naked flesh.

Mitka's eyes were bright as ever, and though numbed by suffering, he had not lost the power to feel; yet when his feelings stirred, he grew wretched and gave himself up to drink, because it was only through drink that he could deaden his sorrow. Firsov had come to him at the very moment when, crushed by Chikelyov's abuse and depressed by his sudden encounter with his sister, he was starting on a drinking bout. The meeting, which he owed to Fat Panama, had been completely unexpected, and he did not know whether to be pleased or sad at this entry of a tender, disinterested love into his life, for his sister's appearance had been both a reproach and a reminder.

Of more than this Firsov had no inkling as he shot out like a bullet from Dmitri Vekshin's cold room.

Fat Panama, who had met Mitka at Nijni Novgorod, where he had spent a week amusing himself, had suggested to him that he should join him on his next little train journey, and Mitka had been attracted by the idea. Vassily Vassilyevich's nickname fitted him well; his body was plump and pleasant, and so was his face, and, like all men who have succumbed to Mammon, he was good-natured and harmless for all his ravenous belly. He turned his appearance to magnificent account, and used to declare, in jest, but with some foundation, that even after he had committed a theft he often succeeded in leaving an excellent impression on his victim, sometimes even rousing his warmest sympathies.

Mitka and Panama got into the early train without exciting any suspicion in the two other travelers in their compartment. These were a chubby-cheeked engineer, who kept fumbling at the pocketbook in his breast pocket the whole time, and a pretty girl with a black bandage over her left eye. Their well-filled trunks lay on the rack and delighted Vassily Vassilyevich with their weight when, with an assumed effort, he laid his empty basket beside them.

They settled into their seats and produced their bottle of wine with a deprecating smile; then they started on their meal, conversing pleasantly the while on co-operative produce societies. At the end of his modest repast Panama, affably but not too pressingly, offered his traveling companions seats at the folding table. The girl refused with a smile; the engineer primly murmured something

about belated invitations and appeared to go to sleep. The
floor had cracks in it, and Vassily Vassilyevich offered the
girl, who was making unavailing efforts to cover her cold
feet, a striped plaid rug; she took it unsuspectingly, without noticing a slightly sinister officiousness in Panama's
neatly rounded phrases.

They drank tea together in the twilight, and Panama
told an amusing story of how he had once played chess
with a married man and won a silver cup from him and
a kiss from his wife. Mitka listened inattentively, for he
was absorbed in watching the pine trees and the snow and
the sparks that whirled past incessantly from the engine.
After they had had their laugh over the unlucky husband,
and had taken precautionary measures against thieves,
they began to settle down for the night. And when two
hours later the rhythmic rattle of the wheels had slowed
down and the girl slept peacefully under Panama's rug
(the slumbers of the engineer had been assisted by some
chloral hydrate), Vassily Vassilyevich carried the passengers' trunks from the carriage, and warned Mitka facetiously not to disturb the sweet maiden slumbers of the
girl.

Panama, who was anxious to make a good impression
on Mitka, resigned to him the larger half of the swag.
With a smile of anticipation Mitka opened the trunk in
his room; as he had just left prison, he naturally considered himself fairly safe for the time being.

In the trunk there were some linen and clothes, several
colored tights, and a variety of innocent odds and ends
with an exotic smell. As he unpacked, he flung the various articles straight on to the floor and pushed them away
carelessly with his foot. He regarded the bottom of the
trunk with surprise and disgust, for there was nothing
there but some long silk cords with firm knots and nickel
buckles. Each of the cords ended in a tight-sewn loop, and
the soft silk shone with constant use. Mitka flung them
away with almost superstitious dread. There were many
aspects of the thief's profession from which he recoiled
with loathing, as he did now.

An iron safe is called a "bear" in thieves' jargon, and
to "gut a bear" simply means to "crack a safe." Mitka
was celebrated for his prowess as a "bear gutter." He must

have possessed some mysterious sleight-of-hand, for he could open safes as easily as a grown-up can open a baby's fist. But Mitka's undertakings were not always crowned with success: there were occasions when neither the straightforward "goose foot" nor the cunning *"balleteuse"* with the tiny, delicate teeth could force an entrance to the treasure. But every time it gave him infinite pleasure to take part in this honorable duel with steel, and to triumph. Mitka's strength thirsted for action and was constantly in search of a worthy antagonist. But here was no antagonist worthy of him.

He shrank back in alarm from the jumble of useless things which his touch had desecrated. He must burn them, or give them away, or fling them into the river; in some way he must dispose of them. It never occurred to him to take the pile of plunder to Artemy the Korean, a receiver of stolen goods, for he found the very thought of him humiliating. At the moment he had a horror of the bursting self-confidence of Vassily Vassilyevich, who used to compare a trunk fancifully to an Easter egg—one never knew what surprises one might find inside. Suddenly an insignificant paper package that he had flung out with the linen caught his eye. He picked it up with a vague misgiving and glanced around at the door. Though stoutly bolted, it nevertheless seemed to provide insufficient security. With a shaking hand he tore the colored ribbon from the blue paper that enveloped the parcel. He found inside nothing but a packet of photographs, but the triviality of his discovery made it the more profoundly shocking.

A flush of shame spread over his face. On top he found a photograph of the girl herself, the same girl who had smiled back so trustfully yesterday in response to Vassily Vassilyevich's professional charm. She was without her bandage, and one eye had a scarcely perceptible squint. She was wearing tights and held smilingly in one hand the very cord that Mitka had just flung away. He put the photograph on one side. The next was a second snapshot of her—but this time the cord was around her neck, and her smile seemed to say "Smile, for now the fun is coming!" Mitka began to turn over the cardboard pictures more quickly. The girl of yesterday, so warm and intimate in his memory, was shown doubled back from the waist at one moment, at another hanging with head downward. His brain reeled; he was amazed by the variety of her poses and her smiles. He flushed hot, and could not tell why. Someone was knocking obstinately at the door and whispering his name, but Mitka did not hear. Suddenly a shiver ran through him from the crown of his head to the tips of his fingers and back again. He sat down and looked straight in front of him. A smile like a sudden spasm flashed across his face.

The last photograph of all, an old crumpled snapshot, faded and dirtied by flies, presented a tiny yard. In the middle of the yard a girl sat on a box in a torn frock with bare feet—it was his sister Tatyanka! And near her stood himself, Mitka Vekshin, the bear gutter and passport faker, an eight-year-old boy then, well built, and smiling in his childish manner. He had smiled without stopping through all those years until life had laid him in the dust and threatened to crush him. The boy Mitka in the photograph had smiled when in the great war the Bavarian infantry had come charging down upon him, the nickel of their eagle-crested helmets glittering in the moonlight. He had worn a smile that triumphed over death when in October, with a dozen lusty youths, he had charged against the grape shot of the landlords. Even a blind man might have felt that smile. In those days he had smiled and flourished, and no grief had yet darkened the blue gleam of his eyes. Yet he himself, the real Mitka, had lived all those years without smiling; for it would have blunted the fineness of his understanding and the imperturbable hardness of his will.

A small yard—there were hens scratching in front of his sister's feet, but two of them had hopped onto the perch at the back. On the left was an apple tree, a branch of which hung down feebly by a thin strip of bark: it had a pathetic look, like a broken arm. Mitka felt again on his face the cool breath that had heralded the wild storm that wrecked the young pine trees at the edge of the forest and did not even spare the apple tree in the small garden that belonged to his father, Yegor Vekshin the pointsman. The whole night through, trains raced madly along the lines and filled the dark silence with their shrill screams and roaring, and in the morning everything that remained alive exulted and flourished. On that very day a wandering photographer had persuaded Yegor to let him take a souvenir photograph of his children. At that time the other one—what was he called?—oh, Leonty . . . was still unborn, and Mitka's mother was alive.

Till late in the evening Mitka sat in front of the faded photograph that still reflected a dim radiance from his childhood. Time, which had vanished irrevocably, opened for him like a book, but not all its pages were equally legible. In the twilight another memory came into his mind. On that evening Mashka, the mare, had been standing behind the corner of the wooden house. In the photograph there was nothing to suggest her presence, but his heart cried: "She is there, she is there!" And she would still be waiting, if Mitka should return after the heat of the day to lead her to the spring. The stupid, patient mare, waiting for twenty years long!

For the first time for years Mitka slept deeply and soundly—but the glow faded under the dull morning light, the enchantment of the square of pasteboard fled. Mitka was ashamed now of the pitiless candor of that document, pitiless as a proof of guilt. He hid the picture with the other odds and ends in the bottom of the trunk and pushed it under the bed.

Then the checkered, anxious days went on, and his restless inertia was a mystery even to himself; he could only ascribe it to his indecision. Should he look for his sister, or write to his father, or, as before, drown his cares in drink?

He felt that his father was still alive, but now sunk in himself, his old head liberally sprinkled with the gray of age. "Do you still go out with a pipe in your mouth to your work on the line, you old Spartan, while the trains go rolling on? I wonder if my stepmother still nags at you for being so hard-up and so proud, or if you still remember your boy Mitka, whom she made you throw out into the world." Mitka saw that his letter would have to be long and querulous, an indictment of life, and so he did not write it.

He could not find his sister immediately, for he had no inkling that she, little Tanya, was the celebrated Hella

Velton. When with surprise he learned this he did not enter the circus, but kept watch the whole evening at the exit, though it was cold and his feet grew numb in their polished boots. A lad selling flowers in the street offered him the frozen glory of his chrysanthemums with a cheeky smile. Probably he thought Mitka was drunk, and he might well have been, for he bought the whole bunch without bargaining, and kept idly pacing up and down the twenty steps to the next lamppost. When Tanya came out, he stepped up to her quickly and confidently, but then suddenly lost his head and let the flowers fall in the snow. Compared with the figure she made in the poster, his sister looked touchingly small and pathetic. Dispensing with a greeting, he at once overwhelmed her with questions: what was the meaning of the band over her eye, what were the black cords for which he had found in the trunk, why had she gone to Nijni?

The long years of separation had wiped out the disparity between their years and made it easy for him, who was two years younger, to catechize her with the insistence of an elder brother. She reeled back when she recognized the thief: her first impulse was to scream, but then she gave a sad smile and made no further effort to release her hands from Mitka's clasp. Their first meeting only lasted a short time, and conversation was difficult and painful for both of them. The ties that had held them together had worn thin since childhood, and she was disturbed and alarmed by her inability to find the few simple, necessary words. All at once she laughed, and in her embarrassment hid her face in her cheap squirrel collar. "Why did you throw the flowers away?" She bent down quickly, delighted at Mitka's awkwardness, which gave her an opportunity to recover from her own confusion. For a long time they could not be simple and sincere toward each other; intimacy came slowly and with difficulty.

SHE HERSELF asked that they should meet again, but Mitka did not immediately agree, for he did not know yet if his sister loved him enough to be able to forgive him his errors. While he was telling her the story of his life in deliberately crude terms, showing himself in the worst light, he concealed his thirst for her affection and forgiveness under a disagreeable smile. Yet he had the feeling that after this meeting he would be able to begin life afresh. It was the ties of their common childhood and home, not those of their kinship, that bound him to his sister. Their conversation took place in Puchov's house—the only spot where Mitka could feel secure against the intrusion of an enemy.

Mitka had not pressed the man who escorted his sister to join them, so he had taken his leave at the next corner. They went hand in hand down the middle of a narrow, empty street, their hearts full of memories. The weather was unpropitious; the gathering clouds trailed low over the roofs; the wind blew, and there was hoar frost on the ground. But in the warmth of their affection they felt well and free.

"Are you cold?"

"Where are you taking me?"

"Wait, I'll show you a real man," Mitka murmured as he led her across the street. "Are they all alive at home? What's the news?"

"I haven't written home once," she confessed curtly, dropping Mitka's hand, which had loosened its grip. "I've never written. Why should I? All that's over, and I've no further use for it."

Mitka was for a moment repelled by the arrogant callousness of her voice.

"But I'll always remember the wooden cottage and the stupid sunflowers in the garden. Do you remember their fat, stumpy stalks, and the way their faces gleamed like sunsets? I'm sure it hasn't changed."

Mitka loved the old house and thought of it as a refuge to which, if all else failed, he might return—the dear old place where he had first seen the friendly sun.

". . . and do you remember the wood owl? And how you treated its broken leg?"

"When?"

"You remember—we went together and found the little thing in a ditch." He stopped and rubbed his forehead in perplexity "No, it wasn't you. It was Manka, not you." This mistake gave a painful check to their mutual excitement.

Puchov was just going to bed when the knock came on his door. He did not recognize Mitka until his sister had been introduced. Then the Master of Blagusha could scarcely control his feelings or conceal his joy. He seized Mitka by the shoulders and shook him and gazed at him with a father's tenderness from under his thick eyebrows.

"They haven't caught me yet, Puchov, so you're not such a prophet after all. Here I am, still alive and kicking!" And he looked inquiringly at the Chinese curtain, from behind which resounding snores issued.

"My nephew's come up from the country," Puchov explained. "He's been making an evening of it: he's asleep now."

The two friends, both taking refuge behind a smile, stood there and tried to find changes in each other; they found them and were silent. In Puchov's eyes there was reproach that Mitka should have avoided him after his release from prison. Mitka's smile said: "Don't be angry with me, old man! I am yours—yours forever."

Before Puchov went behind the curtain and laid himself beside his snoring nephew, he pointed to the still warm teapot and the small cupboard where he kept the day's food. He felt that Mitka wanted to be left alone with his sister, and took himself off. In a little while they heard his nephew, disturbed in his sleep, muttering to himself.

"After I ran away from home I led the life of a dog to begin with. Perhaps a worse life than a dog. . . ." His sister began her story in a whisper as soon as the regular breathing of the other two showed that they were asleep. "It's frightful even to tell you about the first years. An organ grinder taught me all sorts of tricks. You must have seen people do their tricks in backyards for five kopeks? Well, your sister did that. In those days I forced myself to laugh. It isn't very nice, Mitka, when a hungry creature laughs." Her eyes flashed, and Mitka softly stroked her hand, which was quivering with a sudden convulsion of rage. "The organ grinder had a parrot, too, who drew lucky tickets for any fool who wanted them. He was a drowsy old bird, and he didn't always know what was expected of him. Still, it would have been risky to hit him, while one could hit the girl as much as one wanted to. I was hit often, Mitka."

"Did you hate it?"

"It hurt me. He was a bad man. One night I woke up and felt him touching me and tugging at my clothes. . . . You know what I mean? The evening before that his parrot had died, and he had drunk himself tipsy . . . well —I jumped straight through the . . ." She did not finish her sentence, for she felt Mitka's hand twitch with a sudden fury. "For two whole nights I wandered through the woods, famished with hunger, and the whole time I saw a bonfire ahead of me. I went along the road, and the bonfire was burning on my right; then I went farther, and it started burning again behind me, and for two nights it followed me. The third night I slept under a caravan: a traveling circus had stopped there for the night. Do you know anything about circus people? They all live together —men, women, and animals. The clown was called Pugel. He came out in the morning and saw me."

Tanya smiled at the recollection and raised her eyebrows; she was evidently proud of her unhappy childhood. "Pugel asked me what my name was, but I only laughed, for I was tormented by hunger and the heat. 'Matryoshka,' I told him. 'How odd!' he said. 'My old mare was called Matryoshka. Many's the time she's flung me into the sand.

. . . She's left her mark on both my knees,' and he showed me his funny old legs." Tanya fixed her tired eyes on the light in the corner of the room where Puchov's clumsy boots stood. "Then I went into a life partnership with Pugel. I'm staying with him now."

"You're living with him?" Mitka asked, and a deep pity for his sister filled his heart.

"I didn't mean that." She said no more, and no more was needed. She had struggled with the world and won, and she had nothing to blush for; she could even look back with tenderness on the humiliations and failures of her youth. "He's quite old now, and people have stopped laughing at him and begun to pity him instead—that finishes a circus artist. So I took him with me—I was grown-up by then—and he trained me for the circus. It was Giovanni's at Uralsk that first fired my ambition."

She lived again through the privations of her childhood, and bit by bit she told Pugel's sad story, too. Pugel had been a wonderful teacher; he had treated her with a boundless kindness of heart which in these days seems strange and unintelligible, like the words of a forgotten tongue.

In his prime he had earned his living with the help of his children by means of a turn called "The Mill." He had to cling to a trapeze with his feet, his head downward, holding a strap between his teeth. Then he had slowly to draw his children, who were hanging on it, up into the air. There was a roll of drums as at an execution during those hazardous moments, and in the hissing beam of the spotlight the children fluttered up lightly and gracefully above the arena, the meager tinsel of their wings making them twinkle like butterflies. Disaster came in a completely stereotyped form as in a bad novel. When the mill had been drawn right up, the worn-out strap broke just where he held it by his teeth, and the butterflies fell down on the sand. In a moment the liveried attendants had rushed to the spot in a panic, while the father still hung suspended above, with a piece of strap between his teeth, unable, in his horror, to grasp the meaning of its sudden lightness.

The director, a famous horse tamer, cracked his long whip and said: "Clear off, you bungler!" It was a public disgrace, but Pugel still hoped, and whispered, with his eyes fixed on the director's white gloves: "The strap broke!"

Though he humbled himself, it was in vain. The children were unable to take up their work again before the six weeks of their contract had expired, and the disaster had terrible consequences for Pugel. Though he worked now in a provincial circus and possessed all-round skill, his body, enfeebled by drink, could not manage even the simplest salto. So, he exchanged his black and red devil's tights for a clown's costume and breeches with checked seat. He had no ready gift for buffoonery, so he was made into a carpet man—that is to say, he had to creep under a carpet, or rather was covered by mistake with its heavy, stinking folds, under which he had to keep rolling about, while a rain of shouts came from the gallery: "Roll about, ginger knob!"

It was in those forlorn days that he found Tanya under the wagon. He gave the girl twelve lessons in the most elementary acrobatic feats, and led her on to the higher flights of circus craft. She "took the air," as circus folk say, and when she was nineteen she could do feats on the trapeze (*corde volant*) and turns in the air, as well as the average native celebrity. Yet Pugel still protected her from the treacherous chances of a first appearance. It was not until two years later that she was destined to see, from her perch above, the circus bathed in light. Her heart stood still. Then the band blared out discordantly, and everything vanished but herself and the swaying rope under her.

For that evening Pugel lent her the name of his dead wife, the famous acrobat, Hella Velton. Tanya brought no discredit on the name; indeed, she raised it later to still greater glory under the vaulted roofs of Giovanni's, and Becker's, and finally even of Truzzi's. She chose a turn called the "shtrabat," and although this was thought slightly old-fashioned, yet she gave it new luster by adding hazardous variations to it, and the natural grace of her young and supple body turned all she touched to triumph. By the time she was twenty-three her name could stand on the bills without comment or explanation. At twenty-five she was thought to be a Russianized Englishwoman, and received invitations to tour in foreign countries. Her skill encouraged her to reckless feats of daring, which gave her art a strange, wild fascination.

"And are you never afraid?"

"Of course not, you stupid!" How much older she looked now—she seemed almost condescending and indulgent. "Everything is reckoned to within an inch. I could do it all with my eyes shut. That would be rather a good idea, you know!" She stopped. "But they'd never allow it."

"And are you happy? Are you contented?"

"Of course!" she assented a little too hurriedly, and began to tell about the accident to her eye. She had been sitting in the auditorium when a trainer was rehearsing his turn in the arena. A vigorous crack broke off a piece of the whip lash, and it flew over a group of performers and struck her just over the eye. A strange phrase, "thickening of the retina,"—the eye was as good as blind. Suddenly she laughed. "You're good-looking, Mitka: I suppose the women run after you." In her face there was a look of ease and confidence, as if she knew that she had come into the world for predestined happiness.

Now it was Mitka's turn to speak, but the tender, encouraging glance of his sister embarrassed him.

AFTER laboring like a horse, Firsov eventually arrived at a fairly graphic portrait of Mitka, and was even able to identify a minute speck on the map as the pointsman's cabin at the forty-fourth verst from the main station of Rogovo, though it looked merely like a tiny splutter from a mapping pen. There was a spatter of little pine trees sketched around the spot on the map, though the Vekshins' cottage was actually surrounded with curly-tipped birch trees. They soared up gaily and impudently, and seemed more living than mere trees. They were like a band of wild girls, many thousands of them, who had played here one Whitsuntide till suddenly some mysterious, terrifying sound had rooted them to the spot.

The meadows guarded devoutly the secret of the maidens and the riddle of the trees. A wandering photographer once visited those parts—a shrewd, intriguing gentleman with a sack of literature. He roamed around the remote districts, earning his bread and night's lodging with his wonderful art, and wherever he went, he secretly distributed pamphlets among the peasants, inciting them in small type, but rousing words, to rebellion. He was denounced by a rich farmer from the neighboring town of Predotecha, and when the photographer was led past the Vekshins' house in handcuffs, eight-year-old Mitka, who stood by the door, was overcome by a dark, inexplicable bewilderment, and sobbed aloud.

The photographer had straggled from Demyatino to Predotecha, and had lost his way in the sea of birches. The vaults of transparent greenery lured him on and promised him rest and oblivion from his seditious labors. Gently, as with a splashing sound, the branches rustled over him, the birds twittered, and the stillness resounded. Perhaps it was he with his black hat who had scared the green maidens.

Since that time the wind had often ruffled the lush grass, and snow and the revolving seasons had obliterated the footprints of the stranger; yet one birch tree still bore a trace, of which the shy birch maidens whisper. The traveler had dropped down to rest under a stout birch tree, after wandering over many versts of the dusty Russian roads. He had eaten up his small stock of bread here, and with his knife had cut into its soft and sappy bark the words: "Andrey Klokachev. Down with Authority!" When he had finished his meal, he went away, but this mark remained behind.

From those fatal words, scored deep into its pith, the old birch tree sickened. The misery and suffering of men, borne here upon the wind, found a nightly shelter in its long and drooping branches. Through the tiny window of this inscription a terrible canker had forced its way into the birch; the wound swelled, and black and curling growths festered around its lips. The ulcer ate in deeper, destroyed the wood, and, relentlessly advancing, killed the tree. It turned this way and that, piteously rustling its leaves; it struggled against death, and in the frenzy of the spring shed its bark, hoping that it might slough off the accursed scar as well. A hurricane put an end to its agony, for one morning the old birch lay on the ground, its mighty trunk stretching across the whole length of the meadow; it lay in the dust, exposing its secret to the sky, and the torment of its naked roots. In a single night the maidens had grown old and stiff, and their leaves had lost their virgin freshness. The old tree rotted, and covered the whole meadow with debris; the death-dealing words met death themselves, and fell away like a scab. Yet even in death the old tree did not surrender, for from its roots in the spring a slim and fragrant shoot sprang up.

On this birch Mitka had often sat with dark Masha, and planned the games of childhood with a strange, unchild-like seriousness. How often had these unforgettable woods and meadows, full of peaceful flowers and the sound of birds, mirrored themselves in the cloudless blue of his eyes! Just so are the blue sky and the blue thicket of reeds mirrored in the brook; the water never grudges them their image. At that time the world was still for Mitka a play of pure blue color, a mystery still unraveled. Not till later, when his maturer understanding searched for the solution of the riddle, did he begin to see that the Light plays with the Darkness, and that the Darkness is the Light's rival, his equal in power and with him the parent of Life, their eternal child.

Mitka had learned to read in Demyatino, and had deciphered the writing on the birch without trouble. It was oddly consistent with the conversation of the man in the black hat, who had passed the night beside him in the Vekshins' hay loft. The visitor had talked to Mitka till midnight; the world, he explained, was in the toils of Evil, and the soul of Man was crushed down by Authority, and was perishing. His voice had a hollow, passionate ring, but Mitka did not understand a word he said, and had started to cry. All the same his young soul was never afterward able to free itself from the spell of this night's conversation. The fanatical, inexorable eyes of the man in the black hat had stamped themselves indelibly on his brain. Then Mitka had been carried away—the same railway train that he used to meet with his green flag had carried him away from his childhood. Trains, trains, iron endowed with life, with a roar they bored into the flying distance. They tore past, every morning, in their fruitless striving to reach the ends of the earth. The horizon receded farther and farther, but the driver knew neither discouragement nor fatigue. The far call of the engines, wild for their distant goal, echoed through the woods, and cascades of laughter shook the mocking birches.

Men looked out of the carriage windows, and saw how the draft, as they passed, tore at a tatter on Mitka's faded shirt. They all had the same strange, gray faces, stamped with the ennui of cities. Once a passenger—Mitka had a glimpse of gold-rimmed glasses—flung him a three-kopek piece. He picked it up and bought himself a little chocolate bottle he had long coveted at Stepan Dochkin's in Demyatino. He bought it and ate it up secretly. He did not wish to have any secrets, but this secret of the three kopeks had been forced on him and even it was more than he could bear. Now he hated the strange gentleman's twinkling glasses, through which he had spied Mitka in his obscurity at an unknown pointsman's cabin. The three kopeks would not, of course, have added to the welfare of the family, which had learned to make ends meet on eighteen roubles, the measure of official gratitude for obscure service; but Mitka's soul rejected angrily all the plausible excuses of his mind. The seed the man with the black hat had sown grew up.

Meanwhile Mitka's elder sister had vanished without a trace, for it was she who had suffered most from the stepmother. The father had done his best for her; he had hallooed for her in the wood, but had left it at that, for he knew that nothing much could go wrong with a Vekshin. Soon it became clear that Mitka, too, was no longer a child. His boy's shirts became too tight for him, his patched pants too short, and there was not enough money for new ones, as all his father's income went in porridge and cabbage soup, which was so watery that every day you saw in it a dingy reflection of the black ceiling. One day a countryman, who was so crushed by misfortune that he would have curtsied to the cat, passed by and called Mitka "Dmitri Yegorich" in the presence of his father. On the previous evening a railway mechanic from Rogovo had come to shoot in the Vekshins' district. He had deigned to drink Yegor's thin tea with him, and had conversed uninterruptedly on religious matters, for he fancied he derived dignity from such weighty themes. Yegor had listened to him respectfully, sucking in Fyodor Dolomanov's spiritual nourishment with his tight soldier's lips.

Two days later Yegor was sitting on a bench, busy repairing his down-at-heel boots. Dmitri had lain down in a corner after lunch. His father bored the awl in the heel of the boot and raised his eyes calmly. "Well, Mitri, are you pretty tough now?" "Yes, Daddy," said Mitka in apprehension, checking a yawn. His father put aside the boot. "Well, go along to Rogovo today, and ask for Fyodor Ignatich. If you're good at your work, he'll make you an engine doctor." He stroked his clean-shaven cheek at this dismal joke. He had been a soldier and had won a cross for services in the field, of which he spoke reluctantly. He still kept his military bearing, and shaved his cheeks until he was advanced in years; the only indulgence he allowed himself was his mustache. "You'll spend the night in Predotecha," he added firmly.

Mitka's stepmother packed into the wooden trunk everything she did not need herself, so that no one should reproach her with having chased the son out hungry and naked. Yegor accompanied him to the gate, gave him his first eight ten-kopek pieces, and said to him as he left: "Put your best foot forward, Mitri, and trust in the Lord! And remember that weak knees won't carry you far." (Yegor had heard a great deal about weak knees from his company commander in quite different circumstances, yet he had made the phrase a rule of conduct, and passed it on to his son now as the secret of a steady life.)

He waved his hand, and Mitka, stepping out of the door, looked back for the last time at the garden, the house, and his stepmother at the window. Drenched in the calm glow of the sunset, the scene stamped itself on Mitka's memory forever. The sun sank over the distant, clear horizon, toward which the railway line flew on its arrowy way and from which every evening the shades of night streamed across the sky. Mitka's youth ended with that sunset. Suddenly it occurred to him that now his father would have to go out himself to the seven o'clock train. Leonty, his unloved stepbrother, would sit babbling on his father's strong arm, while Yegor stared at the black, oil-sodden gravel of the permanent way and a soldier's meager tear wet his shaven cheek. "Your loneliness will be thrice bitter, Yegor Vekshin, soldier of this Life."

He spent his first night away from home on the road, and, as he went, visited all the dear, familiar places of his childhood. He said good-by to the wood with its strange sounds that terrified him; but the sky was cloudless, and the darkness did not hide it. At sunrise, when the dew steamed up from the ground, Mitka warmed himself at a small fire. Then, with a resolute gesture, he flung all his stepmother's clutter out of his trunk. He felt himself a man now, able to bear his burden and give up his freedom, and with that gesture he renounced, too, the protecting shelter of his home. Three years later he lost the cross on his breast, which his mother had given him.

The distant woods of Rogovo were bathed in the glowing shafts of dawn, and over them the heavens opened in majestic benediction.

"Do you know, her life's a real . . . biography!" said
Mitka in confusion, starting to answer his sister's questions. "When you left, Masha took your place. If you ask
me, Life has the laugh of us—first it's all roses, and then,
before you know where you are, it knocks you over the
head. Lots of people have an easy life, Tatyanuska, as
easy as a song. One man sings, and everyone's delighted;
then another man starts, and his singing's like a splinter
in your heart. No one listens to sad songs. Some people
have everything given them so that bit by bit it may all
be taken away and they may suffer the more."

"Are you speaking of yourself?"

"Of myself and Masha."

As the distant scenes of his childhood flew through his
excited mind, he saw there black-haired Masha, the companion of his happiest years. Her calm beauty had made
her proud and clothed her as in ice; Firsov had compared
it aptly to a snowfield whose snow glitters the purer the
wilder and more furiously the storm rages. In the close
friendship of their childhood they had shared everything
loyally with each other—everything except the chocolate
bottle. When Mitka confessed this to her, she had tried
to console him, and had punished him with a gentle slap
and a loving embrace for his extravagant distress.

Masha, Masha Dolomanova! . . . She was the locksmith's daughter at the terminus where Mitka went to
work. In the summer, when Rogovo seethed like an engine
boiler and the ear was stunned by the ceaseless, deafening
din, Dolomanov used to send Masha on a visit to a third

cousin, who was married to the keeper of the railway bridges in the Vekshins' neighborhood. For a small sum she took the place of Masha's mother, for Dolomanov had been widowed on the day of Masha's birth. He had the reputation of being a decent sort of fellow, though, like all self-made men, he was ponderous and dictatorial, and his hand lay heavily on the whole household. With him lived his brother, a silent toper, who had gone to the dogs, and his Aunt Pasha, who kept house; she was hard of hearing and every night composed petitions to be admitted into the local poorhouse, demanding maintenance at the public cost in consideration of her husband's services—he had been a policeman who had been killed in the troubles of 1905. No one in Dolomanov's house had a single cupboard or nook of his own; the whole house was pervaded by the autocratic spirit of the master.

Only the floorboards ventured to disturb the tomblike silence of the house, and the cat, a good-for-nothing Don Juan, had made repeated efforts to escape from Dolomanov's household, but was always astutely checkmated by the drunken brother—he had a special understanding of this incorrigible libertine. There was a tall and gloomy grandfather clock, in whose glassy depths hands swam around and weights swung. The works were out of order and the hours no longer struck, but when the aged hand quavered up to the top of the dial, a sound went through the room like a malevolent sneeze. To the sound of this sneeze life passed away irrevocably.

The elder Dolomanov, who was kept busy the whole day attending to the ailments of engines, used to enjoy sitting down of an evening beside a glass of cold tea. He would sneeringly retail some office gossip or a discreditable anecdote about the priest Maxim, against whom he cherished, for no reason at all, a bitter enmity. "Maximka's son's turned up again," he smiled, gently scratching the cat, which was sunning itself on his knees. The priest's son, a dissipated young man, who was a student in a seminary, turned up yearly on his father's birthday to start a squabble in front of the guests.

"He went to the pond first and started knocking off the geese's heads."

"With a stick?" the younger Dolomanov inquired ingratiatingly, waiting for his brother's answer as for a favor.

"No, with a bucket," the older brother retorted sarcastically, and after this witticism there reigned a terror-stricken silence.

At Shrovetide Masha noticed that her father's hands trembled as they reached for a pancake. "Well, Maxim's done for," he said, and waited for exclamations of disbelief, but none came. "He ate pancakes with fish and then he died. The doctor said because of twisted intestines."

"Gluttony!" piped the drunkard drolly, and gave Aunt Pasha a kick to show she might laugh too this time.

"Don't blaspheme!" Fyodor Ignatich got up noisily, his eyes flashing, and shook the cat off his knees like dirt. "*You'll* start whimpering when death comes to you. . . ."

Maxim's death disturbed the old man: he himself would not be able to sneak past death, either. He threw a glance at Masha, seeking for sympathy and warmth, but he shrank back from his daughter's aloofness. She had her share of the wild blood of the Dolomanovs, and it was with a sigh of relief that every spring she left her father's house and all its prohibitions.

An iron bridge led over the Kudema, and on both sides of it, not far from each other, stood two keepers' houses hidden in the wood. It was here that the two children met each other.

They met one May morning on the bridge; Mitka was twelve that day and, not without pride, was fingering the tight collar of his shirt, which was as blue as the morning sky. When Mitka stepped onto the bridge, Masha was already standing there on the wooden crossboard with a bunch of wild flowers in her hand. She leaned her chin on the handrail and watched how the wind broke against the smooth, blue waters in darting ripples. Marvellous and beneficent is the wind in May; it helps the little birds to break their shells, and dries the wounds on the trees, and binds hearts together. It whistled through the ironwork of the bridge, and the stiff, metal bands twanged like fiddle strings.

Mitka stood and watched the girl screwing up her eyes in the wind, and every moment tossing the rebellious curls from her face. A red frock clung to her bare legs as closely as if it were drenched through.

"What are those?" asked Mitka severely, touching the girl's silver earrings.

"Earrings." She cast a distrustful side glance at him, but did not run away.

"Why are you wearing them?"

"Well, just because. . . ."

While they chattered together, Mitka forgot the ten o'clock train, and when it suddenly came roaring around the bend, it was already too late for them to run away. The iron rails quivered and groaned and rattled: condemned to immobility, they greeted the flying steel whose destiny it was to rush on tirelessly and forever. Mitka pressed the girl to him and waited for the train to pass. Accidentally their glances met, and that wonderful, daunting glance bound their hearts together forever.

But when the danger was past and left behind it in the air only a meaningless whirl of dust and din, their talk grew more cheerful.

"Do you see that yellow hill there with the fir trees on it? Do you see it? That's Owl Mountain." Mitka pointed at a dull yellow spot in the waving green of the forest.

"Why is it called that?"

"Because owls live there."

"Do they peck?" she asked inquisitively, full of childish awe.

"Of course!" answered Mitka, tugging irresolutely at his belt. "Take them off!"

"Take what off?"

"The earrings."

"All right!"

And the wind swept under the arches of the bridge, dived into the glades of the forest, and, bursting out again, held up the birds in their flight.

"Throw the flowers away, too. I'll pick you yellow ones. They grow over there. No, there!" He seized her head and twisted it in the direction he meant.

"Leave my head alone!" cried the girl. "I can see all right myself."

"Don't be cross! St. Fedya the Ferryman planted those fir trees there. He put money under the fir trees, and people who want anything can take it when they like."

"Why did he do that?"

"You see, he was a ferryman, but he always gave people their money back. He was a fool, but a saint, too. His monastery is over there." (Behind the wood rose up a church with five onion-shaped domes, like a gaily painted wooden toy.) "Don't you know that, either? You *are* silly."

"I'm not silly."

"Well, then, why can't you understand? He died, and that fir tree took his place."

"And then?"

"That's all." Mitka shook his head. His hair was cut in a straight line around the nape of his neck in the peasant way. "Don't be silly!"

This first squabble did not last long, for they had barely left the bridge when she touched his hand in sign of forgiveness. The next day they went to the same place to pick flowers, and all through the summer they met here on every sunny day. She was quick and nimble, and soon learned from Mitka how to climb trees and make catapults and catch crayfish with her hand in the shallows, when they crept into the mud to warm themselves, and pounce on grasshoppers, and many other things. Every day they made the round of their kingdom, and their bare feet left no trace on the grass. The northernmost limit of their realm was the Owl Mountain with its inaccessible slopes. To the left was a field of prickly grass, to the right the limpid waters of the prattling Bikany, stepchild and rival of the Kudema. To the south they could go no farther than the ravine, where once, as they ran past, they had seen a tramp. Masha declared that she had seen a tall pile of gold near him, and Mitka excitedly remembered that he had seen a bloody knife there, too, and this added a thrill to the forbidden darkness of the ravine.

In the autumn Masha went away and left Mitka yearning for the return of the warm days. Winter was dedicated to learning, but as soon as the spring wind began to blow, Mitka was waiting for her on the bridge, even in bad weather, and she never once cheated his hopes.

Yet time flowed no slower than the swift Kudema, and Mitka's cornflower-blue shirt became too tight for him. They no longer spent all their time running around and playing, but often sat side by side leaning against each other and talking in monosyllables.

Masha received Mitka's confession that he had a sister, whom he was fond of, with cold, unchildlike jealousy. Their childish games took on a new and wonderful but disturbing meaning. When Mitka kissed her, only half intending it, Masha shuddered, but she did not feel herself insulted. That evening the sky shed soft vapors of heat, and the scent of a single camomile drugged their senses like the fragrance of a whole haystack. Masha ran away from him, and he could think of no words with which to hold her back. For four days she did not come, but on the fifth they met, as if accidentally, and went together to the ravine as usual. They stayed a long time there and abandoned themselves to the torment of their childish terrors; but there was nothing there except a horses' cemetery overgrown with sorrel, where the horses' bones reposed peacefully under humps of bushy grass. They went around the ravine and extended the range of their territory—but how much narrower had the realm of their childhood become on this evening! An invisible cuckoo counted up passionlessly the remaining days of their friendship in the green wood that glowed in the red sunset.

They had reached the age when the soul in passionate yearning looks for a mate. A strange lethargy weighed on them. They began to feel the stirrings of shame. Masha found her blossoming loveliness an unendurable burden; the shabbiness of Mitka's clothes was an obsession to him. Masha scented danger in Mitka's sharp face, which only now and again was illuminated by a quick flash of his eyes. The storm was ready to break, and the pregnant clouds yearned to be delivered of their riches. Suddenly Masha went away. Her father had sent for her so that she might go to the local school that had been opened in Rogovo— thanks to the efforts of a neighboring landowner, Manyukin.

Next May Mitka went to the bridge again and waited a long time, but no one appeared; it began to rain, but he did not go away. He was sixteen years old that day; he was wearing new boots and a new shirt, and in his hand, which was moist with nervousness, he had a small present for his friend. The money for this gift he had earned in a railway co-operative works in the Vekshins' radius; he had worked for it in the cold autumn rain. It had cost him a lot of trouble to persuade the contractor to take him on. The contractor was a surly man who took pleasure in humiliating his workers, and Mitka had to clench his teeth often to keep himself from planting a blow on the red, mustached face. He brought home a third of the money he had earned, and with another third he bought a shirt. At Dochkin's the draper himself had attended him, sweating with enthusiasm as he displayed before his eyes a dazzling array of satin shirt fronts.

"This, now, is really stylish!" breathed the draper ecstatically, "and so stiff it could stand by itself!" And he rummaged around excitedly, and even tested its strength with his teeth to move Mitka to buy. Mitka chose a showy black shirt, and with the remaining third of his money he bought a small, cheap gold ring, in which a tiny turquoise twinkled forlornly. He had put into this gift all his growing tenderness; but Masha did not come, so, soaked and hungry, he returned home.

Not till a year and a half later did he meet her again, and she recognized him. One hot evening he was returning tired and dirty from the workshop, where he was employed as a waggon cleaner at a salary of fifteen roubles, when he saw Masha, glowing with beauty, coming toward him with a book and a parasol in her hand—the engine mechanic, Dolomanov, always liked everyone to know how liberally he provided for his daughter. Masha called Mitka by his name, and, transported with joy, took a few steps toward him; but Mitka turned away. The evening before he had heard that three men were wooing her: the stationmaster Sokolovsky, the bank clerk Yeldyukov, and the priest in Demyatino, Maxim's son, who was also called Maxim, now a reformed character, and much respected in the neighborhood. Mitka had no wish to be the fourth. In any case he did not remain much longer in Rogovo, for he was not on good terms with Dolomanov, and ended by having a row with him, after which he went into the workshops at the Murom junction. But he was too restless and ambitious to remain there, either, and he made his way farther and farther toward the Urals. Rumor said that after accomplishing the prescribed eighteen thousand versts as engine driver, he had finally become an assistant mechanic; but at that point even the rumors about him died down. It is to this period that Firsov attributes Vekshin's first acquaintance with political parties. Mitka left Rogovo forever, and all trace of him was lost; everyone forgot him, everyone but Masha—bad Masha Dolomanova, who never forgot him.

But already the fifth suitor, who was destined to be the most successful of all, had made his appearance.

THE three suitors, with Fyodor Ignatich and his brother, the toper, who did not count, formed a society, whose basis was their common taste for the pleasures of the bath. It is impossible to say what induced old Dolomanov to erect this temple of idolatry, as the priest in Demyatino called it. The old man was suffering neither from dipsomania nor from any spiritual disorder, yet suddenly, when his daughter reached a marriageable age, he devoted all his savings to building a vapor bath in the kitchen garden. Masha, of course, attempted to dissuade him. "Don't make a fool of yourself!" she said, but Fyodor Ignatich screamed out something about his forty years of work without pleasure, and sent her packing.

Till that time some of them had washed in washtubs, others had steamed themselves on the huge Russian stoves, others had not washed from one summer to the next, but had saved up dirt and soap for the time when the deep waters of the Kudema should have warmed themselves a little. It was not, however, because Dolomanov was not satisfied with the washtub or the stove that he resolved to build this temple of idolatry; it was because the old man had been scared to death. That year Aunt Pasha had finally been granted shelter in the poorhouse. She had taken leave of her nephew and had left the house with a small bag, when on one of the steps in front of the house she collapsed and died on the spot. Her death disturbed Dolomanov so much that for a time he even forgot to quarrel with his brother. He passed a whole month in brooding. Then one night he wakened and pulled a silver rouble out of his pocket. There was a parlor trick that once upon a time he had had no difficulty in performing for the entertainment of his tipsy friends—he would take a coin between thumb and first finger and with two vigorous squeezes bend it double. Now he tried to accomplish this once more, but the coin resisted all his efforts. "You've forgotten how, old fool!" he muttered; he was sweating, and his heart beat with mad fury. He pressed the coin again in his dirty fist; he pressed with force and cunning, but he could not dispel his dark doubts. Then he lit a lamp and, sitting on the bed, contemplated his hammer-shaped fist; it was as it always had been; the mischief lay deeper. Dolomanov's fist, the summary and symbol of his power, had left him in the lurch at the supreme moment. He passed the whole night in torment, and early next morning went out to make his peace with the priest's family in Demyatino. He lunched with Sokolovsky and passed the evening with Yeldyukov. He looked at Yeldyukov thoughtfully as he made up the workers' pay lists. "Fool!" he scoffed in his mind. "You think that that's all you live for." He sat down there a long time, for he was frightened to return to his creaking, sleepless bed.

The ingenious idea of constructing a vapor bath was Dolomanov's salvation. This, Rogovo's eighth wonder of the world, had a circumference of eight or nine meters, and was surrounded by a high fence. The doors were thickly lined with felt. The upper couches were strewn with birch leaves, and Yeldyukov, in painting the stove, had got into such an ecstasy of invention that Fyodor Ignatich would not allow Masha to go into the baths until the steam had effaced Yeldyukov's fantasies. The three rivals, with Masha's wild beauty as a remote, alluring prize, shared the growing responsibilities of the vapor bath. Sokolovsky brought water and split logs; Yeldyukov disclosed a surprising talent for heating the bath in such a way that the heat did not overwhelm the visitor all at once, but insinuated itself imperceptibly into his soul. The priest Maxim went daily to Peter and Paul for twigs and brought armfuls of them, for at that season the birch twigs were particularly smooth and fragrant and lasting.

Nowhere in the whole world was there such a renaissance of the art of the vapor bath. Yeldyukov, who undressed first, would run in, covering his shame modestly with his hands, and splash the walls with cold water so that they might absorb the injurious vapors from the stove. Then he would hang five twig brushes in front of the stove mouth and adjust the bucket. Waves of hissing steam poured over the twigs, which stirred and spread out their crumpled leaves and enjoyed the raptures of spring. Then the others stepped, all four at once, into the steaming, fragrant room and got to work. The pulpy leaves clung softly and firmly to their bodies and forced them to breathe in gasps, almost to suffocate with rapture, to scream aloud with bliss. The toper, who had a bald pate, sat by himself with only his cap on down below in the straw, and shook his head at the unbridled transports of his friends.

On the topmost perch Yeldyukov lay with a stony face and flogged himself ecstatically, while Sokolovsky crouched beside him and gave himself delicious little thrills by sticking the twigs deftly between his legs. His long arms enabled him to reach the back of his neck with the broom in this position. Lower down, Maxim was whipping himself, and still lower down, Dolomanov was dancing about. Then the suitors rolled outside in the snow, returned to the vapor bath, and poured peppermint kvass into the stove. This made the steam sharper, and their temples throbbed madly, yet now the secret essence and inmost meaning was wooed from the water, and the black ceiling of the steam bath spread over them like the vault of heaven. Heated till they flushed an almost dangerous scarlet, they shouted out witticisms to each other, much to the amusement of old Dolomanov, with the result that the heating apparatus, which should have lasted for three years, got out of order in a single winter.

It was wartime, and Masha, beautifully robed and now with the ampler charms of young womanhood, attended the dances given by the young men of Rogovo who had not yet enlisted. The love-sick suitors fawned on Dolomanov for Masha's favor, but she sat in a corner, and no one dared to ask her to dance; for they were all awed by her sulky beauty. Often when she grew tired of crying over her loneliness, she stepped out onto the steps in front of her house in nothing but her chemise, stood there and gazed into the transparent darkness of the snow, listening to the wakeful baying of the dogs. There was a timber wood on a hill behind Rogovo, and the trees there used to sway with a gentle creaking as they gave themselves to night and sleep. The starlight was not reflected on the smooth, deep drifts of snow, but lights came across from the windows of the vapor bath where Dolcmanov was whipping himself with birch twigs in his wild efforts to drive away his presentiments of death. Even in those days, unknown to herself, Masha in her thoughts had already called her terrible lover from the darkness of the woods.

In July the volunteers were escorted to the station. There was a party in the school hall, which was decorated with garlands and flags, and Maxim from Demyatino pronounced the service. Through the open window the evening sky displayed all its tender hues. That July, which was to prelude the first revolution, was rich in storms, and the evenings were heavy with fragrance from the pines (which you could almost feel corporeally), and filled with insatiable yearning. After the service, Maxim gave a farewell address. He spoke of the Fatherland, which had fallen into such distress, and of the spirit of sacrifice which filled the people; of old David and young Abishag. Although they all remembered how, eight years before, he had knocked geese's heads off in the flooded meadows of Demyatino, no one laughed at his pathetic oratory.

"Come, Abishag, bring back the warmth to David's languid body. Pour yourself out, omnipotent young blood, in David's drying arteries," he boomed in an impressively muffled voice. Behind him shone the bald spot on the wall where, some months before, the picture of the last Czar had been torn down for ever.

The volunteers—sturdy, single youths—sweated in their tight soldiers' tunics and stared at the floor in embarrassment. They were escorted to the train, and the stationmaster, Sokolovsky, raised a final "Hurrah!" and gave the signal to start. With a sigh of relief the others returned to the school, where a dance had been arranged. Yeldyukov could play tolerably on the clarinet, and there were four other musicians in the band.

Dolomanova was sitting in a corner when an unknown man invited her to a polka. He was wearing tight boots and elegant, puffed-out breeches. His broad shoulders, his high, slanting forehead, and his uneasy dark eyes impressed Masha disagreeably; he looked as though he had come to do single combat with the world. Merely to flout Rogovo morals, she waltzed twice around with the unknown man. (Yeldyukov had slowed down the tempo of the music, and so the polka had turned into a waltz.) But it was not until the third time around that she observed that strange preparations were being made. All the doors were locked, and Sokolovsky, accompanied by a brawny railway porter, was coming slowly toward her. There was a look of great resolution in his eyes, and behind his back he was holding a rope, whose end trailed along the floor. The couple still circled in the empty hall, and the music ended in a confused noise.

"They're making for us," she whispered, and she felt that her place was beside her partner.

"So I see," he answered, and suddenly he pushed Masha aside and fired a shot straight into the face of the stationmaster Sokolovsky.

She thought she was about to die, and when she came to herself again she hardly heard the stories of the women who stood around her. The stranger in the breeches, having shot off Sokolovsky's ear, had jumped through the window, but the undergrowth below it had eased his fall and the darkness had hidden him from his pursuers. She shrank when she learned her partner's name, for it was a notorious one. He was Ageyka Stolyarov, the terror of two districts, a marauding ruffian.

No one knew where he came from or the name of his unhappy father. He had suddenly appeared with the other harbingers of evil, with the wolves and the smallpox and the general anarchy. He lived in the woods and made friends with animals, it was said. He had been nourished on the putrid blood shed in the war. He was like a bad dream that vanishes at the first breath of dawn.

Those were days of dire need and peril. The land was being laid waste by violence and by creeping villainy. The survivors of the front scoured the broad no man's land between the front and the Hinterland in sinister silence, and a cloud of rebellion followed them. One day at twilight, when the first snow was falling, two boys—workmen's

children from the depot—came to Masha and asked her
for a piece of something red. They had heard news from
their fathers, but the first was obstinately silent, the second merely smiled, absorbed in his secret knowledge.
Masha brought out the old frock in which Mitka had met
her for the first time, and looked on uncomprehendingly
while the two boys turned the stuff over in their hands
and measured its length and breadth. Then she could no
longer stifle the pent-up frenzy in her heart, but abandoned herself to that secret agitation that filled the air
and the wind and the first October snow.

"Let me . . . let me go with you, too!"

She stretched out her arms to them, ready to run off
with them as she was, but they laughed at her impetu-
osity, and, with a glance at each other, hurried away.

An hour later the children of the railway workers were
marching along the single street of Rogovo, four abreast,
though there were twelve of them at most. The wooden
expression on their faces was in keeping with their gloomy
silence, till suddenly, with one accord, they began a tune-
less song. Masha ran out, and recognized in the old man
who was gesticulating with his hands a teacher whom, till
now, no one had suspected. Then she stared at her frock,
which had been torn up and sewn together again into a
long banner. The wind tugged at the frail piece of stuff
as it fluttered and flapped noisily on its flagstaff. Jealousy,
born of her loneliness, clutched at her heart.

She returned home soaked to the skin, and chased away
her tittering suitors from the window. The stationmaster
Sokolovsky went politely up to her and pushed a chair
forward.

"You cur . . . you half-alive cur!" Masha said wearily,
and, scanning him contemptuously from head to foot,
turned and left the room.

Life grew cold and empty, and the winter wore on like a
wasting disease. Spring came, a smell of burning rose in
the air, and every morning a pretty little bird with a yellow breast visited Masha's hospitable window sill. All
Rogovo was deep in the slush of thawing snow, and everywhere you saw peasants hauling at carts that had stuck in
the ruts. More and more often Masha left the house to
wander about in dark, cheerless places. She took a pleasure

in sitting at the edge of the wood beside the river and watching the Kudema toss her foaming mane. Masha wasted with the thawing snow, consumed by the hopeless fire in her heart. One day, when the keen April wind raced over the snowless fields, Ageyka came upon her on the river bank and raped her. She struggled and bit him, but he was able to master her nevertheless. Afterward they sat side by side. Ageyka smoked, and from under his heavy eyebrows observed Masha's tousled appearance. Oh, how she cursed Mitka at that moment for his absence! . . . In the bend of the river the black spring flood seethed beneath her.

All that was left for her now was to spring into the river, yet when Agey proposed that she should live with him, she followed him, for to go with him was as fatal an act as to leap into the icy waters. On the night that Masha left Rogovo forever, Dolomanov's vapor bath was burned to the ground. That was the wedding present of the passionately infatuated Ageyka.

Now all this sank back again into the distance. With hands silently entwined, brother and sister sat on side by side. Their thoughts were filled with that vague, intangible thing that men call life. From the corner, Nikolka's heavy snoring floated through the thick folds of tobacco smoke. The lamp had gone out, for its supply of oil was exhausted, and a brighter light was coming now through Puchov's tiny window. Suddenly, as if Tanya had not heard Masha's story at all, she touched Mitka's hand and asked: "But have you ever killed anyone yourself, Mitka?"

Lowering his eyes, Mitka put out his cigarette between his fingers with an impatient gesture and shook his head.

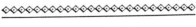
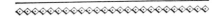
FIRSOV left Mitka alone for the time being and mixed assiduously with the inhabitants of Blagusha. All of them, except Mitka, trusted him, probably because they supposed he had a bee in his bonnet—a theory he took no steps to refute. At first it was Zinka who absorbed him, and he did not rest till he knew what it was that haunted her dreams and filled her waking thoughts. Usually he caught her embroidering, but then she would hurriedly hide her work in the drawer; all the same he managed to catch sight of a pattern of cornflowers and scarlet poppies on a yellow silken ground, which he was not surprised to see later on Mitka's shirt. And yet he knew that Zinka, in spite of her constancy and her abundant charms, had no hold on Mitka.

"Well, enchantress!" Firsov began ingratiatingly as he sat down at the table. "How go the beautiful flowers?"

"Tell me, Firsov"—Zinka gave a loud sigh and blushed like a young girl—"can love break one's heart?"

He laughed meaningly, and opened and shut his cigarette case.

"Love makes the world go round, you know. Mountains crack like nuts and open their treasures. Stars roam the skies yearning to unite and kindle new fires in space. And a heart is a very small thing." He tried to adopt a jesting tone, and she did not know that tomorrow the whole world would see her bleeding wound.

But so it happened. With tears and to the distant tones of a flute Zinka confessed her love to the writer. Her brother Matvey, who shared the room with her, laughed all through her confession. He was a matter-of-fact man, a student, secretary of three organizations, and an employee in an office whose official designation, even abbreviated, occupied a whole line; he was wearing a shabby felt coat, a relic of the front, and in everything—his listless, tired face included—was a complete contrast to Zinka. It was typical of the household that Nikolai, the miracle worker, and Lenin, the leader of the proletariat, should glare at each other from opposite corners. The former had a very menacing expression, but his vis-à-vis did not appear to mind very much.

Often, as he sat with Matvey on the window ledge and watched Zinka's little daughter playing with the rocking horse, Firsov would tease him by talking skeptically about the revolution. Matvey's cheeks would glow and a stream of fiery words would pour from his volcanic soul, but meantime Firsov had already quietly walked off to visit the third lodger, who had lately arrived. Minus was the quietest of all Jews; he earned his livelihood by playing the flute in a cinema, but spent the greater part of the day at home, where no one heard him; only his flute sighed softly for the sorrows of its silent owner. Firsov, who had got to know him by accident, thought himself justified now in spending a few minutes with him every day in the dark corner behind the chest of drawers. It was to the sad tones of Minus's flute that the saddest parts of his novel were composed.

Flute in hand, Minus stood by the window and looked down into the street, a silent bridge between nothingness and nothingness. He played a sad, lingering air, which had come by chance into his head and could not be repeated, and smiled shortsightedly at his nervous fingers. Firsov spoke very little; he sat with eyes closed, and felt the thin trickle of Minus's sorrow filtering through to his heart, and offered no resistance. Sometimes the flute gave out a tender, plaintive sound, then it sang a soothing lullaby, then it had the shrill, wailing note of pain and despair. So does a butterfly dash against the thick windowpanes in its attempt to escape. Through those tones Firsov strove to understand Minus and the soul of his race.

"You may be right!" interjected Firsov absent-mindedly. "If you rush through life in a motor car—or on the wings of fancy, it doesn't matter which—you naturally see everything *couleur de rose*, but if you plod along on your two flat feet, you see the reverse side of the picture. There aren't really any healthy, red-cheeked men in the world, only cripples—and that's what makes the world so wonderful and so sad!"

"Cripples!" smiled Minus, and his fingers pressed the flute still more painfully. "You don't know what you're talking about! You don't know the value and the price of tears and laughter and suffering. You've never wept yet like Jeremiah at the wall."

"Excuse me, but I must be going," said Firsov, suddenly collecting himself, and he hurried out into the passage to fix the weeping Jeremiah firmly in his notebook.

Manyukin, however, was not in the least in a mood for visitors; like a thief he crammed into a drawer a leather-bound exercise book in which he had been writing, and hid himself behind the bed curtain. But Firsov was not to be put off so easily; he entered, and, after standing a moment in thought, caught sight of the shadow of a bottle outlined on the dirty window curtain. Deliberately he took it from the window ledge and made as if he were going to drink it unceremoniously, and immediately Manyukin appeared.

"Excuse me, here's a cup," he said in a constrained voice, stepping out of his concealment.

"Do you drink it neat?" Firsov retorted, and returned the bottle to its place, as he had no more need of it.

"Well, it works quicker if you don't drown it," said Manyukin sulkily, rubbing his hands in sign of annoyance. "But you knew, I suppose, that I was watching you?" He gave in with a laugh.

"I did," smiled the writer.

"You're a rum chap. You experiment with men as if they were guinea pigs. That's like Chikelyov, too. He's all for having me out of the room now so that he can get married. The other day he said to me: 'You should be kicked out as an impenitent parasite, that's the law! I'm going to put a maple-wood cupboard and a mother-of-pearl wall screen where your bed is.' That was all just spite, of course, but yesterday he drew a chalk line across the room and told me I was to keep to my side of it. I never knew there was so much dirtiness in the world."

"Dirt breeds dirt," Firsov snapped.

"Indeed! But you've disturbed me. I'm writing something. No, no, not a novel. I'm only writing about myself." Firsov prudently kept silence. "Have you caught Mitka yet? He's a slippery chap. His way of life is very different from mine. I suppose you're going to cram me in somewhere, too."

"Yes, I intend to," said his visitor briefly.

"Well, you'll make a mistake. You should begin by describing a Manyukin from the earliest times. But you'll just tell how Sergey Manyukin, the parasite and imperialist, is drinking away his life in shame. Today people write just from revenge, and revenge is a poor sort of inspiration." Manyukin rudely blew a breath of brandy into Virsov's face.

At that moment a hairy face was poked round the doorway. "Does the hairdresser, Korolyov, live here?"

"You mean Vekshin?" asked Firsov in a friendly tone. "Yes, he lives here. I'll take you along."

Firsov nodded casually to Manyukin and went out to escort Mitka's long-legged visitor. He knocked cautiously at the door, but when he heard Mitka answer, he waited a moment before he went away.

"In any case, why do you want the hairdresser Vekshin?" he asked, laughing.

"To trim up a corpse," answered Sanka with a confiding grin, for he had often met the writer and was on easy terms with him.

MITKA was lying in bed. The window framed a forlorn patch of sky, and there was nobody to cheer his solitude, for his sister was touring the provinces. Sanka stepped in, clearing his throat. His nickname had certainly been well chosen, for his long, thin body in its ragged coat was topped by a head as round as a bullet, which was always adorned with an apologetic smile. Today his mustache had a swashbuckling curl, and even his mild eyebrows seemed saucy. Mitka inquired the reason.

"I've hooked a wench, master!" he explained with relish. "I'm in love."

"Well, and are you enjoying it?" asked Mitka curiously, rolling over.

"It tickles one up a bit, master." Sanka gave a coy laugh, as if someone had actually tickled him.

"Well, marry her, then," Mitka yawned.

"Yes. . . . And then one'll have kids. . . . 'Are you our daddy?' they'll ask me. . . . And a wife. . . . A wife's not like a mother, one must feed her. I wish we had the old days back again! . . ." He swayed to and fro deferentially from the hips, and in an access of reverence only ventured to hold his cigarette between the very tips of his fingers.

"The other day I was thinking of us riding off together on patrol. Squadron, ma—arch!" he crowed in a high tenor.

"Take your cap off," said Mitka casually and morosely, "and don't bawl!"

"I'll take my cap off . . . a cap keeps one in mind of

one's duty," and Sanka went on to tell how on that patrol he had lost his way, and three times followed his own tracks in a circle until finally he had discovered his mistake. "Then I just sat down in the snow and had my laugh out. The snow blew over me, and the wind whipped me in the face, but I just kept on laughing! Then all at once I stiffened: I thought I saw an eye looking at me out of the darkness and taking stock of me. . . . Lord, what days those were! We've been through a lot together, master."

"Shave your mustache off. It doesn't suit your style of beauty," interjected Mitka gloomily.

"I'll shave off my mustache—all right. One's mustache isn't one's head. Yesterday I met Atashez, our secretary." Sanka sat on the bed and seized Mitka's hand, but Mitka snatched it away. "He tore past me in a car with a little lady cuddled up beside him. Well, well, there's no law against cuddling little ladies, I suppose. She had a nice bit of fur around her neck, and a lovely hat. I nearly bawled out 'That's our chap, the boss's best friend. He's a director now, and doesn't know how many thousands he has. All the same he's been bitten by lice, the same as I have, in his time.'"

"Where did you get that coat?" broke in Mitka again.

"I picked it up cheap," Sanka sighed resignedly. "I kind of borrowed it." And he went on: "Then our eyes met. It made my blood run cold for fear he'd spot who I was. I'd sooner the ground opened and swallowed me up than that he recognized me. 'Why aren't you rolling along beside him, Bicycle?' thought I. 'Can't you roll, too, you old boneshaker?'"

"Perhaps he was ashamed when he saw you," Mitka called out, getting up from his bed.

"Oh, not he!—he didn't even notice me. . . . He had his girl snuggled up to him and a fat portfolio in his hand—business for the whole Republic. And she was a damned fine girl, too—'struth, she was! Well, I often pick up with a girl, too, but only on the streets. You can see me soaking wet, standing in the mud. Off I go with my last cent in my pocket, and then I see one of them with the corner of my eye, sitting alone. She'd a flower in her blouse, to catch the eye—very fetching. Well, I went and sat beside her. 'Excuse me, Miss,' says I, 'if you'll forgive the impertinence, what is the name of that flower you're wearing? It's always been a fancy of mine, that flower.' And she says: 'You're joking—it's just a common violet.' 'Well,' says I, 'I'm very keen on violets. Why are you looking at my mustache? If I shaved it off, it would only grow thicker.' And I saw that the young lady was in a terrible way, as she'd lost her job and gone on the streets to try to earn her living."

"You're a swine," said Mitka, dropping his lower lip with an expression of disgust.

"Wait, master! I didn't half figure it all out to myself, and, as you know, my trade's a peculiar one—till the war I made cobblers' lasts. 'I'll start away at them again,' thought I, 'buy a songbird on the Trubnaya Place, and the young lady'll cook me cabbage soup and wash my linen, and we could set up house together. Anyway, it's better than helping other fellows get rid of their money.' And then before I'd worked myself up to ask her, she'd got up all of a sudden and said: 'What's the use of your flirting with me gratis? Have you any money?' She was a bit put off, master. 'Well,' said I to her, 'I've nothing against it, Comrade. There's nothing like a bit of fun. My name's Bicycle. You're Marusya, aren't you? Come along.'"

"Was she pretty?" interrupted Mitka.

"If she'd been pretty, she'd have found some other chap." Sanka laughed softly, but immediately became silent under Mitka's attentive stare. "There wasn't much about her but her eyes: soft blue, a kind of veiled look about them. We went off. 'If your daddy saw you now,' says I to her, 'he'd fetch you a clip on the ear.' She said nothing. Maybe her family are grand folk. She might be a general's daughter. Generals always have thin daughters with tiny eyes like that." Sanka paused; he was sweating, and looked as if he was taking on himself all the guilt for what happened next, though actually nothing had happened next.

"Well, and what was the end of it?" said Mitka, screwing up his eyes.

"That was the end of the whole business." Sanka suddenly recollected something, ran out of the room, and came back in a moment with two others. These two, Lyonka Zhivotik and Curly Donka, remained standing in the doorway, looking humbly at the dark polish of Mitka's boots. Both of them, for all the contrast of their characters, were united today in their hostility toward the two soldiers, who only through accident had fallen into this doubtful way of life. "Hasn't the fool told you," said Donka, raising his head, "that we met Agey?" He waited until Mitka had digested this sinister name. "He wants to know if you'll join in on a little job with him. If you won't, he says he'll ask Shchekutin." Donka paused to see what effect the name of his famous rival would produce on Mitka.

"Well, come in and take your hat off," said Mitka as he finished putting on his boot.

"We haven't come to stay," Donka said, shaking his curls, and Lyonka coughed agreement.

"Well, then—quick march!" said Mitka, and in the old army way brought his right arm with an abrupt jerk to his side.

This changed the visitors' tone. Lyonka gave a constrained smile to conceal his discomfiture, and Donka tugged at the peak of his cap. They refused the cigarettes Mitka casually offered them, and began jeering at Sanka; their laughter had an unpleasant ring. The four men confronted each other in all the diversity of their characters, each of them pursuing his own thoughts. For Lyonka, Mitka had nothing but contempt: this strange little creature had neither father nor mother, and the thieves held that he had conceived himself. There were stories that his trainer had given him mercury as a child—the popular method of checking growth—and in this way had condemned him to the disreputable but lucrative profession of squeezing through skylights. At the age of twenty he was a general laughingstock on account of his size, but when he was thirty he struck terror into everybody he met. After Fritz, the celebrated acrobat, had excited the wonder of the world by turning the staff of Ambrosius into a walking stick, Lyonka, his pupil, made his debut in the world. Fritz offered his patronage to the talented youth, but Lyonka resolved to be independent, and immediately an unlucky star appeared over his head. Every undertaking he led was doomed in advance to failure, and long months of his life were passed in prison. In the bad days, when the Moscow thieves, bereaved of their leaders, were yearning for new heroes and new deeds of daring, Lyonka tried his luck for the last time, but he was arrested in Astrakhan in the open street in the very act of robbing a foreigner. He was shot at from a boat, but he dived under, and that moment divided his life in two halves. When he swam out, his hair had turned almost gray, but even his gray hair did not save him from the ridicule of his friends. After this he became as greedy as if he were nothing but a stomach. His lack of discrimination and decency in the choice of food and clothes and lodgings betrayed the extent of his degradation.

When Mitka's name came to the fore and his successful exploits got known, Lyonka went to him to pay his respects. Though he was such an incompetent bungler, he always posed as the defender of the thief tradition and all its fetishes. A burglar who omitted to leave his chisel and his iron saw behind at the scene of his operations seemed to him a doomed man. Mitka, who had triumphed in other fields, could afford to laugh at these professional superstitions, but, though he despised Lyonka, he never willingly humiliated him. In spite of this Lyonka envied him as only those can envy who are talentless and consumed with ambition.

Donka was cast in a very different mold; he was curly-haired and gay, and his exploits in love and burglary were always crowned with success. He was a vagabond and a poet, and his poems were sung by the wandering thieves who picked their living in the great cities. His wanton muse was free and unrestrained, and he took nothing seriously, which made women love him. He was a born thief, for his mother had given birth to him in prison.

While Lyonka entered on a detailed explanation of Agey's projected raid, Donka stood by the window and looked out into the darkness. Minus's sad music trickled through the wall, and Donka felt as if a woman were weeping for him. Life and Night mirrored themselves in his consciousness like strange female forms.

"You are blind and void and deceitful," thought he

as he licked his moist red lips, "yet we can't help thinking of you."

"You're muddling it all up," he heard Mitka's powerful
voice. "I'll go to Agey myself. What do you want Sanka
for, anyway? Alexander, have you really made up your
mind to leave the gang?"

Sanka, who had consistently held his tongue in spite
of all Lyonka's allusions to him, got up at these words,
his ears burning.

"I've made up my mind, master."

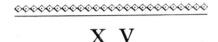
AFTER Masha left Rogovo with Agey, she tried to per-
suade herself that by her elopement with a murderer, she
had avenged herself for her father's despotism and her
whole life in Rogovo; but the same evening wind that
scattered the ashes of the vapor bath over the town was
to disperse all the sweet fumes of her revenge, and leave
her in miserable disillusionment with Agey. She was tireless in her efforts to save him; she poured herself out in a
stream of love and devotion, but she could not drive the
devil out of his bones; it only writhed the more furiously
in his tormented body.

"There isn't a bone in my body that isn't accursed,"
he said with passionate sincerity a year later, after they
had settled in the town. "I'm rotten from head to foot."
He clung to her and hid his hands, which could never be
washed clean, in her lap. But Masha still believed that
love could purify like fire, and only gradually did she realize the uselessness of her efforts. Agey had turned his back
upon the world and passed beyond good and evil, beyond
the reach of human words or sympathy. Nature spewed
him out, and then Masha thrust him from her, though
she still shared the same roof with him, "because," said
Firsov, "there was something pure and human in her
heart which even Ageyka had not been able to pro-
fane. . . ." And it was this humanity that Agey hated
with a murderous hate.

One day he was cutting bread and she was sitting opposite him with her hands on the table. Her gleaming nails
shone pink in the candle light. "You're a sly one,

Manka!" cried Agey, pushing his finger, which did not feel the fire, into the flame of the candle. "Is it true that the more light a man has put out, the worse his death will be?"

"That's a stupid lie. You'll die bravely when the time comes," she answered idly, used to such ideas from Agey.

"And when is the time coming?" drawled Agey, and, aiming suddenly, brought down the knife handle on those pink nails he hated so much. "You mustn't polish them, do you hear?" he shouted, and went on striking, but only on the table now.

A moment later he sought her hand, anxious to ask forgiveness, if only by pressing it in his own. But to Masha his words were like a cry from the pit that had swallowed him. Her soul was steeled by the injustice of life, but gradually there came over her a homesick yearning for all she had lost, for the virginal snowfields that now lay gray and trampled before her. She was young and daunt- less, but there was the stamp of restlessness and care on her dark loveliness, and no one yet had dared to love her. Only Donka had sung "The Snowstorm's" praises from a lodging house in passionate verse.

The husband of the Snowstorm hid in the back room while daylight lasted, but in the evenings he went out to do his work. To Firsov he presented a problem of absorb- ing interest; what were the limits of depravity to which a man might go? Agey recognized no limit, but though he still retained some self-respect—at any rate in physical matters—a stench of dissolution seemed to come from him, as if his soul were rotting.

He sat at home the whole day twisting paper flowers and piling them up in a corner. It was as though he intended to bestow them on mankind, and as though his damnation was postponed as long as they were not fin- ished. There was one grotesque pattern that seemed to obsess him, a huge forget-me-not with rows of wire sta- mens like teeth, which, unlike the blue flower of legend, seemed to symbolize hate rather than true love. Agey did not see any particular sense in his work; it was only his hands that worked, his gaunt, weary hands that did not wish to die. He was used to Manka, but every time he heard a strange step at the door, he started.

On seeing Mitka, he smiled guiltily and, shaking the paper shavings from the stool, invited him to sit down. He almost fawned on him; he seemed frightened that Mitka might take offense and leave.

"I've come about that affair Lyonka's been to see me about," said Mitka, sitting strangely upright in his chair, as if he were frightened that one of Agey's paper clippings might stick to him.

"You're coming with us?" asked Agey.

"Yes, but I'm boss of this show," said Mitka dryly.

Agey bent forward a little, and his hands hung down between his knees, as if they were heavily weighted. Perhaps he had once been handsome, when the first down had bloomed above his lips and before the coarse hair had matted on his forehead. As if in answer to Mitka's thought, he ran his fingers through his hair and laughed joylessly.

"Mitka," he said, letting his hands fall on the chair, "don't turn your back on me! I tell you straight I'd like to be your friend—no, not your friend even, but I'll stick to you! I'm quite alone now. What about my old folk? you may be thinking. Why, my dad himself went to the Cheka. 'Give me a gun,' says he: 'Agey will come home sometime. . . .' There's a nice friendly spirit for you! God, Mitka, I'd not give my old boots for the lot of them. My old boots'll stand by me at least, and not look down on me—for aren't we both black, and one as black as the other! And you've no call to judge me, either . . . you nor anyone else. Can't they just burn me and shovel me out onto the ash pit and have done with it?" He suddenly lowered his eyes mockingly, and said: "Shall I call Manka?" But Mitka shook his head. "No, let you be my judge. I'll take it from you, for you're straight. Is it true, what Manka told me, that there was never anything between you and her?" This was a lie, for she had never spoken to him about Mitka; he had heard about their childhood together from other sources.

"I won't judge you, Agey," said Mitka. "You know yourself what sort of a chap I am now."

"Judge not that ye be not judged!" Agey's laughter writhed through the room like acrid smoke crawling over a marsh. "You're a cute one. . . . You won't judge, and why not? Because you're scared stiff of justice yourself. . . . Oh, it's all a sham!" he shouted, banging his fist so violently on the table that the candle butt fell over (Agey could not endure electric light.) The candle burned on on its side in a small translucent tallow puddle. "Come, judge me, Mitka! What's wrong with you? Why should you hang back from judging me? Shouldn't the good judge the bad?" Agey was sobered by Mitka's cold silence. "Don't be angry, Mitka! You'll be hopping round another hundred years, you silly blighter, long after I've stopped a bullet. With you it's just play-acting, but it's the real thing with me. I'm so low that I'd be glad to lick your boots. I'd give my eyes to meet a chap who'd accept me as I am and listen to me."

Then Mitka told him casually how a week ago he had chased away the writer in the checked ulster, and Agey seemed oddly interested. Suddenly Mitka felt almost sick at Agey's groaning; he stepped to the window and drew aside the heavy curtain. Light and sound poured in, night had not yet fallen, it was still evening. The disorder that reigned in the room spoke clearly of the owner's spiritual decay. The window faced the west, and the dirty snow gleamed under the setting sun in marvellous orange tints. In the tender distances of the sky a strip of sunset glowed delicately and sweetly like the ribbon on a young girl's tresses.

Agey said something behind him, and Mitka nodded without trying to grasp the meaning of his words. Absorbed in his thoughts, he looked out through the window. Had the time come for him to go out into the world and follow the hard road waiting for him? Should he throw in his lot with men who lived in the light of the sun and yoke himself to their hard and honorable toil? Suddenly it seemed to Mitka as if his breast were filled with the sharp resilience of the frosty air, and his feet with the sweet pain of long wandering.

". . . and I know why you're coming with me," Agey's reproachful voice rang in Mitka's ear. "Why haven't you come before? Tell me."

"I said I'd come because I wanted to see Masha,"

said Mitka, almost as if he had learned it by heart. "Is that enough?"

He said this with his back turned to Agey. But suddenly he turned around because he felt the presence of a second person behind him.

He caught sight of Masha and lowered his eyes as if he were blinded.

"Why are you lying to him, Mitka? I know why you're going with him, and I'll tell you, too, but not while he's here. He wouldn't think half so much of you if he knew. He's not your sort. No, it's no good your fixing me with a stony stare: two can play at that game." She turned to Agey and stroked his face tenderly with her finger tips, and only Agey knew how much the careless gesture cost her. "Why don't you give the flowers a rest, you fool? Or you might at least offer your visitor a forget-me-not. Sit down, Mitka. . . . You needn't go yet, need you?" She pointed at the stool from which Mitka had just risen.

"I want to talk something over with him," said Mitka calmly, "and then I'll go."

"You're a queer fellow!" Masha smiled. "There's no need for you to run away like that. I'm not asking you to sit on my lap!" Now that for the first time they met after a long separation, they recognized each other only with difficulty under the masks that life had forced on them. They were well matched for their encounter. Masha stepped to the window and, standing there with her back to the men, played absent-mindedly with the gold locket of her bracelet.

Agey leaned over and nudged Mitka. "There's a woman for you!"

Twilight was coming on, and the glowing embers of the sunset dwindled on the glimmering horizon. Masha gazed for a moment at the empty sky and then turned abruptly from the window.

"Why do you never come and see me, Mitka?" She stepped up to him and touched his chin lightly with her hand. "You oughtn't to forget your old friends. Drop in, whenever you like, and I'll cure you of your dreaming. . . . Won't you even look at me?" Mitka gazed obstinately at the smoke rising from his cigarette.

"Lord! There's a grease spot . . . right on my sleeve. That's your doing, Agey—I wish you'd be careful with your fingers. These spots are the mischief to get out. Do you know if soda's any good with silk, Mitka?"

She scratched energetically at the infinitesimal spot, as though she found it much more absorbing than her visitor. "Mitka, if you think I don't know what you're up to, you're mistaken. It's no good your running away from me, because I've got eight legs and a hundred eyes, so don't try it!" She gave a disagreeable laugh. "Well, I'm glad you've found your sister. Be sure to bring her along here. You're such an old friend, I feel I know her already. Go, Agey, and get ready the samovar, darling. Our visitor's dying for a cup of tea, but he's too shy to say so."

Her husband went off obediently, and Masha fumblingly tried to light a match. "There, it's lit at last! Now let's have a talk, Mitka!"

"Pull down your skirt!" said Mitka, resentfully conscious of her power.

"I believe you're actually frightened of me, Mitka, but I'm not going to vamp you." Her proud, dark face, with its zone of stormy curls, was quite calm, though her painted lips smiled. "Do you know what Agey would do with us if I did? Well, if you want to know, he wouldn't dare to lift a finger, because . . ." She broke off and, running across the room, flung open the door. There stood Agey, a look of terror and uncertainty on his face; in the dim twilight his bowed form was startlingly silhouetted. "Who told you to listen? Go back to the kitchen!" She pushed him back imperiously and slammed the door.

"Listen, Masha, I don't want to quarrel with Agey about you," said Mitka. "I've nothing to gain by making a fool of him. I'm not frightened of you, either, Masha, though I suppose you'll try and get your own back. You're quite right: it wasn't because of you I came today, and, though you mayn't believe it, I dare say I can survive our separation. I'm a strong man, Masha, whatever you may think."

As if to draw his attention, she wiped with her lace handkerchief the hand that Agey had touched, and a heavy perfume filled the room. "I dare say you are, but even strong men have weak spots, and I know yours, Mitka. You're not being as truthful as you used to be. For all I know, it may have been because of me that you came here." She grasped his hand, and the stone in her ring, which was turned inward, pressed painfully upon his fingers, but he smoked on calmly.

"Have you forgotten it all? how we picked lilies of the valley in the Byelyanin woods after the rain? Don't you remember the rainbow over the meadow? It was so near we could almost touch it. You were the first I ever loved . . . I nearly died of joy. . . . And you wanted me, and I wouldn't let you. . . . Have you forgotten it all? Don't you ever remember the lilies of the valley?" She clenched her tiny teeth and laughed. "How very pretty! Wouldn't Agey split his sides over it if he knew! . . . And then I kissed you like this." Suddenly she drew Mitka to her, but as suddenly changed her mind, and did not kiss him. "No, no, I don't want to," she said wearily.

"You're mad . . ." said Mitka, but his heart beat as it had when he had looked over Tatyanka's old photographs. "And it's your fault that it's all turned out like this. When you defiled yourself, you defiled all that I possessed of you, too. But what's the good of talking! I suppose you'll say I didn't love you. My God! Well, then, what about the ring I got you—my grand three-rouble ring? Did you never know about that—and how I waited for you, and waited, in the cold rain?"

Masha smiled. In this half-hour her face seemed to have become longer and leaner. She smoked without a break. "You can't expect to get a girl like me for three roubles, Mitka."

Mitka winced at her heartless gibe; it was the first she had heard of the ring.

"That isn't enough, Mitka. There was a man at the station the other day—I made a fool of him, but what do I care? The man I love must sell his soul for me."

Mitka was repelled and looked at the window, where loose, gray snow lay piled along the woodwork.

"Do you think Agey enjoys being chased off to the kitchen to make the tea, while we stay here together? If you think he doesn't mind, you should just hear him when the children next door make a row. For all he knows, we're kissing and cuddling with our little wings folded together, and laughing at him blowing down the spout of the samovar and dusting it with a rag. We must have everything nice and clean for our dear Mitka. No, Mitka, I'm expensive. I don't suit a poor man's purse."

"What's the use of all this talking? Do you want to marry me, or what?" There was a steely ring in his voice. "One day when I was earning the money to buy the ring, the contractor was going to hit me, but I said: 'Take care, you may get hurt.' But if he had hit me, things would have been different, and I should have asked you why you didn't come for the ring. But we're quits this way."

She had been waiting just for this moment. "You're speaking sense at last. Well, then, tell me why you didn't come to me or answer when I called you. You only lived four doors away in Rogovo. You'll say that creature was with me. It's lies, it's all lies! You were the only one for me in the whole world, Mityenka." She stretched out toward him like a fiddle string tuned to its highest pitch. "Did I kiss you on the bank of the Kudema for nothing at all? You went away from Rogovo without saying good-by—and I'd done everything for you! My father cursed me because of you. When you were in the war, why didn't you let me join you? Did you never feel that Masha Dolomanova was thinking of you?" (The string grew still more taut and sounded thin and high and dangerous.) "You and your politics went down well in the workshop! You were a fine champion of the working classes to take the head of the works, a frail old man, and beat him! But I, his daughter, came to you in the night to warn you. Oh, yes, you hit him because of your class-consciousness, I know. Did you give me up because of your class-consciousness, too? You loved me, my darling, and you still love me, or else why did you send Sanka to inquire for me? Were you ashamed of going for a walk with Masha Dolomanova? Did you think it was treachery to yourself? Why are you all ashamed nowadays of beauty and feeling and your own souls? Why do you prefer to shave off your eyebrows and dress in that dirty coat with three buttons, like a tramp?" She kept it up, but her voice cracked like breaking glass.

"Had your precious ring an emerald in it? If the Party unit had noticed it, you'd have been sent packing. And now you're off with Agey to stop a bullet. And I don't want your ring now. I'm Agey's now, yes, his wife. I'm Manka Stolyarova, the Snowstorm. You've chained me to him forever."

She had begun to speak in a whisper, but then had ceased to care whether her reckless confidences could be overheard in the kitchen.

The room was powerfully heated. Mitka stepped to the window and lowered his eyes in bitter resignation. Suddenly she called him by his name, shyly, almost tenderly, but he did not turn around. In the dusk of evening, lights twinkled in other people's windows, and the first stars came out; a dull glow spread like a canopy over the city and drove away the terrors of the oncoming night. He turned around just as Agey was bringing in a tiny samovar, which he held like a harmonica with his fingers spread out, and once more he was to have evidence of Manka's uncanny power. She looked humbly into Agey's face: it was a wordless thanks, perhaps the promise of a reward, and Mitka thought he heard Agey whisper some confused nonsense into her ear, and a strange fine shaft of pain shot to his heart with a gentle touch and then vanished again; and even fresh joy would not heal the scar it had left.

Mitka had not intended to pay Agey an afternoon visit, so he firmly refused the tea in the low glasses, and the buns and preserved fruit. Agey explained the plans of the proposed undertaking; but his wits had long been dulled, and there was not a spark of his old cunning in him. The goal he had proposed he could only think of reaching through blood and terror. The affair itself was not very complicated; it was a question of "gutting a bear" in a minor company's office—a thumping big bear, they were assured by their accomplice, a clerk in the company, who brought them information about the guard on the building and the number and position of alarm bells, and who, by the robbery, hoped to cover his own private embezzlements.

After Agey, Mitka began to speak, and it immediately became clear that everything would be carried out according to his plan. Agey snorted as he sipped his tea from his saucer and bit a piece of sugar, and Manka listened attentively to the discussion while she brooded over the stain on her sleeve; it was as if she thought her arm had been contaminated by Ageyka's touch. Soon she went away.

In all No. 8 the most remarkable person from a zoological point of view was, without a doubt, Pyotr Gorbidonich Chikelyov, an individual whom Firsov described as a scoundrelly little jackanapes. He based his opinion, odd as it may sound, on Chikelyov's remarkably short legs, which made him look as if he had continually to step over a succession of obstacles. He was never really ill, but continually in a state of ill health. Disasters never happened to him, but every day was full of petty vexations. In his official work it was only through heavy, laborious toil that he ever won the approval of his superiors, although they valued highly his talent for collecting debts. "I can squeeze money from a stone," he used often to say facetiously. On the dull green breast of his coat there always hung an array of tin medals, as a sign of respectability. Every evening he read a few lines in some political manual and learned them by heart, hoping by means of them to reach a higher position. He was crafty and painstaking, and he managed to burrow a modest place for himself in the new society, just as he had done once in the old one. (He had been proposed for the Order of Anna, but in consequence of the revolution never received it.) Now he was chairman of the House Committee, quite a distinguished post for a small man, and his official career still held further hopes.

When Pyotr Gorbidonich decided to marry, he suddenly came up against an insuperable obstacle—Manyukin. He was afraid to drive his roommate into too desperate straits, but he tormented him continually in petty

ways, and Mitka heard him once slyly telling the House
Committee that Manyukin's rent should be raised. He
declared that Manyukin was in the most flourishing circumstances, that he drank daily, and had had the impertinence to buy a new pair of shoes, and actually once had
cooked cauliflowers on the primus—a fact Chikelyov had
personally discovered when he privately examined his
roommate's aluminum saucepan.

"My dear Pyotr Gorbidonich, I'm fat, and excitement
is bad for fat people. . . . I might do something regret-
table," Manyukin whispered imploringly once when he
was drunk and humble and open-hearted. "Don't drive
me to extremities and make me forget myself. Don't
squeeze me so tight, leave me a crack to breathe through.
It isn't the money, for I haven't even got enough to pay
your taxes. But I'm ceasing to be a man and am becoming
a beast. . . ."

"Don't oppose the regulations, citizen!" retorted
Chikelyov crushingly, twirling his mustaches. "One day
you'll see I'll have to come and confiscate your primus.
Besides, I'm entitled to turn you out. My candid advice
to you is: get a job and settle in a community lodging
house."

"They wouldn't take a man like me in there. We've
had our day," answered Manyukin, his voice failing. He
stretched out his hand to buttonhole Chikelyov, but the
incorruptible Chikelyov pushed his hand away. "I don't
know where to turn. I'll go off the deep end some time, I
tell you. Look out! What would you say if I were to spring
at you and bite your ear off, eh?"

"I wouldn't flinch, I'd just defend myself with my
fists," replied Chikelyov, going white in the face, and he
took an imperceptible step back. "My ear is under the
protection of the law. And I shall do what my conscience
tells me. But suppose I were to marry and in due time a
child were to come into the world—and my personal intention is not to have a dozen children, but only one, for
public reasons and the continuation of the species; it
would be an interesting experiment—well, there's more
sunshine in your corner than in mine, and the sun is as
necessary for children as a mother's care. Don't you see
what I'm fighting for?"

Their loud altercation attracted the attention of the other inmates. They crept out into the passage and surrounded the disputants; soon even Mitka, who was a little drunk and therefore ready with his tongue, joined them.

"Ah, Chikelyov!" he said, smiling reproachfully, "you're dressed differently, but your soul's just the same wolf's soul as it was before. Change your soul, Chikelyov!" He spoke of the beauty of pity and mercy in the victor, and uttered cloudy sentiments far beyond the reach of his fuddled brain. Obviously the figure of poor, persecuted Manyukin had been replaced in his mind by his own.

The inmates of the ark listened greedily to Mitka's enthusiastic tirade. The unemployed Bundyukov and his wife winked across at Minus, the musician, who was thoughtfully playing with his fingers on an imaginary flute —"Just look at Mitka!" they signaled. Zinka offered Manyukin something to eat, but he declined haughtily; he was on his high horse and resolved not to be dependent on people's favors. The others waited, fascinated, for the inevitable rumpus. Mitka was seeking feverishly for further arguments, but his thoughts returned persistently to Agey. Zinka's brother Matvey turned the sudden silence to account.

"And what are your views on class war and the dictatorship of the proletariat?" He stepped up closer to Mitka and scratched his cheek. "Or perhaps it's a case of forgive and forget with you, is it?" Chikelyov repeated his words with enthusiasm.

Mitka could find no reply. The same weapons he had just been using to subdue his enemy were being turned upon himself. Yes, he had fought, and which of his comrades could reproach him with halfheartedness? A memory rose up in his mind of a White battery he had taken by assault while it was preparing to pound him with grape shot. Fearless days that never would return! Above the faithless, weeping heavens, below the thundering, unstable earth, and between them Mitka's squadron at a tearing gallop. It had been a battle, an honorable duel between man and man, but the battle was over now, and they were reduced to tale bearing and peeping through keyholes. The times were out of joint, and Mitka had no patience with the host of petty circumstances that hedged him in like hostile legions. Another man might have dominated them, but Mitka's mind could not assimilate so much that was strange and conflicting. For, where he had grown up, life had flowed on like a river continuous and indivisible. He closed his eyes tightly to make the silence still deeper. In his heart reigned now the clear brightness of an autumn day.

Everyone was now making fun of Manyukin, and so Mitka was left in peace. Manyukin, always ready either to laugh or to cry, because he was always on the verge of despair, now put one hand majestically on his hip, while with the other he saluted a nonexistent multitude. During the quarrel he had run quickly to the window ledge in his room, and fortified himself with schnapps.

"Trample on me and overwhelm me with shame, gentlemen!" he cried amid friendly laughter. "I'm the last, the very last *barin* on your earth." He expatiated with pathos on the conquest of Kazan, on the prisons in Astrakhan, on the battle of Poltava, and on a proud man who had once refused to take off his cap in front of the sacred gate of the Kremlin.

"Though my mind has failed and the charms of life have lost their power to please . . . yet I still walk on my own feet and observe with my own eyes. Where is my enemy Chikelyov? Bring him to me, and I will shake his hand. Yes, I forgive him everything—the devil take my slavish principles! Generosity is the voice of the soul, as Alexander Petrovich Agarin used to say. Oh, those days! . . . You awoke, and the little birds were flying, the sun caressed you. . . . Everything did you good. Even a filthy fly was nice, for it flew and it was alive, the dear creature. . . ." This emotional impromptu brought Manyukin to the point of tears. "And in front of the house stands a carriage with four elegant horses, and on the box sits Ivan in splendor, with a whole peacock on his head. And in the carriage sits the master himself, the magnificent Sasha Agarin." Manyukin reeled and took several steps forward. He embraced the air in tipsy enthusiasm. " 'Sasha, is it you?' And we both of us weep over the beauty of our friendship. His mustache tickles my nostrils. . . . Agarin, my dear friend, where are you now? Answer me, my dear friend!" shouted Manyukin pathetically, craning on the tips of his toes. They all laughed and clapped their hands, and then he began to laugh, too, and rubbed his neck good-humoredly.

"Don't make a show of the poor fellow!" Zinka cried in a clear voice. She was a head taller than the others. "Go to sleep, *barin*. . . . You'll have to go to work again soon, too." She dragged Manyukin away to his room. He embraced her and with ridiculous gestures tried to convince her of Sasha Agarin's astounding charms.

Mitka was gradually sobering down and collecting his thoughts. With his eyes still shut, he stretched out his hand and grasped the secretary of the four societies by a button.

"You're studying to be a doctor, aren't you?" he began gently, tugging the button. . . . "In the course of time you'll become a qualified doctor. Supposing you should be called to a priest to cure him—will you give him poison?"

"Excuse me," replied Matvey suavely—he was Zinka's brother, but his voice sounded like Firsov's—"would you mind holding onto this button instead? The other's not very secure. . . . You were talking of poison? Excellent, go on! Who was it you were proposing to poison?"

THIS TIME Firsov was fortunate. He stood now before Mitka, attentive and armed for the encounter, and felt the pleasant touch of Mitka's fingers. He was ready, and there was an almost obstinate look in his face. Mitka raised his eyes in perplexity, and, seeing Firsov, suddenly remembered Agey. Firsov took his enigmatic smile for a good sign, and he was not mistaken.

"Come to my room," said Mitka good-naturedly, and Firsov hurried at once to open the door for him. To make up for his professional intrusiveness, he was almost offensively polite.

He walked up and down the room, rubbing his hands in embarrassment—Mitka's room was always cold.

"What's got you now?" Mitka stepped up to him.

"Your little room's exactly like a prison cell. . . . All you want is an iron grill on the window."

"Sit down and listen. Give me a cigarette, will you?"

"I'm sitting and listening . . . but I only smoke cheap cigarettes."

"Don't make excuses. Anyone would think you had something up your sleeve. Talking of scoundrels, do you know Agey Stolyarov?"

"I do."

"What do you know of him?"

"Well . . . he's a man . . . what's one to say? A pretty tough customer, a night bird."

"Is that all you know? What's wrong with those matches?"

"Oh, we were bathing the child and they fell into the water."

"You've got kids, have you? Aren't they a lot of trouble?"

"Oh, well, I can't say that . . . if it's one's own child, you see. Its one aim and ambition is to make as much row as possible—it's interesting!" Firsov lied with enthusiasm and glanced at Mitka over his glasses. Curiously enough, his lies seemed to win Mitka's confidence.

"Hm . . . well, about Agey. He'd like to see you. He's sick of life, and breaking up. You're a writer, aren't you?"

"I plead guilty," growled Firsov, looking at his spread-out fingers in disgruntlement.

They were both silent, as though beside an open grave. Their mutual distrust was gradually thawing, for a stranger's grave brings men closer to each other. There was not still, it is true, even a breath of friendship between them, but Mitka recognized the man in Firsov, while Firsov no longer felt it necessary to pose as someone else, thanks to his timely fairytale about the child. He shrank from Agey's degradation, and had no wish to act as his father confessor, or to defile his unwritten pages with the spiritual pestilence that streamed from this man.

Firsov explained with businesslike candor that there was now only a single empty place in his novel. "For you, esteemed Dmitri Yegorich," he said, pointing to him impudently. Other people only existed as foils to the heroes, in the old Greek way, and Agey would only block the flow of the narrative and demand a vast display of psychology. But suddenly an idea came into Firsov's mind: in every art auxiliary elements are necessary, stout staffs around which the fragile tendrils of the motif may twine. (Later on we shall see how far Firsov worked out his esthetic). Quite unembarrassed by Mitka's presence, he jotted down in his notebook ideas and episodes that had casually occurred to him. The blood circulated with incredible speed through his brain, yet the pencil could barely travel over the paper at the rate of a child writing on a slate. (It was ridiculous: Firsov hurriedly sharpened his blunt pencil with his teeth, and the gnawed stump was even less disposed to hasten.)

"Do you know I should very much like to . . . Look here, I have an idea"—he struck his forehead—"a very interesting idea has just occurred to me. Can one talk to

him? . . . I mean really talk to him like a human being." Mitka was preparing to go out. "I'm a thief like you
. . . only my thefts are ones that nobody notices."

"You're a fine sort of thief!" Mitka jeered, and handed
Firsov his coat. Then he seemed suddenly to distrust him,
and scrutinized him coldly. "How can you compare yourself with me? You're a public figure, and nobody knows
me but the police."

But Firsov had become absorbed and thoughtful. The
idea, which he had purchased by sleepless nights and humiliating subterfuges, now of its own accord rushed into
his mind. For half an hour they wandered silently through
the streets together. The sky was drenched in pale blue
light by the frosty moon. A church bell ringing far off
called the people to Mass, and there was something perky
and intrusive about the rare, loud footfalls of passers-by.
The sky was brilliant with stars. Lights shone in the
houses. Some fool or other rushed past on a bicycle. And
Firsov had his first chapter ready in his head.

"I'll make them *live!*" he cried, seizing Mitka's sleeve.
"My readers will think they're looking through a keyhole.
I'll *force* them to believe. We only stammer now, and
the fire's gone out, but we'll light it afresh and astonish
the world as never before." Then he rubbed his spectacles, which had been dimmed by the frost.

"You're a wonderful chap," said Mitka condescendingly. "You rustle your papers and believe that you're getting somewhere. But you can't clothe people with paper,
old man."

The other did not contradict him, as at that moment
he was in no mood for argument. He wished secretly that
their wandering might last forever. The snowy twilight
with its stars favored his inspiration. He went to his ren-
dezvous as eagerly as if it were a lover's tryst. One might
almost have imagined that Agey's hoarse voice had power
to bewitch.

At a corner Mitka took a very cordial farewell of Firsov,
for he had promoted this meeting partly with a view to
his own personal profit. He gave him a few pieces of good
advice, and in particular impressed on him the address
where Agey was to meet him.

AFTER the day's work, Puchov withdrew to the small room at the back, and, taking off everything that bore any trace of his contact with iron, washed his hands with caustic soda. Then he put on an old coat, which had witnessed many grave happenings while worn by its former owner and now had loyally to give warmth and protection to Puchov.

People used to knock on his little window as at a porter's door; it was small and dirty, and had not a single pane intact. In front of it stood a bush, which, in the spring, was vaguely recognizable as a lilac tree, and behind was a drain. Puchov never cleaned his little window, for it sheltered his strange way of life well enough as it was from human inquisitiveness and the fetid fumes from the drain. The sun never disturbed the twilight of his dwelling, for all the warmth and sunshine which should have shone for his tiny front yard was confiscated by the house next door, which was madly peppered with windows. Master Puchov's sun was his stove, which he had made in his own image; it was small and sturdy, with a rusty funnel, and it reigned autocratically in the middle of the floor and made movement difficult. It roared angrily when it was fed with fuel, but in return it shed the whole night through a fine, sootless warmth almost like the sun's. For illumination there was a kerosene lamp, which Puchov had salvaged from a heap of old iron. He had lavished his skill and cunning on its perforated sides; it was resurrected now from its disuse, and served him gratefully and loyally.

Puchov sat down by the stove and surveyed his poor dwelling with a paternal glance, and, as he lived alone and rarely spoke to others, he began now to talk to himself. To the stove, which had just swallowed a fat log of wood, he said: "Your throat's growing rusty with growling, you old beggar"; and to the lamp: "Let me finish eating first, and then I'll give you some kerosene"; and to himself, as he lifted the spoon: "Now we'll amuse ourselves, Puchov!"

His diet was practically vegetarian. Puchov did not like meat, but he was fond of vegetables, and had the same feeling for them a scholar has for the printed word. After his meal he fetched from a shelf on the wall a box of tools with sharp, gleaming blades, and threw a few colored wooden discs on the table. He bent over one of them and dug the blade into the soft wood. He loved to be alone with his wood, and silence was balm to him. The chisel rasped as it bored a path to beauty, the shavings rustled as they flew up, the tormented wood complained. Around him life was seething, men fought and died, religions perished and revived again, but Master Puchov in his cellar hole jealously guarded his right to labor in peace at his woodwork, and to laugh at the everlasting turmoil of the world.

For the unusual object that he wished to make that evening he selected a piece of birchwood whose fragrant surface had been roughened by the carpenter's saw. But at that moment the door creaked to announce the arrival of a late visitor. Puchov did not turn around till the newcomer had proclaimed his presence by a nervous cough. "My, here's a fence!" said Puchov, running a friendly eye over his guest.

"All genuine American!" answered Firsov, bowing politely as he squeezed between the stove and a projection of the wall.

"Well, take off your American togs . . . no one will steal them in my house," replied his host. Then he turned again to his interrupted work, and his visitor took off his ulster and galoshes, and smiled as he looked around the room. ("Probity and reserve," he thought as he contemplated the ample joinery of a chest of drawers painted with crude oil colors.)

"Don't be surprised at my breaking in on you like this. Vekshin directed me to you . . . do you know Comrade Vekshin?" He got agitated as he felt Puchov's attentive black pupils fixed on him, and put his hands on his cheeks to cool the burning flush on them. "I called on you once in the beginning of the winter. . . . Why are you looking at me like that? Don't you recognize me?"

"I'd like a good look at you first. I seem to recognize the lower half of your face. Are you a Party man?"

"No, I'm only . . . er . . ." Firsov stroked his unshaven cheeks self-consciously.

In the stillness the head of the pendulum in the clock tick-tocked hurriedly as if it wanted to fly off its rod.

"Is there frost tonight? Is it snowing? There's always a great deal of snow after a dry summer."

"No, it's not snowing. Hullo, cat!" said Firsov with a yawn as the animal rubbed itself against his legs.

"She's from next door!" explained Puchov. "Give her milk . . . there on the windowsill."

Firsov did as the master of the house required, and felt emboldened to smoke and ask the name of the wood, whose rich red was here and there as dark as congealed blood.

"This wood is called amaranth. It grows near rivers in hot climates. The pillars of the temple of Solomon were carved from it. It's a proud tree. It's too proud and disdainful even to blossom," and he carelessly flung a piece on the table.

"You don't say so!" Firsov protested. "I thought everything blossomed some time or other."

"Well, this tree never blossoms," said Puchov with great assurance, and he took a thin board that was dyed through and through with aniline green. (Then Firsov understood why in Puchov's lonely stone cell even scraps of wood should gleam like precious stones; it was easy to understand why captives became friendly with spiders.) "And this wood is called 'Bird's-eye,' the tree bears a great many flowers, long and pink, and the crosses for the two thieves were made from it. You see, there is no tree grows without some purpose. . . . What are you—a fence?"

"No . . . I'm just Firsov."

The visitor shivered as he swallowed a yawn. (He knew

well enough that fence was the term for a purchaser of stolen goods.)

Puchov told him much about trees that evening, about the ancient grass pine, the sage juniper, the exquisite birch and the maple, and he described picturesquely how this last indomitable tree resists the storm that wrecks its foliage, though its soft pith can be pierced by a simple splinter . . . and perhaps it was no mere accident that at this point he mentioned Mitka's name. Then they talked about the growths on the birch, and how, when the tree is ailing, or its roots are rotted by the putrid moisture of a swamp, or it is given a casual blow with an ax, this knotty ulcer clings like an iron lip to the tree trunk.

"It's the same with men: if you get hit once, you wait of your own accord for the second blow. You even pray not to be tortured by delay. A man mustn't let himself be struck even once. But you can't live without strife unless you withdraw from everything." ("Into a dog kennel like yours?" thought Firsov, who was sleeping with his eyes open.) "Look, how painful it was for it to grow!" He cleaned the wood thoughtfully with an iron tool and pierced right into its gleaming, virgin heart, so that Firsov should be the first to see right in. "Look at the way these close rings go round in ripples. That's the way the tree writhed in its struggle for existence: it's a tough bit of wood! Men are like that, too. They've all got some pain in their hearts, and you'll no more heal it than you'll mend the crack in a broken glass. Human progress flies like an arrow, but men grow slowly and tortuously like a tree—ring by ring—that's how it is."

Firsov was aroused by an angry knocking at the door. He mumbled something apologetic about the sleepy atmosphere, then went to the door and lifted the latch. Someone in black and red burst in and pushed Firsov to one side; and heavy boots stamped traces on the floor. Firsov stood to one side and watched Agey's encounter with Puchov. Puchov stood with his hands uplifted in surprise; Agey bent forward, his arms hanging guiltily, as if they belonged to some other body. Neither desired this meeting, but Puchov's glance was clear and conciliatory because he knew only too well the strange origins of human life.

"You've grown older," said Puchov in confusion. "You're crushing the life out of yourself."

"In a million years the earth'll have grown old, too," laughed Agey hoarsely, taking a small chisel from the table and trying its strength on his strong nails. "Hasn't there been a writer here?"

"No one has come for you, Agey," answered Puchov, waiting with ill-concealed impatience for him to leave.

Then Firsov stepped out of the shadow, tapped Agey self-confidently on the chest, and, trying to follow Mitka's advice, screwed up his eyes insolently. "Stolyarov?" he asked abruptly. "Yes? Well, I'm the writer." With deliberately exaggerated dignity he put his hand into his pocket for his handkerchief and drew it out. As he drew it out, a few coins, which had been hidden there, too, rolled tinkling over the floor.

"DAMNATION! I've been always meaning to get myself a purse," he murmured sheepishly. He did not know whether to crawl on the ground around Agey's boots, or to renounce the ten-kopek pieces he had dropped. "It's too silly . . ."

"And I thought you'd have a gray beard." Agey squinted distrustfully at the confused author.

"I'll try to improve my appearance," answered Firsov, irritated at himself and at Agey's red breeches, which glared fierily from under his sheepskin; irritated, too, at Puchov's dumb amazement. "If it came to a pinch, I might take a vapor bath. . . ." And he turned to his ulster, which hung on the chair like a headless body.

Agey took Firsov by the shoulders and pushed him down into a chair.

"I didn't mean anything," he protested in perplexity. "You're all right, too, for all I know. Look at you, you're bubbling like a kettle on the stove already!"

Puchov instantly realized that he was superfluous, and recollected that he had intended to go to the baths. He crammed something into a wicker basket and went away. Puchov, who had seen so much, was never surprised at anything now. An oppressive silence followed his departure, though both of them were quite clear about their intentions. Already a notebook was lying on Firsov's knees, and he began to draw there carelessly with his pencil. At first a pretty girl, but presently she grew a mustache—apparently of her own accord—and the girl's red-cheeked betrayer appeared on the page.

"Do you know why I've asked you to come?" demanded Agey rudely, and observed the girl's betrayer rapidly assuming a beard and becoming still older and uglier.

"I should think I do," answered Firsov nervously, adding an imposing nose and finally scribbling the whole portrait over with amazingly luxuriant side whiskers. "You don't want to die like a beast. . . . I know what you want, more or less, so let's get down to it!" he exclaimed, and his pencil scribbled madly over one page of the exercise book. "Vekshin told me a lot about it, but I didn't completely understand him."

"He told you and you didn't understand him," repeated Agey thoughtfully. He stretched out his hand and shut Firsov's notebook with a snap, for it irritated him. Firsov opened it again, and Agey did not venture to shut it a second time. Something was taking place within him: it was as if a wretched, smoking little lamp had been lit in his sad eyes, which refused to release the light once they had trapped it. Suddenly he blurted out: "Write about me! That's what I want! You can do it—I know you can. One has only to look at your face. I'll explain it all to you. You see, friend . . ."

"My name's Fyodor Fyodorich," said Firsov coldly.

"You see, Fyodor Fyodorich," whispered Agey, slightly disconcerted, "I've got to hurry, for I've not long now, whatever happens. I know when my time's up." A spasm of despair passed across his face. "I'm not frightened of death, Fyodor Fyodorich. There isn't any death—it's just a notion of ours. (Damn you, I can't get used to your black beard.) They've sentenced me four times *in contumaciam* . . . but they'll never catch me, though anyone who likes can do me in and get thanked for it, too. It'll be my girl. She's the one that'll give me up, but I'll show fight all the same. I always fire back, as you may have heard." There was a hint of hysterical laughter in his voice. Firsov looked at him and scarcely recognized him, for his face was dark with foreknowledge, or was it only the agony of foreboding? "My death'll be quiet and sudden. Maybe a beam'll fall on me, or I'll be found smothered, who knows?" He jumped up, and at the same instant Firsov jumped up, too, startled by the look in Agey's eyes. "I want to leave some memory, Fyodor Fyodorich! I want to remain behind in somebody's mind. I always wake nowadays at two, that's my time. I wake up and strike a match, the clock's always at two, and I feel a pain here, something tickling me: it makes me wild. You're a scholar: tell me what a man has here." (He pointed to the region from which the ribs branch out.)

"A neurosis," said Firsov curtly, making an entry in his notebook, which already contained three times as much as had been said. "And have you any other fears?"

"I've a hollow feeling in me. . . ." Agey delivered himself body and soul to Firsov's remorseless pencil. He was terribly excited, and Firsov felt as if he, too, had an oppressive feeling in the same spot beneath the ribs. "Yes, the neurosis, that's where the pain is. Write about me truthfully. Please, please." He took a drink of tea from Puchov's tin can, and his voice became clearer. "I've forgotten everything. . . . I feel as if there was a black hill blotting everything out. Wait a bit, though!" He reflected deeply, in obvious agony. "Yes, it's like a hill, and behind it the sun's going down. It's evening . . . and on top of it I see Pavel Makarich Klopov's windmill, but its sails have been torn away by a hurricane. I wonder if it's still there—what d'you think? There's very little forest left at home. Klopov used to say: 'It's easier to live without a forest . . . without bad thoughts.' . . . He was a prime timber thief," he added with a smile, "but there was a meadow there twenty-four versts wide. . . . It was yellow all around the edge, and there were a few villages on it—Shemyakino, Tsarevo, Paltsevo, and Passynkovo. Write down the names, otherwise you'll forget them . . . and then no one will learn about me. They used to practise the red death in our parts. Have you heard of it?"

"I read about it in some book . . . the old men used to be suffocated with a red bolster . . . some kind of sect, wasn't it?"

"Not only old men." Agey waved his hand and cast down his eyes. "But the folk in our parts are quiet and peaceable. The hares come and play close up to the houses. The bolster business . . . that all happened in old times . . . in any case, what do the bolsters matter? What's the difference whether one smothers a man with a bolster or shoots him with a gun or hacks him to pieces with a sword or poisons him with poison gas? One might even say it's softer with a bolster: it's even a pleasure, if the other party's agreeable. They say that the professor who invented this poison gas hasn't been shot yet, but is still running about. He's one up on me, all right . . ." Agey laughed, but an expression of pain passed across Firsov's face; he did not enter it in his notebook. "Write it down. . . . Why do you sit there as if you were the Mother of God?"

"Please go on." Firsov stretched out his hands as if to protect himself.

"An old man lives there with an old wife. . . . He was as strong as the devil once, but, anyway, you'll see him yourself soon. He was a great believer in God, when it suited him. He was a prime humbug, and he lived happily with his wife. Well, then, the old man sowed a seed in the old woman and a branch grew out of her. It grew and blossomed . . . and the branch . . . was yours truly!" He slapped himself on the chest.

"Didn't you get on well with your father, then?" inquired Firsov in a strange voice.

"Once I took a young hawk out of its nest and spent a whole day playing with it till I got bored and gave it to the cat. That was the sort my father was, too—as pious as they're made, and had ashes on his forehead all Holy Week, but I was half dead when I was taken from him. Do you see my ear? Well, he nearly tore it off me once— that's why we're given two ears to be on the safe side. I've never been frightened of Death since then. Why do they say Death's snub-nosed? Tell me. He isn't." He looked at Firsov with unseeing eyes, as though he were barely aware it was his own voice that was speaking. Firsov hardly dared breathe as he listened to Agey's mad ravings. "He isn't, and I'm the only one knows why. Last year he lived here in Wood Street. He had his cap pulled low over his forehead and a little sharp nose like a bird's. Every time I was in the street I met him going to market or coming out of a shop to go home—Wood Street, that was where he lived, the ninth house from the corner. . . . One evening I followed him and went in." Agey dropped his eyes and paused for a moment. "The next morning I met him, and he was dead . . . though he was carrying petrol in a tin can." He laughed scornfully. "And you've believed everything I said, you fool! I knew what sort you were straight off by that beard."

"I'm off!" threatened Firsov, and was surprised at the hoarseness of his own voice.

"You're a brainy chap with those spectacles. Tell me, is it right to kill—in war or anyhow? While my father had me in his pocket, I used to think that one might kill anything up to a mouse, but nothing higher than that. I had wisdom bitten into my ear. I was a dreamy chap. . . . In the night I used to get up and read, but in the war my mind went off the rails. It was during an attack —a hellish spot called Ferdinand's Nose, a hill full of holes. I went ahead and cut the wire in two and ran in, and up against me came an Austrian officer with a red nose. He rushed at me with his sword, but I took a jab at him with my bayonet. Then I lifted up the butt of my rifle, and he looked at me as you are doing now, in a pleading kind of way. I saw his eyes growing dull. They winked at me and seemed to be wanting something. What did they want, Fyodor Fyodorich? And it's true if a chap hits you with the butt of a rifle, it isn't in the butt that death is, but in the eyes. When he winked at me I thought . . . 'You're cheating,' thought I. 'You want to get into me through your eyes.' . . . And I screwed up my eyes, too."

"It's unbearably hot here," murmured Firsov, who was streaming with sweat, and he got up from his chair.

"Sit down!" Agey ordered him, and pushed his knees down. "A little afterward there was a parade. Our general gave me a cross and praised me, and I began to think of the young hawk. 'But, your serene excellency,' said I, 'I've killed a man.' I was stupid, I suppose, eh? I'm almost ashamed of telling it. And he screamed in my face: 'You fool! If anyone gives you anything, well, you've earned it.' For this bit of back chat I was under arrest for three days —quite the hero!—but I didn't care a damn! 'That's easy work,' thought I, 'and I get distinguished for it into the bargain.' In the end I got a taste for it. I did in seven of them with my bayonet at every attack, and I longed for each attack as if it was Easter Sunday. Once I hacked a man's hand off and brought it to the commandant. Another time I killed a dead man a second time: he was sitting by a gun carriage, and I gave him one just for the love of the thing. And when I'd learned to stomach it, then I had a high old time with medals and crosses. When I'd been given my fourth cross, a gold one, the best of all, I got my picture taken and sent it home. I was so plastered with crosses that there'd have been nowhere for a bullet to get through. I wanted to marry. 'The girls,' thought I, 'may as well start and get sweet on me.' My daddy praised me, too, and when the German war was over and the other began, I thought that I was a hero now and an experienced fellow, and that from now on I could carry on the job on my own. I went back home. . . ." Agey wagged his finger threateningly. "I'm not whining, mind you. You can keep your pity to yourself."

"And hadn't you any pity for them?" asked Firsov, quivering with disgust.

"How can one pity a dead man? They just turn my stomach. I can't even stick the live ones now."

He drew breath, and Firsov used the pause to make notes again. He had a pain in his inside and his fingers were cramped; he wrote rapidly, but he wrote something quite different from what Agey was telling him. In his story the incident took on a slightly different form: at the first outbreak of mutiny in the army Agey struck the general who had rewarded him for his first heroism; he killed him from curiosity, and perhaps also out of gratitude for the wisdom he had learned from him; he killed him and then had himself photographed in the general's epaulettes; this photograph roused the greatest enthusiasm among the folk in his village at home.

"Well, what do you say to this now?" said Agey, and his warm, foul breath misted Firsov's spectacles: he had edged up close until Firsov's back was pressed against the wall. "I've turned myself inside-out for you. . . . Now, what about a 'wet grand'?"

"What's that?" Firsov made an involuntary movement in self-defense.

"It's this, in our lingo . . ." and if Firsov had not drawn back in time, Agey's clawlike nails would have driven into his throat.

"You swine!" Firsov spat out furiously. "None of your tricks, please!"

"All right, all right! You're alive, and everything's merry and bright, even the air you breathe's as sweet as honey, but I've only found the other side of all that. . . . Do you want me to tell you? Oh, very well, I won't. . . . You roar at me, but you're no stronger than that young hawk. An easy life . . . is poison. A man that's poisoned with that hasn't any right to live. He must be destroyed —and the man that destroys him, too—that's logic, eh? You see, I'm not whining or looking for pretty excuses. A man that's doomed like me likes to live his last few minutes on the straight. Who'll kill the last scoundrel, though, if he won't himself? Supposing he doesn't want to leave the earth and all its beauties? Tell me that, scholar."

At that moment the cat, who was sleeping on Puchov's bed, probably had a hungry dream. In quest of food, she crept onto the shelf on the wall, where Puchov kept his more substantial provisions. She trod incautiously on a plate and crashed down, and on top of her fell a small bag of grain with the din of a man falling. So it was that Firsov's book was deprived of Agey's most valuable deductions.

Paralyzed with fear, Agey looked around, waiting for the uproar to continue. In a moment his terror communicated itself to Firsov, and they both rushed to the distant corner behind the stove, and there discovered the cause of their alarm. Pushing away Firsov, who was bending down shortsightedly, Agey prepared to kick the cat, and would have done so if there had not been a sudden knock and Firsov had not hurried to open the door.

Puchov came in, cheerful and fresh from his bath; his frosted hair escaped untidily from under his hat. He went quickly and decidedly up to Agey. "What are you doing?" he demanded, and as quickly and decidedly pushed him to the door. Agey offered no resistance and went as if dazed. "Clear out!" said Puchov, "and never come here again! Get out!"

When he turned to Firsov, he found him sitting, his face drawn with fatigue. Firsov was sickened by the words that had polluted his ears; he hated his notebook in which they were stored. With a senseless, unseeing stare he gazed at the circle of light under the lamp, and understood nothing of what he saw.

"I suppose you've smoked too much," said Puchov. He stood to one side and glanced searchingly from under his spectacles, which had slipped half off his nose. Now for the first time he felt complete confidence in Firsov, for he knew how to interpret rightly his dejected silence.

MITKA made no appearance for several days, and before Zinka went to the beer hall, she powdered the rings under her eyes more heavily than usual. (He was hers only in her thoughts, and yet how she dreaded losing him!) In the Moscow thief world there were rumors that Mitka was drinking hard and losing his grip, and these rumors were partly justified by an actual occurrence that, for unknown reasons, escaped the newspapers. The same evening on which Agey horrified Firsov with his confessions, the burglary at the company's office, which Mitka had discussed at his last meeting with Agey, took place. Shchekutin and Curly Donka helped Mitka in this easy and profitable enterprise, and Agey had his share sent to him afterward in a sealed envelope, for his services as a go-between before the robbery. At this crucial moment Mitka had been deserted by his good sense and had been reckless enough to insult Agey in this fashion.

Mitka had come to his decision after a detailed discussion of his plans with Shchekutin, and it was to divert Agey's attention that he had engineered the meeting with Firsov. While he was taking his leave of Firsov, he kept looking at his watch, for he wanted to visit his sister before the robbery; she had invited him by letter to her first appearance after a long interval in the Moscow circus.

The performance dragged on drearily. A man in a frock coat, so immaculate that it made one yawn, was trying to force a white horse to kneel down before the audience, but the horse merely scraped its hoofs on the sand and would not obey. Mitka sat in the gallery; down below, the rifle shots of pseudo-Khirghiz riders blended with the make-believe belaborings of the clowns and the tactful applause of the audience. Mitka listened absent-mindedly to the echoes in the dark vault of the cupola.

During the interval Mitka went to his sister's dressing room. The circus attendant, some Ivan from Kostroma disguised in brass buttons, showed him the way. From behind the door with Tatyanka's stage name, there was a sound of thin, unreal laughter like peas rattling on paper. It was the laughter of an old man, whose black cap heightened the pallor of his face. In the light he looked so well scrubbed as to be almost transparent. While he rummaged in the trunk, he kept telling Tatyanka something funny, at which he found nobody to laugh but himself. Mitka's sister was standing in the middle of the room in blue tights and a magnificent glittering blue belt. A woman in gray, with hopeless eyes, was massaging her neck and shoulders. A small looking glass, lit by a row of unshaded lamps, reflected Mitka's features, which were drawn with fatigue.

He was terrified by Tanya's inward composure. "I'm still stealing," he was about to reply facetiously when she asked him what he was doing; but his sister suddenly forgot her question and stepped out to see to her apparatus. In her gray dressing gown she was a stranger to Mitka. There was a trace of masculine positiveness in her movements, and Mitka waited vainly for her to betray her hidden agitation by some involuntary gesture.

The old man, on the other hand, suddenly started to bustle about excitedly; he picked up things from the floor and immediately let them drop again. "Tell me, are you the bookkeeper? Yes, yes, Tanya has told me about you," he added, summoning all his attention. Mitka made to stand up, but Pugel held him firmly by the shoulders. "No, sit you there! So fine a young man! *Ach*, if we were not young, then should we not grow old. Yes, yes. *Ach*, how untidy! Dunyash, Dunyash!" he called behind the door, but no one came, only a tiny whimper of muffled music crept into the room. "Excuse me, I am vairy excited. I am not going in." He smiled engagingly. "That 'shtrabat,' that's a turn! People like to amuse themselves, but want vairy moch for their money. The sheep! What

do they know? When my children fell down, they hissed
me off! And why?"

The door burst open and a wave of brassy music surged
into the room, and again the senseless rattle of drums
hammered at the door of the green room. Tanya entered.

"Are you the first turn?" asked Mitka, getting up, but
he started when behind the door a bell rang insistently
through the whole house.

"I must go now."

His sister flung off her dressing gown while Pugel
adjusted his little black jacket. There was a proud look
on his face, as if it were he who was destined to sway the
hearts of the audience. As he left, Mitka turned again to
the deserted room and lowered his eyes. Pugel stood on
the tips of his toes, looked at the ground, and made the
sign of the cross over Tanya.

Mitka returned to his seat in time. With an uneven
hail of applause the circus greeted this woman who could
transform their terror into rapture. Mitka did not clap.
Colored spotlights crept along the black noose that hung
down from the cupola, and with a painful feeling of
estrangement Mitka recognized his sister in the shapely
circus artiste who was bowing with proud courtesy in all
directions. She threw her black cloak to a passing attendant and climbed lightly into the air with a smile on her
lips.

A deep silence brooded over the tiers of seats which
rose in widening circles to the top. The string instruments
soared up into a thin, agitating melody. A cornet sounded
warningly. In the radiance of a blue beam of light (which
for some reason or other seemed to Mitka orange-
colored), Tanya crouched down and put something hurriedly to rights. "She's tying her shoelace," said a stout
young man in a box. Mitka could only see the back of his
head, which was curly like a sheep's rump. His lady had
a voluptuous figure, and her breasts looked like a couple
of sugar melons. She was peeling an orange with the
brightly polished nails of her little fingers. "What a long
time it's lasting!" she said, and suddenly he saw again the
buckled straps on his sister's shoes, whose purpose he had
not understood.

Miss Hella Velton kept the "shtrabat," the leap from

the noose, for the end. She arranged mechanically the blue hood in which her hair was confined: suddenly she stretched out her arms and circled round the trapeze. Then she, the unapproachable, sent kisses to all who had come here because of her. A voice near Mitka made him start. "Now for the 'shtrabat'!" said the squire of the lady, who was still peeling her orange.

There was a loud blare of trumpets and everything grew still. Only the soft hissing of the spotlight and the strained gaze of the audience broke the stillness. Mitka raised his eyes furtively. The Velton, strange and pitiless, stood high up there with a noose around her neck, and carefully measured the space between her and the yellow, expectant sand. The stillness grew more profound. Someone got up to go away. A woman's voice cried out: "Enough!" Mitka looked across at the box: the lady was no longer peeling the orange, and her momentarily arrested nail vied in brilliance with her diamond ring, which shot beams of light into Mitka's eyes. It lasted only a moment . . . and the nail of the tiny finger tore again at the orange peel. The clapping and the noisy blare of the orchestra announced the end of the turn. His sister stood below in the sand, bright and supernaturally blue: around her shoulders a cape hung loosely, and the silk cord still swayed over her head. As she went away, Mitka saw in the arena Stassik, the circus artiste who had escorted Tanya to her first meeting with her brother. The dogs stood in a semicircle, pressed close together, and looked up sharply and nervously at their master.

Mitka ran out of the circus with his fur coat flung open. He found Shchekutin at the card table in a third-class thieves' den, and they left immediately—Donka had previously been sent to reconnoiter. Some hours later, the sun not yet risen, they parted from each other, having made short work of the company's "bear." When Mitka was alone again, he dropped down on a seat in the boulevard. A strange apathy had come over him, his brain worked sluggishly, and his thoughts moved with difficulty. The lighted windows seemed to swim toward him mournfully over the snow. The stillness of the night lay heavy on the city, but already there was a dull white radiance on the snow, and round about there were tiny noises of awakening. Mitka roused a coachman and ordered him to drive to Blagusha in the hope of finding Agey there still.

His intention had been to make his peace with Agey and then settle down quietly in the country. (For some time Mitka had not been able to banish the evil thoughts that kept rising in his head.) So he drove on with coat flung open and tried to think of nothing. The runners of his sledge made a complaining sound, and he listened absent-mindedly to their monotonous refrain. "What is she to me?" the runners seemed to say. "She's a stranger, a worn-out woman, Agey's wife. Why am I dragging myself off now to this damned place Blagusha instead of going to bed? To make my peace with Agey? Nonsense! Just because I want to have another look at the man for whom Masha Dolomanova threw me over!" In a secret corner of his fancy he imagined to himself the happiness he had lost, a happiness full of pain and wounds. He, Mitka, as Masha's husband! In the same house in which the old man had held his despotic sway unchallenged Mitka might have enjoyed a placid family life in Dolomanov's luxurious feather bed. It would have ruined him in a year. On Sundays he would have gone to church in Demyatino with his wife, and then to Maxim's to eat pies. Yes, however hard he might struggle against it, Mitka would have been destroyed by the downy softness of the beds. But, on the other hand, the whole of the reviving glow of Abishag in which Ageyka now warmed his numb limbs would have been his.

He jumped from the sledge and, to the amazement of the driver, pressed a handful of snow to his heated forehead. The thought of Masha would give him no rest. He felt ill, he was shaken by cold, a feeling of oppression weighed on the back of his neck, and his heart beat jerkily as if he had been poisoned. He put his hand under his coat and, feeling a fat packet of money, coldly recalled all the details of the crime that a week later was to baffle the world. Suddenly he was seized by a painful fit of coughing.

"Is THERE any equality in the world?" said Puchov, smiling. "I tell you people are only equal in greed, and then when they've had their fill they've no use for equality. In the vapor bath I've been taking a look at people's navels. In one man the navel has a jolly look, in another it looks as if a spiteful eye was squinting at you."

"But all the same they're all equally navels," said Mitka, stepping nearer and throwing off his fur coat. "It's cold. . . . Put some more wood on, Puchov! Well, have you talked it out with Agey?" He shivered, and his thoughts circled around uneasily.

"A strange customer!" replied Firsov between his teeth. When Puchov greeted Mitka, he had scanned him attentively.

"Are you cold? (I was beginning to think you'd stopped a bullet somewhere.) What about mixing you a little drink? I've got a lucky touch!"

"I'm racked from head to foot with this cough," murmured Mitka. "Can't you let me be with your medicines? I suppose you think you're going to cure me with hydrochloric acid. I expect I've been smoking too much."

Puchov said nothing, but suddenly a glance like a sunbeam flashed from under his eyebrows. Firsov thought that at last he understood Puchov's secret. "In this world we're all of us play-acting one way or another, all but Puchov, and there he sits, calmly looking on." This thought passed through his mind and vanished again. Sure enough, the master of Blagusha had a snug corner here from which to contemplate the world. Even the tiny, splashing waves of life did not reach here, while the great breakers rolled roaring high over the roof. Suddenly Puchov got tired of joking.

"Fyodor Fyodorich, you said a man will get crushed if he doesn't keep in step with progress. But I say . . . wait a little. People will get sick of it all and they'll start saying: 'We're tired of building ourselves a cage.' My dear chap, you can piss in the grass just as well as anywhere else: it doesn't do you any harm, and it's good for the grass! I'll tell you a parable. . . . Father Agafador, who shared my cell, told it to me once in the night. Well! After the Fall, Adam and Eve were chased out of the garden with brooms. Then they sat down on a hill and wept, because they would have to go to bed supperless. They cried and started reproaching each other. Then the Tempter stepped up to them. 'Don't cry, Comrades!' said he. 'There's another way into the garden. Get up! Time is money! I'll escort you myself,' and he led them." Puchov bent his head thoughtfully. "He's been leading them ever since. First of all they trailed along on foot, and then he put them in a carriage, and today he drives them about in airplanes. He drives them and flogs them on. It's a long way round, and the door they'd give their eyes for isn't even in sight yet. But the old Adam is still pressing on. He has become small and moldy and stinking, but nothing can quench his thirst. Marvellous, isn't it?"

"And good, too!" exclaimed Mitka passionately. "But when we get there, we'll become the masters ourselves. You're on the wrong track, Puchov. Men must go on advancing farther and farther. . ."

"When the black angel crashed at the beginning of time he, too, flew farther and farther with his head down. In that place, my dear chap, there's no above and below. One can't even stop when one wants to. Yes, and why should one stop, if grass and vegetables grow there without sowing, and there are no beggars, and nobody has pock marks, and the primus stoves never break?"

"You're just carping," Firsov flashed at him.

"The truth always sounds carping, my dear fellow: it's only lies that wheedle you." Puchov got up and brushed Firsov's cigarette end off the table into his palm, and threw it into the stove.

The soot that had gathered on the lamp globe reminded them it was time to leave. The frost flowers on the window gleamed blue. They stood up and spoke a little more about small, trivial, everyday things. And while he was putting on his coat, and was getting into a frenzy of exasperation at having stuck his arm behind the lining instead of into the sleeve, Firsov overheard the following scrap of conversation from behind the curtain:

"Stay with me. I'll teach you how to solder saucepans, and lots of other things, too. The bread you earn will taste sweet . . . and I'll get you out of the way of smoking."

"I'd shrivel up with you, Primus," Mitka turned him off jokingly. "I must have my fling first. You've no idea what goes on inside me."

It was bright and frosty now; the February morning promised to be a wonderful one. Veiled in the blue light of dawn, Blagusha reposed in deep snow. Trees and air glimmered in the prickly hoar frost, and the snow crackled pleasantly under the hurrying feet of the rare passers-by; it was like music, with not a single superfluous note. The sun rolled up, sluggish and coppery red, from behind the thin vapor. But no, the purple splendor of the morning snow in Blagusha cannot be described.

They paused to light cigarettes, and Firsov remembered that gray morning when he had landed in Blagusha for the first time. He had not at that time even begun his work, but now the crammed and teeming pages almost seemed more than his mind could master. He cast a furtive glance at Mitka, who was fumbling in his pockets for matches, and then breathed in joyously the frosty February air, and thought: "I have invented you as men later will know you. I have drawn you out of the darkness. You think with my thoughts, and the blood that flows in you is mine. Everything—this fine skin coat, though it's yours, and your face, which the world finds so terrifying, and these birds that seem to sway pensively in the blue frost, and the whole of this morning, which is never to recur again—all this comes from me, and I myself am it all."

Yet Mitka's face at that moment had an ill and wasted look.

CHAPTER

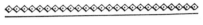

X X I I I

MITKA was in high fever. The moment was a splendid one for arresting the thief in his defenseless state, but no one paid him the slightest attention. A small dog barked at him in the street, but its barking did not reach Mitka's clouded mind. As he passed a baker's shop a warm, appetizing smell filled his nostrils and he paused, but he did not realize that he was hungry; so he went on, driven by his fevered fancies. It always seemed to him that in the very next street he would find something of the greatest importance for himself. He had wandered about in this way from early morning like a drunkard, and only his lucky star saved him from an accident. His reddened eyes were blinded by the brilliance of the snow, and streamed distressfully. Suddenly he fancied that Manka the Snowstorm was walking near him, but he did not turn his head, for he knew only too well that she was there. She was putting questions to him and reproaching him, and he had to answer her.

"Yes, Masha . . . the hero lost his pants at the last moment and the affair ended painfully. Thank you, Masha, for loving me and suffering for me. I know, of course, you can't take anything seriously, it's your nature. No, Masha, I'm unshakable: I'm made of Carborundum." This pompous word pleased him, and he repeated it several times. "I suffer a lot, Masha, but then one's got to if one's going to do anything. You say I've dished the revolution, but haven't I dished myself, too? And yet maybe I'll come alive again. I'm not out to be a 'gentleman thief,' Masha—that's not my game. God knows I've sunk low.

But it was all such a confused business, my mind couldn't keep pace with the speed—I lost my grip, do you see? But listen to me. I'll not mind dying if I've got to, but what I can't do is look through a keyhole. . . . And I won't either. And if I don't want to, a mountain won't make me. Haven't I fought, too? How my head aches!" He wanted to seize her by the arm, but his hand struck empty space —Masha had vanished. He found that she had been playing a trick on him (she had spoken a great deal herself, but not allowed him to tell her what was in his mind). He ran around a corner and clung to a post to keep himself from falling, but Masha wasn't there, either. In his delirium he fancied that she had slyly run up some steps to hide herself from his reply. Hurrying and stumbling and breathing heavily, he walked up the steps looking for her; he stepped through a wide door and stood still, full of amazement and suspicion.

A crowd of people were sitting at desks, their heads bowed busily over papers. They were all silent and as if crushed, and in the room there was a buzzing as though a huge paper fly were flapping its wings. Manka was not here; but he had already forgotten her. Certainly he had been here once not long ago . . . last week? . . . in a dream? . . . yesterday? That was where the wire for the alarm bell was: it would have to be disconnected before he and Shchekutin . . . Oh, yes . . . they had gone in then. Shchekutin had searched for the switch along the wall so that he might attach the electric drill. ("The work will be carried out at the employers' expense," he had said facetiously.) Mitka walked in slowly between the desks, and nobody stopped him. In the passage he turned to the left and stopped in front of a door with an enamel plate, which said that there was no admittance except on business.

The dusk of morning still prevailed, but no one had dared to turn on the lights. A spirit of misfortune brooded over the whole building. The cash desk with its glass walls recalled Mitka, as he passed it, from the chaos of his delirium back to reality. A policeman was sitting there, in the dark, too, as if he were guarding the melancholy ravages of Mitka's art. Mitka tried to laugh, for he felt strangely cheerful, but the laugh stuck in his throat; it sounded to him like a hoarse barking. Still wavering between indignation and laughter, he opened the door to the director's office and almost ran his head into two men in leather jackets. They apologized politely, they had not seen Mitka distinctly in the darkness. He waited until their steps had mingled with the general din in the passage and then stepped in. Atashez himself, the one-time secretary of the regimental cell, the loyal mustachioed friend, was sitting at a large table on which four telephones were ranged at his disposal.

Everything had the same superior look as the bushy white beard of the exalted founder of the establishment, whose portrait hung on the wall in a heavy frame. Mitka took off his cap, and immediately a thin man in a suit of foreign cut, with a pipe in his mouth which spread an aromatic smell, began to take his leave in pedantically halting Russian. Atashez was gay and amiable, and his teeth glittered as resolutely and busily as the foreigner's.

"Good morning, my dear fellow!" Mitka interrupted them both hoarsely, smiling at Atashez's surprise, and flinging himself into a soft and elegant easy chair. "I'm still living, you see, still living. . . . I've come to pay you a visit."

The other made no reply, but stared at him as at a dead man. He recognized Mitka immediately—they had lived through too many adventures together, the same shrapnel had too often stretched out its deadly claws over them both. It was only the presence of his visitor that prevented him in the first moment from expressing his joy at seeing Mitka again. But even after the stranger's departure, Atashez's embarrassment continued. The first outburst of joy was over, and the first words that were spoken had a flat sound. Atashez spoke casually about some trivial matter, while Mitka stared fixedly at his manicured, terribly efficient hands, his tie and his close-cropped mustache. "Devil take it, what a fine mustache he had once, and now he's cut it short, the fool, and hung some sort of a pound weight onto his face instead of a beard," thought Mitka inconsequently.

"Where are you now? . . . It's all such ages ago . . ." said Atashez in embarrassment, and his eyes roamed restlessly about the table.

"I'm working at the Co-operative . . ." mumbled Mitka importantly, and coughed in the hope that his voice might recover its lost ring. "I've been traveling the whole time, always on the move. Yesterday I lost my voice on the train: I got into an unheated carriage. Well . . . it's not so bad . . . it's interesting enough work!" He improvised some figures and platitudes which had stuck in his memory from the newspapers. "Who was that with you?"

"A foreigner. Business, you know, business. The reconstruction is going full steam ahead."

"Eyewash!" Mitka gave an indulgent wink. "No, that's not what I meant. I don't mean the foreigner, but just before him two men in leather jackets went off."

"Oh, them?" The Director shot a glance from his black eyes at Mitka, surprised at his strange question. "Yes, yes, my dear chap, sixty thousand roubles were stolen last night, in one night. These are two men from the C.I.D. who have just been with me. Mitri, you should take some medicine, or you'll lose your voice altogether. You knew Bachtin, didn't you? Well, he lost his voice, too, and now he can only croak."

"Did you gamble it away," asked Mitka gaily, bent on infuriating Atashez, "or was it with the girls?"

"What are you talking of?" the other said, frowning.

"The sixty thousand roubles. There *are* such things as girls and cards, aren't there?—but I was only joking. I've just read about it in the papers." (Mitka was lying, and if the Director had had time to glance at the papers that day, he could have caught him at once.) "Yes, a lot of money! And the worst of it is that this money will be chucked away on clothes for some wench. We had twelve thousand roubles stolen from the bank in Vetluga, too. I think it must have been the same two thieves. Bold boys, especially the older one. Ask them about me: they'll remember me right enough. Say from Vetluga—'The Red Sower Co-operative.'" He lied at random, as if his only object were to stay longer in the luxurious armchair. "Is it stuffed with down? I've never sat on anything so soft. Chaps like us have to put up with stools."

"Ye—es," drawled the Director inattentively. "Here's a clue. It was found near the cash desk." He unwrapped a paper that lay on the table, and showed Mitka a ring with a small blue stone. "That's the way it lay, rolled up in paper. It interests me, because I think I've seen it somewhere before. Where was it, though? At the front, I think. Yes, Kazan! That was where it was!"

"You saw it on me," said Mitka softly, taking the ring and slowly letting it drop into his pocket. "Have you forgotten? Let me have the paper, too."

"Are you sure it's yours?" The Director made only a feeble protest, for he did not dare to disbelieve Mitka. (At that moment the telephone rang. "Hullo! wha—at? Who's drunk? Wrong number . . .") "It was found near the telephone—no, devil take it, near the cash desk, I mean. The man who broke open the safe must have dropped it."

"You make mistakes sometimes, Atashez, even if you are a director and have had four telephones installed!" Mitka smiled impertinently, and rattled off a glib little story about how the ring and his purse had been stolen from him together at Vetluga. "Don't you believe me? If I say it's mine, what more is there to say? . . . It would be the very devil if one were to come here as a harmless visitor and then get arrested and be told 'You've broken into the safe.' "

"You're awfully changed, Mitri," Atashez began in a curious voice. (Suddenly the telephone rang again. "Is that Katya? As far as I'm concerned let it burn! No! I've got a friend sitting with me here. Do you remember once I told you about the night before the battle of Lukoyanov? Well, this is the man. Well, all right! In twenty minutes. . . . I'm going again to the C.I.D. . . . All right, I'll pass it on to him." "My wife sends you her greetings. I've told her a great deal about you. She's as fond of you as I am, for some unknown reason . . . *in contumaciam,* I suppose!"

Mitka seemed not to have heard Atashez's little joke. "On the night before Lukoyanov . . . yes, a great night! You came and lay down, and were very tired. Then Pyotr came with a mandolin and twanged out our song, 'The Little Apple,' and you jumped up as if you were off your head—with your 'boorka' flying around you. And then you were off like a rocket. That was an evening! There was a hard day in front of us, but that evening we sang more songs and danced. You see, that was why we liked you, Atashez. Then we both sat side by side with our arms around each other, and I teased you about this ring. Do you know what's hidden in this ring? Myself!" He stood swaying in the middle of the room. "It's all over: it's all gone west now, Atashez. There's nothing left now but the shadows dancing on the walls from the old fire."

The Director glanced at him keenly. "What are you jabbering about, Dmitri? Have you lost the use of your eyes? Nothing's over: it's all just beginning." He had not expected Mitka's attack, so was not equipped to defend himself.

"Beginning, is it?" asked Mitka, and raised his eyes. "But what's beginning? Your Katya has a red hat, I know, but you're one of the respectable ones now. You just sit there and say yes to everything." Suddenly he seized Atashez by the shoulder. "Where have you thrown your old coat, your 'boorka'? The nice, warm, shaggy 'boorka' we slept under together the night before Lukoyanov? You say it isn't over yet. Well, then, sing the song of 'The Little Apple' again! Dance and sing, Atashez. I'm not ordering you to the barricades, but just sing our song! Dance, you devil, or it'll be the worse for us both! Take care the cutlets don't get overdone! Take care!"

"You've gone off your head, Dmitri!" whispered the other in consternation, for Mitka's rage had both shocked and incensed him. His jacket flapped wide open, as if it were the famous skin coat—but the jacket wasn't the "boorka" all the same. "What is there to dance about here? This isn't a public house. . . . They can hear us here. . . . Someone might come in. I'm the Director here, the chief director. I've to answer for a hundred puds. No, that isn't what I mean. You think that everything's over? What's wrong with you, Dmitri? Don't you see, we're beggars, we're saving up one kopek after another and flooding the land with electricity. We're building, and our bricks are dearer than other people's because we knead them with our own hands. No one has helped us, they've all despised us and hindered us, but did you see just now how that chap with the pipe in his mouth bowed to me? Do you understand now? Yes, we wear smart suits, and we'll put on top hats if we've got to. We'll grill cutlets, too, because cutlets must be well grilled. We've had as hard a time as anyone has ever had in the whole history of the land, but we don't complain. The new century began in the year 1917. But what's the use of talking? It would be all up with us if we believed your arguments, and they have a powerful effect as you put them. The only thing that's worrying me is the sixty thousand roubles." He frowned at this disagreeable recollection. "You're very ill, Dmitri. Sleep well and drink wine, and then come to me and we'll have some fun together. I'll explain to you why one can't always tear about with a sword. In the crush one might strike one of one's own fellows. . . . You think a different heart beats under the 'boorka'? No, it's the same, my friend. . . . It's only that it beats more slowly because we're economizing. We even have to economize in heartbeats. Now, go, go!"

Mitka did not hear his last words. His rising fever made his head swim.

The Director led him tottering to the door and looked into his face as he said good-by. "Are you crying?" he asked unguardedly.

Then Mitka straightened up and pushed back the Director. "I'm crying for your sixty thousand roubles, Atashez." He turned his back on him and stepped out into the corridor.

He walked swaying down the steps. During the half-hour he had spent with the Director he had grown very much worse. He wanted to drink, and made for a place where one could abandon oneself carefree to rest and revelry and sleep. But as he went away, he felt clearly his right at any time and "without announcement!" to return there . . . if it were only to make another effort to rouse the stiff-necked Atashez to a dance. At that moment Mitka did not remember the thirty thousand roubles that weighed down the pocket of his open coat.

Firsov's professional conscience carried the day over his
personal distaste, and the very next day he went to Agey's
house, where he made the acquaintance of "The Snowstorm." Agey's desire to be immortalized in Firsov's narrative was so strong that he agreed straight off to take the
writer with him to Artemy's den. For his visit Firsov put
on his usual disguise. He wore thick felt breeches thrust
into worn, goat-skin top boots, while under his jacket he
had a gaily embroidered shirt, and when over all he put
on an evil-smelling sheepskin, the effect was superb. In
fact, when they met at the appointed crossroads, Agey
only recognized him by his spectacles and his villainously
shaggy beard.

They stepped into a droshky. The driver was a friendly
little old man, who grumbled and exclaimed without stopping about the hard times. They drove through the most
animated streets, but the whole long way they did not
utter a word until, as they crossed a great square, Agey
gave his companion an unexpected dig in the ribs.

"Do you know who'll be there?" he asked in an important voice, bending close to Firsov's ear.

"Who?" Firsov came to himself with a jerk, for his
thoughts had been far away.

"My father," Agey whispered into his ear. "I'm telling
you between ourselves. You see, I wrote to my father that
I'd bettered myself and got a fine post as business manager." Firsov disliked Agey's brand of humor, and did not
trouble to conceal his frown. "I wrote to him: 'Come and
see the life your young hopeful's leading, and we can make

friends again, too: the apple that falls stays under the apple tree after all.' I'm his son still, the old devil's son, aren't I?" he added scornfully. "It isn't good for a man to live always at war with his father, is it? What do you think?"

"No, of course not . . ." Firsov stammered, and in his heart he cursed the day he had become a writer. There was an ugly tremor in Agey's voice which disturbed him. Was it revenge? or was it perhaps really reconciliation? "It's hard to guess the spot where the sun stands in a November sky." Firsov remembered the words he had written at the beginning of his third chapter.

Cradled in soft clouds the waning moon rose above the dark streets. In its greenish light the blackened chimneys with their swirling smoke stood out sharply against the sky. It was freezing, and indoors people were piling on the logs. The two-storied houses huddled together in a frost-bitten row, one lower than the other, for the wretched street fell away steeply in the middle. Under the light of a street lamp Firsov cast a furtive glance at Agey's face, and was astonished at its peacefulness. His eyes were smiling, as if they saw with the calm of foreknowledge a final goal to which the feeble little cab horse was bearing him.

"Tell me, Fyodor Fyodorich, is it really true that the French eat toads?" asked Agey suddenly.

"Well, not exactly toads," muttered Firsov dryly, and fidgeted as he reflected whether it would not be more prudent to run away in time. "Actually, they only cook frogs' legs and eat them . . . with sauce."

"But that's rusty, too," Ageyka interrupted. He was silent for a few moments, as if he wanted to give Firsov time to reflect over the different thoughts that can occupy two men, even when they are sitting side by side. "Puchov said to me once . . . he wanted to prove to me what a bad chap I am . . . 'Every metal,' said he, 'has its rust: copper green, iron red . . . aluminum quite white.' 'And what sort of rust have I got?' I asked, and he answered: 'Black.' No, Fyodor Fyodorich, my rust isn't black."

"That's how it is . . . the air eats iron, time eats man." With these words the old driver turned around. His fares made no answer, and he stopped talking, too—without feeling offended; but he began to urge on his little horse more vigorously.

As they got out of the sledge at the end of a long, nameless street, Firsov was once more surprised and alarmed by Agey's unaccountable behavior. "Listen, old man," he said as he paid the driver, "there's another five kopeks for you, buy some oats for your horse. Buy some oats and let it eat them. Do you understand? Off with you!" (Firsov later on understood the real reason for Agey's strange behavior.)

A water carrier brought them into a dark courtyard, and Agey, after exchanging a few remarks in thieves' jargon with him, stepped through the wide-open door. In the yard two small cottages were hidden behind some trees—it was a clever piece of deception, for later on, one saw that they weren't so small after all—and around them some very innocent-looking sheds were grouped. The haphazard arrangement of the buildings gave the impression that some drunkard had flung them down here and then run away from the disfigured spot.

Two chained dogs greeted the newcomers with a raucous barking, and someone appeared on the staircase, apparently a woman, and said a few words to Agey. Then he took Firsov in.

"They're just starting boozing. . . . Mitka's here. And he'll find he has me to reckon with tonight," he muttered *sotto voce*, and, suddenly stumbling, let fly some unsavory oaths.

The door was half open, and they went in through a clean, respectable-looking dwelling, and then . . . Firsov later on could scarcely recollect how Artemy's den was furnished: he saw everything that took place after he entered the room as though through thick bottle glass. The shadow on the steps now revealed itself to be a tidy, respectable-looking woman with a small handkerchief around her head, and, shutting the door behind them, she vanished as quickly as a real shadow. A lively hum of voices and the noise of some continuous movement came through the passage, which was divided off by a cheap curtain.

This was where Artemy's den began, the secret scene of drinking and debauchery and recuperation from the excitement of the dangerous life of every day. Here, as they drank away the loot of yesterday, the thieves concocted plans for new raids on the world and its inhabitants. Here, too, one could gamble away one's booty, and Artemy only asked half per cent of the stakes. Into this room only the older and more experienced ones or, among the younger, only those who had already given proof of their talent in thieves' craft, were admitted. Artemy, the patron of thieves (who was called "the Korean" on account of his successful escape from Saghalin by the Korean Straits), received his guests in person in the anteroom. His small, restless eyes were parted from each other by a sharp, thin, powerful nose, which gave his face an almost diabolical expression. His eyes were instantly at work on Firsov, endeavoring to ascertain whether he was dangerous or useful.

"Please, please . . ." said Artemy, after he had heard Agey's explanation. "We never show the door to a guest who's friendly. It's a good thing to describe us and the air we breathe. Maximka used to write about us, but that's a long time ago. Oska's here today." He passed his clumsy hand over his thin beard, which was so black that it looked artificial, and over his well-greased hair, which was cut like a coachman's. His hair, so many times shaven in imperial convict settlements, had retained its color and thickness. Artemy helped Firsov take off his short coat, and, secretly feeling his pockets to assure himself of his guest's harmlessness, laid the skin on the chest, as all the hooks were already loaded with clothes. Artemy's threadbare jacket smelled strongly of camphor.

"Please step in," he said as he pushed back the curtain with a perfunctory gesture.

Firsov now for the first time observed at close quarters the milieu he described in his works. Yet he did not notice anything out of the common: people were amusing themselves, that was all. A few noisy lads were energetically throwing an insignificant little man up in the air, so that his striped breeches got torn and his collar, which had come loose, hopped about like a little bird on his stiff, starched shirt front. In any case, the little man offered no resistance; he tittered, and was deeply touched by this stormy testimony of camaraderie.

"Why are they doing that to him?" Firsov asked Agey.

"Because they're very pleased with him," Agey explained smilingly. "That's Oska Preslovuty—haven't you heard of him yet? He's a famous man. Take a good look at him—you collect freaks, don't you?" Thereupon Agey left Firsov with the remark: "Well, then, amuse yourself as you like."

Not till later did Firsov get to know Oska's story. Osip Preslovuty, an hereditary coiner, was the fourth of his famous family. He was nimble and meager and more like a corkscrew than a man. Long ago Alexander the Second had rewarded a brave soldier with a twenty-five rouble piece that Oska's famous grandfather Larion had minted, and Larion's descendant justly considered himself as at least the equal of a count in rank. Today he was celebrating a new issue of coinage: he was entertaining his friends and some women and at the same time cultivating new acquaintances. It was his object to be as agreeable and as sociable as possible.

Not till now did Firsov see that it had been a mistake to appear here with Agey. As soon as Agey was recognized, a chill, a feeling of constraint, fell on the company. But new guests arrived, fresh bottles were uncorked, and soon Firsov was drinking out of the glass that Sanka pushed toward him, and quietly and silently observing the furniture of Artemy's den. The guests went to a table, on which stood a careless disarray of plates, dishes, and drinks; they took what they wanted and went on amusing themselves. Someone boasted of his successful *coup* as he drew a cork out of a bottle with his penknife, and a woman was singing in front of a looking glass, which was scratched over with people's signatures and mottled with age. Everyone amused himself, and unburdened his soul in his own way.

"It can't go on like this. Look, Fyodor Fyodorich!" whispered Sanka. He was almost tearful with drink. "What's to come of it? My master's here, too—have you seen him? They're going at him from all sides. . . . He won't listen to anyone. . . . Come and look at the master, the way he torments me." He drew Firsov into the little room next door, which was divided off by a curtain and a stout door. The card room looked more sober and serious. The two blind windows were adorned with green curtains, and the floor, which in the adjacent room was only strewn with sawdust, was covered with a sort of carpet.

In the thick, sour-smelling tobacco smoke, Mitka was standing to his full height at a green baize card table. Firsov recognized him from behind by the straight, stony lines of his back. Ruined gamblers, drawn by curiosity or sympathy, looked on in melancholy fascination while Mitka lost his money to a meager, sad-faced Jew. The Jew won without a break, and, putting his money in his pocket, repeatedly tried to escape, but somebody in the darkness (the lamp hung low, and the corners of the room stayed in gloom) always pressed him down by his shoulder and forced him to stay. "I can't . . . I can't go on," groaned the Jew, who was dripping with sweat and excitement.

"Pirman, you keep the bank!" Mitka's voice had a quietly imperious ring.

Pirman kept the bank again and, in growing despair, won Mitka's crumpled notes. He did not understand Mitka's recklessness. He had come here to earn a trifle from a drunken thief, but had had insane luck, which had made him the hero of the evening; and now he cursed his luck.

"Has it been going on like that long?" whispered Firsov, going forward a little so as to be able to see Mitka's face. But immediately they began to hiss, and so he remained standing in his place. . . . "That's the twelfth thousand that he's flung away!" Sanka whispered plaintively in his ear, and ran wrathfully from the room.

Before he left the room, Firsov succeeded in making two more observations. Mitka's dim gray eyes strained from under his lifted eyebrows, but his face was calm and blanched with illness; only by his fingers that drummed upon the table could Firsov detect his inward agitation. A thick stubble of beard covered his cheeks like a smear of dirt. Secondly, Firsov noticed that every time he drew money out of his pocket, Mitka straightened the tiny blue ring on his finger. The ring seemed to be unbearably tight.

And suddenly Firsov felt that here something very extraordinary was taking place—something that would never happen again. Only at the crossroads between two epochs, and in a moment of colossal reconstruction, could one behold the agony of a . . . yes, of a . . . planet flung out of its course. This stifling smoke, these wild passions born of the tedium of life, Oska's mad debauchery, and Mitka's cruel scorn of his fortunate opponent—they were all the flashing of the same fly wheel. When Firsov went into the next room, where Oska's laughing tenor rang through the air, he loosened the tight collar of his fanciful embroidered shirt. One had to admit that Artemy, in his endeavor to supply his friends with a cozy home, was not at all sparing of fuel.

In his blue silk shirt, his face pale and bearing the traces of sleeplessness, Donka read his poem to the end. His verses had nothing particularly striking about them, or any special preciosity of meter; he simply sang of his unenviable lot and used his heart as his ink pot. He sang of the morning on which his wretched annals would end—a morning which, though gray and ugly, he would greet like a morning in May. On that day the strong arm of the law would seize him, Curly Donka, "like a wild beast, or Kolchak the admiral." The others drank, and treated the poet and a small guitar player with a pimply face. The guitar player needed no pressing; it was almost as though he wished to drown his marvellous gifts. ("I should have gone to the Conservatoire, and now I have to strum country dances at weddings," he complained bitterly to Firsov, who had complimented him on his playing.) He twitched at the strings with his short fingers, and Firsov furtively entered in his notebook under the table: "The most devoted lovers in the ecstasy of love could not fuse so utterly as this guitar player and his guitar. Now he stroked the strings with the deepest tenderness, then he flung himself upon it with the fury of an animal, and his fingers tore at its tense and twitching body as if he wished to rend its last tones from it and make it soundless forever. No one knew the name of the piece he was playing, but everyone saw a sinking ship before him. . . ."

"What are you jotting down there, Comrade?" a sugary, insinuating voice suddenly whispered into his ear. It was from Oska that the attack came; he was only moderately drunk, but in a quarrelsome, contentious mood. The danger was soon averted, however, for those who had already met the writer in the beer hall took his part. In a moment Firsov's star was in the ascendant; they were actually on the point of tossing their new visitor up to the ceiling, and had started pulling him about, much to Firsov's alarm, when Oska himself came to his rescue.

"Write, write about us!" Oska had become excessively gracious, and proposed a toast to Art—Art in general, not only his own branch. "Write that we're all human," he went on, passing some sweets soaked in wine to Firsov. "Look at me! Who am I? I'm an individual, if you want to know."

"Is that good or bad?" the others shouted.

"It's middling! . . . Osip Preslovuty, an individual. My God, I'm a great man, though unknown to fame! Here's something to remind you of me." He drew a note from his pocket, to convince Firsov of his artistic skill. Firsov, who was overwhelmed by all his new impressions, got out of it by stammering something facetious.

"Someone said to me lately: 'I hear you looted a flat, Oska!' I, Osip! . . . Lord, but I'm *the* thief! . . . In all Russia there's only we nine, and I'm the fourth. Ask whoever you like: 'Who's the fourth?' And they'll all say: 'Oska.' . . . And then to be thought a bloody amateur! What would my grandfather say to that?" Oska actually began to weep.

The hubbub swelled and spread. In the center of the room Curly Donka was still dancing with a set face, and broken glass was crunching under his feet, while tumblers tinkled mournfully on the tables. Firsov turned around to answer Oska, but instead of him saw a tousled, emaciated woman, whose eyes had a strange gleam, sitting beside him. She drained a glass of wine at a single draught, and cried out into the hurly-burly: "Here comes the *barin!* Here's the *barin!*"

Oska had already risen to greet Manyukin, who had turned up unexpectedly. He pressed some notes into Manyukin's hand and assured him that they were genuine, but Manyukin, who was already rather tipsy, pushed Oska's insistent hand to one side with a noble gesture. The most noteworthy sights in the room now were Mitka's empty, hopeless face, peering from the other room, Manyukin's turned-in toes, and Artemy's broad, slotlike mouth. Artemy escorted Pirman to the door and pocketed his percentage with a scornful smile; then someone handed Manyukin a glass of wine to cheer him up.

"*Vielen dank*," said Sergey Ammonich nonchalantly. "What are your commands?"

Then Curly Donka came up. "*Barin*," he said quietly, looking at the ground, as though he were frightened to utter what he had to say aloud. "*Barin*, tell us about a woman . . . the woman one sees only in dreams. . . ."

"At your service!" Manyukin straightened himself obediently; suddenly he looked around with wide-open eyes and began: "Well, the story, how I . . . converted . . . the . . . the . . ." (he reflected a moment) "how I . . . I . . . converted the famous Stasska Kapustnyak to Christianity. . . . Would you like that?" He was met with an acquiescent silence.

"That's about the woman, is it?" asked Donka, as if he were half asleep, and stretched out his legs.

"In my young days I was an amazingly good-looking young fellow . . ." began Manyukin in a lisping voice like the rustling of moldering pages. "I confess it openly . . . when I was thirteen I almost seduced the wife of our chaplain—only a miracle saved me, and I see in it the hand of Providence." He suddenly became conscious that his thoughts were wandering. A cold sweat covered his face, and it was sluggishly and with unwonted delay that his fancy got to work. "There I sat one evening . . . I was bored. . . . I went to the telephone. 'Put me through to Lieutenant Agarin.' 'Is that you, Sasha?' 'It's me!' he answered. 'Stop drinking!' I shouted, for he smelled so strongly of wine, you know, 'and come across and let's blow off steam!' After ten minutes Sasha burst into my room in full gala dress with ribbons and orders and shoulder straps. 'Where are you off to?' 'To the club,' said I. 'They've got some tip-top lobster there.' We hurried off. They were playing *chemin de fer* when we got there. In a jiffy we had joined in, and toward morning we were both of us plucked bare. I sat under the chandelier . . . I remember that exactly. I felt as wretched as if I had lost my childhood's innocence. I hadn't a centime, and my skull felt as thin as an eggshell . . . and the rosy dawn crept through the window like pink wadding. Then in the pool of wine on the floor I saw a hundred-rouble note swimming. 'Pick it up?' thought I. . . . 'Perhaps I can win something back. . . .' But I was ashamed." (This was Manyukin's story, but no one saw the pool under his feet in which Oska's crumpled note lay; they saw only the hundred-rouble note that Manyukin mentioned.) "And suddenly behind me I became aware of the eighth wonder of beauty and elegance. It was as if an electric current ran through all my nerves. 'This is she,' thought I, 'of whom for twenty-four long years I have dreamed in torment before going to sleep. My God, must my wretched youth end at the feet of this beauty?' My joints cracked . . . but I didn't dare turn around. I clenched my teeth"—Manyukin ground his teeth—"I turned around, and all at once felt that death had come and seized me by the throat with its hands. And what do you think?" Manyukin swung back his body from the waist with a majestic movement and crossed one leg over the other. . . . "There sat a fat peasant, if you please . . . the fat sagged off him in rolls, and instead of a face he had a huge, lilac-colored tomato. It wasn't a man, it was just an adenoid, if you'll pardon the expression. And beside him"—Manyukin flung a sharp, anxious glance at Donka, who was groaning—"her tender arm around his neck, sat the woman. Terribly pale, and her eyes, her eyes . . . blue, like . . . blue steel. I stood there as if rooted to the spot, and waited for my end. I tugged Agarin by the coat, my blood was glowing hot, my limbs were racked with pain, and I whispered to Agarin: 'Who is that? Speak, or I'll shoot you!' 'That man there,' he answered, 'is Giga Mantagurov, a well-known man; he owns a racing stable and oil wells. Do you see those fiber trunks? Well, he carries his money around with him in them: there's an ocean of naphthalin in each of them.' 'You're lying.' 'God strike me if I am.' 'Sasha,' I said then, 'weep for me and pray for me, for I'm done for. . . .' All around was wild confusion: bronze chandeliers lay on the floor, cards floated about in pools of spilled wine. . . . And there she was sitting . . . there she was sitting . . . like an alabaster chalice . . . and a coolness . . . a coolness streamed from her as from mother earth. I got up and squared my shoulders, my eyes were flashing. I went up to Mantagurov, and banged a bottle on the table. 'Bonjour,' I said, 'I'm Sergey Manyukin. . . .' He was alarmed, of course, and offered me one of the trunks, but I . . . 'No, no, Giga,' said I majestically, 'everything depends on how one feels at the time. Look at me. I never did any harm to anyone, not even to my dog, but all the same you're going to fly up to the ceiling in a minute.'

"He stared at me, and saw a handsome chap with a nasty look in his eye: he understood and went pale. 'Look here,' said I, 'either we'll play for her, this fatal beauty you don't know how to value, or you'll fly up to the ceiling with a bullet through you.' He began to laugh, his red gullet began to hop like a bird in a cage. 'And what do you stake?' he croaked. 'I stake the Kuznyetzky bridge in Moscow,' cried I, beside myself with passion. 'It won't do,' said he: 'my stake is higher.' 'The Tverskaya street as well, then.' 'Too little.' 'Dorogomilovo as well,' said I softly, raising my index finger. Then he gave in. . . . 'Let's play Polish Bank, at seventeen,' he roared. The beauty was seventeen. Two servants unsealed the cards. I dealt—left, right, left, right . . . stop!—two queens. The second pack —stop! . . . two tens. Sasha hissed: 'Give it up, you bastard, give it up! You're losing.' I went on dealing. My face altered, it altered . . . my face altered."

At this point something happened to Manyukin. He looked stupidly in front of him with a dull stare, and a stifled sob broke from his open mouth. He cut short the tale he had invented, for it seemed to him that someone who was not there had blown in his face; it was like a tender breath of wind. He struggled heroically to continue the story, but he had forgotten, forgotten everything, suddenly and catastrophically. He did not grasp the meaning of the glances that were directed at him as he wiped his face in embarrassment. The loneliness of his inglorious old age was more than he could bear.

Then he got up slowly and went to the door. Artemy ran after him.

"Let him be! . . . It's hard lines on him," somebody shouted.

"Put some snow on his breast," cried the lean woman.

In the universal hubbub no one noticed a sturdy, respectable old man with a peasant's clothes and beard entering the room. The curtain was pushed to one side by some ready hand, and at the same moment Manka the Snowstorm appeared in bizarre splendor. She wore a pink silk dress with flounces and a starched Antoinette collar. She glanced around imperiously, scrutinizing the faces of the company. Everyone understood and was silent, and two men drew aside to clear the path to Mitka, who was leaning apathetically against the wall. Agey got up with a loud sigh, pulled his clothes straight, and went up to the old man. Firsov looked at the round clock that hung above the door into the card room; the hands pointed to twenty-five past one. Without knowing why, he got up excitedly, but instantly sat down again on the hard, uncomfortable sofa. Manka the Snowstorm gave him a quick, friendly smile as if to say: "Well, Firsov, so you're one of us, too!"

MANYUKIN was quickly forgotten and left to himself (he was lying in bed somewhere in Artemy's house), and they all watched while Agey calmly and resolutely went up to his father, kissed his hand, and introduced him to the thieves, who were waiting in tense expectation.

"Here, this is my father, Finogen Stolyarov. Allow me." They all bowed, for no one could guess at first what Agey intended.

"Peace to the honored company!" said Finogen with modest dignity, and fumbled in his coarse gray coat at the spot under which the heart beats and where notecases are usually kept. "What is the occasion you are celebrating?"

"We are celebrating a feast day, little father," cried the thieves in chorus. "We are celebrating Maxim the miracle-worker's day!" They had begun to see what Agey was up to. . . . "But take off your coat, little father."

"In winter? Saint Maxim? But Maxim is in the apple season," muttered the old man to himself as he took off his coat, which Artemy immediately carried away behind the door. The old man sat down, and the thieves pressed around him. Those who could not get near, looked over the heads of the others at the blunt, honest face with the gray eyebrows. A girl began to titter, and Agey gave her a merciless dig in the ribs, after which she preserved a terrified silence till the end of the evening. She did not even venture to complain about Agey to her freckled squire.

"I never heard anything before about a Maxim's day in winter."

"But of course," Donka improvised rapidly. "Don't you know the saying:

> "'Wintry Maxim, when you poke,
> Up the chimney drives the smoke.'"

"It's certainly very cold outside today," said the old man, and crossed himself as he took a glass of wine which was passed to him. "It seems the days are drawing in." He drank and cleared his throat, hiding his mouth politely with his sleeve. His eyes wandered around looking for Manka the Snowstorm, and he was not content until he found her. He saw her gazing fixedly and keenly at Mitka's listless face and shaking her head.

At a wink from Oska a stalwart youth poured expensive wine into the kvass glasses.

"Well, well!" began Finogen afresh, considering the silence of the company as a mark of respect for his age. "And we thought that you townspeople were at your last gasp. You've got into a fine muddle here. My friend Pavel Makarich Klopov from Passynkovo told me . . ."

"Is Pavel Makarich still living, then?" inquired Agey dully. His face was becoming more and more gloomy.

"He died last spring, he died beautifully. He brought trouble on nobody," said Finogen, and looked at his son. "And Pavel Makarich prophesied, while the European war was still on: 'Grass and mushrooms will grow on the streets of Moscow, and one man will take a wide circle to avoid another. . . .' But you live still, you breathe." Finogen smiled crookedly.

"But let's drink and be friends, Father!" his son interrupted him.

"Let's drink, Ageyuska!" said the old man gaily. "Why shouldn't I take pleasure in my son's company?" All the same he hesitated to drink, but gazed long into the depths of the brimming glass. "Is your name Maxim?" He turned to Artemy. "Then I congratulate you on your name day. May the Lord send you many years and let you survive us all."

"*Merci*," piped Artemy scornfully.

"You've got a little business, haven't you?" The old man turned to Artemy, whose beard inspired especial confidence. "Are things dear now?"

"I deal in buttons, Daddy. But there are different kinds of buttons. One kind one hides, the other kind one wears on one's jacket for everyone to see. . . ." Artemy was making fun of the old man to his face.

The new game would have gone on longer if it had not been for Agey. He stood up, and his face was sinister and swollen and had a leaden look.

"Here you, sergeant!" he rudely addressed Artemy, who was looking at the old man with twinkling eyes. "Some soup here! Quick march! . . . What kind? . . . Cartgrease soup, of course, you fool!" He sat down, and turned his face away in a temper from his father, who shook his head reproachfully.

Oska, Donka, and several others had already vanished; some had gone out with women; only those remained who had nothing to draw them out into the cold, unfriendly night. Agey silently took a pear, the ripest of all, which squirted juice through his fingers as soon as he touched it. He smiled quietly at some thought, licked up the sweet juice, and flung the pear under the table. "Aha, rotten, you see, but sweet!" he muttered to himself, and jumped up in a sudden frenzy of excitement. "Why are you gaping at me? Have I suddenly grown horns or what?" he cried, and the dumbfounded revelers fell apart in confusion.

"Sit down, Agey, and hold your tongue! They're laughing at you," ordered Manka, picking a grape from the bunch. "Now's your chance to describe us all, Firsov! Something snappy. Take our little Mitka here: 'From Commissar to Cad.' Do you think they won't allow you?" She frowned as Firsov shook his head. "Write the truth, and they'll allow you, all right."

Artemy arrived with the soup that had been ordered and slapped it down on the table in a painted wooden tureen. "There! Put it away, m'lord!" he flung rudely over his shoulder.

This soup was a special concoction of Agey's with which he was accustomed to test the devotion and obedience of his few friends. It was a disgusting mixture of beer and vodka, with lemon slices and cucumbers floating on top to add to its horrors.

"Let's be friends, Mitka. Come and sit with us!" he began, passing Mitka the wooden spoon. "Let's eat together

and bury the hatchet. I'll forget the way you treated me.
. . . Oh, you don't want to, eh? Then the devil take you
and break your legs!" He gesticulated wildly. Finogen did
not for a moment take his watering eyes off his son as he
struggled to grasp the change that had taken place in him.
"Well, devil take it . . . I've done my bit for the party,
too. . . . I've strangled a bishop! Yes, I have, damn
you! . . ." Then Agey's pent-up wrath broke out in a
storm against Sanka. "What are you gaping at? You want
to marry, do you, and have a lot of squalling kids? Papa!
Mama! Clear out, damn you!" He followed Sanka with a
sharp stare as he withdrew, then suddenly made a petu-
lant, discontented gesture. "Why did I turn him out? He's
not my enemy." Then he pointed at Mitka, who stood
there in a feverish dream. "All right, no need for you to
get excited. You'll sleep with her before I'm cold. She'll
take the life out of you and burn you to a cinder."

The next moment Agey ran wild, and struck out right
and left. The noise of breaking glass mingled with the
screams of women; a chair was overthrown; somebody trod
on the guitar, and a discordant screech from its torn
strings rang out and died. Under Artemy's leadership the
enraged thieves made for Agey, who stood ready to defend
himself, scarlet with passion. But now their blood was up.

"Let's get out of this. Take me away," said Manka to
Firsov, and, without waiting for his consent, seized him
by the arm. "You've seen all there is to see. They're going
to start fighting this is no place for you now."

"Got another lover, Manka? Stay here, or it'll be the
worse for you!" screamed Agey over the heads of the
others who stood around, and his body writhed as if in
torment.

The last thing that Firsov saw was Agey's flame-red
pants as he towered above the rest on the table. Deserted
by all, old Finogen sat on his chair as if it were a pillory,
and looked all around him with a helpless, lost expression.
Firsov, who had just put on his coat, threw a glance at the
clock: the hands were creeping on inexorably toward two.

It was still night when Manka the Snowstorm stepped out of the den with Firsov. It had just been snowing, and everything looked strangely soft and virginal. The sky was full of stars, the moon shed rays of intolerable sadness, and cold shadows played over the glistening snowdrifts. In the dark corners crouched terror, and silence lay in ambush in the streets.

Manka the Snowstorm gave Firsov a sign that the street was quite free. In her astrakhan coat and her white fluffy scarf she seemed to Firsov like a vision of his heated fancy. A wildly romantic mood seized him. The keen, bracing frost and the sight of the untouched snow had a refreshing effect after the squalid adventures of the night. Excited by the lateness of the hour, Firsov became sentimental and banal. But he pulled himself together and offered Manka his arm, on which she leaned gratefully. He looked at her profile with its icy pallor, at her rebellious curls above her high, clear brow, at her dark, restless, ever smiling lips. He was happy, because he did not understand what had happened.

Suddenly she clung to him convulsively. He looked at her in surprise, blinking through his glasses; then she gave him a long and passionate kiss.

"Kiss me, kiss me . . . you fool!" she breathed into his face imperiously, and planted a second kiss on his thick, chapped lips. "Can't you see who's coming?"

Firsov returned the kiss distractedly. Not till a moment later did he grasp the situation, and his sudden realization put to flight the wild and blessed magic of the night. Not far from them was standing a closed car, which looked as if it were observing the silence of the street attentively with the pupils of its extinguished lamps. Firsov turned around instinctively. A file of men, all exactly like each other, were pouring through the door of the house from which Manka and he had just issued. Firsov realized that this was a raid just before he noticed the reinforced patrols advancing toward them. He bent with clumsy ardor over his unexpected conquest, and did not notice that he was scratching her face with his spectacles.

"What's that you say?" he asked excitedly.

"Your spectacles . . . take them off! Have you ever seen a lady killer with spectacles?" she breathed into his ear, and drew him down on a bench beside a high gate.

Though they were still in danger, Firsov was delirious with excitement. Once more Manka's cold lips were pressed upon his cheek as a patrol advanced toward them. The nearer they came, the closer she clung to him. The proximity of danger seemed to increase her passion.

"Hot stuff, eh?" said a policeman approvingly, not without envy; perhaps he was thinking of his own sweetheart from whom his duty had torn him. "Look at the way she's cuddling him!" and the others growled agreement.

Manka gave a little squeal of pretended dismay, as though ashamed at her raptures being observed. Their hurried escape seemed drolly natural. They now doubled on their tracks and, running into a churchyard, hid in the porch; at the same moment, quite close to them, a shrill whistle sounded in the darkness, echoing in the silent street. A cloud veiled the moon, and the enchantment of the night was over.

The danger was past, and Firsov, with a feeling of relief, tried to draw Manka to him, but she slapped his hand and laughed.

"Don't be a fool!" she said dryly. "I thought a man who wore spectacles would have some sense. You've only tasted once and now you want more, do you? Button up your coat, or you'll catch cold. Whatever do you suppose there is about you that could attract me? You write, but what else is there about you? I barely know your name." There was a strange softness in her voice. "Is your wife old?"

"One's own wife is always old, even if she's young," said

Firsov touchily, and passed his tongue over his lips. The
stone wall against which they were standing sucked in
greedily the warmth of their bodies, but Firsov felt as if a
hot wind were blowing. "Love me—just love me. At the
first glance I saw through you, I found you out . . .
you're lonely, I know it. But I can do anything for you—
anything. I can build towns, and create men and worlds
out of the void." He gabbled a great deal more nonsense,
which only his overwrought state could excuse.

"Aren't you frightened Agey might be waiting somewhere and watching you seducing his wife? . . . All
right, I was only joking. He won't do any more watching
after this." This callous hint brought Firsov to his senses
and sent a chill to his heart.

"Let me tell you this, though. You write about women,
I suppose, but what do you know about them? A woman,
if she's a woman at all and not a dummy, remains young
as long as she isn't afraid of growing old, and a young
woman is like dust in the wind. Grab her, you fool, or
she'll escape, and the more attractive she is, the slyer
she'll be. . . . But we don't want to spend the night here,
do we?"

They went to Mitka's flat to wait for Manyukin. Without knowing why, they were both of them sure that the
harmless storyteller would succeed in escaping. Their
hopes were not cheated. When the windows were growing
gray in the light of dawn, Sergey Ammonich appeared with
a pallid face and sunken eyes. As usual, he was wearing
a woman's coat, and a woolly cap like a pancake, cocked to
one side at a dashing angle, sat on his head. He was longing to fling himself into bed, but they dragged him to
Mitka's room and began their catechism.

"They all know me, you see," stammered Manyukin as
he reported the details of his escape. Mumbling his words
in his confusion, and making patterns with his finger in
the dust on Mitka's table, he told of Agey's last moments.
Artemy had shot at the patrol, which had returned the
fire, and the first shot had struck Agey. All that Manyukin
could tell of Finogen was that the whole time he had sat
there with an apologetic smile, murmuring: "He's having
his revenge now, my gift from God." And then the
old man had turned over his dead son with his foot, and

stared for a long time at his stiff, cold face. All this may have been just Manyukin's imagination: he had estimated the strength of the patrol, for instance, at a hundred men. In any case, the old man had a perfect right to say farewell to his son as he chose.

"A quick death, an easy death . . . but you, every day you must die, every breath may be your last. Nikolasha, my friend . . . Nikolasha!" Manyukin moaned in despair, heedless of those who stood around him. "I haven't any friend called Nikolasha . . . I'm lying . . ." said he after a while, and reeled to his room. "Pleasant dreams, Signori!" he called out to them once more in deep despair.

"Who's the Nikolasha he's talking about? What's happened?" Zinka rushed with these words into the room. She could not go to sleep while anyone was talking of Mitka in her neighborhood. The soft whiteness of her shoulders shone through the torn wrap she had hastily flung over them. Firsov went to the window.

"Mitka has been killed," said Manka harshly, going up to Zinka. "It got him here," she added, and she rudely put her hand on Zinka's forehead, which was bowed in horror.

The mischievous trick was completely successful. Zinka did not cry; she sat down and gazed at the foot of Mitka's bed with a face that had suddenly grown old. She was frightened to ask Firsov, but Firsov turned around of his own accord and shook his head in denial as an answer to her wordless appeal. Zinka understood him: she jumped up, she could scarcely contain her rapture, and fluttered up and down the room like a great, restless fly. The reeling frenzy of her joy was almost terrible to see. Suddenly she came to herself and went up to Manka.

"You're wicked . . . oh, you're wicked!" she said, shaking her head and shedding tears. "You black-hearted woman!"

A sparrow alighted on the windowsill. It puffed itself out, looked at Firsov's sad, sleepless face, picked up a flake of snow, and flew away. It was free and could fly where it wanted to, this stupid, happy feathered thing, this sparrow! With a scarce audible chirping it hailed the dawning day, which was to feed it and warm its frozen wings. For even the most wretched day will bring a little sun and a little dung for a sparrow.

BOOK
2

CHAPTER

I

"IT IS entirely on your account, Nikolasha, that I have decided to describe my life and thoughts from the rosy days of childhood to their wretched end today. Should my writings escape being used for packing cucumbers and fall into the right hands, then read the confessions of your father, which were dictated by the beatings of a dying heart. I shan't try to excuse myself or to preach at you: at the end of his life a man knows less than when he is just beginning it, for the child draws his knowledge from the fount of his own youth. I bequeath these scribblings to you in memory of your father. Add up the entries and make out the total, for the time is come, and no one will challenge your conclusions.

"Inconstant is human destiny, my little angel. The storms have died down and the wrinkles have passed from the face of the cloudless sky. (What poetry! It ought to be put to music.) In front of my window I see the scaffolding of a new building (a lie, already; I don't see any scaffolding before my window. It's night, Nikolasha, and if I strain my eyes, I can only see in the empty distance the tiny cottage in which the priest of the next diocese lives). And here I sit, quiet and alone, on the ruins of my past, and contemplate the precious and meaningless fragments. What am I today? 'The scum of humanity' you called me at the angry climax of the breach between us. But even in moments of calm you had an unbridled tongue. But I don't listen to your insults or quail before your sullen stare. No one can insult me now, Nikolasha. There is no organic form of life without its distinctive scum, and each of us must be prepared to act in this boring and ignoble capacity.

"My skull is already white and round as a bullet: you could play skittles with it! It is wrinkled, but intelligent thoughts (like yours, I mean) have no place in it. But listen for a little all the same! I assure you, my angel, it is not for our country to return to its old ways that I yearn during sleepless nights. It is for some order in life that I yearn, old and incompetent as I am! Everything is in confusion, and every man's hand is against his neighbor. You will say, perhaps, that the train is still racing through the darkness of the tunnel and has not reached yet the light at the other side of the mountain—but isn't the tunnel rather long, Nikolasha? Has it an exit at all? Look out, in case the darkness crushes you! I'm not asking you to despair (though it's only fools who can't despair). There is nothing to return to. What has been destroyed in streams of blood cannot be cemented together by blood again, and why should it be? (Imagine what would happen if someone started attacking the peasants and began to scream at the top of his voice: 'You have built your houses out of my wood. Away with them!' The ruined peasants would wander around the ashes of their homes: they're used to wailing and lamentation. 'This was my well!' someone would cry. (Revenge is a fool's game, Nikolasha.) The navel cord that binds us to the past has been cut, and the old gods have been overthrown and insulted too deeply for them ever to return. One cannot rejuvenate the dead. No, as you're at it, bore your tunnel to the end! Bore through the rock with your skull, my little angel! Struggle on, I keep whispering to you, but do you hear me?

"I whisper to you because it's night and next door my savage roommate is snoring, as if he were blowing a trumpet or gnawing at a piece of glass. I have covered the lamp with a sock so as not to disturb his well-earned slumbers. I sit up the whole night, for I cannot go to sleep. My heart bounds and knocks too violently, right and left and up and down like a child's rattle. I am growing old: only with an effort can I endure my life, and my breath fails me at every step. With heavy labor I can still earn a little drink to force my aching heart to be quiet. Yes, Nikolasha, if a man's heart is heavy he can't bring himself to shout 'Hurrah!' As you see, I have remained true to myself—I still drink. But the time is coming when only by rousing pity will I be able to earn my bread: my wonderful lies won't help me any more. I've lost my grip even there. Often I break off in the middle of the story and stand helpless, and don't know what I should say. Don't be alarmed! I'm not asking for pity . . . Sergey Manyukin is still alive. Only I want to relieve my heartache just a little.

"Perhaps you have long ago ceased to live, Nikolasha. Perhaps in the years that have elapsed you too have been murdered, like so many others. You had so many colors —white, and black, and green, and red. . . . Perhaps the fate that I await myself with indifference has already overtaken you. But even if it is so, give me a sign, raise your voice, lift your eyes, look around you. Look at me! Perhaps in the sadness of the tomb it will cheer you a little, and lessen your dread of men. But if you are alive, keep going on, keep going on, Nikolasha. If you are dead, then you have overtaken us all anyhow.

"It is my heart that is speaking to you, but do you hear it? The bitter tears cool my cheeks and lips: do you see them? Ah—devil take you, Nikolasha—may God judge you! I feel that, living or dead, you expect a reckoning from me. I do not see you, I do not see you, but I feel that you demand it, screaming and stamping your feet. Take, then, my pitiless Caesar, what is Caesar's!

"I can describe our family only as far back as Jeremy. Farther back the branches of our stock lose themselves in the mists of obscurity. This Jeremy, an interpreter, the ancestor of both of us, served the Russian crown, and fell in the Battle of Poltava. For his heroism he was raised to the nobility after his death, and rewarded with the estate of Vodyanetz. Do you still remember that little spot on the banks of the Kudema, Nikolasha? Do you still remember the Owl Mountain and the gay woods that lay around it, the scene of my childhood and of yours? Does the curly maple still stand in front of the window of your nursery, or have the peasants already cut down the tree your grandfather planted? Does the rushing Bikany, the lovely Tartar daughter of the Kudema, still flow by our manor? (Oh, I'll give you heaps of poetry, Nikolasha, and won't ask even a scrap of bread in return.) Often on the banks of the river have I heard your toneless laugh, like that of an old man. Once you fell right into the Bikany, but the switchman pulled you out of the water. (I'm keeping my eye on his son, who lives here in the house with me now.) How much terror and agitation did your boyish escapades cause us! Once I remember you cut yourself on the hand to see if a child's blood would flow. Then you ate yourself sick on a basketful of cherries which had been prepared for stewing, and which you had stolen. We made ready to read the prayers for the dying over you. We tortured ourselves with the question of how we could go on living if you should die. But Heaven was pleased not to take you from us, for we gave you castor oil. At the age of three you cut a little dog out of paper (or was it Pelageya Savichna herself? I can't remember now), and everyone declared you were a deep child, and loved you all the more. You were a weak child, but you grew up contrary to all expectation and in defiance of the doctors. We all loved you, because we were always dreading you would die. Yet you did not die, but lived on, so that there should be someone to judge me, me, the inglorious monument on the grave of the last Manyukin.

"I did not mean to laugh: forgive me, Nikolasha. It's my nerves, I suppose: they've been shattered by despair and misfortune, or perhaps it's because I can't control my face any longer. It sags in and puffs out now like an empty cardboard box. Yet listen all the same to the cry of my genuine despair. Why were you killed, if you aren't still alive? And why are you living, if death has spared you during these terrible years? Forgive my long-winded lamentations, Nikolasha.

"Jeremy's son was called Vassily. I found the following in the parish register, compiled by Father Maxim of Demyatino, who preserved the family records after the house in Vodyanetz was burned down. This Vassily added laurels to the crown of the empress Elizabeth and won himself a glorious name. He was killed at the age of twenty-eight during the Bashkir rebellion at Orenburg. The empress had no opportunity of rewarding the heroism of her loyal subject, for her ill-fated nephew came to the throne. Jeremy's grandchildren, Vassily and Sergey, fought as lieutenants for the glory of the Russian eagle. One fell in the inglorious Danish war, and the other, your great-great-grandfather, in Persia in the time of Catherine. So we, too, have played a modest part in incorporating Derbent and Baku into the mighty Russian empire. Be proud and glory in it, Nikolasha! Even now the new eagle draws petroleum from these wells.

"There is no need to enumerate the glorious deeds of your other ancestors, Nikolasha, and, besides, I am tired of them. All died sword in hand, and left behind them a numerous progeny. And now we come to you, Nikolasha. How will you justify hereafter the great expectations of your forbears? Above all things, be honorable, my little angel. One can be honorable anywhere. In our family there have been idlers and gluttons, despots and great sinners, my little angel, but no cads. Cads can do no good, Nikolasha: they can only stink, and suffocate in the rays of other men's glory.

"Life proceeds according to an inscrutable law. The generations differ from each other, they fight with each other, and encounter life and death, and do not know that the one can neither be nor come into being without the other. They do not reflect that the young can only build their giddy structures on the firm shoulders of the old. They have no inkling that they too will one day be trampled underfoot by a grateful and businesslike posterity. My tongue is venomous and ill-natured, Nikolasha: it is wry with gall. Be generous, young man, and forgive me my senile grumblings, but mayn't one look back and take stock at the end of one's days?

"I return to the more recent past. Your grandfather did not fall in battle, although he held the rank of lieutenant of the guards. (But you see, my little angel, it wasn't even a rank, it was only a title, for he was never with the regiment.) Ammos Petrovich, after he had graduated in political economy in Yaroslave, entered the civil service, but that did not lie heavily upon him. He stayed comfortably on his hereditary estate at Vodyanetz, grew new sorts of strawberries, and farmed his land. I remember clearly how he used to putter around his well-kept, tidy beds in chamois-leather gloves. The bronze medal that, as a child, you used to drag about the garden paths—well, he won that for his achievements in that sphere. The apples you

used to like so much were improved by your grandfather—
of course with the gardener's assistance. Your grandfather
was no ordinary man. When he was a justice of the peace
in the reform days of Alexander II he used to attend sit-
tings in a velvet top hat such as used to be worn in the
days of Nicholas I, and a uniform with strips of a dull-
colored fur. His body servant, Yegor Matveyich—he was
also glazier, floor polisher, bath attendant, and storyteller
—used later to maintain jokingly that he poured his master into the uniform in spoonfuls. Ammos Petrovich was
peaceable but firm. I remember an anecdote my mother
once told me. Ammos used to supervise the compulsory
labor, and always found the same thing: the men idled.
Then he laid his opera glasses on a tree stump, threatened
with his finger, and went away. The opera glasses stayed
behind as though to keep a close watch on the peasants
through both ends, and the peasants labored and sweated
as if their master were there himself—until a cunning lad
had the idea of covering the opera glasses with his cap.
Then the peasant song rang out again in the meadows,
and our good old orthodox idleness blossomed anew. Ammos Petrovich passed away in the apple season: it was his
own fault, for he stayed too long in the vapor bath.

"I can remember only one day in my childhood. We
were going to Mass. Andrey had harnessed Arlekinka, the
mare, and was waiting outside, his hat with the peacock
feathers in his hand. His hair was liberally greased, his
black mustache looked like wire that had been nibbled at.
We drove out of the village. In the night it had been raining, and the leaves shone on the trees . . . and on a
branch a grasshopper was sitting and rubbing his eyes with
his little legs. It was morning, the sinless morning of life!
I jumped out of the carriage, and raced around madly in
the grass, the July dew gleaming on my shiny jack boots.
The church was cool and dark inside: the deacon was
booming, and the candles flickered in the sunlight. Ammos Petrovich stood in the choir on the right, next to the
ikon—representing a lean peasant in coarse clothes with
tousled black hair, St. Fedya the Ferryman—and intoned
with the priest: 'Timon, Parmen, Prohor, and Nikolai!'
They all came to dinner afterward. The priests sang something short and rather gay to suit the occasion, and then

began to eat and talk politics. We ran into the back passage, where Dunka in her bright clothes was turning the refrigerator, and amused ourselves there till Yegor Matveyich in his plush breeches and with boots on his bare feet served the festal cake. After the meal, the priests sat on drowsily, lolling in their chairs, and we ran out into the wood, where so many childish responsibilities were waiting for us. The day seemed endless, and it was as though the flowers were blooming again in the beds in honor of the feast day. In the evening the children were put to sleep in my grandmother's room. There was a different smell in every corner of this room—in one corner of raisins, in another of snuff. Our dreams were very light and brittle at first, then they grew thicker and thicker, and suddenly they were no longer dreams, but something rich and strange and sweet . . . an ethereal gingerbread.

"I love that day, which has stamped itself so deeply on my memory. I make no secret of my weaknesses, Nikolasha, for I'm not a candidate for a position in the civil magistracy of today. But I'm not bragging, and have no intention of seducing anyone with alluring pictures. You will build yourself a new Mammon, and adore it passionately, for man cannot exist without idols. Why should I hide anything from you? I have sunk deep, deep. My neck is already half wrung: give it the final twist, little son!

"At the start of my confessions I may as well admit that my life is a miserable one. Once I tried my hand at inventions. I invented a dye for chamois leather and a lamp shade for night work, but nothing came of them. I tried to start a business—first with carpets, galoshes, cocaine, and pictures, and then with little crosses and finger stalls. I hadn't sufficient experience. I learned to play tunes on a wine glass as on a flute, but nobody liked it. Now I tell lies for money. When I go up to a table I am never certain whether I'll get a tip or a blow in the face. I've reduced my fee already to a quarter rouble, and yet I go to bed more often than not with an empty stomach. I can only eat half my fill, but I am more liberal to myself with drink. Only one course is left to me—to die, to fall from the tree like a ripe apple in autumn. But my misfortune is that I am fond of this tangled tree, and would like to hang on it just a little longer.

"You were the first and only son of your parents. But you have another little brother, Nikolasha, and I am his father. You are not the only one in the world who is ashamed of his father. I am keeping watch over your little brother, my progeny, from a distance (I'm becoming stupid, but I can't leave off)—an old man's inquisitiveness. I shudder to guess how it will all end. Our breach began, if you can remember, on that fateful evening when you surprised me with a strange woman who was not your mother. She became the mother of your little brother, whom you do not know. Her husband, a switchman, was in the hospital at the time in Rogovo, and she was scrubbing the floors in our house. She was a fine woman, and I was, as you know, a weak-willed man: well, what tree can resist a hurricane? You surprised us, and began to rage and scream, so that we were frightened you would have a fit. You were a thoughtful child, though. You wanted to know a lot, and you worked your way into our secret. So, as a child, you got to know your father's shame. Yet I presented you with a remarkable young brother, my little angel. . . ."

And so the venom of Manyukin's grief was poured out in writing.

"Tear yourself away from your writing a moment, will you, Sergey Ammonich? . . . And tie my tie for me, please . . . a small bow, if you can: I can't get it right," his roommate bawled into his ear, looking over his shoulder at the exercise book. Manyukin turned around angrily, and began to tug at the tie around Pyotr Gorbidonich Chikelyov's craning neck. "Tighter, tighter! Otherwise it always slips down, and one sees the stud. It's a very important occasion . . . a decisive battle. What is it you're writing there all the night long? Won't you show it to me? I'm so fond of reading." Chikelyov made a slight gesture with his fingers in the air. "Tighter, please! . . ."

"Where did you buy these fantastic ties?" asked Manyukin rudely, turning his face away from Chikelyov's stale breath. But Chikelyov was already running up and down the room in tremendous excitement, and making thousands of different preparations: he polished his shoes to make them shine brighter, cleaned his collar with spirit of ammonia, scraped his teeth with the scissors, looked out of the door, listened to the clock to see if it was going, and arranged his books on the table. To stick to the literal truth, there were only three books there—a book on the laws of taxation, a collection of interesting stories from the lives of eminent people, and finally a lexicon of difficult words, which he used in the composition of letters (for the sake of good tone and modest polish). Fortunately they were books of a comfortable size: a single one of them would last him to the end of his life.

After Chikelyov had pranced up and down until he was

tired, he drew his chair close beside Manyukin's. Manyukin closed his book once more, and glanced in exasperation at his smartly dressed roommate. Chikelyov sat there at his ease, and moved his neck so that his narrow tie creaked up and down over his starched collar.

"Citizen," said Chikelyov solemnly and with restrained emotion, "for half an hour I've been wanting to speak out my mind—I'm boiling with emotion, if you'll be so good as to note—and you've been busying yourself with calligraphy. In my opinion the pleasure you derive from it is not particularly great. The only advantage I can see in it is that it isn't in conflict with the law. That's a fact."

"Go on, go on, Pyotr Gorbidonich," replied Manyukin politely. "It's a pleasure, so to speak. . . . And I myself, if you'll excuse my saying so, am exceedingly interested to hear the causes of your . . . er . . . transformation. Go on!" he exclaimed in real goodness of heart.

"I've nothing to 'go on' about," retorted Chikelyov coldly. "I come to you in all civility, and you bark at me like a dog—and that's typical! In Heaven's name, can't two intelligent men talk reasonably to each other for an hour?"

"But please, Pyotr Gorbidonich, it's only a minute so far," exclaimed Manyukin in embarrassment, for he thought he actually had offended the man. "I am always ready to lighten, to the extent of my power, any weight that lies on your mind. If you're in need of my advice or my experience . . . well, I'm older than you are."

"I don't want advice at all . . . and what sort of advice could *you* give me?" answered Chikelyov cuttingly, emphasizing every word by beating time on Manyukin's knee. "What sort of advice, be so good as to note, could you give me, seeing that you yourself are the type that ends by going out of his mind or committing suicide?"

"No, no—I'd prefer suicide. You're always joking, Pyotr Gorbidonich." Manyukin smiled miserably.

"It's something else I need. I want someone to listen to me, for nobody listens to me. The days are past, please note, when anyone can ignore me. They are indeed! I am so constituted psychologically that I would be prepared —and this is typical of me—to embrace the whole world out of sheer happiness, but under the condition—"

"Well, do it, then!" implored Sergey Ammonich, crossing his arms over his stomach in expectation of his roommate's confession. "I wanted to myself some time ago, but I was shy of—"

"Of course you think: 'Chikelyov is a spiteful chap. He wants to marry, the fool. He's an office drudge,' or, perhaps, 'a bandy-legged scarecrow,' or 'a Chinese samovar.' Don't mind me. In the office they have other names for me. And why not? Since his childhood Chikelyov has been tyrannized over, and Chikelyov has adapted himself to circumstances. But be so good as to note, Chikelyov knows his own value. . . ." He grew more and more wrought up as he went on.

"But please . . ." Manyukin, who was already on the verge of tears, got up.

"First of all, what is a wife? A wife is for me the means of satisfying the requirements that stand in the foreground of my life," announced Chikelyov unctuously, and waited hungrily for Manyukin's comment.

"What requirements are you talking about? . . . I suppose you're speaking of the esthetic aspect," Manyukin interposed in embarrassment.

"You're a fanatic. I always guessed you were that type," exclaimed Chikelyov reproachfully, jumping up.

"What has that to do with fanaticism? What do you really want from me, you hopeless fellow?" Manyukin clasped his hands over his head. He had given up all hope of understanding Chikelyov.

"Just wait and I'll tell you everything," threatened Chikelyov. And he opened his mouth, but immediately jumped up, and began to run up and down again. "She's there, she's there . . ." he repeated in consternation, running to the door, but presently coming back again. "The gas bill, be so kind as to pay it—the gas bill!" He tapped his fingers on the table and snorted with rage, then he vanished.

The spring, the spring had confused Chikelyov's senses. The day before, a mangy crow had cawed the whole day long on a telegraph pole right in front of Chikelyov's window, as if it were calling someone who obstinately refused to answer. The day was measuring its strength against the night, and it was winning. From the windows of the bake shops dough larks with currant eyes peeped out; the snow was becoming black and melting away. The human race, which is yearly rejuvenated in the spring, struggled with all its strength to hasten on the course of these dull and empty days. A light snow fell in the bright sunshine and melted almost as soon as it touched the earth. It was as though a monster of the skies had breathed his living breath over the city. For unknown reasons the crow of yesterday had died during the night. Boys on their way to school, filled with high spirits, threw it up into the air, but it always fell down again with its wings stretched out. Men's hopes for something extraordinary increased tenfold. It was as though they were expecting someone to come and shower happiness all around in handfuls, stupidly and generously.

And actually that morning the crisp clouds began to round themselves in balls in the empty spring sky. Toward midday the sky completely cleared; the sun triumphed over yesterday's conqueror and trod his victim beneath his feet. In the fields the shrubs grew pink, and black ice holes gaped on the frozen river. Between the double windows on the sunny side of the houses the flies revived again, awakened by news of offal. The sunbeams streamed in gay profusion over Manyukin's open book; then they left the table and crept across his bed to the door, which they covered with a brilliant patch. Suddenly behind him Manyukin heard the click of the opening door.

On the doorstep stood Klavdya, Zinka's little daughter; the child used often to come here in Chikelyov's absence and amuse herself on the floor with all kinds of chips and rags, while Sergey Ammonich buried his nose in his papers. Bathed in the sunlight, the child smiled softly, and waited for permission to come in.

PYOTR GORBIDONICH had no face, but only a mask that altered its expression according to what insane devil had temporary control of him. His flagrantly colored tie and his way of doing his hair, like a coffee-cream cornet, far from being embellishments, lent a crowning touch of the grotesque to his appearance. In front of Zinka's door he drew a corner of his colored handkerchief from his side pocket, composed his features into a dignified expression, prepared his voice, and tweaked at the little medal on his breast, which twinkled back obediently as though it were the most illustrious decoration. With the confidence of a conqueror, Pyotr Gorbidonich flung open the door.

But immediately a wave of self-distrust came over him again, and his squinting eyes roved around dejectedly. He took a step forward, then a step back again. Zinka was putting away some clothes, and to judge by the twitching of her shoulders she was crying; from time to time she sniffed at a small bunch of violets. But Pyotr Gorbidonich did not completely lose his composure; he went around the table, and ventured at last to smell the violets. He was preparing to smile, but no sooner did Zinka raise her weeping eyes to him than he shrank back again into almost complete inconspicuousness.

"I've already paid the rent, Pyotr Gorbidonich," said Zinka dully, blowing her nose. "And I simply won't clean the back stairs. I never use them. . . ."

"You must certainly clean the back stairs, but that is not what I've come to talk about," retorted Chikelyov, blinking obstinately and sitting down. "How can you talk

of stairs, now that April and spring are with us!" (Pyotr
Gorbidonich sighed, moistening his finger with spittle,
and secretly rubbed a scratch off his shoe, which spoiled
its shine, under the table.) "I'm excited—that's typical
of me now—I saw some little birds yesterday in the market square, a pair of finches, and I said to myself: 'I'll buy
them: they can amuse themselves in a room and enliven
our Soviet existence.' But, be so good as to note, I didn't
buy them. They were very small, I know, but they were
disgustingly dirty. . . . Well, what I said about the little birds is only an introduction, for I want to speak
about myself." (Zinka sewed on a button, and went on
wiping away her tears.) "Now, the question is, What am
I? I grew up without a daddy, and have gone through life
without a mammy. 'Pyotr Gorbidonich, come here! Pyotr
Gorbidonich, go there!' That's the way they pushed me
and ragged me and tormented me.

"Then I asked myself: 'What did I come into the world
for, anyway?' 'Aha,' thought I, 'just to bear things.' You
beat me, and I endure, and I'll go on enduring. What was
it a field marshal said to his soldier? . . . He cuffed him
and then he said: 'Endurance is the shortest path to pro-
motion.' (Oh, what an admirable little book, and it only
cost thirty kopeks, and yet something good on every page!)
I say, this thing here, it's a case in point, will you accept
it as a little token of my feelings—if you'll excuse me?"
He dug his nails into his palm, and, bracing himself for
the effort, placed a gaily colored box on Zinka's knees.

"What's this?" smiled Zinka through her tears; but she
took a chocolate and chewed it, still weeping. "How sweet
they are!" she said automatically.

"Liqueur chocolates, and just look at that little ribbon! We're already on the way to prewar standards of
production. Don't throw away the ribbon. It might come
in useful. . . . Give it to the child to amuse her. It's typical of me, I have an extraordinary affection for your little
girl. . . ."

"Are you going away somewhere, Pyotr Gorbidonich?"
Zinka smiled sadly, picking out a piece of chocolate that
had stuck in her teeth.

"I'm on the point of setting out. I'm about to embark
on a boat and 'sail to the isles of the blessed.' (An excel-

lent song: no one sings songs like that now!) and I want
to ask you to come with me. I'm a clever seafarer—a serious seafarer, please note. I would even like to call myself
a thinking seafarer. Don't mind my behaving rather masterfully now and then: I'm really a simple, good-hearted
fellow. But I'm a firm character, and my habits, if you'll
excuse me, are like granite. You'll get a tram car to leave
its rails before you get me to leave my habits. For example, I like water very cold, but for me tea must be piping
hot. You may strike me dead if you like, but you'll never
get me to change. Apart from that, what I value in a
man is mind. For a man isn't an animal—that's typical
—who just eats and has a nice little family. A man has,
before anything else, to perform his duties for which he
is paid, like me, for example. But if I'm paid, that means
that I'm needed. So that people can't get on without me.
(Of course, that's only theory, it may be different.) What
it implies, though, is, that I'm 'pivotal,' if you see what I
mean. . . ." Now that he had got into his stride, Chikelyov could not stop. One might have fancied that he had
three times the normal number of teeth in his mouth,
they glittered so continuously while he went on talking
rapidly. "So I can (of course, without its coming to the
knowledge of the authorities) have my own opinion about
things, too. For example, be so good as to note, I'm not
fond of flowers, I like combinations of abstractions better. I can't approach a flower as I would an animal, let
alone you. . . ."

"Don't be so learned, Pyotr Gorbidonich. I'm an uneducated person . . ." said Zinka softly, looking up at
Chikelyov with moist eyes. "My brain doesn't work easily. . . . I've just come back from the prison: I was taking things there."

"Aha!" Pyotr Gorbidonich patted his knees with a
spiteful expression. "It doesn't matter. Go on sewing: I'm
very fond of watching needlework. Well, then, I'll continue. You are a lady without any male support or protection, and I am, please note, a homeless orphan. And
—it's a case in point, even if it's unpleasant to speak
about it—I'm still virgin! I've admired you for four
years. . . ." Chikelyov tugged excitedly at his collar.
"You are beautiful. You're a dangerous woman! You

beckon, and the whole world lies at your feet (the male part of it, I mean.)" Zinka was silent, her mouth half open. Suddenly she slammed down the lid of the chocolate box and put it on the table. "I read once in a novel that the Duchess of Bourbon commanded her squire to bring her her father's head—a moody woman! And he brought it, he brought it! No, one should forbid such beauty, forbid it in the name of the higher morality . . . so as to prevent such fatalities. One should nip such beauty in the bud. Why, anyone might become a parricide in a jiffy!" Chikelyov stood up straight, waved his arm eloquently, and looked for a moment straight in front of him.

"The way you talk! . . ." gasped Zinka, and her long lashes quivered. Chikelyov grew more and more impassioned. "I can only sing songs," said Zinka.

"And love, you can love, too, as no one else can in our days. I know it. . . . You're crazy about this Mitka (only a passing fancy, of course, but still it's very strong). You visit him in the prison hospital, you wash his linen at night so that no one can see . . . you cry for him . . . and I torment myself in the room next door, I whisper to you, I whisper: 'He's an unreliable fellow, an outcast, a thief, an irresponsible good-for-nothing!' He won't even be grateful to you. He'll put you in the family way, and then leave you in the lurch, as your first one left you and gave you a child to remember him by. Listen to me, I implore you! If Chikelyov, Pyotr Gorbidonich, offers you his hand and heart, that means that he is ready for action. That means that Pyotr Gorbidonich has become gentle, and wants to live at peace with the world. The withered tree blossoms again . . . excuse me, what's come over me?"

He looked around him, as if he didn't know where he was, and sat down in his former place.

Zinka threw her head back, as if she wanted to flaunt before him derisively the charms of her fair white throat, and laughed loudly at Pyotr Gorbidonich's love.

"You!" cried Zinka between busts of laughter. "You want me, do you? Why, I shouldn't think your arms are long enough to get around me even! Do you know how much I weigh, you poor weakling?" She gave way to peals of unseasonable merriment. "Oh, my belly's sore with laughter, I can't stop! I'm to wash your linen for you, I suppose? You'll never get into prison, I'll be bound, you'll never get drunk even. Why, you haven't even the spirit to catch a cold. You want to make me into Madame Chikelyova, I suppose. How could you understand my unhappiness? Mitka! He's the only brave, unhappy man in the world. You aren't worthy to tread in his footsteps, but here you come hopping along like a sparrow courting a cow! You God-forsaken fool!"

Pyotr Gorbidonich cast a wounded glance at the chocolates.

"As far as God is concerned, apply to your brother! He'll explain it all to you according to the latest scientific conclusions. In any case, what does 'God' signify? Lenin lies in the 'Red Square.' . . . I can go there and convince myself of the fact, but where is God?" He could not keep up this tone, however. "Oh, if you lived only a week with me, you'd see what kind of a man I was. It's a pity you never read any stories, for there are some very instructive ones. Tears flow in them, tears, don't they, now? Yes, for many centuries the kind sun has been shining, but all the same it has never yet been able to dry mankind's tears. And yours are only beginning to flow now."

As he was going away he looked out through the window into the yard; the two other windows faced the street. Boys were running about wildly in short breeches that barely covered their cold blue knees. They ran across the yard, spurred on by imaginary riders, and shouted.

"Hi, there!" shouted Pyotr Gorbidonich through the ventilator. "None of that running about! What are you running about for? Are you off your heads? I'll give you . . ." And as he was already in the doorway, he said: "Well, I take back all the nonsense I talked . . . it's to be as if nothing had happened, you understand? It's springtime, and every man's a fool in springtime. I am, too. . . . But that doesn't interest me at the moment. Yet all of us chase happiness after all. But we've not advanced so far yet that all men can be made on one and the same pattern, so that they might all be the same size and weight, and so on. When that time comes, if anyone grows up too strong and pokes his head too far up into the air, then he'll have his wings clipped. There will be no pain in the world then. Everything and everyone will be the same. If a man collapses, it won't matter: if he dies, he'll just be forgotten. Animals and everything else will be built on the same plan!" (the warlike shouts of the boys playing came through the ventilator, which Chikelyov had forgotten to shut.) "I don't like boys, either. A grown man is something different: he has an office, he votes at meetings, reads the newspaper, visits the circus, and pays taxes. . . . I can't bear any noise, I can't bear any noise, I tell you!" he screamed out suddenly, and took himself off in almost equivocal haste.

CHAPTER

I V

WITH Mitka's disappearance life in Number Eight seemed suddenly to be extinguished. All the same, Pyotr Gorbidonich expressed his disapproval of the modest hiss of Manyukin's primus stove and the insinuating creaking of the oiled doors. Every day he introduced improved new rules to perfect the running of the block: often they claimed to be rules for the conduct of life. It was an inward triumph for him that the group of humanity most closely contiguous to him could not move except on its tiptoes and in constant terror of transgressing a paragraph in the regulations. The snub he had received from the beautiful Zinka was the only blot on his divinity. . . . Pyotr Gorbidonich bit his lips and lay low like an enemy in front of a beleaguered fortress.

By shrewd inferences (and once by personally tracking her) Chikelyov had learned the truth. Zinka visited Mitka in prison, she stood in a line there and begged and humbled herself and made herself ridiculous, imploring permission to visit Mitka and bring him presents. She did not spare herself, she sacrificed herself recklessly, and found her wretched happiness in this. Mitka, who had fallen into a strange state of lethargy and indifference, received Zinka's presents apathetically. Now and then he looked at her sharply, as if he could not guess the reasons for her boundless devotion to him. But Zinka never betrayed during those visits her hopeless yearning, which is so unbearable to the man who does not return it, although her constrained, shrill laugh pointed to a secret sorrow.

On the day on which Chikelyov offered her his hand and heart she had not been allowed to see Mitka. A young peasant in a military cape had been touched by Zinka's tears, and had explained to her that Dmitri Vekshin's sister was already waiting in the audience room. Filled with a vague tenderness, she had anxiously scanned the crowd of visitors, but had not found any face that reminded her of Mitka. Then suddenly she had seen Manka the Snowstorm leaning against a wall, and had realized the deception. She could almost have screamed at this impudent imposture, but instead she had gone up to Manka and asked her some trivial question. The scornful stare she received was less painful to her than the failure of her errand and that her parcel had not been delivered. When she returned home, she sent Klavdya across to Manyukin, and cried the whole day long till the return of her brother Matvey. Her hopeless love, embittered by jealousy, darkened her life, and destroyed her happiness. She grew quiet, stopped quarreling with Matvey, and even tried to ingratiate herself with Chikelyov. Her suffering, strong as her body, lent her art new and terrible vigor. She asked Firsov, seeing that he was a writer, to compose songs for her. He agreed, nor was it merely his fear of losing her goodwill that prompted him. Zinka was one of the main characters in the story he had begun, but the Zinka of his midnight labors was a clearer, more definite figure. In his story he incorporated the songs he had composed for her, and in his desperate attempt to test the validity of his art, presented Zinka with his ingenious portrait of her.

Now she had something to sing, and the regular clients of the beer hall had something to hear. "I perish in vain! The spring has become my autumn . . ." sang Zinka, clasping her hands over her head, and all were struck dumb by the exposure of her sufferings. "As a man breaks a little twig in a stranger's garden and flings it away, so have you left me!" It was the wild blossoming of a poisoned body, where the poison has not yet started its work of destruction, but has only lashed the hectic blood to frenzy. Spotty Alexey thought that the artificial flowers in the pots must burst into blossom under Zinka's passion, and the musicians sprain their fingers. In her expectation of a meeting with Mitka, Zinka lived as in a dream, and slowly wasted away with the fever in her blood. The months passed, and in the warm May evenings she often sat by the window and watched the dying light and the slowly lengthening shadows. Oh, she knew too well that the night must soon end! She knew that after the darkness, the light of day must invade the sky again. Klavdya sat on a stool at her feet, and with precocious concern watched the changes in her mother's face. Matvey was the only one to disturb their peace. He blocked his ears with his fingers so as not to hear his sister's dreary sighs, took a glance now and then at his Lenin, and sank yet deeper into his scientific studies.

At that time Zinka was Mitka's only link with the outer world, which had rejected him. Apart from Zinka not a soul visited him. Puchov was a confirmed recluse, and far too Russian a character in his relations with his friends; and his sister Tanya was at that time undergoing a severe emotional struggle. Even Mitka's best friend, Sanka, did not visit him, for he, too, was suffering a strange revulsion of feeling. The spring had its effects on all alike: it was the spring, too, that changed Zinka's anguish to a light, and beautiful, and not unbearable load.

One Sunday Mitka asked after all the people who had forgotten him. Zinka offered gladly to inquire about them and let him know on her next visit. Then Mitka fell into his former lethargy, and broke off the visit before the time was up. On the way home Zinka cried; she thought he was tired of her and had had enough of her. . . . In the evening she sat by the window again; twilight was falling, and the child was playing on the floor. Matvey peevishly stopped his ears with his fingers, and absorbed wisdom from his thick, learned book.

"Matvey . . . !" cried Zinka softly when the first storm of grief had subsided a little. "Look, Matvey, how striped the clouds are!" She pointed at the feathery, sunset clouds behind the dusty glass. "Life is a strange business! Just think how many things are crowded into one minute—laughter, and tears, and cries. . . . Do you know, Matvey, why people drink? (While I'm singing I watch them and think it out.) When they're drunk, dreams come nearer, so near that one can touch them with one's hands. . . . But you're working . . . shall I stop talking?"

"No, go on chattering as long as your tongue isn't tired," said Matvey, and looked at his sister in surprise.

"Do you never dream that you're flying, Matvey? I do. I often dream that I get up on the window ledge, and fly . . . not as a bird does, but standing upright. . . . Suddenly my breath fails, and I wake up." Zinka longed to tell someone of the sweet torments that consumed her. "And it's a good thing that I don't fly, that I only get ready for flight. . . . I saw a thing in the theater once: the woman was in love with the man, but he wouldn't have her, and she put her neck in a noose. It's all a lie and a cheat, the theater is. If he turned her down, well, he was within his rights. She ought to have taken a good night's sleep, and the next morning, if she had anything else to lose, to cry for that. The first night with a man is like a hundred years. Love dies, but hope never dies. You don't know what love is, Matvey. . . . And I feel as if I had music always sounding in my breast."

"Love?" exclaimed Matvey, jumping up in a fury. "Here you have all about it! Read about love there!" He turned the pages over angrily, looking for those pictures and explanations which would outrage Zinka most. "Do you understand now? There are no mysteries, there's no flying; there's only the mutual attraction of the sexual glands. I can't stand all this talk: it's like a fly buzzing. When one day men discover everything, and measure and weigh and calculate everything . . . when they get to know the numbers, the temperature, and the color of things . . . when they are in a position to change everything, then there will be happiness. Happiness, my dear, can be manufactured as easily as galoshes or that electric bulb there." He jerked his head toward the spot on the ceiling where a meager bulb struggled weakly with the twilight. "One must learn, and then happiness without suffering will come."

"Happiness without suffering, you say?" Zinka went up to her brother, and, with a caressing smile, passed her fingers through his untidy hair. "Then happiness is to be manufactured in factories, is it?" she inquired laughingly, but Matvey looked at her so furiously that she walked away. It was already time for her to change her dress for the evening.

She lay awake the whole night long, and listened to the beating of her heart. A spring in the child's sofa kept up a maddening creaking, and later on rain pattered on the windowpanes. Matvey talked wildly in his sleep, the mice gnawed, and Zinka heard everything—everything except her own sighs for Mitka, which were like the rising and sinking of continents. At daybreak she fell asleep and dreamed. . . . In a great empty hall, formless, discordant music resounded: a dense and palpable light filled the room and gave it a menacing solemnity. Zinka looked at a couple, the only one, revolving in an unintelligible dance; their faces were known to her, but do what she might she could not recognize them. She ran down a steep, winding stair, and all those obstacles that one encounters only in dreams met her on the way. When she had reached the bottom, she went more slowly, and, screwing up her eyes, stared straight in front of her. The couple were standing near the exit. They held each other in a close embrace, laughed, and pointed their fingers at her. Their eyes gleamed unnaturally: she would never forget that gleam. . . . At the last moment she recognized them both and screamed aloud.

She awoke with a splitting headache. Matvey was already gone, for he always left early. The child was playing about on the floor, barefoot and in her chemise; she was trying to build a high tower out of bricks, but every time it clattered down. The noise awakened Zinka, and she got up exhausted and cross and with dark rings around her eyes. Spring was no easy load for her to bear. Moreover, in her lonely, isolated life she believed in dreams and forebodings.

ZINKA did not succeed in executing Mitka's commission, for one morning Klavdya cut herself while she was playing with a knife in the kitchen, and later on there was a disagreeable incident in the beer hall. Then a few days passed by unnoticed; there was an unceasing drizzle, and she felt moody and dull and sleepy. On Sunday she remembered Mitka's request, and, in a sudden outburst of fury, resolved not to go anywhere.

The summer had already come with its hot days and sultry nights, and Zinka spent her evenings in dumb misery by the wide-open window; on the window stood a cactus plant in a pot, a strange abortion that had shriveled in captivity. Zinka gazed straight out: at the window opposite sat a thin young man with his wife, who was wearing an embroidered blouse. They had put on headphones, and were listening to the wireless together. Beneath the window young lads wandered past in groups, playing the mandolin. One of them was roaring out bawdy songs in a breaking voice; one might have thought that this beardless youth had loved ten women at once, and deserted them all, and only carried away with him the sorrow and satiety of life. . . .

> "You're my dandy, you're my joy!
> You're a pipi, you're a ka-ka,
> You're a saucy boy. . . ."

came into her mind. Meanwhile the sun was sinking behind a huge building that looked like a prison or a hospital. Zinka could not repress a yawn; she got up and went to drink tea with the Bundyukovs.

At the beginning of summer Matvey got a practice. His sister escorted him to the station and even gave him a little money, so that he might not starve during the first few days before the new life absorbed him. She baked cakes for him, patched his clothes, and even cried when Matvey said good-by.

"You're as fat and round as a turnip, and you believe in God . . . there's no place for you in the life of the future, but you're good . . . you're good. . . . Good-by," said Matvey, touched by Zinka's solicitude, but he drew back from her embrace. "Don't cry for me: our relationship is a pure accident. Keep up your spirits, and be jolly, and let your thief go hang, for, apart from everything else, he's a lazy devil. Don't come with me to the train. I don't like that sort of thing."

But in the end he became sentimental himself, and had no inkling that the very next day Zinka would shift his chest into the kitchen, and buy a new iron bedstead. Chikelyov instantly noticed what was happening. The presence of the new bed plunged him first into grim speculations, then roused in him a feeling between rage and appehension, and finally set him off on an offensive campaign. There was no time for delay. But his first move was a most disarming one. He brought the little girl quite a nice little hood, and then some shoes and galoshes. Of course the hood was not suitable to the season, but Pyotr Gorbidonich had the winter in mind, and added a box of moth powder.

Chikelyov's new habit of taking the little girl every day for a walk seemed to Zinka a mere caprice. (They used to walk far outside the bounds of the city, where there were a great many trees, and Chikelyov used always to impress tenderly on the child's mind: "Breathe, breathe deeply when you pass a tree!") One day a week later they had returned to the house from a walk. They entered solemnly, and stood silently waiting. Chikelyov tittered, the girl beamed; she was so quiet, one might have thought she was frightened of scaring away her pleasure by an incautious movement.

"What are you so pleased about?" her mother greeted her.

"We've just come in from a walk . . ." answered Chikelyov mysteriously, rubbing his hands. "Yes, talking of pleasure, it's typical that it's always to be had everywhere if you only look for it—a man must be able to find it himself. For instance, three days ago we sat in a train next to a nasty old gentleman. Klavdya asked me: 'Where has the old gentleman put his nose?' I answered: 'In his pocket.' We looked at him the whole time, and didn't in the least allow him to damp our spirits. Isn't that a pleasure?" Chikelyov's whole body twitched with ecstasy, and he went on happily. "A tax collector, my colleague Filimonov, had reddish hair. . . . He ate raw sturgeon flesh and died. Well, it might just as well have been me. Please note, I'm no longer in my frivolous youth. There you have another pleasure! Every day for me is a day of pleasure. . . . I don't wait for pleasure to be splashed over me from a bucket. . . . I look for it myself, myself. . . ."

"It's a wretched sort of pleasure: one forgets it the very next day. . . ." Zinka smiled absent-mindedly, and noticed for the first time the straw hat on her little daughter's head. It was a very cheap hat, but it would have been quite nice if it had not had an appalling green ribbon. Pyotr Gorbidonich adored green.

Zinka stared at the hat gloomily; she was a neglectful mother, and she felt the reproach it conveyed. Chikelyov had started on his siege cleverly, and even if he still shrank back from the assault, he had all the same reconnoitered the approaches.

"One must love children . . . they are life's flowers. I should like to have notices like that pasted up everywhere. . . . Certainly nowadays children are precocious plants. . . ." He made ready to go, yet still stood rooted to the threshold. "It can't go on like this: please note, it's raining outside, and the child's running about in shoes with holes in them. . . ."

"Will you be off, you wretch!" Zinka screamed, beginning to cry.

"I'm going, I'm going . . . it's typical of me, I'm always on the go," murmured Chikelyov as he shut the door cautiously.

Klavdya began to cry; it was as though she thought Zinka wanted to rob her of her pleasure, and her mother had great difficulty in calming her. The next few days Zinka looked on jealously while the little girl cleaned Chikelyov's presents; she breathed on them first and took other little tender precautions. Zinka was capricious in her treatment of her child, but Klavdya was older than her years, and submitted philosophically to being alternately stormed at and caressed. Zinka noticed that in Pyotr Gorbidonich's presence Klavdya could be merry, and that her pale cheeks then turned a lively red. She saw, too, with disgust, that Pyotr Gorbidonich was fumbling excitedly like a thief for the right key to the child's heart.

One night in the beginning of June her door was standing open. Zinka walked soundlessly down the corridor, but did not go into the room, as she heard Pyotr Gorbidonich's voice. She thought that Chikelyov was telling the child a fairytale while he put her to bed. For some time Chikelyov had, of his own accord, taken over the responsibility of putting the little girl to bed. . . .

". . . I grew up a small, silent child, and everyone treated me unjustly, just because I was small and quiet. I hadn't even my little fists, I had nothing. My mammy ran away with Uncle, and my daddy ran away with Aunty. I lived with my grandmother. My grandmother said to me my mother was dead. We lived in poverty. We had a cat that ate out of the rubbish heap and was the fattest of us all. Men can't eat out of the rubbish heap or they'd be laughed at."

"And hadn't you any nuts, either?" asked the little girl in a curious voice.

"We had nothing. We hadn't even bread. I used to go to a boy to play, and he had lots of toys, mountains of them. As soon as he left the room, I began to kiss the toys. I wanted to have some, too, but I told no one anything about it, because people called it jealousy, though it was only that I was hurt. After my grandmother's death I went back to my mother, but she wasn't fond of me, and she had begun to drink, for the new Uncle had run away with a new Auntie. I wrote letters to my grandmother on little pieces of paper, and stuck them behind the holy pictures. I always thought that 'old squiffy' " (this was evidently his name for his grandmother), "would read them. Now I could buy any toy I wanted, but it's too late: people would laugh at me. They always called me Petya, but now I'm called Pyotr Gorbidonich." (His voice was hoarse with emotion. Zinka stood behind the door, and smiled disgustedly.) "Sleep, little girl, sleep!"

"Where's Mammy?" asked the child drowsily.

"She's gone to the beer hall—she sings there," whispered Chikelyov soothingly.

"And why doesn't she sing at home?" the child went on.

"She doesn't want to sing at home. . . . Go to sleep, go to sleep. And so I became Pyotr Gorbidonich. I grew up and began to get to grips with life. I was given an Order, a small medal, to wear on my breast on feast days. I thought people would begin to respect me if I put on the medal, but then times changed, and all medals were thought useless and silly. When I put on my Order now, people just laugh at me. People like to laugh. Other peoples' troubles are always a good joke. Are you asleep? Well, go to sleep, go to sleep!"

Zinka stepped into the room with a feeling of nausea. She did not look at Chikelyov as he jumped up.

"The general committee meeting takes place tomorrow . . . to decide about the water supply . . . and other current business . . ." he announced, and his face turned sharp and pale.

"Are you amusing yourself?" Zinka gave a dry smile. "Why are you corrupting my child, Pyotr Gorbidonich?"

"I was looking for sympathy," answered Chikelyov sadly. "Our souls have become small: our souls have dried up, but children can still understand one and have pity. Oh, it would be better if our souls died altogether. One puts one's neck into the noose on their account," he added in a whisper, but suddenly a shudder passed over him and he ran to the door before Zinka had time to fling him out.

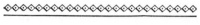

At the end of the first part of his story Firsov was faced with certain difficulties. The plan of his work demanded a diminution in the number of characters, so that Mitka might be drawn in greater detail. So, in the pangs of literary creation Firsov was compelled to remove from his narrative Matvey, Zinka's brother, and Lyonka Zhivotik. This corresponded with the actual trend of events, for Matvey got a practice, and Lyonka was arrested on some absurd escapade, and disappeared from the stage for a long time. Firsov was planning to marry Stassik to Mitka's sister, and to contrive some timely escape for Mitka, when suddenly life itself burst in and tore to shreds the subtle figments of his imagination.

Firsov loved life with its sharp odor, its tartness and sweetness, its light and shadow, its ordered chaos. In his notebook every tiny detail was recorded with the fidelity of a mirror, for to Firsov it was a record of miracles. The grass on the pavement in Blagusha was a miracle, so were the poplar flowers which at this season hung in the air like tender snowflakes; even the sober, imperturbable crow of the cock was a miracle. And Firsov himself in his cold and busy preoccupation with life was not unlike the cock. Encountering with rapture the naked rays of reality, he did not distinguish between their colors, or draw any conclusion from their reciprocal play. He, who was fire itself, was reproached with coldness; but the critic was not altogether wide of the mark who maintained that in Firsov's melting pot even the most worthless refuse could be made to look like gold. Firsov, at the end of the first part, wrote in his defense: "The river is beautiful even by night, if only a tiny patch of it reflects a star."

In the night, when his scraping steel pen and the thin Soviet ink and his own exhausted brain were warring with each other, Firsov would often take refuge in a new invention. It was a cunning and unbridled amusement; it built for him whole towns with imaginary suns and interminable rows of streets, and then set him down in the middle of them, and the men he had himself created laughed at him with his literary doubts and his checked ulster. One day that spring Firsov sat staring sadly and angrily into the stove, in which his half-finished story and his notebook, which was too fat to catch fire all at once, were slowly smoldering. He poked at the paper with the poker, but the fire slowly chewed its way through, and the sparks flew up lazily. Then he turned from the precious ashes back to reality, and battled again with himself and his momentary exhaustion.

In his fancy he imagined a square in which the thief, Mitka Vekshin, was to be drawn and quartered, as in the old days. The crowd that surrounded the place of execution looked on in grave silence while the earthly body of Mitka was dismembered. Firsov was present in the crowd, and another more significant spectator, as well, who attracted all his attention. Nikolka Zavarihin had appeared soundlessly; he had come silently out of the darkness of the countryside, and attached himself to reality. It was not till he was quite close that Firsov remarked his broad smile.

And in actual fact no one except Puchov had noticed Zavarihin's sudden appearance on the scene, for at first glance it was not in the least surprising that he should open a wretched little shop with only one window on a derelict site not far from the large market place. A month before, Nikolka had been going around peddling fancy wares and had not scorned even the meagerest profits; he had come to terms with life. Quite accidentally Firsov, who used to go out into the market place to get a breath of fresh air, came upon him peddling, and was so astonished that he could not take his eyes off him. That had been in the early spring.

"What do you want, citizen? Would you like something to smarten yourself up, or somebody else, perhaps? What about a little ribbon for your beard?" Nikolka had a knowing wink for Firsov and for everybody else.

"I should like a comb," mumbled Firsov gruffly, and he reminded Nikolka of their first meeting. "Do you remember? In the beer hall?"

"Oh, Lord, yes! but you didn't take it seriously, did you? It was all nonsense! Now I'm beginning with proper work at last. Lord! We have to lug our whole stall around with us on our bellies!" Nikolka broke off, and began in a serious business voice to recommend his wares. "Have that, citizen. It's foreign wood. Palm wood that grows by warm rivers." (He, too, evidently, had not been able to escape Puchov's lectures on wood, but he had turned them to good account for his struggling little business.) "It's specially suited for your beard. Comb it, comb it. . . . There's nothing like it when you're bored. . . . Let me tell you, one day you'll come to me and thank me for it." He became familiar, for his shabby customer inspired him with contempt. "A first-class variety, only sold privately. Only I and Puchvostov, Zotey Vassilich—perhaps you know the old man?—sell these goods—no one else. Between ourselves, people turn them out of birch wood, polish them, and then ask a rouble for them, but I'll let you have this one, and with pleasure, too, for fifty kopeks." (In some odd way Zavarihin's glib falsehoods seemed only half consistent with his character.)

"Right you are, then! Give me the palm comb," agreed Firsov when he had heard him to the end.

Zavarihin did not have to support his pedlar's tray on his belly for long. (Once Firsov saw him hung round with colored toys. The fragrance of the woods streamed out from him, and he himself was like a bunch of wild flowers. Chikelyov, who wanted to buy something for Klavdya, was standing by, so Firsov, who did not want to meet him, walked past.) The newly opened shop at the derelict corner was called "The Pedlar's," and from behind the window Nikolka was looking out over the heaps of knick-knacks. Firsov went in, but Nikolka was as cool as a king. Even his smallest movements expressed a haughty condescension and dignity. "Much obliged for your visit, but if you should die, we should be able to survive it." Something like this rang in Zavarihin's voice. But Firsov saw a hidden strength in him, too—the strength of swollen waters dashing with violence against a dam.

"It's still spring," sighed Firsov, sitting down, "and it's hot already."

"And summer's coming, and it's not a bad thing either," observed Nikolka. "They're plowing already in the country. Yegor's Day is the great day for plowing. The grass grows, and the birds sing. . . . You must go into the country to hear the little birds. You ought to. It would be amusing for you, seeing you're not used to it," he said jeeringly, and with a rag he put a polish on the little bottles of eau-de-Cologne in the window for the millionth time.

They often sat together like this; they understood each other and did not get on each other's nerves. But it did not escape Firsov that in a very short time Nikolka had accumulated far too many wares. They lay everywhere—in corners and on shelves and in the hand-made chests. At midday, when the sun stood high over the market place, its beams caressed Zavarihin's shop, and his treasures became alive as at the wave of a magician's wand: the cotton and silk stuffs flared like colored flames. Firsov suspected that there was something shady beneath it all, but he had no wish to probe deeper. He loved this aimless loitering in the silent shop with its fragrant smell of calico, through which a tiny sheaf of sunbeams crept.

NIKOLKA had changed a great deal since he had permanently settled in the city. Only yesterday one could not have imagined him without his orange leather tunic. But suddenly the germinating grain burst its husk, and he bought a smart leather jacket and a striped cap; so now, except for his gaily embroidered shirt, no one could have guessed at his humble origin and simple-minded tastes. The little grain swelled, struck its roots into a chink in the asphalt, grew strong, and strained upward. Nor was there any shortage of chinks in the asphalt, which had been well cracked in the storms of the preceding years.

Zavarihin laughed at Puchov's deviation from the intelligent path of existence, for, in his estimation, to live was to fight and to win, to live was to guard one's powers so that they should not rust through lack of use.

"Well, Puchov, a crab has a poor sort of existence now, hasn't he?" chuckled Nikolka as he drank tea with his uncle. "I was eating crabs the other day with some pals in the beer hall."

"Why are you talking of crabs?" asked Puchov.

"Because you're like a crab, Puchov. You just sit in your shell and don't care a damn for anyone else." Nikolka laughed heartily—he had no fear of giving offense, for a wise man is never offended by the truth. "Anyone can fling you into a saucepan, Puchov, and eat you up. Nowadays there are two sorts of men—those that get eaten up, and those that do the eating." Nikolka laughed again, for it pleased him to be able to class himself in the second category.

Presently he stopped his visits to his uncle in Blagusha altogether, and forgot his gray village, although he was in no hurry to break off all relations with it. It was pleasanter to pass a free hour with friends over a glass of beer, and chat about business. But even friendship had no deep roots in Zavarihin's nature; the lonely independence of his character safeguarded him from any wasteful squanderings of his powers on friendship or other unprofitable attachments. If a misfortune happened to a friend, Nikolka would have turned his back on him without any twinge of conscience.

At the end of the winter Nikolka had an all-night carouse with his friends in the beer hall to celebrate the opening of his business. He treated the whole crowd of them, and got blind drunk, much to their amusement.

"Now we've the power, we can do anything. I've nothing now, but I'm going to take everything I want, and no one will break me, I can tell you. . . . And I can wait. I'm treating you, though I've nothing to gain by it, because I want you to understand what sort of a fellow Zavarihin is." There was a sharp, unpleasant ring in his voice. "I came into the world with my fists clenched, and I'll be top dog before I'm done. I'm ready for anything, and my head's screwed on the right way, too. I've only to leave my felt boots behind me in the shop and no one'll dare put his nose in! . . ." (His friends smiled at Nikolka's boasting, and winked good-humoredly at each other.)

"Go it!" laughed the only man with a beard among them. "Go it! There's great stuff in you: you'll be a great man yet! You're a cute one, and there's no nonsense about you, either!" This friend was a job master and wore a beard parted in the middle. None of his friends could ever afterward forget Nikolka's threatening face (even if it was a little absurd), or his pugnacious fists. They did not know that he was not drunk with beer, but with elation at his first victory. The world seemed to him a spacious, pleasant place, which only needed him to balance it. He liked it: it was soft as down, and as pleasant as an obliging customer.

When the company got tired of sitting in the beer hall, the bearded man suggested that they should drive to the circus. They all four got into a droshky (the snow had already half melted away), and they drove down the boulevard to the circus. Nikolka sat silently on the knees of the man with the beard; the others hiccuped and struck up a song. It made one merry merely to look at that gay mass of singing, shouting humanity. As they were simple folk they wanted seats in the gallery, but there were only stalls left. The appearance of the acrobat Velton always meant a full house.

The friends were resigned to try another entertainment, but they were squeezed closer and closer to the box office, and before they knew where they were, the tickets had been bought, and they were pushing excitedly into the circus. Zavarihin sat in the stalls, thinking to himself that he had the whole world in his pocket, and stared haughtily into the arena, where boneless, half-naked men did feats that seemed to surpass the limits of the possible. Zavarihin was in high spirits, and bent on enjoying an entertainment for which he had paid a solid rouble. ("If I spend seven roubles on breeches, then I must wear them for seven years. But if I wear them for eight years, then that means that for a single rouble I get both pleasures," he said with complete gravity.)

During the *entr'acte* the friends went into the buffet. Nikolka remained indomitably cheerful, although the music was playing something as sad as a dirge. At the end of the piece there was a soft sigh from the flute, and the music started again, the violins began suddenly to blend and twine nimbly through the solemn rattle of the kettle-drum, and Velton made her appearance. The beam of the spotlight strayed, as if intentionally, and fell on Nikolka; and, with lips pressed tight together and brows raised, she bowed to him. An inner voice told him that not so long ago he had stood close to this woman; and now she met him with her blue-eyed, laughing stare. Suddenly a silence fell, and with it a decisive moment in Nikolka's life.

"Let me have a look at the program—who's this girl?" roared the bearded friend into Nikolka's ear. Nikolka gripped his hand, and held it fast. "Let go of my hand, you lout! You'll break it before you're done with it!" grumbled the other, brushing Nikolka's ear with his beard.

Not until Velton stepped under the dome in her blue tights did Nikolka recollect Mitka's splendid fur coat and the fat *barin's* chatter, and a lot of other unimportant things. His hands caressed impatiently the crimson velvet of the seat. It was as though, by the mere power of his concentration, he were forcing Tanya to soar higher and higher, right up to where a noose slowly swayed backward and forward, awaiting her touch. He loved her already and so he waited for something extraordinary from her.

The silence was interminable, it drove Nikolka to his mad act, drove him into an emptiness where every support failed him. A violent longing overmastered him, a longing more powerful than love. At the last culminating moment he jumped from his seat, and screamed aloud. . . .

When the police were leading Nikolka and his suddenly sobered friends out of the stalls, he scarcely repented what he had done. During the interrogation in the manager's room he stood upright, honestly offended, and unconscious of having done anything wrong. Could he be sentenced just because his heart had burst with rapture? . . . He screwed up his eyes and smiled. Almost touching the paper with his nose, the policeman translated the consequences of Zavarihin's rapture into cold-blooded official language.

In this police record it was asserted that Zavarihin, in a state of intoxication, during Hella Velton's performance (Tanya's real name was put in brackets) had cried out "Fall!" The exclamation might have had fatal consequences for the artist. In stiff handwriting without any flourishes Nikolka signed the document. He stood up in the room a head taller than the others, and, scratching his chin with his fingernail, looked around for his friends, but they had already disappeared. The room was full of artists who wanted to see the criminal; only the plaintiff was absent.

A seedy little old man in a clean black suit, whom Nikolka did not know, kept jumping at him like a small wave battering against a cliff.

"You knew what you were doing!" he screamed in broken Russian, driveling with senile joy at Tanya's escape. "You might 'ave killed 'er. We're just poor artists and you're a chentleman. You pay a rouble, and you want to buy death for a rouble. It's morder. . . ." He went on crying in German, and the policeman looked with interest at his mouth, from which a torrent of strange sounds was pouring.

"How much? How much does it let me in for?" Zavarihin interrupted, pursing up his mouth. "Must I pay immediately?" He wanted to draw out his wallet on the spot, but did not do it because they had all begun to laugh at his eagerness.

The clouds veiled the stars and the cocks were crowing loudly in the poultry yards of Blagusha when Nikolka knocked at his uncle's door, where he was still living. While Puchov was getting up, Nikolka betook himself to the middle of the yard and, standing there, contemplated the heavens with his legs apart.

"Fall down!" he repeated suddenly, not with the commanding voice that had shaken the circus, but sadly and beseechingly. "Fall down, so that I may love you more . . . so that suffering may enrich me. Fall, for how else could you shake my soul?" All this lay implied in the two words. He repeated them once more, and listened to the echoes and images they called up in his mind. A homeless dog sniffed around his legs; it barked and tried to bite him more than once. Before Puchov opened the door, Nikolka had seized the dog furiously by the long hair on its back and flung it into a dark corner of the yard; the dog neither barked nor whined again. Puchov let in his nephew and stepped out into the yard to look at the night. When he returned, his nephew was no more to be found, only his great snoring hulk lay there in his place. Nikolka's soul dissolved in sleep as a lump of sugar dissolves in the calm hot depths of a glass of water.

CHAPTER

V I I I

Firsov's manuscript, which had been started afresh so many times, lay peacefully in the cardboard portfolio on the shelf, under a layer of dust. A portly garden spider sedately took up her residence there to ambush flies and rear a family. At first she spun thin, sticky threads backward and forward, then a yellow pellet the size of a pea hung from them; later on, the soft shell suddenly burst, and a swarm of helpless spiders crept out into the wide, free world. The master of the house could not bring himself to sweep them away, and so the young spiders rampaged at liberty about their paper home.

Firsov had other things to worry him: things were happening for which he himself was partly responsible. In his story he had deliberately altered the circumstances of Tanya Vekshin's first meeting with Zavarihin. According to him, Nikolka had followed Tanya several times, until one day she had stepped up to him and asked why he was dogging her so persistently. Nikolka mumbled something fatuous; Tanya laughed, and then he laughed, too; and this laugh was to give rise to their tragic intimacy. The improbability of the incident was obvious at a glance.

What actually happened was that Tanya visited Puchov to inquire after her brother, and there met Nikolka, though they had already known of each other's existence before this. Puchov was away, and there was no one to interrupt their *tête-à-tête* until Firsov dropped in in passing; he watched with amusement Zavarihin's agitation as he pumped oil into the stove to make the tea and zealously washed Tanya's glass under the tap. The colorless flame hummed obediently, but the glass fell to pieces in Nikolka's too eager hands: he was terribly excited. They avoided looking at each other in terror of betraying themselves by their eyes: their silences were awkward. Tanya offered several times to tie up the cut in his hand, but he refused. It was only a scratch, he protested, and, getting some spider's web out of a corner, he stopped the bleeding in the traditional way. "What are you doing? Why are you doing that?" asked Tanya, flushing and biting her lips. "That may give you blood poisoning. . . ."

"Well, we all must die one way or another," murmured Nikolka awkwardly, and he rubbed the spider's web right into his cut. He gave a mighty yawn as he poured the tea into glasses. "We must all die, mustn't we? What do you say, poet?"

Firsov was tactfully silent, and observed with pleasure the inward agitation of these two strong young creatures. Perhaps it was only in the interests of his preposterous experiment (the interplay of art and life) that later on he persuaded Nikolka to make his apologies to Tanya for his behavior in the circus. He even put it into Nikolka's head to buy her flowers, and sapped his resistance by tales of Tanya's fame, and finally gave him her address. The writer did not, indeed, make a single false step. Nikolka valued friendship with those to whom fortune was kind, but in his nature was an unconscious revulsion from death and disaster and disease, for his lot was to be strong and ignorant of suffering. He despised all those who roused his pity, because it robbed him of his strength and undermined his security. With sincerity he longed for the speedy destruction of all the weak. The strong, like Nikolka, love only the strong.

During his very first visit he gave himself to her, and was strangely delighted at this unusual extravagance. On the way he had bought some beautiful full-blown roses. The spring was at its height; fluffy little clouds flew across the sky, and in the air echoed the solemn Easter hallelujah. Everything that day—the slow swaying of the branches with their fresh spring leaves, the falcon flight of the wind, the vague, friendly glances of the suburban folk, and the motley gaiety of the sunlit streets—everything contributed to Nikolka's cheerful mood.

He rapped smartly on the door, stepped gaily into the anteroom, and almost pushed over Pugel, who gazed at him in bewilderment. The old man would have been scared out of his wits by Nikolka in his old-fashioned merchant's dress, which sat oddly on his great shoulders, had not Tanya appeared at the same moment. She stood in the doorway, dressed in somber black, and through the window a sea of cool green light streamed in.

He tore his cap from his head and stood there with his arms hanging down. The smell of his cowhide boots announced him more eloquently than his words. Pugel, whose fatherly jealousy had been roused by an infinity of details, rolled his eyes excitedly. "Is dat you?" he called out, seizing Nikolka by a button.

"It is, sure enough!" said Nikolka, beaming and self-conscious. He cautiously pushed aside Pugel's hand. "It's a holiday today and so I've come without being asked," he added, and tried to catch again in Tanya's half-turned face the enchantment of the fateful evening at the circus.

Tanya made an embarrassed gesture. "Come in, as you're here. Put your cap on the table. You take it, Pugel dear!"

Nikolka parted reluctantly with his cap, for his big, clumsy hands became dead and meaningless when they had nothing to fiddle with. Although he fought against his embarrassment, his gaiety had abandoned him. He sat in a deep armchair and scowled suspiciously at Pugel, who was busy making the coffee, at the walls, which were hung with brightly colored circus posters, and at the carpet, which seemed to him to be looking superciliously at his clumsy boots. Tanya's room was as impersonal as every room that only serves as a temporary refuge.

"Are all of those you?" Zavarihin pointed at the posters.

"All me," Tanya smiled and looked at her guest more closely.

"And wherever you look, there's the noose. Have you had it a long time? Have you been earning your living with it for a long time, now?"

She took him up quickly. "Ages . . ." And she shocked

the old man by the unusual ring of her laugh. "Do you smoke?"

"No, I've no use for smoking!" said Nikolka with a grimace.

"I suppose you come of country stock, don't you?" she asked after a short pause. It was hard to say whether she was offended.

"I'm a peasant," declared Nikolka even more defiantly. "A peasant, one of those whom people despise, but who aren't proud, and can stand a lot. Nowadays the peasant is only the seasoning they put in the broth to give it a good savor. We deal in small wares—little crosses and soap and ribbons . . ." It was a lie, for only yesterday Firsov had remarked the suspicious quantity of goods in Zavarihin's shop; but Nikolka was disparaging himself deliberately. "All this talk about the bourgeois! And where are there fat bellies left to knife now?" He flung her a piercing glance, and blushed as he met her steady scrutiny.

Tanya slowly turned her eyes away.

Now they both looked through the window, behind which the dazzling noon rode past. As the wind shook the window frame, scattered patches of light ran loosely across Nikolka's face.

"Phew, how hot this chair is! It's like sitting on a bog," he said, and got up. "It's splendid in the woods now— the leaves rustling, and the wind rustling . . ." His nostrils dilated, and he glanced aside. "Come into the country with me," he said suddenly. His eyes sparkled with anticipation, and he promised her so many country pleasures that were new and strange or forgotten that she agreed.

She liked his rough, firm strength and his simplicity and directness.

She put on her big cape—it had a strong, friendly smell of india-rubber, which Nikolka could smell a long way off—and then her small hat with the blue veil. Her appearance flattered Nikolka's vanity. Pugel accompanied her to the street door. He was wearing an apron and holding a feather brush in his hand, for with the restlessness of old age he dreaded the repose he had earned.

"Pleess!" He seized Nikolka by the sleeve, for Tanya was already coming down the steps. "Look after Tanya!

She is breetle as a tweeg. She is breetle: yes, yes, I know it, I'm already vairy, vairy old." He was moved, and raised his lashless, protruding eyes to Nikolka's face.

Nikolka cut the old man's mumblings short. "Right you are . . . all right!" he said, pressing his lips together. "Cut along, Daddy, get busy! You'll give us coffee another time." He fumbled impatiently in his pants pockets. "Here you are . . . for tobacco. . . ." He pushed a coin into Pugel's astonished hand, and banged the door behind him.

They were already on the street, walking intentionally some distance apart, before Pugel had closed his fingers on Nikolka's half-rouble piece. Suddenly his mouth twitched into a sly smile; he ran into the room and put the gift with its value mark uppermost on the most conspicuous spot on Tanya's dressing table.

"A peasant, yes! A scarecrow . . . And what a scarecrow!" he said, shaking his head. His toothless mouth distorted the words even more than his German accent.

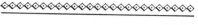

Nikolka had conceived his plan as he ran clattering down the stairs after Tanya. She waited for him and squinted her eyes to face the wind that swept down the street.

"Let's go that way," he said, pointing in the direction from which the wind and the breath of spring came to meet them; the houses there were smaller and lower. "The air is purer there." (Tanya was surprised at something fresh and unspoiled in Nikolka's words.) "Oh, I'm no good at talking . . . but if I had a harmonica! . . ."

"Do you play, then?" asked Tanya. She was shy, without knowing why.

"I'm the best harmonica player in the district," boasted Nikolka. He stood for a while irresolutely, then suddenly disappeared through an old, half-ruined stone doorway. "Wait here a moment," he called out to her from the depths of the yard. "I'll be back in a moment."

The promised moment dragged on indefinitely, and Nikolka's delay began to be tedious. Tanya was on the point of walking off in resentment when suddenly she heard behind her the clatter of a horse's hoofs and the soft rolling of rubber wheels.

"Step in . . . quick!" cried out Nikolka, holding in the horse. He grinned savagely as he tugged at the reins, and the horse came to a standstill, snorting.

"I'm going to take you out for a drive, not to get anything out of you, but just because I'd like to," he shouted, showing all his healthy teeth.

He did not say (and Tanya did not ask, for it made the adventure all the more wonderful) that in the house behind them there lived the man with the beard parted in the middle who had sat with him in the stalls on the memorable evening of the scandal, and that from him Nikolka had hired a horse with a hogged mane for the whole day. He spat on his hands, and sat upright on the seat, and the light, well-sprung trap rolled out of the side street.

Skillfully plying the reins, he drove into the main street with its roar of traffic, and there gave the horse its head. The regular beat of the hoofs, the flashing of the bright spokes, and Zavarihin's loud, self-satisfied shouts excited the angry stares of the passers-by. The cabmen, crouching sulkily on their boxes, gave him a wide berth, and did not even have time to fling an oath after his flying wheels.

"A horse is a fine thing. . . . There's nothing like a horse in the whole world!" whispered Zavarihin excitedly into Tanya's ear.

"My brother used to like horses, too," she cried, shielding herself from the wind with her hand. "But you knew him, didn't you?"

"Of course." Nikolka smiled perfunctorily, and steered the trap past some lumbering trucks. "We had a little scrap together . . . but that doesn't make any difference: often the friendliest way of all to meet is when you have a set-to with someone with a knife in your hand. You get to know another chap fighting. In our village at home the only way you could make a pal was with your fists."

Her long, intimate stare was like a caress; it seemed to challenge his virility, his power and strength . . . but his hands were tied by his timid, helpless love. He flinched from her glance like a whipped horse, and relieved his feelings in an outburst of bad temper. "You mangy hound, I'll run you down, I will!" he screamed at a policeman who stood in the street, and, in a spasm of rage, shook his fist at him. He managed the reins cleverly and drove with his left hand only.

The policeman drew back and looked in stupefaction after the tearing carriage. Then he jumped on to the footboard of a passing truck and shouted something into the driver's ear. Suddenly they were in the thick of an adventure. As they tore on as fast as the horse's legs could travel, Tanya clutched her hat tightly, and kept looking around at the truck, which came rolling and rumbling and belching fumes behind them, all the time emitting a hoot that was like a sob. She felt a sudden, overwhelming terror of Nikolka, and it seemed to her that his lips had disappeared and the wind was beating vainly against his sealed and empty face. His left hand, blue from the reins wound around it, lay on the lacquered dashboard of the trap. He was intoxicated with joy at his race with the dead, blind force that tore behind him.

"Do you want me to stop?" He turned around to Tanya, his face distorted with excitement.

"On! On!" implored Tanya's eyes, and her lips feebly echoed them.

The wind that seared and stung sounded in her ears like a terrifying scream, and her heart contracted into a helpless little ball. For a few moments she offered her breast to the wind exultantly, but soon she grew tired, and leaned back, indifferent to everything. Nikolka raised himself a little, and, with a faint smile, began to slow down. The horse, covered with foam, obeyed the slightest twitch on the reins, as if it understood the strange nature of their game. Now it went at a trot, and flung its legs forward cheerfully and surely, and, with ears pricked, listened to the sound of the rolling rubber wheels. The trap came to a stop with a jolt, and Tanya jumped up from her seat.

"Stay where you are!" Nikolka roughly pulled her back.

"He's coming," whispered Tanya, drinking in the wind with open mouth.

"He's putting his best foot foremost." Nikolka gave a sardonic smile, and patted Tanya on the knee familiarly. "He'd give his eyes to catch us, you bet!"

The policeman had jumped from the truck and was running toward the trap, the flaps of his coat flapping against his knees. Then there was a moment of tense excitement. The horse's legs and its graceful body leaned forward slightly; the next moment the trap tore on and the policeman ran after it, pursued by the delighted jeers of the street urchins.

"Ho, you mountains and valleys!" shouted Zavarihin, and he sighed as he tore at the reins. "Ho, you dark forests!" he cried, still more dolefully, and in his exaltation

Tanya felt an almost magical power. (Nikolka's grandfather must have shouted like that when he drove the government *troika* through nights and forests.)

The horse's hoofs ate up the miles and left clear fine
tracks behind them on the damp earth. A cock fluttered
to one side, dogs yapped. The factory suburbs gradually
grew smaller and sank far behind. A great hill crept toward them and disappeared. In front of them on the horizon the Moscow fields spread out with their scanty little
woods and small ravines, and gaily singing birds hovered
invisibly in the air.

"The birds there . . . surely they're not siskins?" and
Tanya tried to outscream the wind.

"The siskin likes being up high."

The wood bent off to the left, and a grove ran out to
meet them, as tender and transparent as if it were about
to flutter up into the gray-blue of the spring sky. The trap
plunged into the moist coolness of the grove; the horse
walked slowly along the still wet road, and his dark coat,
on which the foam mantled, steamed and cooled. The
grove breathed heavily, as if it were heaving a tombstone
from its breast; the silence was rhythmic and expectant.
In the meadow a bird catcher lay stretched out indolently
on his cloak, and near the empty bird cage a bottle glittered in the sun.

"I don't like machinery," said Nikolka with a gloomy
look as they got out and sat down on a tree stump. "A
machine won't help you if you get into a mess, and you
can't coax it." He broke off a twig covered with leaf buds,
and rubbed it between his fingers, and smelled it. "It's
got a fine smell . . . you get a better smell from a tree
than from any flower." Then he remembered the flowers
he had bought for Tanya on the way; he found them
crushed in his pocket, with half their petals off, and sinis-
ter-looking smudges on the remaining ones. "They're
smothered . . . the flowers. It's all nonsense, though!"
he said reflectively as he held his stricken bouquet in his
hand. "The writer put me up to buying them."

Tanya looked at him again, and all at once she became
glad and free in God's world. She joked and laughed, ready
for any childish prank. For the first time in her life she

had become a careless child to whom the spring was a free and healing gift.

"Let's shout so that it rings through the whole forest, shall we?" They laughed till they were tired; they shouted so loud that it seemed to them that the whole world would hear it; they mimicked the owl, and scared the bird catcher, who was busy drinking. Their voices dispersed into a thin fume of sound, and the wind bore it away in its huge embrace. But the climax of their abandonment was a positive and significant action that could never be undone. Yet it could not have been branded as lewdness. On their way back, Zavarihin proposed to her in crude, clumsy words that henceforward they should live together as man and wife, as they had that day. He was scared by the rapid march of events, and he accepted her consent in silence. He had always been afraid of women, and this single intimacy had given him the torment of satiety. He lashed the horse on in a fury.

He took off his cap and let the cleansing wind sweep across his head and free it of all its cares—even of the madness of love, the latest of them all. They drove along a bad country road, the wheels sank in the glistening earth, and the trap was spattered with dirt and had lost its polish. As they were descending into a hollow, Tanya seized Nikolka by the sleeve, and her hand weighed on him like a seven-ton weight. The sun was veiled in the afternoon vapors, and the city rose up flat and colorless and inevitable. At the edge of the suburbs, as they were passing through an evil-smelling cloud of dust, Nikolka flogged the horse once more.

"Soon I'm going to change into new rooms, and I'll invite you to come and see me," he said as he took his leave, his eyes not meeting hers. "Well, so long! You must be tired, I'm sure," and he disappeared with his trap into the twilit peace of the street.

Tanya gazed into the dimness after her lover, and brooded over her joyless life and the fickle winds of spring.

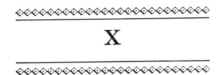
SEVERAL days later Tanya, who had learned Nikolka's address from Puchov, visited him in his little room on the third story of a long, dirty-looking house. The window looked out on the courtyard and offered a view of roofs— a whole panorama of wet roofs, for the spring had changed its face once more and a nasty rain pattered monotonously on the windowpanes. Tanya paid her visit on a Sunday, so as to be sure of finding him at home.

He was sitting at the table, eating boiled eels and spitting the bones into a jam pot, and he seemed rather to be enjoying his solitude. He was intensely embarrassed by Tanya's visit, for even the thought of marriage was a nightmare to him. He rushed about the room in embarrassment, with the eel's head in his hand, until Tanya burst out laughing, and he stood still, his mouth twitching, waiting gloomily for her to speak. As Tanya had no grounds for suspecting that his feelings had altered, she hung her coat calmly on the nail and put her hat on the bed.

"Take your things off, if you like," he said gloomily, with an effort of composure. "I've been living here a week already, but I was always afraid to ask you over. . . . We've a lot of bugs here," he added with bantering solemnity.

She ignored this observation. "So this is where you live? . . . Well, it's all solid enough, and you've got all that you want at your elbow, anyway," she said, casting a fleeting but friendly glance of approval at the sloping walls of

Nikolka's little room. Nikolka watched her keenly to discover her real opinion.

The room was still empty, but it fully expressed the man its owner was to become; there were no flowers in the window, no pictures on the walls, not even a fragment of looking glass. Instead, a gaily ornamented harmonica hung on a strap over the bed, which was covered by a striped country blanket, and on the low head end lay an old newspaper, carefully folded.

"Do you play?" asked Tanya, embarrassed by her lover's silence. She pointed at the harmonica.

"I play on holidays . . . tunes," returned Nikolka curtly. "But I told you so before. Have you forgotten?"

"No. I remember everything," she answered meaningly. "Am I in your way?"

"I've had my dinner," answered Nikolka, shrugging his shoulders. "You're not in my way: today's a holiday."

"Well, in any case I'll sit down," said Tanya with a slightly different inflection in her voice, looking gravely at Nikolka. "But if you like I'll go away again. You said amazing things to me that time we went into the country. Perhaps you were drunk, though?"

Zavarihin stared at Tanya dully, like a stunned ox, brooding over her dark dress with its high collar and her soft, fragrant hair; he could have lifted her with one hand. With slight irony he glanced at her expensively simple shoes, and tried to picture her carrying manure in the country in clothes like these. But at the same time he remembered her triumph in the circus, and wondered how the thought of her could have disturbed him for a whole week. "But she's young and charming . . ." he reflected slowly and comfortingly. "She's famous," shouted ambition. . . . "She has money," whispered covetousness, and his cheeks grew red with shame. He cleared the table, and wiped it with a rag, his eyes turned away from her. He still had the strength of youth and could not surrender to mean considerations without a struggle.

"Sit down, and we'll drink tea. The tea'll boil in a moment in the kitchen. Shall I get a lemon? There's a fruit stall down below." His young bass voice went on talking, but he was still ashamed of his thoughts.

"Just listen, Nikolka, do you regret it?" She stretched out her hands to him, which he grasped apprehensively. They were hot and moist.

"Look here!" He scratched himself behind the ear, and for a moment his voice sounded like a boy's. "I've never been in a situation like this before. Tell me if I do anything not quite . . ." She smiled, and he went on excitedly: "There was a woman in our village they called Mavra the shepherdess, because she used to get hold of the young shepherds and corrupt them. She used to get them into the bathhouse and amuse herself with them. She began to treat me to cakes, too . . . and one fine day . . . there she stood, bare as my fist, in front of me."

"And what did you do?" Tanya bent her head.

"I? . . . I let her have a whack on her bare belly with my stick and took to my heels." He laughed loudly and cruelly, and Tanya no longer saw the boy, but the full-grown, keen-witted youth, from whom a thief had tried to steal the most precious of all possessions. "I ran into the garden and my heart laughed in my body. I sat down, ate the cakes, jumped up, danced . . . and ate again. Wait a moment, what was it I was leading up to? I'm laughing, but God knows there's little enough to laugh about. I haven't been to see you because I'm so worried. I'm stuck for money, but I could pull off a thing or two if only I had the cash. For instance, I've had an offer of some goods dirt cheap—'black' goods, but chaps like me can't be squeamish: you'll get nowhere with the white goods nowadays."

"And do you need much?" asked Tanya, becoming interested. She was afraid of offending him by saying more, but the hint was enough; it staggered him, for not even in his dreams had he hoped for so simple a way out of his difficulties. This time Tanya was stronger than he, and that instantly attracted him to her.

He began enthusiastically to form new plans and walk about the room in excitement; for the first time he showed genuine pleasure in the visit of his betrothed.

"I'm glad you've come," he stammered, and before she could stop him, he ran away to fetch a lemon. He knocked over a chair as he did so, and forgot to shut the door.

When Tanya was alone, she began to walk up and down the room, and her eyes fell on Nikolka's pathetic possessions—a kitchen table, a stool, and a Viennese chair, made in Moscow.

She sat down on the hard bed and then looked under it. There was a little chest with an old-fashioned lock, and a pair of shoes stiff with age. Everything here was so open and unabashed, she felt she knew all Nikolka's secrets already. A cold shudder ran over her as she thought that a great future was in store for Nikolka, while she herself, it seemed to her, was finished and done with.

Suddenly peculiar noises came through the door. She got up; the noises were not repeated. She went to the door, and again there was a teasing repetition of the noise. Then she went out into the dark and malodorous passage: something sticky clung to the soles of her shoes. Nearby someone was crying quietly and wearily, as though the first bitterness of despair were over. Tanya took four steps on the uneven, well-worn landing, and stood before a strange door. She struck her foot against something long and flat which leaned against the wooden wall, and it began to fall slowly down on her. She clutched it in the darkness and, with a beating heart, held it fast in her hands; it was like the lid of a trap. Paralyzed by the silence of the passage, Tanya listened to the conversation behind the door.

"You're a fool! Can't you see you're free now, and on your own at last?" a deep, impersonal woman's voice scolded. "Now you can pay calls or sleep the whole live-long day. Do you think it's nice always to have to listen to your child whimpering, and you carrying on like that? . . ."

"She died: she lay there like a rose," wailed the other woman's voice. "She lay on her back and went to sleep. . . ."

Tanya glanced again at the object she held in her hands, and almost screamed when she saw what it was. At the other side of the wall, then, the dead girl must be lying! There was a menacing premonition in the trivial episode, which she could not shake off. The toneless voices of the women called up strange and frightening fantasies in her mind, and they seemed to multiply and drain the strength from her body. She thrust away the coffin lid—its cheap lace border caught on her hand—and ran into Nikolka's room, back to light and life. He found her sitting on the bed, but did not notice the expression of terror and pity in her eyes until he had cut two thin slices from the lemon.

"I'm frightened, Nikolushka," she whispered through her sobs, while he sat beside her and stroked her trembling hands. "I'm frightened of everything in life. In the circus I'm never frightened: there I know that any mistake may mean death, but in life there are worse things than death."

He embraced her clumsily, spreading out his fingers shyly, and at the moment he hated her for her incomprehensible, humiliating tears.

"It's all nonsense! . . . Aren't you with me?" He laid his terrible fist, clenched till it was blue, on her knee. "They can get around me, but . . . my fist is hard: there's no nonsense about it." He thrust out his chin aggressively: a man who insulted him would regret it for the rest of his life. "I'm a strong man, and everything about me is strong. When I see a tree, I feel I could tear it up, root and all, with my teeth. . . . When I'm with you, there's nothing in the world you need be frightened of."

"You're so warm!" Tanya pressed against him. "If anything awful ever happens to me, will you help me?" She did all she could to win his tenderness. "It's odd, I'm already using my second noose in the circus: the first has got past using. . . . And it's my life to me! In all these years there has never been anyone near me, even as a friend. It's always seemed to me that I haven't been fair to Pugel in robbing him of the best thing in life. . . . He's a marvellous old owl: not long ago he washed my stockings. I'm ashamed, and it isn't a good thing either that they're all so fond of me. I'm lonely because everyone's fond of me, and protects me . . . from what? You don't understand me, and that's why you're so strong . . . because you don't understand the stupid, dismal pettinesses of life. And you shouldn't ever try to understand it, Nikolushka." She looked fixedly into his uncomprehending face. "Do you know, I'm going to leave the circus for good? I'm frightened . . . when I think that in the evening I'll again have to . . . My feet turn cold. . . . Why is it so cold here, Nikolushka?"

"It's summer, too . . . but perhaps it comes from the

stone floor." He pressed her to him again cautiously; he was afraid of crushing the expensive material of her dress. "I'll give you just one piece of advice. Don't worry! All that doesn't matter. If you remember it a year from now, you'll just laugh at it. And don't be worried about your money, either, I'll pay you interest. At the moment no one will lend me anything because I can't give any security. . . . I've nothing but what you see in this room." He lowered his eyes contemptuously. "People don't trust me. 'And if he died!' they say. Stupid fools! Do they think Zavarihin is going to die?" He laughed angrily and tonelessly, and then was silent.

In the stillness that ensued she looked at him with a sudden fear of estrangement, and her face seemed to plead for mercy.

"What sort of interest? How dare you . . . to me?" She jumped up, intending to leave at once, but it seemed to her that as soon as she opened the door, the lid of the strange child's coffin would clatter down on her. In her mind she saw the two men who stood nearest to her, Mitka and Pugel. Pugel, with his perverse, intolerable belief in her "star," and Mitka, her seven-days brother. . . . Wasn't he nearer to her than this strange youth, who was stretching out his relentless arm over the world? She stood up, but then sat down again; it was an unconditional surrender to the mercy of the conqueror. And this end to it all even pleased her, for to the weak, surrender is the sweetest part of the battle. "Why did you speak about interest, Nikolushka? Haven't I given myself to you utterly?"

He sat there, silent and embarrassed, contemplating his red hands, which had been charged so unjustly with avarice.

"Good accounts never injure friendship," he said sullenly. "Don't be cross with me for the country saying, but plain words are best. . . ." He drew her to himself masterfully without any fear of crushing her dress, "You're my lizard, my slim, blue lizard."

"A lizard?" she repeated, half scared, yet thankful for his spontaneous caress. "Now we'll marry and you'll put me at the cash desk so that I can pay out the money and not eat your bread for nothing. But I'm not much good at money matters, Nikolushka. . . . Pugel does all that for me. . . ."

"You . . . at the cash desk?" Nikolka raised his eyebrows in surprise, and instantly lowered them again. "But if you don't want to yourself . . . No, you're Hella, after all. I'll never call you anything but Hella."

They drank tea, and Tanya tried to imitate Nikolka, who sipped his tea in the peasant way from his saucer, and then blew on it. But she could not keep it up, and began to laugh. The tea had grown cold, and but for the lemon it would have tasted like dish water. Then Nikolka told her about his life, and there was no trace of self-complacency in his tale. He took his own powers as a matter of course.

"How do you manage to do it all?" exclaimed Tanya admiringly.

"I suppose it's just a trick like yours in the circus, Hella. I'm nobody now, anyone can haul me off to the police station: all the same, I can squeeze a man till he looks like a piece of chewed string. They say strong men don't cry, but if you ask me, the strongest'll cry if he can't find a use for his strength. . . ."

Later on they sat together on the bed like a pair of lovers.

At the beginning of summer Tanya finally left the circus, though they still hesitated about marrying, for Nikolka's business demanded his constant attention. Tanya's belief in herself had utterly dried up, her nerves were shattered, and the smallest thing could throw her into a state of exasperation. When she perceived Pugel's worried gaze, she would scream at the old man, and weep.

"You're always so in a hurry, Tanya," he said once as he watched her nervous movements.

"And you always annoy me, Pugel," she flung back at him rudely.

"My girl, always 'ave I nursed your fame. You 'ave become Hella Velton, but one leetle scrap is mine, yes, yes," exclaimed Pugel.

New traits of quarrelsomeness and jealousy appeared in Tanya's hitherto calm and equable temperament. There was not a single one of her circus colleagues now on whom she lavished her former gay, friendly smile. It was as if her performances had become only a dangerous, pointless routine, a tormenting drudgery to win her daily bread. Her decision to leave the circus was not suddenly taken, for her contract in any case came to an end at that time.

She lost her nerve shortly before her meeting with her brother. Before packed houses she would run up the rope, nimble and blue, and gaily confident of what was to come: the orchestra would be silent, and the beam of the spotlight would envelop her, and then a moment of grim silence would ensue, in which one had to forget everything, and after it a half-moment of superhuman resolution . . . and finally the wild applause of the multitude would burst out in gratitude for the instant of ecstatic horror they had lived through.

Then one evening someone sneezed at the moment when the drums stopped. The pit hissed, and then the gallery hissed at the pit, and something akin to madness swept over the assembled thousands: but silence was restored when Tanya made her first movement of preparation. A few moments of uncertainty slipped by, Tanya stood up above holding on to the rope, as if she were frightened of crashing down into the sand, and had suddenly realized the danger and the futility of her turn.

Everyone saw how nervously she stroked her neck, which was poised for the swoop down to the cord. The dim spots of faces far below, waiting excitedly for the miracle to happen, seemed vague and far away. The ray of the spotlight wavered unsteadily, as if the tremors of the acrobat had infected it. Someone ran to the manager's room to report the approach of a fiasco. Pugel stood, pale as a corpse, behind the scenes, listening to the applause. Then Tanya with a wailing, animal scream flung herself down. (The noose should have stayed her flight through the air with an elastic touch in the muscles above the collarbone. Then from the vertical position, with her head downward, she had to describe a semicircle, and free herself from the noose as she drew herself up with her arm.)

Tanya had not heard her own terrible scream, and so was able to muster strength to bow to the silent public. Pugel embraced her in the arena, as if he wished to shelter his foster child from the disgrace of failure. His tears, which they regarded as a father's, touched the audience: never in all his life had Pugel received such a frenzied ovation. It was a fiasco without a parallel in the whole history of the circus, and only out of respect for Tanya's reputation did the management remain silent about the disagreeable episode, although it was privately decided to substitute another turn for hers.

Her will was paralyzed by her terror of the inevitable. She trained every morning in the circus more eagerly than ever, so as to discipline her limbs to the utmost pitch of obedience. Often it seemed to her that the accident had been merely a short-lived rebellion of her body, the immediate consequence of overexertion. She must have an interval of rest, as had been necessary some years previously, when her self-confidence had been shaken by similar warning symptoms. She did not appear for two days, but the elasticity of her muscles, which was the foundation of her spiritual health, had not yet returned. Pugel could not bring himself to realize that his protégée might have to leave the circus, and deliberately tried to ignore Tanya's exhausted nerves. The fiasco merely roused his contempt for the audience—"Block'eads," he repeated several times that evening to the clown. "When the serpentine dancer 'op round them they clap, but when a girl jump to 'er death then they 'iss!" And yet he resolved to advise Tanya to take at least two months' holiday.

Once when Pugel was away from home on business of hers, Tanya thought of a way to cure herself. She put a stool on the table and began to take down the circus posters that formerly had stimulated her courage, but now only alarmed her. She threw the last and dustiest on the heap, and looked down: she began to sway, and would have fallen if she had not supported herself against the wall in time.

She crouched in front of the stove and began to burn up the paper, which now was of no use to her—the dishonored small change of her fame. It was a warm summer night, and there was scarcely any draft in the stove. Tanya experienced a marvellous feeling of relief, for while she was consuming her fame to ashes, she was ridding herself of her past and herself. Her heart beat fast and gladly at the thought that soon Nikolka would lead her away to his village, where no one would recognize her as a runaway circus artist. Suddenly she visualized her fancied happiness: a rough peasant's room . . . Nikolka in a gay shirt drinking tea and crunching sugar with it . . . without the father's knowledge she is giving a tidbit to the child, a second Tanya, her little daughter. The oval looking glass behind her husband shows her reflection—a peaceful and colorless one. It seems to her that she has become more womanly and found her real vocation. Over her head is a warm, firm roof, and under her feet solid ground.

Pugel found her asleep by the stove in the smoky room;

part of the dead ashes had fallen on her knees. He struck a match and approached her on tiptoe. There was a peaceful smile on her face, as though she had at last attained the safe shore she yearned for. It was late. Outside the window the hoofs of a droshky nag rang in the street. His eyes twinkling, the old man lit the lamp, and noticed now, for the first time, the uncanny emptiness of the room. On the faded wallpaper gaped the empty patches left by the posters. The old man shuddered, as if he had been robbed or was preparing to spring at his robbers. His knees gave way; the walls swayed before his eyes, and he swayed with them. It was quiet, and Tanya was asleep.

He knelt down in front of her, and looked long at her calm, closed eyelids. The lips, which she had bitten till they bled, were smiling, and her perfect peace—this seemingly eternal peace—shocked the old man. His tongue lolled out of his mouth, and his eyebrows almost met perpendicularly.

"Don't smile, don't smile like that!" he moaned, and turned away from her in anger and pain.

She awoke slowly and reluctantly, as if thick folds of sweet and heavy water divided her from reality. The bareness of the room and Pugel standing over her reminded her of what had happened, and a look of pain came over her face, and the flush of sleep turned to an ashen gray. She straightened her dress and sighed doubtfully. There was nothing left for her to do but to fly to Nikolka, and, though it were only for half an hour, to catch the infection of his tireless health. An odd feeling of distrust made her reluctant to lay bare her weakness to him, but her pain was stronger than her scruples.

"Why don't you ever come to me?" With these words she shook him out of sleep. She looked for her reflection in his sleep-dulled pupils. "I'm so sad. . . . You can't love me much—you've got business. But do you love me a little? Take me soon, Nikolushka, and keep me with you."

"Come, come, that's all nonsense! . . . It's all right!" he whispered comfortingly, and, fighting back his drowsiness, rubbed the places that had been stung by bugs. "I'm sorry: I don't like speaking about it. You must have a little patience, and we'll get married soon. My affairs are gradually getting straight. I'm expecting a big bit of good news tomorrow. It's going on all right, little Hella! Aren't you frightened that they'll crawl on you, too?" He laughed and scratched his skin.

At night it seemed as though Zavarihin's ceiling had sunk lower and the walls had furtively receded into the darkness. A gloomy corner, but it was warm and soothing for Tanya's nerves. He yawned again comfortably, and his fireproof finger played with the flame of the tallow candle. Tanya grew bored and she hurried away down the passage, past the rows of staring doors.

The forlorn emptiness of the city by night seemed in accordance with her suffering. She liked to wander through the sleeping streets, to look into strange windows, to guess at the easy life that went on behind them, envying it. . . . And if there was a drizzle of rain, Tanya felt the weariness of her limbs still more pleasurable.

It was in some such expedition that she met Firsov. He had come from a party, was slightly tipsy, and hummed a little song as he went.

"Mademoiselle! Mademoiselle!" he called out facetiously, doffing his disreputable hat. "What gloomy Fate has driven you out of your warm, virgin alcove into the gloomy night?"

"Yes, driven—that's it." Tanya smiled sadly at his disheveled appearance.

A melancholy gas lamp contemplated this unusual encounter. A tipsy band of men drove past, holding on their knees women who shouted out obscenities. An astonishingly lean dog ran past. It was raining.

"I wager you're returning from an assignation. The tender passion has you in its grip." He realized that he was drunk, and consciously turned it to account. "And we've been drinking . . . a random mob of poets . . . nothing but Mozarts and Salieris. Mademoiselle, wisdom can't endure noise: wisdom loves solitude. But creative thought can't endure the cold: it needs human warmth to nourish itself on. And here, behind this scarecrow façade of mine, twenty-seven men are living." (He tittered affectedly.) "You live in my heart, too, even if it's only in a subordinate place. Yes, nobody cares about writers nowadays, nobody except the tax collector. . . . Our age can't be bothered with such trifles. But   all the same, it's we who'll count up the reckoning."

"Listen, Firsov!" Tanya held him fast by the damp sleeve of his ulster. "Try to be sober just for a moment. I'm going round and round looking in at strangers' windows. Why, why is life so beautiful so long as we look at it from outside? But if one goes in, it's spoiled in a moment. Look for yourself!" She led him to the window of a cellar, and pointed at the dirty window panes. "Look . . . the mother's suckling her child . . . and look at the way it's clinging to her!"

"I'm ashamed to," Firsov simpered ironically, and covered his eyes with his torn sleeve. "It's night now . . . and all the people are probably sitting about half naked . . . and I've a wife, you know."

"Firsov, be sensible! You know you're as sober as a judge. Look, she's lit the little lamp . . . she won't go to sleep before she has suckled the child. . . ."

"Aha!" croaked the writer, and, with thievish curiosity, flattened his face against the window. "Now let's go into the matter. The dear little child is sucking at its mother's breast, and stretching out its little angel hand. . . . What is it holding in its hand? A lily? No, it's a piece of sausage. Or am I lying? I am not. And you, Mamselle, are as naïve as this poor cherub, in whose sickly body there isn't even room for doubt. And what is that standing on the little chest? A cooing dove? . . . No, it's a half-empty whisky bottle. . . ." He grinned wearily. "Life, my dear Mamselle, can't be reckoned up correctly without cooking the accounts a bit, and our mistake lies in this: that when we grapple with great things, we never take the human coefficient into consideration. All the confusion comes from that. . . ." Suddenly he recollected himself and pulled a face. "Excuse me, I'm chattering away, and I've forgotten a most important thing. You asked me to introduce you to Zinaida Petrovna Balduyeva (a remarkable woman: she should be painted . . . with a bunch of violets in her hand). I quite forgot about it. Oh, I wish these twenty-seven people had never been born in my confounded skull! I'll call for you the day after tomorrow, in the evening. . . ." As he took his leave, he gave her hand a friendly squeeze. "Don't be upset by the coefficient, Mamselle. It contains all the savor and glamor of life. Otherwise every lout would just drink up life to the dregs, and then put a bullet into his brain. . . . Because then his brain would ask for something beyond life. . . . No matter what happens, keep on living, Mamselle. A living human being is, after all, Nature's most beautiful creation."

A sharp retort was on the tip of Tanya's tongue, but she did not manage to utter it. Firsov's spectacles flashed eloquently; turning around, he hurried away. On the wet pavement the line of street lamps cast a glittering reflection like a string of glassy pearls. Leaning against a lamppost, Tanya looked after Firsov with a smile. The writer's sudden onslaught had relieved a little the cold pain at her heart.

Firsov had agreed to visit Zinka on Friday, but he spent the preceding day profitably, too. As soon as he wakened in the morning, he had a vivid picture of himself knocking loudly and smartly on Dolomanova's door at five o'clock. And so it turned out. It was the beginning of June, and by midday the air was glowing as if about to burst in flame. In the evening a brilliant fiery cloud appeared on the horizon; and from the fact that the hens were busy cleaning themselves by the fence and that a woman was taking down the washing from the line in the yard, one could deduce that a storm was not far off. Firsov knocked; he knocked again, and then kicked the door with his boot.

There was a sound of someone moving cautiously behind the door. Then a face, swollen with sleep, appeared in the narrow crack.

"Ah, the author!" said Donka, admitting Firsov and giving an affected cough, for it was only in front of Firsov that he felt no shame at being a flunky.

"Is Manka Fyodorovna at home?" asked Firsov somewhat dryly, and, without thinking, pressed his shabby hat into Donka's hand.

Donka silently escorted him through the cool darkness and opened the door into an ill-lit room that seemed to be full of tiny secrets. This impression was confirmed by the prevailing disorder.

"Are you asleep, my charmer?" asked Firsov, shutting the door firmly.

"Hullo, Firsov!" Dolomanova's voice came listlessly

from behind a screen. "Come in and amuse me! What's the news?"

She was lying on the sofa. Her Chinese dressing gown fell open a little in front as she sat up to put the book she had been reading on the table. Firsov winced, for it was the collection of amateurish stories which he had published before the war. Her dressing gown was rumpled up, and Firsov saw her stockinged legs and a suggestion of lingerie. Dolomanova was never embarrassed in his presence, and this exasperated him, but the intimacy of their friendship permitted them to be casual with each other. Firsov laughed and lowered his eyes in embarrassment.

"Well, how's your film work going?" he asked crossly, offering her a cigarette.

"I'm at it morning, noon, and night, and I'm bored stiff, Firsov!" she cried, suddenly laughing, and supporting herself on her elbows. "Our studio's looking for a bandit, Fedya, a specialist in arson and murder. . . . Will you take it on? You'll get paid: it's not for love. You'd do very well with your beard and all—what do you think? But you're such a queer creature! You're a famous author, aren't you? and yet you never wash or shave—I wish you'd tell me why."

"Don't mind me. Any other remarks you'd like to make? About my ulster, for instance? I don't dress for effect, I dress for decency, and, after all, I didn't invent the fig leaf!" And, with a theatrical gesture, he displayed his torn pockets, which shone with grease and looked as if a dustman had been warming his hands in them for a month.

"There, I'm making fun of you again!" she went on, drawing her black stocking tighter, "but, all the same, I'm very fond of you (that's why I've been studying your prewar work)—or rather, it's not you but your mind I'm so taken up with, so you needn't get conceited, Firsov. You're so full of ideas." Someone crept in noiselessly and hid behind the curtain. "That you, Donka?" said Dolomanova. "Well, run away and play till I call you. You needn't bother your head about this old fogy: he isn't Mitka." The next minute they heard soft footsteps and the angry creaking of the door. "I'm sure he's been writing poetry while I've been making you a declaration. He had a premonition that all wasn't as it should be. 'Lay your hand on my breast and tear my heart to tatters!'" she declaimed with ironic pathos, and laughed. "There's a whole pile of his poems from his army days over there on the windowsill. He's quite gone to pieces. . . . The awful thing about love," she said thoughtfully, "is that it puts you at other people's mercy, though actually most people enjoy being trampled on."

"Won't you pull down your dressing gown?" said Firsov in a pleading voice, frowning slightly, for the tobacco smoke had crept behind his glasses. "There's no need to expose your knee caps!"

"What's wrong with my knees?" asked Dolomanova sullenly, and in spite of the summer heat a wintry chill seemed to radiate from her eyes. She got up and stood regarding him coldly. He had fallen on his knees before her, his face twitching with passion. With one hand she firmly drew her dressing gown more tightly around her. She was afraid of Firsov's eyes.

"Stand up, Fedya. . . . I like you all the same," she murmured half in alarm, half in annoyance at his humiliating and senseless declaration. "Stand up . . . for you've got a brain, you're better than all of them."

His glasses were lying on the carpet beside his knees, and, marvellous to relate, remained uninjured to the end of his declaration. For the first time Dolomanova saw Firsov's short-sighted gray eyes; they had a glint of yellow in them and were honest rather than kind, yet they were his only attractive feature.

"Don't I mean anything to you, then? All these last six months I've been swearing I'd never come to you again, and yet here I am. You asked what I had to give you—but haven't I got power, too, of a kind? Yes, and more than all the others have—the power to create, power to embrace the world with my thoughts, and all the people in it. Your Mitka is in me, and many hundred Mitkas, past and to come, and the creative fire that flashes through my body is yours to have, yours alone. I cling to you as Mitka's sister clings to Zavarihin, because life is terrible to me without you. Listen to me, Manka, I implore you."

But his words were like a wave beating against a rock against which many waves have beaten.

"Look here, Firsov, pass me an orange, will you?" she said curtly. "There, on the table—a big one, please."

He staggered up. First of all he put on his spectacles, without which he always felt undressed, and then brought what she asked, looking inexpressibly foolish and humiliated.

"I'm thirsty," he said querulously.

She tore the orange in half and threw one half to Firsov, who turned away in embarrassment to cram it into his mouth and gulp it down.

"Looks like a storm," said Dolomanova. "I love sitting at a window in a storm, and I love to suck oranges, don't you?"

"Oh, I love oranges, too," he replied in the same tone, trying to conceal his mortification. "If I may inquire incidentally . . . what particular claim can Donka advance for residing in your rooms? The rights of love?" he asked, and wiped his hands, which were sticky with orange juice, on his pants.

"Not a question one asks, Fedya . . . especially after an unsuccessful declaration. By the way, you're writing about me in your book, aren't you? Well, if you ask me, it's not me you're in love with, but the other lady. . . ."

"What lady?" asked Firsov.

"The one in the book. Isn't that true, more or less?"

"After the sad demise of the late lamented Agey"—he choked down a more bitter retort—"you've become more subtle, Manka Fyodorovna: but I assure you that after you so ingeniously freed yourself from that somewhat incomprehensible attachment, I have positively made myself sick adoring you."

"Now you're in your element!" she said, laughing at Firsov's rage. "I'll give you some good advice, though: don't tease me with pin pricks. They're no use. Also you must never mention that name in my presence again, do you hear?"

She shut her eyes for an instant, as if she had suddenly grown tired. "What's the good of you? Why, even Donka here, if I said to him: 'Donka, fix up Firsov for me—take him for a ride! . . .'"

"Charming vocabulary! I congratulate you!" Firsov spluttered with rage. "My God! In the old days women like you were immured in convents. It's a disgrace that you should be allowed even to mix with respectable people."

She yawned and went to the window. An orange-red sunbeam broke through the bank of clouds, and fell through the window into the room, so that Firsov saw again through the thin fabric of her dressing gown the strong, supple lines of her limbs.

"Do you like thunder, you respectable citizen?" she asked, without turning around, but he did not answer; he was bitterly regretting his visit. Dolomanova did not repeat her question. "Is it true that Mitka's sister is leaving the circus? There was talk of taking her into our studio. Is she pretty?"

"Oh, quite," murmured Firsov, and began to take notes.

"Well, bring her along. I should like to meet her. What are you writing there?"

"Only something about a fool and a she-devil."

Dolomanova smiled. "Have you a child, or is this to be your first?"

In the stillness a cock crowed, apparently from boredom. The crow sounded as though it came out of the earth. Thunder rumbled not far off, preceded by a flash of lightning. A cold draft blew in through the window and puffed her dressing gown a little apart. It began to grow dark. Firsov hurriedly slipped his notebook into his pocket, and ran to the door. Dolomanova did not hold him back. For a long time he fumbled with the lock, he stormed and scratched his hands till they bled, and finally Donka came to his aid. They went together down the steps. The clouds were rent with thunder and lightning, and the cool July rain poured more torrentially through the torn clefts till the yard, with its foaming puddles, was like a big washtub. In a window, which gaped like an ugly mouth, a gramophone set up an outrageous braying, while in the sky the flat background of clouds grew blue, and the maple before Dolomanova's window saluted the cloven heavens majestically with arms upraised.

"I'll bet she's tormented the soul out of you, too,"

whispered Donka, blocking the writer's way. "And what has she done to me? I've become a flunky, and worse—a scoundrel. Has she kept you hanging around her for nothing, too?" Firsov's face writhed as if he had a toothache. "She said to me: 'Live there in the little room. You'll be able to help me in various ways!' Oh, I ask you, mate, where are my curly locks now? My hair's falling out, Fyodor Fyodorich. And I've torn out a good lot myself. I remember in Zvenigorod I met a girl I could have twisted around my little finger. But her there . . . what's one to say about her? I live in that little room like a pet pug." He sobbed, but no tears fell; he licked his lips greedily and looked past Firsov to the doorstep, as if he could see there the pitiable fate of the seducer who was seduced. "You sit there with her, and perhaps you stroke her breast . . . and I write away in my little cupboard. . . . No, listen to this poem of mine. . . . Perhaps I'll write it on her back with a knife."

"Oh, to hell with you, you damned fool!" Firsov cut short the unwholesome tirade and stepped straight into a puddle beside the steps.

He might have been completely drenched before he got to the gate, but July storms do not last long.

Zinka's name day was in the middle of October, but her birthday was in July, and on this day Firsov had invited guests, and the neighbors prepared presents. Chikelyov arrived from the office with a large bag of red currants, but when he opened the door, he let out a groan of dismay, for Manyukin's behavior had positively passed all bounds.

On the floor Sergey Ammonich half lay, half sat, in an exceedingly undressed condition, cleaning the stains on his ragged suit and, what particularly outraged Chikelyov, singing as he did so. A little bottle and a glass of water stood beside him, and from time to time he sprinkled the spots with them.

"What are you cleaning that with, your excellency?" asked Chikelyov, sniffing and squinting at Manyukin's outspread garments.

"With spirits of ammonia, your serene highness!" Manyukin, flushed with enthusiasm, raised his perspiring face. "And, in places, with the needle."

"Well, and what's to happen if someone comes to see me?"

"Who should come? You haven't any relations."

"Well, and if a taxpayer who's behind with the cash should come to me to bribe me? . . ." Chikelyov grew warm. "Shouldn't I stamp my feet then, and fling him out and insult him? . . . Shouldn't I do that?"

"You should, your grace!" agreed Manyukin pacifically, and busied himself once more with the stains. "Even the law enjoins you to." He raised his finger reverently.

"But where is there room for me to do it? How can I stamp my foot if the room reeks of spirits of ammonia, and a naked man is lying on the floor?"

"I'm sitting, Pyotr Gorbidonich, I'm not lying," retorted Manyukin, stammeringly but logically.

"You'll regret this, your excellency!" screamed Chikelyov, turning away.

The rest of the preparations went off without a hitch. The wife of the unemployed Bundyukov baked appetizing cakes, and the fragrant smell streamed through the passage into the street. Even in the eddying clouds of dust raised by the evening wind one could still follow this mawkish stream with one's nose. Nikolka fell in with it on his way to the party. He was alone, for Tanya had gone on ahead with Firsov, and the sweet smell quickly put him into a holiday mood, for he was extremely fond of any kind of a spree. He walked with a cheerful, firm step, as if the whole world were asleep and only his boots, which had stolen a march on it, were up and doing. He walked . . . and, exactly as he had done ten months before, he suddenly stopped dead as if he were stunned.

The woman in the black dress, the same one who had tricked him on the platform, but more proud and stately now, passed just before him through the door. Scarcely had her steps echoed down the darkness of the entrance passage than Zavarihin rushed in after her; he had found again what he had lost, and had no intention of letting her escape him a second time. She could have taken warning at the scraping of his soles, and easily saved herself from pursuit, but he came up with her on the stairs. Panting heavily, he blocked her way and looked at her with eyes narrowed, as if he were aiming a shaft at her guilty head, but he did not venture to say a word.

In the dull light of the staircase window he saw her questioning smile, which was indulgent rather than angry. He had already forgiven her everything, and only wanted to hear again the voice that had bewitched him.

"What is the number of this house?" he said hastily, passing his hand awkwardly across his forehead. She made no reply. Nikolka edged still closer to her. "You . . . are you the same . . . or her sister?" he whispered, feverish with excitement.

"Sorry, no relation, I'm afraid!" smiled Dolomanova, and passed on—but it seemed to Nikolka that she passed through him, and he had not the strength to stop her. He wandered up and down the staircase in a stupor until he caught the sound of lively voices through an open door. He was too exhausted even to show surprise when he saw her at Zinka's table, where she drew upon herself the universal attention of the company. (Zinka had just handed her a cup of tea, and Zavarihin saw how her hands quivered and the tips of her ears glowed.) He did not hear Firsov's facetious introduction of her to the other guests. He looked at her, but did not recognize her.

"She's the same and yet different. The other one I pitied, but this one—it would be nice to carry her away somewhere quiet with her arms tied behind her back," thought Nikolka as he looked at the Bundyukovs' cracknels, which resembled plump, twisted female arms. "Would she allow it?" he said almost aloud, and, in his embarrassment, took a handful of red currants and ate them, biting off the separate berries with his teeth. The big bowl with the red currants—Chikelyov's present—stood under the lamp, where their ruby hue gave no hint of their astringent taste.

"I've never heard Mitka tell a lie," said Tanya defiantly. (She had already been speaking, but Zavarihin only caught the conversation now.) "Mitka is an honorable and good and open-hearted man . . . and that's what he'll remain, whatever becomes of him. And this is the last place I should have expected to hear anything different . . ." She emphasized the last words, and flung a burning glance at Firsov, who backed her up with an embarrassed nod. (Zinka sat at the corner of the table, pale-cheeked under the full glare of the light, and followed the conversation trembling with excitement.) Tanya was agitated and could not find words strong and sharp enough with which to vindicate her brother. A soft curl fell across her eye and obscured her sight, but she did not notice it. (Nikolka was the whole time alternately exasperated and tormented by the conflict in her face, until at last the mystery became clear to him.) "I'm not asking you to worship Mitka. . . . Nowadays one has to put up with what one gets.

. . . I was only asking for a little justice toward a human being."

"And have you known your brother for a long time?" asked Dolomanova in a strange voice and without a trace of mockery. "When I said that your brother could hardly be called generous, I was thinking of something you know nothing about. Mitka's life has been rather—well, eventful!" (She tapped the tumbler carelessly with her fingers.) "You don't wish to say though, do you, that such a sister as you can't have a bad brother?"

"I was twelve years old when I left home. . . . I met my brother for the first time this winter," said Tanya, with dry lips. She realized that Dolomanova had some private knowledge of Mitka which entitled her to speak of him in this way. She looked restlessly around at the guests. Zinka was pulling at the fringes of the tablecloth, Firsov was biting his nails, and Chikelyov was alternately jumping up and sitting down. Tanya caught a malevolent glance from Nikolka, and grew more and more embarrassed. "Perhaps," she added shyly, "you mean that Mitka is a thief—but I've known that for a long time. People like telling tales about each other, but I thought you were going to tell me something bad about my brother which I didn't know already."

"No, that wasn't what I meant," said Dolomanova patronizingly.

"If Manka Fyodorovna knows anything, then it can only be from hearsay," remarked Zinka, flushing.

"Not only from hearsay," Dolomanova smiled, and allowed a cruel pause to elapse. "We're friends from childhood . . . that's to say, Mitka and I used to play games together as children. Then life parted us, and each of us went on with his own game. If you insist on it, I can tell you what I was hinting at . . ." She threw Tanya a friendly smile. Tanya flushed under her smooth insolence.

Then Nikolka stepped up to Tanya and asked her in a whisper what had happened to her eye.

"Oh, Nikolushka, I'm almost blind in this eye, it was injured by a whip," she exclaimed impatiently, disregarding her lover's curt, strange laugh. Then, going to Dolomanova, she touched her hand beseechingly. Her face

twitched. "You'll tell me later . . . between ourselves,
just me . . . about my brother . . . not in front of
everyone . . . or if you like I'll come and see you." In
her hurried words there was a prayer for mercy and
silence.

"And I should personally be obliged if you would tell
us all about him now," cried Chikelyov loudly and dic-
tatorially. "As chairman of the lodgers' committee, I'm
curious to learn the truth about one of the lodgers. Please
don't stint the colors."

Then Firsov resolved on a daring step. From several
symptoms he distrusted Dolomanova's outward composure.

"Mamselle," he began, "there is no need for you to be
afraid. Set your mind at ease . . . all of us here are fond
of your brother."

"With certain exceptions," screamed Chikelyov defiantly.

"I was only thinking of human beings at the moment,"
Firsov flung at him. "Your brother hasn't left the city, as
I told you yesterday, he's in the prison hospital. That's
always the way: the higher a man rises the more painful
is his fall." Firsov spoke with an effort, as if the words
stuck in his throat. "But which of us got through the revolution without some stain on his character, or even carried
on to the end cheerfully?"

"Here, just go on with what you're saying, citizen!"
Chikelyov leaped up excitedly and banged his fist so heavily on the table that the glasses rang. "I myself, and that's
a case in point, have been struggling for a long time to get
to the bottom of this fellow, but I couldn't lay my hand
on anything definite. Creatures like that ought to be
hanged, they ought to be turned into soap. Speak! I demand it in the name of justice."

"He doesn't pretend to be anything he isn't," Firsov
went on speaking. "But . . . in our days a thief, or 'bear
gutter,' in the language of this charming lady, who herself—"

"Firsov!" said Dolomanova severely, her voice raised,
and Firsov immediately sat down and passed his hand
across his sweating face. He looked at her reproachfully

like a cowed beast, and Nikolka's eyes shone with joy at Dolomanova's victory. "Why have you got up this scene? Why did you invite us all for the same evening?" (The Bundyukovs slipped unobtrusively out of the room. It was because of their congenital terror of noise that these peaceful people had brought no children into the world.) "You'd better have stayed at home in your armchair thinking out justifications for Mitka's 'exploits,' to give them a pretty name. You know quite well that Mitka's more than a thief: you told me the plot of your book yourself. Have you forgotten what happened to the man at the front? I was going to mention that, but I was interrupted. I was also going to say that he's not responsible, he's a . . . sick man."

They all hated her, not so much on account of her words, but because of her frozen and fearless beauty. Nikolka fidgeted uneasily in his chair, ready for any crass stupidity, and, casting a glance at Tanya, saw that she was crying. He pressed her close to him, and whispered to her: "Don't worry, poor little One Eye!" But she felt his pity like an equivocal insult.

"I'm sorry, I've spilled my tea!" Dolomanova broke the silence by turning to her hostess and standing up. None of them could shake off their embarrassment. Firsov unconsciously crushed a bunch of berries in his hand, and then confusedly wiped it in his pocket handkerchief. Dolomanova glanced again at Tanya, who was leaning toward her as a scorched twig leans toward the fire, and went to the door. "Don't you offer up rather too many victims to your wretched novel?" she said meaningly to Firsov from the doorstep, and went out. She did not catch the coarse insult that Zinka, half beside herself, flung after her, for she was already walking down the stairs.

The cause of the scandal lay, strangely enough, in words that had not been uttered. Zinka stopped screaming. Powerless to thrust aside the bitter cup that Dolomanova had passed her, she gasped for breath; she could only open and shut her mouth like a huge fish on a sandy beach. Klavdya, who had come out of Chikelyov's room in nothing but her chemise, embraced her mother's knees and silently shook her, as though imploring her to be calm.

"I see it was the devil led me here, Zinochka!" said the old woman in the corner, who up to this time had done nothing but sip her niece's thin tea in silence. They all looked at her in amazement.

"No, CITIZENS!" Chikelyov bestirred himself and flung a sharp glance at the old woman, of whose existence a moment before he had not had an inkling. "It can't go on like this! Noise is forbidden in this life: as chairman of the lodgers' committee, with an intimate knowledge of all the regulations, I can assure you of that. Now I propose we close the meeting, and open it again as if nothing had happened. The motion is before the meeting that tea be drunk: please raise your hands."

"Might I have half a cup?" said the unemployed Bundyukov politely, for he had crept into the room again.

"No, excuse me, please!" said Chikelyov. "You must ask someone else. There are so many ladies present, it's a case in point, that I feel entitled to disappear for a moment. I've got a surprise!" he shouted. "I'll soon restore your spirits with a surprise!" Then he went out of the room. During his short absence not a word was spoken. He did not, however, keep them waiting long, for he soon came back, with the air of a thief. He had his remarkable secret hidden under his jacket.

Pyotr Gorbidonich went to his place at the table, looked around him mysteriously, made a gesture with his hand, and again concealed the object, which Nikolka noted with disappointment was a fat exercise book bound in oilcloth. Pyotr Gorbidonich knew how to work on the nerves of his fellow men when he had the upper hand.

"A book!" exclaimed Zavarihin loudly; and while he stroked Tanya's hand, in his thoughts he christened her with the name of Dolomanova, who had just gone from him forever.

"All books are written from evil motives," observed Bundyukov politely.

"This is only an exercise book"—Chikelyov blinked slyly. "And yet what type of an exercise book is it? Is it a simple account book? Perhaps it isn't such an insignificant little book after all . . . with its eighty-five numbered pages? No, I reply: it's very entertaining reading matter . . . it's the diary of a one-time landowner. It is, if you please, a secret which no one must know. . . . The surprise is that you will have to guess the name for yourselves." Chikelyov wriggled with pleasure like a child.

"What are you going to do, Pyotr Gorbidonich?" asked Zinka timidly. (She blushed when she remembered how beautiful she usually looked in moments of distress.)

"I want to entertain your guests," he answered, swaying on his heels. He felt so completely at home that he almost started to pick his nose. "There are the most extraordinarily interesting things here . . . about beggary, about Russia, and so on. Real philosophy!" Bundyukov gave a sycophantic smile. "Just a moment . . . the bit I wanted was somewhere here, I think. I got interested in the matter once when he had forgotten to lock the drawer. . . . Devil take it! . . . there's the page with the ink stain on it. . . . I can't find the other one; I marked it with my fingernail . . ." he muttered, fluttering through the familiar pages. "Yes, yes, here it is!"

For the last time he appealed to them to be quiet, trying to elicit some sign of interest, even if it were only an unguarded smile. But no one looked at him except Firsov, who stared at him through his dark spectacles, and, with an effort, repressed his indignation.

"Why do you look at me like that . . . so angrily?" He scanned Firsov impertinently with a sharp glance, and cautiously covered his exercise book with his hand. "In the future state, which will come in a thousand years, there will be no secrets. Anyone, please note this, will go to anyone else you like, at any hour of the day or night you choose, and personally inspect his life through a magnifying glass. The other man may be entertaining the idea of destroying the whole human race, for with the progress in science, death rays, tear gas, and so forth . . . one can blow up the globe before you can say 'knife.' Each little man will be kept under observation, he won't be allowed to run around without control. There will be no secrets, but: 'Oblige me, citizen, by exhibiting here publicly in the town square your breathing apparatus!' Then everyone will be forced to be honest. Whether you want to or not, you'll have to put up with it. If I was, let us say, the president of the globe, I would have a machine put on everyone's head, a machine with a ribbon, like in a telegraph office. Every morning a specially appointed clerk would have to read off the ribbon and enter up his conclusions . . . and in the same way one could look into his skull, too. . . . Thought, that is the cause of suffering. The man who can eradicate thought will be held in everlasting remembrance by a grateful mankind. . . . Why do you look at me like that? Do you think you'll frighten me and make me cry?"

"What has a sneak like you got to cry for, except when your dirty schemes don't come off?" said Firsov, quivering, and he went to the window, followed by the disapproval of the company.

"Keep your tongue under control, citizen!" Chikelyov shouted after him, and fluttered nervously through the book. "Listen instead . . . perhaps you'll hear something that will do for an article."

Outside the window the leaves of the poplar tree billowed and glistened moistly, and from the station near by there came the long-drawn scream of the engines, sad as eternal farewells. Down below, someone shuffled in and then shuffled out again to some unknown destination.

In a voice that sounded like the smack of a wet rag, Chikelyov began to read from the mysterious exercise book. Nobody interrupted him. Everyone was thinking about Dolomanova's dark insinuations, which had never been explained: only Bundyukov waited patiently for an opportunity to laugh, and looked at Pyotr Gorbidonich's mouth. Zinka's aunt breathed noisily; she was apparently making ready to go to sleep. With a feeling of disgust Firsov leaned out of the window, as Mitka was to do many months later, but even there Chikelyov's exasperating voice reached him.

"It is no humiliation for me, Nikolasha, to have to stand in the street with outstretched hand. It wasn't out of weakness that I decided on this easy and degrading means of earning a livelihood. And yet I'll admit (why should I tell a lie? Won't I soon be dead and buried?) that I bought myself a few days ago a tiny punnet of fresh strawberries. There were four in it. I went through the streets of Moscow, ate them under everyone's eyes, and spat out the stalks onto the snow. . . . I did not buy them because I wanted to recover my dignity, but because I had such a craving for strawberries that I could have cried. Old people and pregnant women resemble each other: both are carriers of human disease. Once I was offered a job at making slippers, they said it wasn't difficult. Judge me if you like, but I refused the work, although as a joke I had a shot at it. I couldn't get the needle through the felt, and that was the end of it. I pushed it, but it wouldn't go through: there was nothing to do but hammer it through with a stone. . . ."

At this point Chikelyov stopped, and skipped a few lines. Bundyukov laughed, and Nikolka shook his head.

". . . So then, my dear Nikolasha, my status was a beggar's. With the confusion in my brain, how could I possibly do myself justice in my storytelling? I reduced my fee to twenty kopeks, then I brought it down to ten. . . . I even sank to reproducing the Old Testament stories in a comic form. Once I fell among coachmen, Old Believers, and barely escaped with my life. If you should ever have to stand at street corners, as your father has to, never lose heart, my little angel! I can bequeath you neither bank notes, nor Caucasian estates, nor stout peasantry, nor your grandfather's portrait to cheer you: but I can give you a piece of well-seasoned advice. If you stand at a street corner, do not stretch out your hand like a turnpike, but keep it on your belly, keep it on your belly, Nikolasha! You mustn't tremble or whine: today people have stopped believing in whines or death rattles. No, be honest, open your modest eyes wide, and stand calmly as if you were enjoying the evening air. They will give you alms out of charity. Nothing can kill this reactionary virtue, for men will always have pity for others and indulgence for themselves. Try it, humble yourself only once, and then it will be as smooth as butter, you'll like it immensely.

"Think out some amusing way to behave—as amusing as possible. For instance, lately I applied to a man who had the stamp of a bureaucrat all over him: 'Comrade monarchist, lend me ten kopeks till the restoration of the fatherland.' And he was so pleased, he gave me a rouble right off. With a father's love I bequeath you these hints on conduct so that you may hold high the honor of the Manyukin family."

The listeners were more than a little surprised that that merry fellow, that reckless old drunkard, Manyukin, was capable of scribbling such a lot of gloomy stuff. But all of them, except Tanya, laughed. "I've made new acquaintances, too, in the gutter. On my left stands a beggar with a military past, the blind Sergey Sergeyich. He is really blind. I once actually tried, between ourselves, to test him, and let some coins drop near him. On my right stands a lady of fifty. Imagine, she is the cousin of Alexander Ivanich Agarin! She is a flighty lady, who in the heyday of her youth was once in love with me, sought out every opportunity of meeting me, and even wanted to fling herself into the Kudema when I married your mother; she didn't throw herself in, and to this day she regrets it. After the revolution she was set to doing up parcels, and then to a lot of other things . . . and then to parcels again. But she couldn't get used to working, so she was thrown out, and took her stand at the street corner, but in a hat, and on this hat—just imagine the elegance—a bedraggled little bird! Then next I met another man in the street. He wore a Turkish coat, and earned money with his beard (people gave him alms on account of its length). And who should it be but General Tolstopaltsev himself (the aide-de-camp in Petersburg who was always yearning for Europe, and posing as a liberal). I addressed him, but then I recollected how once, at a public dinner party, he let off a fine one: it sounded like the report of a gun (it was an election day, and there were three hundred people present, just imagine!), so I began to laugh. I've grown short of laughing matter now, and so coarse, my little angel. I'm not in a position now to give myself airs. 'Even a cherub won't come out of a puddle clean'—that's what my roommate says of himself, Pyotr Gor—"

"That's a lie, I never said anything of the kind," commented Chikelyov, and he skipped two pages.

"Don't you pay any attention to him!" said Bundyukov consolingly. "The main thing is to hold one's head up. Remember the saying: 'Mud doesn't stick to an honest man.' "

"Do you say that this man has been dead a long time?" asked Tanya softly, and all of them heard the quiver in her voice.

"That's just it, citizen . . . He's still alive, and nosing around somewhere!" cried Chikelyov with rising enthusiasm. "After his death we'll put the manuscript into the archives, but now we want to enjoy it. And all this psychology! He's out to tell our authors what's what," Chikelyov flung in Firsov's direction. "Yet it's all seriously meant. . . . It's quite indifferent to him, of course, but a great many interesting reflections on Vekshin occurred to me while reading. By God! I ought to take up Pinkerton's profession. I hold all the threads relating to this case in my hand, but I may add that the said Dmitri Vekshin is not simply a Vekshin . . ." He broke off and put one finger to his forehead, which shone with sweat. "Answer me, citizen, as a friend of your brother's. . . . Your home is somewhere on the Kudema? Aha! And wasn't the property of the landowner Manyukin in the neighborhood?"

"Why do you torment me?" exclaimed Tanya, and tore herself free from Nikolka's arm. "Say straight out what you mean, you vile creature!"

"Just a moment's patience and I'll submit all my conclusions to you," said Chikelyov with noble forbearance, pressing his hand to his heart. "You have just tried to defend him (as if he were your blood brother) . . . I confess I was greatly touched, but actually the circumstances are quite different. . . . I was just about to explain them." Carried away by his eloquence, he came closer to her and pressed her hand, which lay feebly on her knees. "Let's suppose that the property is adjacent. . . . We know these properties well enough! There's a garden there . . . all kinds of birds. . . . The nightingales warble (they stuff themselves chock full with flies and then, out of sheer lack of occupation, start to sing away). . . . The air is very good, first class: please note that! And all this has a powerful effect on a young man who is married to an invalid wife. . . . And then—now this is typical—there appears in seductive guise, like a heavenly vision, a woman who begins to scrub the floors."

These insinuations would have gone on longer if they had not been interrupted by an unexpected incident. Suddenly in the passage there was a loud hubbub, and the door slowly opened. They all got up in tense expectation of some important occurrence. Zinka's aunt, roused by the sudden silence, cried out and crossed herself. Chikelyov raised his arm.

"There you are . . . I said so . . . it's what I told you!" he exclaimed triumphantly.

A FEW minutes before, through the fog, Firsov had been able dimly to distinguish two figures on the pavement, strolling slowly in the direction of the house. In the murky light it looked as if below him a compact four-legged mass were advancing.

"I can't think why I don't dislike you," said a voice that reverberated flatly in the fog.

"It's instinct, that's what it is," returned the other voice cheerfully. "And besides, we're relations, though distant ones." The first voice made no reply, and the second went on: "All men are related to each other, only they're ashamed of each other. They pose as strangers . . . and one injures the other . . . in the name of justice. . . ."

The men passed by, and Firsov closed the window; as he did so, he noticed with annoyance that Klavdya was still sitting at Zinka's feet in nothing but her chemise. A few moments later he understood the real meaning of the conversation he had overheard. Behind Chikelyov's back Zinka signed urgently to Tanya not to believe the ingenious theories of the chairman of the lodgers' committee. Tanya's face was pale, her eyes glittered, and Firsov had already stretched out his hand to Chikelyov's shoulder to stop her martyrdom, when the door opened, and the mass he had seen through the window rolled in.

It was Manyukin, very much the worse for liquor, his face aglow with happiness. He was soaked through, and his clothes were in the greatest disorder. He was leaning amicably and securely on the arm of Dmitri Vekshin, who helped the old man more or less to keep his balance. Vekshin had on his sumptuous fur coat, but it was already shabby and torn in places and stained on the sleeves with lime. They stood still, holding on to each other, and there was something frightening in Mitka's deep, clear gaze, which stamped itself forever on Tanya's mind.

"The twin stars," stammered Manyukin, and bowed, "greet the single stars." As he spoke he slapped Mitka on the chest, and then slapped himself on his worn two-buttoned waistcoat. "Well, here we are! We've come to the party, too, and on the wings of an adventure. I've just been chucked out of a beer hall with a kick on the seat. . . . Up I flew, and thought I was flying to certain death, but suddenly I struck on something wet and soft, and hung on to it. I hung there in a perilous position, and then slowly began to slip down. 'Now,' thought I, 'this man will give me what-for, too, for I've probably dirtied him.' And I even made a guess where he would hit me—on the back?—there's enough fat there. On the skull?—there's nothing but bones there. . . . 'Well,' I thought, 'supposing he gave me one on the belly?' . . . I raised my eyes in terror, and whom should I see in the darkness of the gloomy night . . . but him? There he stood in his fur, musing in the rain. 'Dmitri,' I cried to him, 'Dmitri Yegorich, Prince of Denmark . . . help poor Lear to get up!'" Firsov pushed a chair to him and he sat down.

They passed a chair to Mitka, too, but he walked around, greeting all the guests except Chikelyov. He was silent and kept his head bowed. But when he got to Nikolka, he stood still, and, holding Nikolka fast by the hand, fixed his eyes on the point on his forehead where the hair began: he remembered their previous meeting.

"This is my fiancé. I want you to know each other," said Tanya excitedly, pressing her lips together. "I'm soon going to be Madame Zavarihina." She wanted to give this information a jesting turn, but her brother was silent, as if he had set his face against her resolve in advance. He stood by the table, a look of sickly abstraction in his eyes. Manyukin still sat as if there were a wall in front of him through which strangers' eyes could not pierce, and his red fingers tapped nervously on his knees.

"Sergey Ammonich—would you like some currants?" asked Zinka.

"The currants are excellent," put in Bundyukov, with his mouth full and his face screwed up, "but they leave rather a wry taste on the tongue."

"I bought the currants myself," flashed back Chikelyov sharply. "Of course their flavor is tart, but what led you to consider that it leaves a wry taste?"

"Did I say that? Really?" said Bundyukov in alarm. "But I said just the opposite. . . ." He caught Mitka's eye and became still more confused.

Mitka looked lean and pale, but well-washed and clean-shaven; he sat upright and scarcely touched the plate that Zinka handed to him. He was far removed in spirit from all that was happening; now and then he raised his head and stared indifferently at something or other. Tanya tried to lead him into conversation and asked him about his prison life; she turned to him with special tenderness because she knew that stories were being circulated about him, but her efforts were of no avail against his monosyllabic answers and his inattentive nods. Then, suddenly disregarding Tanya, he turned to Manyukin and suggested they should have some soup together.

Roused from his coma, Manyukin turned around irresolutely, and stammered: "Good: I'll ladle out a small plateful. . . . I've drunk enough today, but I haven't managed to get anything to eat. See, my pulse has stopped again . . . but that will pass. It's really extraordinary, that man over there, the author fellow, told me lately that my eyes weren't the same size, and then I said to him: '*Your* eyes seem to be rather at cross purposes, too, Fyodor Fyodorich. . . .' Nowadays everything's at cross purposes. . . . Don't be cross with me, Pyotr Gorbidonich. . . . I'll pay you my rent, all right. I haven't drunk today at my own expense, you see. Some absconding clerks, about five of them, treated me. It's extraordinary, the tipsy feeling's gone, but I've got an awfully done feeling, as if someone had beaten me. Did someone hit me over the head today, little brother? . . . I don't think so. . . . They didn't have any use for me, although I did several parlor tricks, and even lay on my belly and crawled around

. . . very entertaining, they said. . . . I'll show you how I did it . . ." and he slowly got up from his chair.

"Oh, hell! it makes one ill even to look at you," said Firsov sharply, and he scowled. "You treat us as if we were cads who wanted to humble you: it's damned insulting. You're being entertained, you're being given tea and cakes, and you . . . God knows what you've sunk to!"

"Why's it insulting?" exclaimed Manyukin in surprise. His voice quivered, and he thrust out his underlip. "Excuse me! If I made a show of myself before those swine, why can't I before friends? It's you who are insulting an old man!"

All the same, he did not try to lie on the floor, but shuffled his feet where he stood, and looked at Chikelyov, who laughed heartily at the antics of his drunken friend.

Actually Manyukin was not looking at Chikelyov but at his elbow, and even that was not what he was actually looking at, as it turned out in a moment. For he went up to the table quite close to Chikelyov, and then they noticed that he was not by any means as drunk as he pretended to be.

"Have you read it?" he inquired with exaggerated cheerfulness, and the muscles of his face began to twitch in rivalry, but the one half could not catch up with the other.

Chikelyov at first did not understand what Manyukin was asking him.

"Certainly, certainly: we've read a great deal out loud. . . . I've always been curious—that's typical—so I got hold of the manuscript privately, and looked into it . . . as chairman of the lodgers' committee. . . . And I must openly confess I had expected nothing of the kind! You've risen very high in my estimation. . . . That style! . . . What a style, by Jove! And it's amusing, too, how the words flow on, as you read them . . . like in a newspaper. And with gifts like yours, do you really lower yourself to roll about on the floor? What a disgrace!"

"I'm exceedingly grateful . . . your excellency," smiled Manyukin, rubbing his bald head, as if it had been overwhelmed with disgrace.

"Only, in places, a lot of it ought to be improved . . .

it shouldn't all be in such a gloomy note: it ought to be a little brighter. If I were in authority I should order all authors to describe life from its cheerful side, for everyone ought to laugh. I would even impose laughter on the whole globe, under penalty of being torn to pieces by wild beasts if you disobeyed. I read once in a newspaper that in America people treat despondency with castor oil and electricity: the first outwardly, the second inwardly . . . that's to say, if you'll excuse me, the other way about. A contact is established inside the body . . . and so a cheerful mood ensues."

"The bit about Tolstopaltsev is really rich . . . it's enough to make one crack one's sides," commented Bundyukov helpfully, delighted that everything was passing off so easily.

"And I should like to give you just one more piece of advice. You should collect a few more stories like that . . . from the lives of generals and counts and bishops, and bring out a little book for purposes of propaganda. You'd get very well paid . . ."

"Quite . . . quite . . ." stammered Manyukin. His face was covered with shame as he stretched out his hand for the manuscript. "Will you give it to me, please?"

"A moment. . . . Your Nikolasha there seems to be a cute one, what? You've let us see all the ins and outs of him all right. Wait a moment, I'll show you the place. . . ."

"Give it to me, I'll find it myself," said Manyukin, his face blotchy with terror, and there was a dead silence.

"No, keep your seat, please, keep your seat!"

"But—"

"No, certainly not!" said Chikelyov. But, looking around, he saw Firsov coming toward him, and immediately clasped the manuscript to his breast.

Tanya had never yet seen Chikelyov so pleased with life and so abominable.

"Sergey Ammonich," said Firsov distinctly and politely, "don't you think it would be really satisfying to give a cad a black eye?"

"Oh, impossible!" answered Manyukin in his most matter-of-fact tones. "In the first place, my dear chap, he's stronger than I am. In the second place, it would be a disgrace for me to wrangle with him, Fyodor Fyodorich. I'm an old man . . . and in spite of everything a nobleman," he confessed with a laugh.

"Well, I come of a humble stock, so I'll have a try," said Firsov in a fury, and launched his hand clumsily through the air.

There was no sound, and the writer seemed to have missed his mark; nevertheless, he had soundlessly and unerringly caught Chikelyov exactly on the jaw. Then, scarlet in the face, Firsov went into the front room, and, in his excitement, even forgot to take his leave of the company.

"Oh, re—eally?" called Pyotr Gorbidonich after him with poisonous politeness when he had recovered from his momentary shock. "Would you like to try it again, perhaps? Just try it, will you? . . . and I'll ask you all to look on and pay attention." He looked around for the Bundyukovs, but they had already withdrawn into their rooms.

The other guests left, too, and when Zinka went into the front room, there was nobody there. On the staircase Tanya asked Firsov what it all meant.

"That was the coefficient at work, Mamselle," Firsov snapped back in the darkness, but to tell the truth he was not particularly troubled by remorse.

NEXT morning the events of the previous day seemed, to those who had taken part in them, nothing but a bad dream that had left a heavy head and a feeling of nausea. Before Pyotr Gorbidonich left for the office he visited Zinka twice to ask her in confidence whether Firsov's conduct had been so insulting that a legal action should be brought. His line of thought was as follows: he had been struck, but not knocked out; he had only had to put some iodine on the scratch. Neither the Bundyukovs nor Zinka would dare to spread the story further: Zinka would be all the less likely to do so because of the fact that Mitka had spent the night in her room, his own having been taken over for another purpose during his absence; and Chikelyov was, after all, in a certain sense, a kind of guardian of morals. One could settle the matter by a duel, and put a bullet through the cad's head—but dueling was forbidden. And, after all, what did it matter getting a smack on the head? The chairman of the lodgers' committee wasn't a people's commissar. No one would be dismissed from the service because he got a cuff on the head. It was wiser to have no enemies, for without enemies one could hop around like a sparrow, giving pleasure to everyone, and no one would think of throwing a stone. In a word, Chikelyov was in a desperate panic.

Zinka got up early, tidied her room, and went to the market before Mitka was awake. After she had cut the remnants of yesterday's baking for breakfast, she went into the kitchen. Her little daughter was absorbed with the cat and, when Mitka opened his eyes, was trying to tie one of its paws to its tail with the pink chocolate-box ribbon off Chikelyov's liqueur bonbons. His awakening was heavy, the numbness of sleep giving place to the numbness of reality. The weather was splendid, for the morning wind had swept the skies clean and brought gaiety and freshness to the little strip of grass which could be seen through the window. A heavier fragrance streamed from the poplars. It was not hot; the sun stood so still that it seemed fixed to its place.

"Can't you manage it?" Mitka asked the child, whose frock was like a little gay patch of red light moving about on the floor.

"The stwing's too short," said the little girl unsociably, and let the cat go. It immediately darted behind the door, taking the precious little ribbon with it. "Come back, I want to take off the wibbon," whispered the child. She did not run after the cat, though, but stood by the window and looked at Mitka putting on his tight boots. "I know who you are," she said gravely.

"Who am I, then?" asked Mitka, raising his head.

"You're a thief," said the child gravely. "Are you going to be my daddy now? She's bought you a bed, and Uncle Matvey slept on the chest." Klavdya was silent for a moment. "Mama is good . . . she's fat . . . you won't hit Mama, will you? My other daddy hit her always and said she was a . . ." The child used a foul word, which sounded strange on her lips.

"Run away, child," said Mitka indifferently, and stood up. Once more the dull veil of yesterday blotted out from him the sun-washed morning sky. Zinka brought coffee, but he refused it. From the chest of drawers he took the linen cap her first husband had left behind, and stood for a moment in the middle of the room without answering Zinka's voluble stream of questions and complaints. He seemed changed; his gaze was strangely clear and thoughtful, suggesting alarming and hidden potentialities. Then he quietly opened the door into the passage, as though hesitating whether to leave the house or not.

He wandered about the whole day. First he went to Sanka, who, he had learned in prison, lived at the opposite end of the town. He found his door in the basement of a dirty alley. Three rotten steps led up to it. "A. Babkin, Maker of Wooden Lasts. Customers' material may also be employed," stood on a tin plate fixed in with three-inch nails. Underneath it was pinned a scrap of paper announcing the inventory of a sale on account of change of address. The humble household furniture was precisely numbered and catalogued: a kitchen table, a card table (with three legs), a mincing machine, a balalaika. . . . Number eight comprised two aluminum saucepans; under nine was written the sentence: "Inquire within." With a wry smile and stifling his inward agitation, Mitka opened the door and entered.

An unglazed window dimly lit up the damp walls. In the corner of the lobby dusty pots stood on a shelf, and underneath them logs of wood, from which Sanka earned his daily bread, lay piled up against the wall. The room behind the door would have been uninhabitable had there not been traces there of an industrious woman's hand. All the same, it was some time before one could get used to the fetid vapors of the damp masonry, to the dim greenish light, and the oppressive stillness of the cellar. In front of the single window hung a patterned muslin curtain, and from the ceiling hung a bird cage, but during Mitka's visit he heard no sound from it. There was also a cactus plant, a pathetic little abortion under a glass, and on a splinter of wood, which had split off from the veneered wood of the chest of drawers, a key hung naïvely. Near the chest of drawers sat a woman sewing, ingeniously using the light reflected from the whitewashed wall of the house next door.

"Is Babkin at home?" asked Mitka shortly. When he noticed the woman's terrified look, he took off his cap, but even then he did not greet her.

"What a fright you gave me!" said the woman shyly, pressing her hand to her heart. Her solitary, precious possession, her shy, bright smile stamped itself on his mind. "Shura isn't at home: he's with a customer, but he'll be back soon. Take a seat. Have you come from Lozhkin about the goods?"

"No, I've come on my own account," Mitka answered sullenly. He sat down on a stool and took a cigarette from his pocket.

The woman became agitated. "Please don't smoke

here," she pleaded, with a propitiatory smile. "My lung isn't quite right yet, and the window's tight shut. We don't open the door ever, either, for in the hot weather there's such a strong smell from the cesspool. We only air the room in the evening."

"All right, I won't," and, without knowing why, Mitka blushed. Then he took up a pair of scissors and looked at them attentively. "Probably it's that woman he picked up on the boulevard . . . she's frightened of me," he thought. He jerked up his head. "What did you say?"

"Are you one of Shura's . . . old friends?" she ventured to ask, gazing ingratiatingly at Mitka's shiny boots.

"I'm Vekshin, Dmitri Vekshin . . . perhaps he's told you about me?" he answered. He spoke his name with emphasis and hid his boots under the stool.

"Vekshin, did you say? . . . No, he never mentioned that name. . . ." She bent again self-consciously over her work.

Mitka went to the chest of drawers, and looked at the photographs pinned on to the wall. In the middle hung an old portrait, spotted with age, of a distinguished old gentleman in a braided uniform with a long face and side whiskers.

"Who was he? A police official?" inquired Mitka in a lowered voice.

She turned around in alarm. "No, that's my father, he was a Senator . . . he sat in the Senate."

"And is he still alive?" Mitka went on to ask, without knowing why.

"No," she said softly, but Mitka noticed how nervously her fine, transparent fingers manipulated the needle.

("I've put my foot in it again," he thought uncomfortably. "I'm sure she's stopped counting her dead long ago, but I expect she remembers each one individually. I'll be bound, too, she washes her own linen and scrubs the floor, but her hands have remained as delicate as they were at first. Yes, they're fine, quiet, good hands. . . .")

"My father died at the very beginning," she said.

"And what was it like"—Mitka moved his fingers awkwardly—"there? . . . in the Senate . . . was the work hard?"

She looked at him steadfastly, and their eyes met; it was

as much as they could do not to laugh. They both felt more cheerful, and, with a sudden confidence in her guest, she began to speak of the horrors of the first month of her married life, when Sanka had broken off his relations with the thieves. Mitka learned that Sanka wished to forget his past, and that in the last few months he had had more orders (all the wooden lasts had been turned into fuel in the famine years). So they had made up their mind to leave Moscow and settle down in a tiny little town, "the smallest in the world." There they could start again, as if nothing had happened. Mitka listened to her story with mixed feelings of contemptuous pity and alarm.

Sanka came in a moment later and instantly everything became more cheerful, even the pan on the oil stove bubbled more gaily, and the invisible bird began to eat hemp seed, so that the shells flew recklessly through the air. Sanka's thin and unshaven face had lost its sickly, puffy look, and, browned by the sun, looked handsome. He wore, like every other craftsman, a linen jacket and cheap shoes. Though he was sweaty and unkempt, he was the same unforgettable Sanka Babkin, the comrade of Mitka's long past years.

"Master!" he cried out, and shrank from his friend as from an apparition. Mitka's straight gaze seemed to confound him. He could only point with his hand at the meager amenities of his hovel. "Master!" he repeated, barely audibly, and, in his joy at Mitka's visit, began to cry.

It was painful to see his friend crying, and Mitka's face grew sad and gray. He looked around suspiciously at the woman, who was watching the reunion in timid bewilderment.

"Pull yourself together, you big clown!" said Mitka, pushing his sobbing and swaying friend away. "And you call yourself a last-maker!"

Sanka sobbed all the more; his heart would not be comforted. Mitka looked at the photographs over the chest of drawers, the Senator and the pretty young ladies with their little white aprons . . . the house with the terrace, on which well-dressed amiable people were drinking tea.

"What sort of a bird have you there?" asked Mitka irritably, turning his back on his friend.

"A crossbill. I bought it the other day . . . it's pretty," muttered Sanka curtly, and he called back his wife, who was about to leave the room so as not to be in the way.

After a whispered conversation, his wife took a few coins out of the chest of drawers, and disappeared. When Sanka turned to his guest, his face was blotchy and covered with embarrassment at his sudden effusion of sentiment.

"Take a seat, master," said Sanka, annoyed with himself. "Or have you done enough sitting about already?" he added facetiously, remembering Mitka's prison sentence.

"No, but I'll sit down all the same." Mitka sat down with a satirical smile, and Sanka realized that he did not want to talk about prison.

"Well, I'm still alive, as you see," began Sanka with a self-conscious smile. "I can't complain. I'm making good. Here I am with all my goods and chattels . . . only Xenka's always rather seedy."

"Is Xenka her name?" asked Mitka in surprise. "And I thought her name was Katya."

"No, Xenka. . . . It's damp here, and she's ailing, too, she's worn out. . . . No, don't think it's as bad as that!" he added violently. "I got her away just at the right moment. . . . I tell you, I'm glad of it . . . the last few years I've been living like a beast, and now I've done something good . . . don't you see, master?" As Mitka kept on looking him straight in the face, he became embarrassed again. "Lord, it's hot! . . . even the flies are dying of heart failure."

"Do you intend to settle somewhere else?" asked Mitka casually.

"I can't shake off my friends any other way." Sanka pushed his stool nearer and seized Mitka by the hands. "Xenka and I have agreed that we'll go off to some tiny little place—with two church steeples—and we'll live there like Darby and Joan. The trees will . . . rustle. The doctor says that Xenka will get better there. And there we'll stand on the steps in front of the house in the evening—silence . . . and peace." Sanka closed his eyes, as if he were composing a poem about all the things that were pictured in his soul in vague colors. "The sky's like a shell, the torn clouds are resting, a bird flies up noisily, the moon is rising behind the ravine . . . and the night, the night . . . white as cream! But best of all, nobody ever comes, nobody brings his dirty presence our way. Master, there's no dirt in nature, all the dirt comes from man."

He opened his eyes with a sudden self-conscious look. "Can you beat that? A chap who has been a thief spouting about little birds!"

"I'm a thief still," said Mitka sharply, and drew away his hand. "I don't like talking about these things, Bicycle, and I haven't any use for all this mushy talk."

Sanka looked toward the door in alarm. "Don't call me that, master . . . she might hear it. . . . And is it all mush, then, about the little birds? I was a great bird-lover in the old days. I'm so fond of birds that I can't eat them when they're cooked: I feel as if I was eating myself." He blurted out these words violently, and Mitka smiled at his sincerity. "At the front I ate them . . . but it was because I forgot. . . . I forgot everything there, even my own name. . . . Did you ever hear a starling teasing a golden oriole, master? Listen!" And, pushing out his lips, he mimicked the gentle, soothing twittering of the birds.

"I help a priest. I give him porridge now and then. The priest is a drunkard, he's drunk away the gold cross at his breast, and for twenty kopeks he'd spit on an icon . . . but he's a great one for birds: they're his only tie to the world. Often when we're sitting and chatting together, I feel as if the birds were sitting there in the bushes and waiting, waiting . . . What do you think, master—are the birds waiting for me?" he cried.

"You're gabbling nonsense . . . you've become an utter fool since your marriage," said Mitka bluntly, and he decided it was all due to the woman's influence.

"No, it isn't nonsense. You shouldn't ask me to give up my soul, master! I'm not just a dumb brute!" He himself was alarmed at the menacing note of his voice, and suddenly again was ready to yield to his master in everything. "Donka came here the other day dead drunk with a girl. We had a row . . . and then he broke the pot plant to bits, and seized the key and let fly at Xenka's breast. . . . You should have seen it whizz! Was that right? . . . with a key? . . . on the breast? Why don't you say something, master? . . . Or people come here and ask for money, and then make a row . . . and I can't chuck them out, for they're all old friends of mine," he said bitterly, and his lips quivered. "And now I never take a drop. . . ."

Mitka smiled to himself and cracked his fingers.

"When are you going?" he asked finally.

"It all depends on the money. . . . We're trying our hardest, and going short, and Xenka's embroidering little rugs with bourgeois patterns. We've saved fifty roubles already, master! It'll be a hundred by the winter, and then we'll sink into peace as a stone sinks into water. I'm only telling you out of friendship. Nobody else in the world knows anything about it."

"Hm!" His visitor rocked backward and forward, and bit his lips. "Well, but you can't shut yourself up altogether. . . . Will you bring off a 'show' with me?" He smiled oddly.

With a suddenly altered expression Sanka retreated to the wall and sat down upon the bed. His hands, outstretched as if he wished to thrust something away, expressed horror.

"Don't ask me, master! I won't go," he said in a smothered voice, as if someone had him by the throat. "Don't be angry with me . . . I won't go. . . . I've sworn I won't. . . ."

"But I'm not asking you," Mitka flung at him coldly. "I only wanted to test you. I don't need you. . . . Stay by yourself, and live on in the way you think fit."

"Do you mean it?" Sanka jumped about delightedly and gave an unnatural laugh, looking as he did so toward the door, in case his wife were already coming. "I sent her for some kvass. We can get kvass here in the provision stores for sixteen kopeks . . . and it really prickles when you drink it. . . ." He ran to the petroleum burner, and put it out. "I knew straight off, master, that you were joking, for what could you want me for?" With a jerk he clutched at Mitka's knees, and looked into his eyes with the despair of a suppliant. "And you mustn't come to me again, you mustn't! I'll keep you in my heart . . . I'll kiss your hands, only don't waken me from my sleep!"

His distorted face and hoarse voice moved Mitka painfully.

"All right!" he said softly, and slowly got up.

Sanka's wife came back just as Mitka was about to leave. Sanka ran out into the porch with the uncorked bottle in his hand. The door, which had a brick hanging on a chain, shut of its own accord, and Mitka had already got his hand on the latch of the outer door when suddenly he turned to Sanka.

"Why are you standing there with the bottle?" His eyes fell on Sanka's leather belt, the very belt on which he had stropped his razor at the front—the belt that had once tied fast his drunken hands.

"A drop of kvass, master . . . have a drop of kvass, do!" murmured Sanka, almost dancing in his terror that the lord of his life might go away without hospitality or a friendly word.

"I don't want any kvass," said Mitka, and watched the end of the famous belt swinging to and fro. "You say you've saved up fifty roubles?" He took the dangling end of the belt in his hand, and so put an end to Sanka's excited dance.

"Yes, fifty," repeated Sanka in an awed whisper.

Mitka wrapped the belt around his finger and drew Sanka closer to him. Something prevented him at first from raising his puckered eyes to Sanka's; then he looked up, and suddenly braced himself for a decision.

"Give me thirty . . . or at most forty!" he said harshly, without faltering, and without letting go of the belt. "I need forty roubles at once. I could have as much as I wanted, but I need honest money—money that's been earned by honest sweat." He was silent, and suddenly loosened his hold on the fateful belt.

"Do you want it at once?" whispered Sanka, shyly hoping. He was holding the bottle askew, and more than half of its contents had already escaped. "Xenka has it . . . wait here!" he whispered conspiratorially, winking slyly; but Mitka was not embarrassed. Sanka disappeared behind the door, which sank back heavily and majestically into its former place.

The minutes passed uneasily, and suddenly Mitka felt that enough time had elapsed, and, turning around to the door, looked at it angrily. At the same time there was a hasty rustle behind it. All at once Mitka's mind seemed to be overcast by a cloud, and, as though impelled by invisible hands, he quickly kneeled down and looked through the keyhole. The key was not in it, and he saw a piece of wall pasted with newspaper, and then something dark covered his field of vision—it was Sanka's eye. Both of them remained for a moment at the keyhole. Then Mitka drew back, as if struck in the chest by a gust of wind; the keyhole appeared again, like a white spot in the hairy felt of the door. He stood bolt upright, the brick on the cord arose, and the door slowly opened.

"There it is!" whispered Sanka triumphantly, and held out to him a tiny package sewed into a piece of rag. "I've got it! I've got it!" he repeated exultantly, as though he had just stolen the money from someone. He was cheerful and poor and generous once more, as he had been at the front. "Let's cut it open with a knife," he almost sang with joy. And he drew the gleaming blade along the seam of the mysterious packet. "Out you come! Where are you hiding yourself?"

"Don't cut the money, though!" whispered Mitka, infected by Sanka's excitement, but Sanka was already drawing it out of the rag. It was wrapped up in clean notepaper.

"Take it, master! Has Sanka ever done you any injury? Take it!" He pointed to the door behind which his wife sat. "I've told her everything . . . all we went through together. She's crying . . . women are stupid. . . . Take it, take the rag and all!"

Mitka put the clean and carefully counted money into his pocket, and, for friendship's sake, refrained from thanking Sanka. Deep in thought he walked out into the yard, and did not turn around until he heard Sanka calling him frantically.

Sanka was standing at the door. "Master!" he called out gaily, the bottle with the much praised kvass in his hands. "Don't go without a drop of kvass, master!" and he showed him the glass, in which the drink seethed and foamed invitingly. But Mitka refused it with a gesture, and vanished around the corner.

THE SUN flooded with scorching heat the uneven pavement of the empty street along which Mitka walked. There was not a living soul to be seen, not a cloud in the sky; it was an effort to breathe. Up above, the deep blue sky shed a blinding glow, and the chaos in Mitka's mind grew more confused every moment. Suddenly he had a feeling that Sanka was running after him with the glass in his hand, and he turned around in such fury that he wrenched a muscle in his neck.

But soon he forgot all this, and stared at his own abbreviated noontide shadow. The cobbles that lay in it gleamed bright lilac, so intense was the heat, and every detail in the street fastened itself on Mitka's mind and drained him of his strength. A spasm of pain convulsed his face. "Murder," he whispered suddenly: "thou shalt do no murder . . . but you can't be guilty in the eyes of the man who is dead. Your guilt can only be toward the living, who look you in the face. Murder isn't the destruction of life, it's only the annulling of guilt as far as the man who is murdered is concerned. There is no higher law to stop one . . . but . . ." Suddenly he remembered Agey's words: "What's the good of pitying dead men? They just turn your stomach. I can't bear them even when they're alive now." He was dripping with sweat, and his clothes clung to his skin. Then the unbearable stillness was shattered by a sudden noise.

On the yellow street a procession appeared, swaying to right and left and raising swirls of dust. A touch of red lent it a solemn appearance, and soon it became clear why this unusual hour had been chosen for the procession—a red coffin was lying on the catafalque. As the procession drew nearer, the musicians put their glittering instruments to their lips and blew from their trumpets vague, discordant sounds. At the same moment groups of women and children, enthusiastic patrons of any street function, streamed out of the houses.

All at once the horse drawing the hearse stopped for a few moments to relieve itself. No one was surprised at this, for a horse is a living creature. Mitka stepped closer. A boy in a little blue shirt was sitting on the box and whipping the horse, which his father was driving, with a little stick. He looked about six years old, and he was sitting cheerfully on a folded coat, for he had no idea what was going on. Mitka observed the boy with interest and, following the procession without noticing what he was doing, was soon walking close behind the catafalque. The blue shirt and the child's small, lightly freckled face teased him as if they were in some way painful and familiar. In the dry noonday heat the feet of the mourners stirred up lazy swirls of dust, which mixed with the noise and glitter of the trumpets.

The gates of the cemetery were already approaching when an untidy but bustling man with a lot of pimples on his face came up to Mitka.

"You're from the district station, I suppose, Comrade?" he asked irritably, and tried to embrace Mitka, but was coldly repulsed. "The devils . . . they promise to come and then don't. It's a damned shame!" he said in an offended voice, and walked on beside Mitka. "Who's to give the address over the grave? It isn't right to bury a man without one. It's like saying to him: 'Well, we've brought you this far, and now you can shift for the rest of the journey on your own.' Every man, even the humblest, deserves something after all. . . ." He gesticulated with his dirty fingers, and pushed out his lips. "Now, wouldn't you oblige? I can't do it, for, as it is, I represent the commandant and the priest and the widow. That's enough for me. In my opinion one should bury the dead at night and then everyone would have a good excuse for not coming." He looked into Mitka's gray face, shrugged his shoulders, and dissolved again into the hot, yellow background.

Leaning against a trellis fence in the shadow of an aspen, Mitka still thought of the boy and his little blue shirt. His mind was tormented by a stream of recollections . . . and suddenly he saw before him, so that he could almost touch it, the bridge across the Kudema, the shaggy, racing clouds, the flowing ripples of the water, Masha's little red frock, and his own shirt of cornflower blue . . . the memories, in all their disturbing clarity, ran painfully through his brain. The Kudema, the free and rushing river, had torn away with it Masha's little garland of sweet youth . . . had rubbed it away on the stones of its bed, and strewn it on its banks.

At this moment of despair he loved wild Masha; she alone, he felt, could understand his suffering. The shadows of the tree moved up and down across his face.

Then the child gave a shrill scream, and Mitka shuddered and opened his eyes. A little group stood around the grave, which was hidden by them. The music played more softly, and, soothed by the sad air, the boy suddenly became quiet. At the same time a dull sobbing beside him caused Mitka to turn his head. A little old woman was crying, because no one else was crying. She baked holy wafers, and, after escorting so many of her dear ones to the grave, only remained alive herself by a miracle. Now she was thinking of all those who had passed through life with her.

"Look!" she said, bursting into tears: "they stick a man in the ground and no one sheds a tear for him. He's just covered up like a piece of wood so as not to lie about the roads. . . . No, little son, nowadays there's no respect for human life. It's shameful, that's what it is!" And once more she abandoned herself to her tears.

Slowly Mitka picked his way through the graves and went away. The riotous colors of the late afternoon numbed his brain and blinded his eyes. When he remembered Zinka, who was pining for him at home, a feeling of satiety came over him. In his imagination the circle of mankind contracted, and outside it somewhere stood Masha, smiling sadly at his sufferings. She alone possessed the precious key to his recovery, and so he resolved to go' to her that he might catch in her eyes a glimpse, a bright reflection of the past that had vanished without a trace.

A gust of wind blew on the back of his neck and brought a few fragments of the address to his ears: ". . . you made experiments in the domain of stock breeding. We think" (and the speaker deftly reproduced a sob) "of that irrevocable day, when at the general meeting of the . . ." Then the wind thought fit to shift. It was a playful little wind that lived with the birds on the cemetery trees.

The heavy sun had crossed the zenith. The tops of the trees were still, and their stillness was more appropriate than words to the loneliness of the tomb. It was this that made Firsov write in one of the early chapters of his novel that trees were nobler than men.

WHEN Mitka caught sight of the brightly painted Turk on the signboard, he realized that it was not Dolomanova he wanted. Through the open door a fine metallic hammering could be heard.

"Well, do you think I'm going to make your pan eternal for five kopeks?" Puchov was asking a stupid woman, and did not greet Mitka until he had finished her copper pot.

When they were alone, they embraced each other. Puchov did not trouble him with questions, and this encouraged Mitka.

"Everything the same as ever here, I suppose, old Primus?" he asked, bowing his head submissively before Puchov's unchangeableness. "Is your old maggot still going strong?"

"Yes, yes, still crawling," grumbled Puchov as he locked up his workshop for lunch. "Now come in and pay me a visit!" he added, and gave Mitka a slap on the shoulder. While he prepared his lunch, he inquired casually when Mitka had been let out of prison, and what he was thinking of doing now, but, apart from that, asked no further questions.

Mitka began to eat in silence, but soon stopped. A fit of sadness came over him, and he put his spoon on one side. He looked on as Puchov pumped up the primus, put the well-known teapot on the fire, and washed the crockery.

"Why aren't you asking me any questions, Master Puchov?" asked Mitka reproachfully.

"We haven't seen each other for half a year . . . how am I to ask you questions? You've become a different person. You become a different person every month now!" Puchov turned around, shaking his wet hands.

. "My whole life's gone dead. I can't understand what's happening out there," Mitka said abruptly, and his eyes were dim as if from a thousand sleepless nights. "What's going on in the world, Puchov?"

"The world's all topsy-turvy!" laughed Puchov, and the humming of the primus could be heard above his voice. "All the old names and labels have got in a muddle, for nature hasn't any use for them. You see something on a tree and say 'There's a beetle!' but do you think the beetle knows or cares? And now we've all lost our labels, too —that's all that it amounts to."

He broke off impatiently, and, letting the teapot alone, sat down beside Mitka. "Well, let's hear about you, anyway. What's your trouble?"

"I'm frightened, old Primus, I feel as if I was fumbling in the dark," answered Mitka evasively, glancing up to see whether Puchov was smiling at him.

"It's only the blind, Mitka, and the dead who aren't frightened of the dark," said Puchov, smiling.

"You're always playing with me, trying to get something out of me." A muscle twitched furiously in Mitka's face. "If you're fond of me, then order me to do something. I've got everything I ever wanted, Puchov. When I was a kid I wanted a little chocolate bottle: I hadn't any need for it, but someone threw me the money . . . the little bottle broke. Then it was an officer's horse took my fancy, a chestnut . . . a beauty, and I got that, too. For two nights I slept in the emperor's bed: . . . it was soft, but it didn't do me any good, and so I got up in the morning and was off. I thought the best thing of all was to have power over one's fellows—and then there was a night at the front . . ." (The Master of Blagusha had stopped smiling while he listened to Mitka.) "I've been through everything and done everything, Puchov, but what good had it done me? I'm always wanting to be able to forget everything, as one can in one's childhood. I was talking to Firsov once, and he said to me: 'To kill a man means to kill oneself in him.' Then I said to him: 'If I don't kill him, he'll kill me. . . .' What is there particularly sacramental about killing? . . ."

"Mitka, you're ill, you're very ill!" The locksmith looked surreptitiously at Mitka's restless fingers. "You must take a rest. . . . Look what a fine gentleman you are there in your photograph, gloves and all, and now you're dressed any old way and never shave."

Mitka rocked backward and forward on his creaking chair, and the dim light from the window played on his lined forehead.

"I was let out because I'm supposed to be ill, but I'm well enough. I'd like to know, though, if anyone else has ever hated himself as I do. Wherever I go, I think of Agey —and I think of the world as if it were a diagram on a desk . . . and I'm standing somewhere else and studying it in my mind—and if you ask me, it works better on paper than in practice."

He told Puchov all his thoughts and feelings, and Puchov watched him sadly. The evening was already coming on, and on the dirty windowpane there glowed an orange reflection.

"You want me to give you orders," said the locksmith as they drank tea together. "But that isn't the right way to set about it: a man should be able to lean on himself. . . . After my military service was over, I went into a small monastery and nearly died of boredom behind the high stone walls. I was serving brother to the hermit Agafador. I thought to myself: 'Let the wise man take the responsibility for me and my stupidity.' My work was very hard. In the night he used to waken me: he used to say: 'You're always sleeping, Yemelka: read me the song of praise to gentle Jesus!' I began to read sleepily till the letters got mixed up together and my face got damp and swollen, but he sat on the edge of the bed and cried. Next to the monastery there was the market place with a merry-go-round and little hotels, and while we rang our bells, they played their harmonicas—every man to his taste! Then I took to roaming, and I climbed the walls and saw that the world was very beautiful . . . for fools! I took walks and smoked and amused myself. . . . I made the acquaintance of a market woman and ran off to her every evening . . . (there was a ladder against the wall)."

"What are you driving at with all this?" Mitka was already bored with Puchov's long-winded story, and yawned.

"One time I was climbing back. It was twilight, and the old man was sitting on a little bench, breathing heavily and coughing, but with God's help he had taken away the ladder and laid it on the ground. I turned to run away, but he'd spotted the prodigal. 'Jump, Yemelyasha, jump, it's nothing!' 'But the ladder!' said I. 'It's nothing! Come on!' Then I raised the skirts of my habit . . . and the next moment found myself sprawling in the ditch. . . . Two months long I lay in bed with my broken leg, and the old man sang the song of praise through by heart every night. He made a cripple of me, but he was a wise man all the same."

"Well, and what then?" Mitka's face was gloomy and aggressive.

"Well, and just this, then," said Puchov irritably: "another man's will can turn one into a cripple. Nikolka told me once that the wind used to drive bears to them. Well, it must have been a big blast drove you along this way, my dear boy. You've got great power in your paws, but what have you got in your head? You can't understand your own self properly . . . so what can you do between the upper and the nether millstone? You have no wish to earn your bread with your own sweat, and save yourself from the abyss. Now, I ask you: Could you build a bridge that would stretch across the abyss and carry all the loads that would tear across it at a high speed? Or could you describe your life in a song, so that everyone would cry and sing?"

"I haven't room to turn around in my bear quarters, old Primus, and now I'm fed up with being bullied and laughed at, though I haven't got the hang of things yet. Why do you confuse me with talk?"

"Mitka, we're not related to each other, but you're more than a son to me. My dear boy, if you're going to tackle lions you've got to be a lion yourself. Sleeping in the emperor's soft beds isn't good for anyone, not even

the strongest. You asked me to tell you what to do.
. . . Well, it's your burden and you must bear it. You
must suffer, Mitka, till the fire of your soul burns you
clean." He clenched his fists as if he were kneading
Mitka's soul and wished to press the blood from it like
juice. He spoke in this way because he loved Mitka, but
his love was perhaps as possessive as Agafador's.

The sun had already sunk, but the twilight still
gleamed transparently. Puchov evidently did not want to
open his workshop again; he fetched his scraps of wood,
and set himself to his usual work.

"Look here!" said he, after a long silence, "here you
have a healthy piece of wood: it's straight and clean. And
here you have a piece of wood that got slightly damp and
then was nicely dried in the sun. Look! . . ." He bent
the wood and showed Mitka the winding course of the
yellow and blue wood fibers, which were like the veins on
a man's brow as he thinks. "Do you see, that wood was
sick, but it's kept as hard as a bone. Try, scratch it with
your nail!"

Mitka was silent, but suddenly he groped in his pocket
for Sanka's money. His already half-forgotten resolution
came back to him with renewed strength.

"I want to send my father some money . . . good,
honest money. He must remember Dmitri! Do you intend to start scolding me again?"

"One shouldn't judge a man by his happiness, but by
his sufferings," said Puchov, barely audibly; he did not
appear to approve of Mitka's decision. "Isn't Puchov a
father to you?" In spite of the twilight he noticed the
flush on Mitka's face. "You've got fine side whiskers. . . .
Your father'll be ordering you now to shave them off."

"Shave . . ." repeated Mitka awkwardly, and stroked
his cheeks with his fingertips.

"You're a smart boy, but you're frightened of your dad.
He might throw you out of the house, and what would you
do then?" the Master of Blagusha said banteringly, but
Mitka got ready to leave.

They stood in the courtyard. In the sky the half-moon
hung shy and tender as a love signal.

"Yes, you all come to me to be patched up," grumbled

Puchov gruffly. "I'll just leave you all to yourselves and go off to Turkestan."

"What have you lost there?" smiled Mitka hopefully.

"Vegetables are cheap there, at any rate," Puchov flung after him, and turned his back.

MITKA did not go straight home, but wandered about the streets, which lay steeped in the dusty, sweltering heat of evening. While he was standing by a bright shop window, he fell once more into a brooding trance. The passers-by pushed against him crossly, and one of them, whose lips were as green as if he lived on grass, made straight for Mitka, but Mitka stepped aside in time. "There is no guilt, for the man one has killed no longer exists to accuse one. There is guilt, because the guilt is a matter not of the dead but of the living: guilt before the third person. . . ." This thought flashed through Mitka's brain, and suddenly in his imagination there rose the picture of a simple little woman. Her eyes were tear-stained, and she was tugging at a little ribbon with her fingers.

This picture had already been haunting him for a long time, and now he thought that he saw the woman on the other side of the street. Unable to fight down his malicious curiosity, he crossed the street. But he could not believe in the reality of the woman, even when he caught up with her and could distinguish the lilac stripes on her dark dress. When she smiled, he thought little dimples would form on her cheeks, which would be as colorless as she was herself.

His imagination took full possession of him. He saw the steps of a brick house, the front room (at this moment the woman turned around and it seemed to Mitka that she recognized him), and after that a poor little room, through whose window a cluster of roofs were to be seen. They sat down, and he told her how it all had happened.

She bent her head, listened to him, and her lips moved. (Then Mitka heard distinctly the words: "God will punish you!" the very words which a moment before he had put in the mouth of the old woman of his imagination—a woman like the one he had seen in the cemetery; she was only returning to him his own words.) He drew himself up expectantly.

Someone clapped him on the shoulder. The traffic roared, the first lights flashed out, and, as if they had risen from the ground, Fyodor Shchekutin and Vassily Vissilye-vich Panama the Fat stood before him.

"Ah, whom have we here!" panted Panama delightedly. Shchekutin smiled condescendingly. "Well, why are you standing there as if you'd been struck silly? I say, Fedka's just back from Irkutsk . . . when did they let you out?"

"You didn't recognize me," said the other in a deep bass voice, and kept his hands in the pocket of his leather jacket.

"We've a lot of news for you!" crowed Panama excitedly, and his Adam's apple jumped up and down in his shirt opening. "Zhivotik's been caught messing up a job and Prince Babayev was picked up because of a smelly old corpse on his hands . . . He put her in a tub, but didn't scatter any salt over her, so a leg crept out of the tub. It's God's truth, when a man's down, even the beggars give him the go-by! The Snowstorm has gone on the stage: she's got Donka fairly in her clutches. Fritz was here a few days ago, too, he was asking about you . . . he wanted to take you abroad with him. Yes, and by the way, he showed us a German goosefoot . . . a lovely piece of work . . . a real bird! . . . You can't compare our Soviet work with it. . . . And an electric borer! . . ." Words failed him for rapture; he blinked and shuffled his stumpy feet in their fashionable boots.

"Something like that would come in handy with a little friend of ours," laughed Shchekutin dryly. "Just turn around, Mitka!"

Behind them flashed the window of a jeweller's shop full of expensive, tasteless gewgaws: rings and brooches with stones that looked like well-licked sugar candy, monstrous watch chains, cigarette boxes with pictures of popular heroes and girls, and a lot of other things, all merging in one gleaming metal surface on which the electric light was reflected. Over a black silk screen a terrified, mustached face was visible, and with some surprise Mitka recognized Pirman.

"There's a dial I'd like to spit on!" laughed Vassily Vassilyevich, without turning away from the window. "What about going in and scrounging a drink off him?"

"You're an optimist!" said Shchekutin with conviction.

"Go on! He won't refuse *me*," said Mitka indignantly, and went to the door of Pirman's shop. "Let's try!"

They stepped noisily into Pirman's dusty premises. Shchekutin was behind Vassily Vassilyevich, and Mitka closed the procession. There was a stamp of solidity on the business: the silver and the inferior gold shone, the clocks on the brackets buzzed and ticked in different tones, and a geranium stood on the counter for elegance.

"Good day, Yefim," said Shchekutin graciously. "We wanted to pay you a little visit."

Pirman said nothing and, in his embarrassment, completely forgot the presence of his wife (a lady rather to Vassily Vassilyevich's taste, who had a weakness for the monumental), and of his customers (a Soviet official and his emaciated wife). Finally, however, he succeeded in making a sign to his wife, and she unobtrusively edged nearer the door. Nobody interfered with her, but when she had got quite close to it, Vassily Vassilyevich, just as a matter of precaution, blocked her way.

"Every inch the lady," said Panama amiably, and trod on the tip of her patent-leather shoes. "A lady like you (pray excuse me), like a tea rose, suddenly to go off for a policeman. . . . Madam, you'll be the death of me yet: laughing is bad for my health. . . . I can show you a doctor's certificate. . . ."

"Allow me, citizen," stammered Pirman, pale and uncertain. "For hygienic reasons my wife has to go out."

"Make an end of it . . . will you come to the point or not?" screamed Vassily Vassilyevich in his face, and instantly everything became lively. Mitka grew cheerful, Shchekutin gave a toneless laugh, and even the miserable wife of the Soviet official looked at Panama and smiled.

Mitka went, with nervous haste, to the counter.

"Be a sport, Pirman! It's a sad heart that never rejoices," he said mockingly, and added a few words in thieves' jargon, which normally he never used.

"I don't understand you . . ." said Pirman, and his face was dead white.

"Mitka's saying you should give us a fiver for beer," Shchekutin explained to him gently. "No more of your tricks now, Yefim! You brought your own pack with you that time, but you left one card behind you on the table. It wasn't a nice card, either, it had pimples on it. . . ." Shchekutin drummed thoughtfully with his fingers on the glass top of the counter. (Actually he was lying for the fun of the thing. Pirman had played with genuine cards, though he was a practised sharper.)

"I've taken money off nobody," whimpered Pirman, as if on hot coals, and pointed to the patched sleeve of his canvas jacket. "I can't even buy myself a coat. . . . I can't even pay the taxes."

A painful silence lasted for a little.

"Then I'll choose myself a watch chain," said Vassily Vassilyevich gloomily. "I like that one. Have you any lockets?—with a girl's picture or a landscape? . . . What a pity, Yefim, what a pity!"

"Allow me, I'll pack it up for you." Pirman's wife hurried up: she had wisely reconciled herself to the loss. "A very pretty chain!" she said with a seductive glance and a gracious gesture. "You've got excellent taste!"

"Now you're flattering me," simpered Vassily Vassilyevich, winking and lightly patting her plump hand.

The attempt had come off, and Pirman hastened to open the door. Then Mitka, his face pale and twitching with emotion, caught Pirman by the jacket. The canvas jacket was crumpled irreparably in the iron grip of his fingers.

"You swindler!" Mitka whispered in disgust, shaking the jeweller. He remembered Sanka and the little packet, and the recollection increased his rage a thousandfold. "You louse! Out with the fiver! I'll annihilate you! . . . Who are you, anyway, you swindler?"

"I'm . . . a human being, aren't I . . . and a . . . radio fan, too," stammered Pirman, as if he were out of his senses.

The position of the jeweller was perilous, but Vassily Vassilyevich took the matter in hand.

"Mitka!" he said reproachfully, and in his voice there rang such noble wrath that Shchekutin turned around curiously. "You'll wreck his business. Ah, how really Russian that is!" he added caustically. Mitka, in disgust, loosened his hold on the jeweller.

"Go on living, then, you swine . . . and drain us dry, drain us dry!" Mitka flung his last words to the shop at large, and stepped out into the evening heat.

So THE first day passed. Lifting his legs with an effort, Mitka climbed to the second floor, which was filled with a sweet and sticky smell, for the Bundyukovs were cooking jam on the sly. Chikelyov was putting the little girl to bed, and telling her some story or other in a soft singsong voice, but when Mitka appeared, he turned his back on him sulkily. Mitka began immediately to look for ink, but could find no trace of such a thing, for Zinka never had anything to write about or anyone to write to. Then he asked Chikelyov for some ink, and, with a sudden access of generosity, Chikelyov produced his whole writing outfit.

"It's a case in point, how like him you are," he said impulsively. "I really marvel at your angelic simplicity, Dmitri Yegorovich."

"Clear out, will you?" said Mitka, wearily closing his eyes.

Now at last he really made up his mind to write to his father; in the morning he had only intended to send him money, so as to remind him of his existence. His plan had taken shape while he was still in prison, when his mind was straining to find a beam of light in the twilight of reality.

The gloomy, terrible world appeared to him like a great empty barn, in the corner of which his wounded consciousness had hidden itself. "It is the sadness we feel," wrote Firsov, "when at night we gaze into the sky as if we saw there our distant home."

The following was the gist of Mitka's letter:

"Greetings, father. I expect you've made up your mind that Mitka has rotted away long since in some communal grave. No, father, I'm alive, still alive. I'm sorry I forgot you, but I've had no time even to think of myself. You will understand me, for you're good, and I've never heard a shabby thing about you. I dare say you'll hear gossip about me, how I've gone to the bad, but don't be in a hurry to think the worst of me. I remember that about 'weak knees' . . . and I'll make good yet, Yegor Vekshin, if I've got the strength. I'll justify my wretched existence even if I've to give my life for it. . . ."

At this point it occurred to him that his words were neither sincere nor convincing. He read the ill-written lines through once more, and found the tone of his writing cringing and disagreeable. Chikelyov sat beside him and watched his labors attentively.

"You're a dreamer!" he said in a whisper, so as not to wake the little girl. "But I've my thoughts, too, when I look at you. How strangely like him you are!"

"Like whom?" Mitka turned his face to him.

"Your father," remarked Chikelyov informatively. "I'm really a friendly fellow, though, typically speaking, I ought to hate you. . . . You were present, for instance, at that unpleasant affair with the author. . . . You even smiled at it, though I'd done nothing to deserve such treatment. In a threefold capacity I had a right to be interested in the matter: as a roommate, as chairman of the house committee, and . . . also from the fiscal standpoint. (Perhaps one could sell the manuscript, and make up the arrears for rates.) I am a social factor and consider any assault on my person as an injury to the foundations of the State. A blow on the ear is of no importance to me personally, of course, but—"

"Well, you're going the right way to get one from me, too." Mitka squinted his eyes in the light, and covered the letter with his hand.

"I don't mind . . . within limits, of course." Chikelyov blinked huffily, and suddenly jumped away from a bluebottle that was buzzing around him. "That's typical of me: you're a marked man and yet I'm interested in your fate. It once occurred to me that Zinaida Petrovna liked to think of you as a martyr. What would happen, though, if there was a slight turn in your affairs: supposing, let us say, it was to come out that you weren't Vekshin at all? . . . But don't be alarmed, I've a special weakness for that lady and I can be silent, too. Of course, I never for a moment doubted that you were Vekshin . . . but, please note, every circumstance is like an egg, and one never knows what will come out of the egg. Have you never thought of that?"

"No, never . . ." Mitka uttered the words with an effort, and, to the accompaniment of Chikelyov's unceasing chatter, wrote his letter to the end.

"I find it rather odd to think that the chair here mayn't be a chair after all, and that Vekshin mayn't be Vekshin. My dear chap, everything depends on our point of view with regard to a thing, and that accounts for differences in culture, too, in my opinion. I say to myself: Pyotr Gorbidonich, if a cucumber thinks itself an apple, as chairman of the lodgers' committee should you not give the matter your attention? That's typical, there's no doubt about that whatever."

"Come to the point, will you?" said Mitka, sticking down the envelope, which contained Sanka's money. "And make it a bit shorter, or I'll fling you out!"

"Well, in that case you wouldn't hear what I've got to say, so you'd be the loser!" Chikelyov cautiously withdrew out of range of Mitka's fist. "But I must check my deductions by a few questions." He took out his small notebook. "You were pleased to come into the world in the government of N——, I believe. Very praiseworthy. I'm a great admirer of that government myself . . . all the little gardens and pools."

"That's all rubbish," said Mitka patiently. "There aren't any gardens."

"Oh, come, now! Surely there must be gardens there with at least two hundred trees." Chikelyov fluttered his little book. "It isn't nice to tell a lie to a man older than yourself."

"Oh, well, there may be gardens like that on some of the estates. In our neighborhood there was an estate, I believe," admitted Mitka, grudging Chikelyov his little score.

"Ah! Well, so far, so good! I feel I'm on the scent now, and I'll nose out the truth, and I won't need a bloodhound, either. Tell me, is your father's name Yegor, and was he a switchman? I've had fifteen years' experience, and that experience teaches me that a man likes to hoodwink his fellows. A successful piece of cheating exalts a man . . . but I'm straying too far from the main theme. Now attend! Your mother . . ."

"I can't remember my mother at all," Mitka interrupted him coldly.

"But I have a few dates about her. I'm passionately fond of getting to the bottom of any matter. I wake up in the night and whisper: 'Pyotr Gorbidonich, in civil matters you're a real Pinkerton.' Then I calm myself again and go to sleep. I'm always dreaming that I'm unmasking somebody, and ferreting out secrets. I investigate, refute lies, and unmask the guilty party. It's much the same sensation as in tobogganing. (To be accurate, I have never tobogganed, but I can picture the feeling to myself.)"

"I'll bash you to a jelly if you don't take care, Chikelyov," said Mitka, shaking his head.

There was nothing for Pyotr Gorbidonich to do but to speak clearly or to beat a retreat. For the first time in his life he overcame his cowardice; the stake was too high, for it meant robbing Mitka of the halo with which Zinka had invested him.

"Don't try to frighten me. Have a little patience. Don't I put up with you here in the house, although I might be accused of concealing you? One night you might rob the whole house, who knows."

Chikelyov trembled with hatred, but forgot his terror of Mitka's hands, which lay on the table as if turned to stone. "How could you forget that the neighboring estate—"

"Vodyanetz!" recollected Mitka with an effort.

"Yes, Vodyanetz . . . it belonged to Sergey Ammonich, my roommate. (Later on I'll give you a small exercise book of his to read.) Your mother was, according to Manyukin's descriptions, a very . . . beautiful woman. When your father lay in the hospital of . . . Rogovo, she used to scrub the floors of the house at Vodyanetz. That was shortly before you came into the world." Chikelyov scratched the back of his head in exasperation. "If only I could find out how old this Nikolasha is now! . . . I bet you anything you, like Nikolasha, is only an alias!" he exclaimed with a sudden inspiration.

Mitka sat helplessly opposite Chikelyov, while the latter jotted down various dates on a small piece of paper. A mad wish to find out what was going on behind Chikelyov's dirty, malevolent brain overpowered him. Suddenly Chikelyov jumped up and ran to the door, for the danger of continuing the conversation had become apparent to him.

"The affair is not yet really ready for discussion, but in a short time I will reveal everything. Oh, my imagination will be the death of me!" He made a gesture that looked as though he were kissing his hand to Mitka, and Mitka shook his fist at him.

. . . Zinka came home late. She was angry, and still was wearing the Eastern trousers in which she had appeared in the beer hall. She withdrew behind the curtain that divided the room into two halves, went to bed, and forgot to ask Mitka if he was hungry. Presently she extinguished the light, and a few uncertain minutes passed. Young people with guitars passed by on the street, and Mitka lay on his back, and made an effort to decipher Manyukin's allusion to their relationship. A subtle thought flashed through his brain and fluttered away again. Suddenly Zinka stirred noisily.

"Aren't you asleep yet?" asked Mitka softly. Zinka did not reply. "I've lost that hat of yours somewhere. . . ."

Again no reply. The night was cool and drenched in moonlight. Toward midnight Mitka heard unmistakable sounds of stifled sobbing. He sat up; he had a foreboding of something terrible and disastrous. The sounds continued. He went over in his bare feet to the curtain, without noticing his shadow, which was clearly silhouetted on it. The moon flooded the room with light. Terrified by his forebodings, Mitka tried to peer over the curtain, but at his touch it slipped from its nail and fell on the floor. Mitka straightened himself like a thief caught in the act.

Full in the moonlight, Zinka sat on the edge of the bed with her arms clasped around her knees. Her eyes were bright with tears. The utter helplessness and despair of her posture awoke Mitka's pity. Her luxuriant hair fell over her shoulders, which were as round as two moons. She did not stir, for the pain she was enduring was greater than her sense of shame.

With a painful presentiment that all was lost, he seized her by the shoulders. It was as though the wind were embracing an unresisting cloud. Filled with wild desire, he set his teeth and fought against her power, but wherever he looked he saw Zinka countlessly multiplied by his feverish midnight fantasy.

"You'll waken Klavdya, you madman!" she whispered, exulting in his downfall.

With this misunderstanding in the moonlight began the whole affair between them.

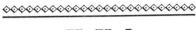
IN THE morning the letter was posted; then dark days followed. Mitka began to neglect his appearance, and from morning to night paced up and down his room in galoshes and an old shirt from earlier, happier days. Now and then he broke off a piece of black bread and chewed it with the slow deliberation of an animal whose wits have got dulled by lifelong imprisonment. He was waiting.

For a whole month no one came to see him but Curly Donka, who brought an open note from Dolomanova inviting him to visit her. For a full quarter of an hour the ambassador did not look at Mitka, but in a flat voice he repeated his spiteful charges against Sanka. He dwelt with ill-concealed malice on Sanka's defection from the thieves' gang.

"Sanka's staunch and honest as the day. . . . Why did you smash his cactus? . . . Did the cactus hurt you? Don't twitch like that!" shouted Mitka, enraged by Donka's insinuations.

"I can't endure the petty bourgeoisie," answered Donka as he went away. "And the reason why I twitch is because I've got malaria. I've been stung by a poisonous fly."

Mitka's attempts to have a talk with Manyukin did not meet with success. Sergey Ammonich was visibly declining. He set to work every morning all the same on the manuscript Chikelyov had profaned.

His desk was often left unlocked as before, so Chikelyov had an opportunity to notice that Manyukin's handwriting was becoming less and less legible.

THE THIEF 281

Manyukin usually did not go to stand at his street corner until three o'clock in the afternoon, when the streets were filled with a crowd of officials. He went there stealthily, and came back stealthily, and whenever they met in the passage, he used to make a facetious bow, which greatly annoyed Mitka. On his return from his street corner, Manyukin used to fling himself flat on his bed.

Mitka did not speak to Chikelyov, and Chikelyov, too, was stubbornly silent. The unemployed Bundyukov had somewhere or other unearthed the news that Chikelyov had been promoted in the office. Every evening Pyotr Gorbidonich came to give Klavdya a kiss before she went to bed and a sweet to send her to sleep, but without relaxing his cool, Olympian severity. (Zinka stayed all day away from the house.) It was very hot, and Mitka felt as if he were in a vapor bath. He was waiting.

One day toward sunset a barrel organ was playing in the courtyard, and Mitka swung himself onto the window-sill to listen. The listless voice of the street singer reverberated against the glowing brick walls. He was singing an old song about the great warrior who had watched the burning of the conquered capital from the walls of the Kremlin. A tiny wind ruffled Mitka's hair, and his thoughts fluttered back to his childhood like a wounded bird—to a half-forgotten moment. . . . He saw a cool, clear fish pond in the wood, and in the sky the menacing sun. There was a stillness in the air, and in the stillness the dragonflies, hovering motionlessly, gazed down on the smooth mirror of the pond. Masha was sitting on the bank, laughing gaily at Mitka, who was romping and splashing in the water. They used to catch fish by digging up the mud and forcing the fish to take refuge on the surface of the water. The organ grinder turned the handle of the machine slowly and irregularly, so that at one moment it sounded like malevolent laughter, at another like the slow sigh of a dying man. . . .

Mitka did not look up until his sister had called him for the second time, and then he turned around and smiled without showing surprise. She was wearing a simple light dress and an old straw hat. Tanya never knew how to dress; her unaffected smile was her only attraction, and excused everything. She accused her brother of having completely forgotten her.

"Nikolka wants to visit you: he wants to be friends," she said, looking away. "He's got a big deal in hand at the moment, something in corn, and wants to contract something, too."

"Friends with me? . . . That's mighty flattering! Where does he get the money?"

"I gave it to him . . . I had money." Mitka's satirical glance embarrassed her. "I don't know anything about his business: it's not in my line. . . ." She was vexed by the turn the conversation had taken, and changed the subject. They could not get married for about two months, and this again was due to Nikolka's business. Shyly she announced the joyful news that she had left the circus forever. She glowed with happiness when Mitka was not looking at her, and her joy shed a strange, reflected glamor even over Nikolka.

"D'you think I'm right?"

"You mean about the circus? I do indeed," said Mitka. "We've to pay too dearly for our fame, both of us!"

"No, I mean my getting married," corrected Tanya cautiously. "I've worried myself to death about it. Often I've trudged around the streets like a homeless tramp, rather than go back home and fret about it the whole night long." She sighed and added gloomily, "I can't afford to pick and choose. I'm not so young now, you know: I'm a year older than you."

Mitka brought a bottle of soda water from the cupboard, and drank it alone, as his sister did not wish to drink with him.

"I'd make it worth his while to leave you if I thought he'd see reason, but he wouldn't. You say you're happy, but if that's happiness, you'd be a damned sight better without it. I'd exchange it all for a little solid contentment. Sister," he went on bitterly and tenderly, "before I knew you existed I didn't suffer for you, but now I'd sacrifice myself for your happiness. Everyone should have something for which he can sacrifice himself without question. You'll understand me, you're so gentle."

"Gentle! . . . And the other day I screamed at Pugel because he broke a glass. You expect wonders from me—

and that frightens me. You ask wonders from me in return for your love, but what if I can't do them? . . . Everyone's the same, they burrow in each other's souls, looking for something marvellous, and then, when they don't find it, they feel they've been let down. What sort of a miracle is it you're expecting from me?"

"I'm not asking for miracles—there aren't such things. The world's a dreary place," said Mitka quietly, but a muscle twitched in his face. "You'll never be happy, and that's why I'm fond of you."

A flush of embarrassment deepened on her cheek, and to hide it she went to the window. Suddenly Mitka heard a muffled laugh, the soft laugh of a girl who has attained her happiness.

"What's amusing you?" he flung at her crossly, and, going up abruptly to her, pressed her finger firmly against the windowsill. "Is it your sweet little romance? Well, either he or I will have to clear out: there isn't room for us both. And there's a lot more in it than that, too . . . more than meets the eye. That's why you'll never be happy." But even as he said it, he realized that his last remark was untrue.

"I'm afraid of you," whispered Tanya, hurrying to the door.

Yet in a moment they were reconciled again—his gray, unshaven face was too near and dear to her: she loved him both as a human being and a brother.

"What a horrid thing to say—'amusing me'! Mitka, why can't I have the happiness I want, instead of a made-up one of yours? And that's why you're ill, if you ask me—from making up a love for yourself that doesn't exist."

"Leave that alone!" cried out Mitka, jumping up from his chair. "That's got nothing to do with it. . . ."

Then Zinka came back, and the conversation was broken off.

For some little time after that night, Mitka had a feeling of shame and inward desecration. (Firsov in his story simply made him say that he had defiled himself with Zinka.) But gradually he became inured to his shame, and this seemed to him the most sinister symptom of all. (Firsov commented cryptically: "The fruit forms when the flower dies.")

He did not love Zinka, but his mistake became a habit, though he dishonored both himself and her with his joyless caresses. She did not notice it, for she was happy, and only occasionally became conscious that it was not Mitka she was embracing, but his shadow, which became fainter from day to day. Mitka deteriorated before her eyes—he ate a lot, did not wash, became untidy and irritable, and, except on the well-worn paths of desire, never showed any affection for her.

Zinka did not want him to see her tears, so it was always in the kitchen by the primus stove that she gave way to them. Then Bundyukova used to draw her like a child to her bosom, and console her with eager, coaxing words. Bundyukova had gathered her experience from three marriages, and knew all the secret springs of life.

"I don't sleep a wink the whole night," moaned Zinka once, grateful for the least sign of affection. (Actually this was only a way of speaking, for she slept admirably.)

Bundyukova whispered in her ear: "Don't you know that for a hundred and fifty years Adam tried to resist Eve? . . . And yet Eve won with the apple! She only made him bite it once, and yet to this day he's still chewing her raw little apple. The fool can't leave off for anything." But the reason for Zinka's tears lay deeper than Bundyukova guessed.

In the very thick of her emotional crisis new regulations were issued by which the beer hall programs were to be strictly censored, and only songs on the most edifying topics allowed. Zinka was told she must go, for she sang of frailties for which there was no place in the new era, and so the very evening when the curtain dropped between her and Mitka, she lost both her work and her income.

Pyotr Gorbidonich was the first to learn about the introduction of enlightened programs in the beer halls, and immediately he started to walk with a dancing, hopping motion, as if he were getting ready to fly; nor was his triumph premature, for after two days, Zinka put her pride in her pocket, and came to him for money. She found Chikelyov brooding over the book of anecdotes concerning great men.

"As a man I sympathize with you," he said phlegmatically, after he had taken a good look at her, and noted her embarrassment with satisfaction. "It's typical of me that if I was absolutely at my own disposal it would all be as clear as daylight, but as a responsible member of society . . ." He stood up and moved his hands irritably. "I have no right to connive at immorality."

"Don't be frightened: there'll be enough for you, too," said Zinka with a wry smile. She was standing, but he remained sitting comfortably and solidly, as if he were going to give her request a month's consideration.

"Excuse me, I haven't yet got to the end of what I was saying. As a responsible member of society, kindly note, I deprecate immorality, for I am only a brick in a given cross section, and a mere brick must not have feelings, or else mischief may result. But all the same, I'm Pyotr Gorbidonich Chikelyov, too. I'm weak . . . and can't altogether trample under foot the Pyotr Gorbidonich in me. I'd have him executed, but he pokes his head up again. He hasn't got the better of me yet, though: someday I'll slash off his head from his shoulders, the rascal, and then you'll see what you'll see! I'll cashier him, and humble him, and dishonor him in every possible way."

"Will you give me the money, or won't you, you beast?" Zinka screamed at him, almost reeling with rage.

Her cry roused the chairman of the lodgers' committee from his dream of self-conquest. He lowered his eyes, smiled, and blushed faintly.

"Does a beast remain a beast when he does something good? You're different. . . . I could almost commit a crime for you!" He ran to her, his face distorted with passion, but she thrust him away. "If only you would try to understand me! Pyotr Gorbidonich is trampled in the dust already . . . he's just a brick, a brick. There aren't any geniuses in the world, and a good thing, too! We're all dingy and all the same, and we've one common denominator, and that's Bread. Do you think I want a genius to show me what's what? No fear! I don't want any fireworks. I'd just put the lot through the mincing machine! I'll show you a little picture . . ." He handed Zinka a photograph of a group of Soviet officials of all ranks. "Look at them—and there isn't a pin to choose between them, is there? There are the bigwigs pretending they're reading the newspaper, and here am I standing beside them and looking as if I was yawning . . . as if I found it all very boring." (He gleefully poked one of the dignitaries in the nose.) "Yet that one there has two foreign university diplomas, and seventeen years' subterranean political work behind him . . . and once Alexander III banished him for five years to Siberia—and there am I, all the same, and we're both of us much of a muchness!" He threw the picture into the corner. "That's one up for the little brick—just you watch him sprout!"

"I came here to ask a favor, so I suppose I must listen to you," said Zinka, lowering her eyes.

"I'm thrilled at the new prospects I see opening up for Chikelyov. Yes, you can have the money: I suppose Mitka'll want it for tobacco and soda water. People have the oddest tastes! I read once in a book of a man who loved a tree stump, and went out for assignations with it every night. Odd—wasn't it!" He rummaged in his bed, where his savings were apparently hidden. "I've given him the little manuscript book on the sly: it'll amuse him."

He gave her the money this time, and on several other occasions, too, generously and graciously; he did not even plague her beyond bearance with his disquisitions, for, in the depths of his heart, there was stirring a vague hope of happiness. Gradually Zinka came to depend on his money, and for the time being he refrained from speaking. She recovered her spirits, but she was silent for days on end so as not to annoy Mitka, who sat motionless by the window. Once she began to sing; she felt a pain in her chest, so strong was her desire to sing.

"Stop that!" said Mitka irritably. He was eating salmon, which had been carefully shredded into thin slices. "Why do you buy rotten salmon?"

"It's only a bit dry on account of the heat, so it costs a good deal less," she said with a blush, and cursed her yearning to sing.

"Then I won't eat it!" He got up impatiently.

In the evening, it was true, he felt he had been wrong, but it was not he who begged her pardon, but she who had to beseech him to accept her forgiveness.

"You're big . . . and you crawl and fawn," he reproached her softly.

"My love drives me to it," answered Zinka. "I'll lose you soon, so I'm struggling as hard as I can. Even in my dreams I see you with her." (It was no longer mere jealousy, but the bitter presentiment of her loss.) "After you, I'll despise everyone else. I'm in a bad way, Mitka."

"No good man prospers nowadays." Mitka remembered Puchov's words. He listened.

"It's only the child talking in her sleep," said Zinka. "Do you know, she calls you 'Daddy'?" She saw the discontented look on his face, and put out the light.

"She must be pretty well used to daddies by now!" were Mitka's last words.

Mitka was steadily deteriorating, and his inflexible will was smoldering away like a smoking wick.

Mitka's days were dreary and saturated with heat and boredom, and his nights were ruts along which his disturbed dreams lumbered inexorably. Zinka's love was like a millstone around his neck. Often in the night he struck a match, and in its flickering light gazed at her powdered face, which he had begun to hate. Then he sat down at the table and opened Manyukin's manuscript. Manyukin's obscure notes confirmed Chikelyov's hints, and Mitka's reactions to them were as violent as that painstaking schemer could have hoped. The page of the manuscript where Manyukin wrote of Nikolasha's brother was soiled with constant handling and stained with candle grease; yet he did not yet guess the truth. "It doesn't matter: father knows about it all and will tell me when he writes. Now I must go to sleep. . . ."

And once more a disturbed, insubstantial sleep enveloped his marrowless thoughts.

Even by night he waited for his father's answer. During the day he ran to the door as often as there was a ring at it, and in his imagination saw a hand respectfully passing him a letter—but it was only his neighbors returning from their work. Once he opened the door and Chikelyov came in.

"Leave the door open," said Chikelyov in a friendly way. "Daddy's climbing up after me. (Well, perhaps he is somebody's daddy, who knows!) It's terribly hot today . . . it's touched Daddy in the upper story. Wait and you'll hear!" He slipped past, and immediately afterward Manyukin appeared, panting heavily.

Mitka did not move out of his way, and Manyukin was preparing to make his usual bow, but for some reason checked himself.

"This heat's absolutely bowled me over. . . . I had to get a policeman to tug my heel out of the asphalt." Mitka was blocking his way, and Manyukin wished to gain time. "I raked up seventy kopeks today, and made a lady cry. Say what you like, but people can still cry. You remember the old ruffian who said: 'It will be very odd when people can't cry any more!' Not long ago blind old Sergey Sergeyich stood there and whispered to me: 'I'll drink myself tipsy and do myself in!' For he hadn't any tears left: they had all flowed into the ground."

"You're mighty proud, Manyukin!" said Mitka gloomily. "Your guts are hanging out of you, but you still despise us all. . . . I've been wanting to ask you for a long time why you despise me."

Sergey Ammonich gave a forced laugh and raised his eyes.

"I wanted to ask you something, too," he said. "Have you found my manuscript book? It's gone and lost itself. . . . I used to jot down various observations in it. There are one or two pretty smart things in it, too, in a humorous way." He thought that Mitka would deny it and was trying to drive him into a corner.

"Yes, I've got the manuscript book," answered Mitka simply. "Chikelyov gave it to me."

"What! Chikelyov?" Manyukin recoiled in surprise at his candor. "And I thought the cat must have gone off with it. You know, cats are very fond of going off with paper. At Alexander Ivanich Agarin's home, you know, a cat ate the family archives: they'd shut her up there to catch the mice, then they shot her. . . . Does my style interest you?"

"No, but how old is this Nikolasha?" asked Mitka with a beating heart. "How many years older is he than me?"

"Leave me alone!" Manyukin thrust off Mitka with his hands. "There isn't any Nikolasha. That's only a literary trick. Everyone's a Nikolasha. Leave me alone! . . . Oh!" He suddenly guessed and laughed scornfully. "Now I know what you're imagining. But that's an unworthy, beastly supposition. Why are you so bent on passing for my son?

What good would it be to you, citizen? In the old days if a man insulted your mother you'd strike him. I'm referring to our 'member of society,' Pyotr Gorbidonich, that scourge of humanity. Go and bring me my book, citizen: bring it, please." He gave an offensive laugh and left.

Mitka slowly turned to go, his bare feet moving soundlessly. He opened the door, but did not enter, so as not to interrupt Chikelyov's conversation with Zinka: there was a savage tenderness and an emotional quaver in Chikelyov's voice which betrayed the poignancy of the moment.

". . . I trample my secret underfoot. I turn the lash against myself gladly, joyfully. I give you money . . . and for what purpose? To support my enemy. But I give it all the same, and will give it till the end of my days, because I only think of you—even during office hours," he added in awed tones. "And that is the secret of my love . . . the sacrifice of the evening of my life—but there isn't any secret about it!"

"You're always at me about it, Pyotr Gorbidonich," said Zinka submissively. "And yet if he were to order me to die . . . and not only to die . . . if he were to say to me: 'Marry Chikelyov!' well, I'd marry you, and I'd wash your linen for you."

Pyotr Gorbidonich never allowed himself to be intimidated by a woman, so he proceeded: "But if there isn't any secret, why do I hand over the money, eh? It's simply because I adore plump women from my very heart. That's the weakness of my youth and the tragedy of my age. There's a different lining to every secret. The lark, let's say, flutters up in the dawn and twitters . . . Is that a secret? Far from it, for what has the brainless creature to sing about? 'Mamselle Lark, tomorrow a hawk may eat you, and you'll never know why you've come out of the egg.' It's all stuff! I'm forty-two, and I've believed in this secret for twenty-five years. But where is it, I ask you? And if I can't enjoy its beauty now, in the evening of my life, well, at any rate, I'll have my fun trampling on it."

Then Mitka came into the room; the riddle which had been puzzling him had been unexpectedly solved. Zinka screamed and sprang to one side, while Chikelyov looked around and tugged at a button on his coat.

"How much has he given you?" asked Mitka in quiet, vibrating tones; the flush of shame upon his cheeks was hidden by the merciful evening light.

"I had to have something to live on," said Zinka awkwardly.

"Go and buy some wine," ordered Mitka. "Why did you never breathe a word of this to me, Zinka? It's as if you wanted me to behave like a scoundrel—did you think I'd be more manageable then, or what? . . . Twenty-five years, was it, you said you'd believed in that?" he turned to Chikelyov. "Well, what about celebrating the occasion?"

But Chikelyov had already vanished.

"Shall I spend all the money on wine?" asked Zinka, her voice trembling. She turned and went.

The stillness of the twilight came on, and Mitka went to the window; Zinka was crossing the pavement, her head covered with a shawl. The street was dry and gray and gave out a dead heat, and the sky raced eastward, covered with clouds and charged with storm. In the corner of the room Klavdya contemplated Chikelyov's new present, a little cart with a cheap, gaudy music box that sounded as if it had colored glass rattling inside it. A storm approached, and the lightning flashed soundlessly across the sky.

It grew quite dark; there was a noise, and Mitka turned around. In the open door the gray patch of a face was visible.

"Have you brought the wine?" asked Mitka, but did not get any answer. "Who's there?" he exclaimed abruptly, and had a feeling as if a breath of cold hostility had blown in from the darkness.

"It's me, master!" the gray patch announced itself, and shyly took a step nearer.

"LORD, you gave me a fright! Why do you go wandering around in the night? For all you know, I might be sitting here naked," said Mitka in a curious voice, but he was unspeakably rejoiced at Sanka's visit.

"I'm worried to death, master," said Sanka in a whisper.

A flash of lightning relieved the tension and lit them both up as they sat side by side at the table in friendly reunion. Mitka lowered his head and picked his teeth, and Sanka sat half leaning toward him. His first words were almost drowned by a loud peal of thunder.

"I've brought it, master," whispered Sanka, nodding his head.

A wet, cold draft crept through the window.

"What have you brought?" asked Mitka suspiciously, and then Sanka began to talk; in the twilight his gestures seemed grotesque and meaningless, his voice broke in his excitement.

"The ten roubles . . . that were left over from the fifty—do you remember?" Unguardedly, he touched Mitka's fingers and jerked his hand back abruptly as if they had burned him. "Yes, I'm worried to death. Lord help me, when I think how we used to be always together, and now I've left you, it gets me cruel, master, it does: I feel as if I were being strangled." Mitka clenched his teeth; he wanted to fling Sanka out for flaunting his loyalty so pointedly. "I was at my wits' end what to do with the note. I'd half a mind to throw it into the fire, but I couldn't raise my hand. It's enough to make one's heart bleed to see my wife—she's so poorly and low . . . but I say to her: 'I'm the master's now, and if he tells me to go to hell for him, to hell I must go.' " Sanka became so emotional that there seemed something disingenuous about his candor. "When I'd thrown it into the cesspool it was a load off my mind. It was a shame . . . for a whole half-year we looked after it, and put it out in the rain, and all at once there was an end to it! . . . but breaking things is nice and easy, master!"

"But what did you throw out?" asked Mitka contemptuously, and his face grew gloomy.

"The cactus!" screamed Sanka with a malicious laugh. "Now I've nothing left, master . . . not a pot, not a jot . . . only your friendship. Take the ten-rouble note . . . take it, I'm ashamed of keeping it any longer."

He forced the crumpled note into Mitka's reluctant hand, and Mitka took it, for he could not understand this instance of Sanka's devotion. In a minute he had forgotten where he had put it, for the episode had meant nothing to him. The stillness was broken only by the spasmodic tinkle of Klavdya's music box.

"I don't like your jokes, Alexander . . . I'll chuck you out again!" Mitka paced up and down the room, turning around sharply at the corners like a beast in a cage. "Look, there's a cloud like an anvil! . . ."

"You'd never chuck me out, would you, master? Me? You're an odd chap, and always were." After a while he sniffed and said: "It smells like a drugstore!"

"Mummy's taken dwops," said the child. Klavdya was sitting at the table and listening to the conversation of the grown-ups. Her hands made little white patches on the checked tablecloth.

"Go to bed!" commanded Mitka furiously, and the child went obediently, though without hurrying herself, into the corner in which the divan stood.

Zinka returned with her purchases, and had barely time to shut the window before a torrent of rain poured down. The lightning flashed almost without a stop, and an unearthly light lit up the room and its inmates. Sanka sat with his head lowered as if he were asleep. Zinka went up to Mitka.

"Don't be cross with me, Mitka," she said, standing close behind him. "I've been without work for three weeks, but I think they'll take me on at the theater as dressmaker. I don't know anything about it, but I'll learn all right, I expect. You'll have all I earn so long as you're ill."

"Who told you that I was ill? Fetch the bottle and light the lamp," said Mitka.

The rain splashed, and the gutter in front of the window bubbled monotonously. On the table in the circle of light cast by the lamp stood the bottles and the food. Manyukin had arrived, too, of course, but nobody laughed at him at this impromptu evening party.

"Drink, Alexander, drink to the old life!" repeated Mitka dully. He himself drank without stopping. "We're neither of us up to much—dying's about all we're good for now, maybe—but we're not asking to be pitied or forgiven, Lord no! Drink!"

"I drink to our eternal friendship," whispered Sanka, as if he rejoiced to see the old fearless blue coming back into Mitka's dull eyes.

At the other end of the table sat Zinka, comely and flushed with wine, embracing Manyukin.

"When I'm drunk I'm good, I'm cheerful and talkative," said she, flinging back her head. "You're a *barin*, and my mother was a washerwoman, but you should listen to me all the same. I'm Zinka, and I sing songs, but if anything happens I'll go back again to my mother's washtub. What's wrong in my singing songs, *barin*? I sing songs— no, I only cry for my unborn happiness, but people look at me as if I was a tart. Is it better to wash other people's clothes than to sing songs? Do you respect me, *barin*?" She looked fixedly into Manyukin's attentive eyes.

"Duchess!" he said, and made a pathetic gesture with his free hand, spilling the red wine from his glass.

In the course of this sober and respectable banquet the plan of an attack on Pirman was discussed and decided upon. In undermining Pirman's comfortably established prosperity, Mitka saw a pleasant diversion from the dull round of his existence.

Sanka was silent for at least two minutes before he frowned his agreement.

So it was that Chikelyov's twenty-five years' belief in dreams and the sweet secret of love had a drab feast to celebrate them.

THE sun lit up the litter of crockery and empty bottles on the table. Pollen from the poplars blew in through the open window. The air was fresh, and the celery that lay in the shopping basket scented the room, for Zinka had already returned from market. Mitka noticed a letter on the chair, and in his excitement it never occurred to him that the letter could be from anyone but his father. He contemplated the address with great impatience and the elegant flourishes of the handwriting did not alarm him, though he expected a simpler, more untutored hand.

"Firsov's here . . . shall I let him in?" asked Zinka, coming in with the coffee.

The writer was already looking into the room over her shoulder, and swinging his hat. He was in an extraordinarily excited mood, and filled the room with cries and laughter and bustle.

"My prince!" he called out tenderly, casting a side glance at the letter Mitka held in his hand. "Everything in this world is wonderful. The city in the morning is beautiful. This old planet will last for a long time yet, my prince. And at last I've found the human creature I was looking for: I've discovered a really naked soul. This is the third day now that we've been wandering through the worst quarters of the town, and he's telling me everything. Manyukin's nothing to him! Manyukin can't even lie properly. Just listen to this! In some small provincial town he was given a contract to build a coronation pavilion, and what do you suppose he built it of? Of any old rubbish! The city fathers were delighted—it was so nice and cheap.

They held a service in honor of the new emperor, they shouted 'Hurrah!' and . . . the pavilion collapsed. They laughed when he told the story in the beer halls, but he hasn't got any fancy for joking, he's a gloomy fellow . . . eats eggs, shell and all. He had to run away from the little town, it was a scandal through the whole of Russia! He was considered a hereditary Czar murderer. . . . Then he served in the navy somewhere. He calls himself Anatoly of Ararat—a marvellous name!"

"You find everything marvellous," laughed Mitka. "What have you come about?"

"Well, just a friendly visit, I suppose—but I've an ax to grind, too. I'm still hard at work on my story. There are a few rather interesting little episodes have cropped up in it." He cast a side glance at Mitka to judge the extent of his forbearance. "I'm interested in the technical side of your craft. I should like to get first-hand—"

"What do you want to know—something about house-breaking?" Mitka raised his eyes and took a cigarette out of Firsov's box.

"Yes, some small details . . ." Firsov cautiously touched Mitka's hand, as if he were pressing on a very dangerous spring. "Tell me about it, but in as much detail as possible."

While they drank coffee, Mitka told him about the "bear" that had been the means of exalting Pirman to his present comfortable condition. From his story it seemed that one of the packs of bank notes which Shchekutin had flung on the table had upset the ink pot, and that the paper money had been drenched with ink. At this moment Firsov puffed a wreath of cigarette smoke from his mouth with a knowing air.

"Tell me, now," he whispered, "might it happen that actually a whole pack of notes could get soaked? . . . That is to say, in my story one of these . . . these . . ."

"Spies," Mitka suggested, looking at him curiously. "Speak out!"

"Yes, one of them showed himself to be a traitor."

"Yes, he 'peached,' as we say. . . . In that case he must be made to pay for it, he must be brought before a thieves' court, or, as you say, put on his trial."

"But—" Firsov stopped and cast a penetrating glance at Mitka. "Then it turned out that he was completely innocent, for the ink-stained notes were traced, and he was arrested in the middle of the night by the police. . . . Do you understand what I'm driving at?"

"All that's too subtle," smiled Mitka condescendingly, pacing up and down the room. "We do it more simply. I don't understand, though, why you want to dirty your pen with our life." They left the room together. "One should only write about things that don't exist at all. You ought to lie and flatter people: people love what's nice, and like to think that everything all around them is in perfect order. And then, if you want to write about me, you must have something of Mitka in you yourself. It isn't with ink one writes, after all."

"Oh, but we're all Mitkas, Chikelyovs, Manyukins," murmured Firsov. They went down the steps. "I've been a lot with Marya Fyodorovna"—Mitka stood still and was silent. "On picture postcards one often draws carrier pigeons with ribbons. Well, I'm a little pigeon like that. Marya Fyodorovna asked me to call on you. . . ."

"The Snowstorm never asks, she commands," said Mitka, and stood where he was, for he had an unpleasant suspicion.

"Well, then, she commanded . . ." Firsov bowed his head and went on crossly in an uneasy voice. "She commanded me to convey her compliments to you and congratulate you on your family happ—"

"What?" Mitka's eyes narrowed.

"On your family happiness," Firsov shouted angrily. "In which direction are you going?"

"I'm going to the right," said Mitka cheerfully, for he guessed that Firsov had made up this message himself.

"And I go left."

They parted coldly, not as friends.

"We're still taking each other's measure," said Mitka smiling. He had left his room with the intention of bragging to Dolomanova about his father's letter. His duel with her was in full swing, even though it was waged invisibly and only in his thoughts, and the letter was his heaviest trump.

". . . She isn't at home and I don't know when she'll be back," announced Donka perfunctorily through a crack in the door.

"Perhaps it's only you I want to see," retorted Mitka. "Let me in. I won't do you any harm."

The door opened and Donka's sleepy face appeared.

"You'll lose your beauty if you go to sleep in the daytime. You've got a puffy look already," said Mitka facetiously.

"I'm fat enough without that," mumbled Donka. "This is my little cupboard. Is it good enough for you?"

In the little room there was only a bed and a table, on which some scraps of paper lay untidily. There was a little window, just large enough to poke one's head through in moments of poetic frenzy. The air in the room was thick and the maple outside filled it with green light.

"This place is like the bottom of the sea," said Mitka. "Isn't there any room for you in *there?*"

"She doesn't let me in," admitted Donka apathetically. "I write flunky poems here. May I read you one instead of offering you something to eat? For instance, the one about livery, it's very amusing. . . ." (His apathy seemed ready to explode.)

"No, I'd sooner rest a little."

Donka was going to pieces, but in his idleness and despair he had flung all his soul into his poetry. Now he stood over the table that was the silent witness of his creative frenzy and fumbled awkwardly among the closely written sheets.

He agreed straight off to take part in the robbery of Pirman's shop, as he wished to restore his prestige in Dolomanova's eyes by flouting her orders.

"Sanka's been complaining again about your kicking up a row in his house. It's not right, and the next time I'll make you sorry for it," said Mitka severely when their discussion was ended.

"Wait a bit, and I'll start complaining, too," whispered Donka, and flung himself face downward on his bed on top of the scraps of writing which he had swept carelessly from the table.

Into Donka's solitary poetic brain neither heat nor any known voice could force a way. Time passed, and Mitka

went on sitting idly on his stool. All at once he felt uneasy;
Dolomanova had not yet returned. Donka was asleep and
his shirt was rumpled up, exposing his sinewy thighs.
Mitka drew the letter out and angrily tore open the envelope.

"To our first-born little brother, the honored gentleman, Mitri Yegorovich, hearty greetings and profound
respects." This was how the long letter from his home
began. "Heartfelt greetings, too, from your brother and
devoted servant Leonty, who writes this letter. Our common father also sends you his greetings and his blessing,
but he constantly sits by the stove and chews something, for he is the hero of many years of toil. Since you
left the house, he has got worse and worse. He com-
plains of pains in the chest, wants to have a talk with a
doctor, but can't visit him alone. Moreover, we haven't
any money. That's a fact. We've come to such straits
that we've sold the coat that belonged to us in common.
Forgive us, for the Lord Jesus' sake. Father has attacks
every day, and mother has a swollen leg. . . .
"Forgive me for disturbing your peace. It is said
around here that you have a raccoon coat. That is splendid: a raccoon coat keeps one magnificently warm. I
have read your letter to father, and he said that I should
answer you in the same style. He is very weak, but his
brain is quite clear. And we're living very badly—there
isn't a scrap of sugar or a leather boot in the house. We
hadn't any colored eggs at Easter. Honored Mitri
Yegorovich, I got a position plaiting bast shoes, but
they want to sack me because I work too slowly, and can
only plait fourteen in the day. Please answer this letter
and don't despise it, and if it should be possible, please
send father more money for shoes. You've got enough
and to spare, and all our life we'll work and strive for
your favor.
"I had a mind to marry Parashka from Demyatino.
She is a real sweet girl, but nothing came of it. Why?
Because we haven't any money. Mother says if we sold
the cow, we could marry. But how can one carry on a
farm without a cow? You know it is so yourself, little
brother. And then one is frightened, too, of being

blessed with children. Peasants are fruitful. And there's another little difficulty there, too: I should like to marry Praskutka, but Aksyuta is very pretty, too, and I am passionately fond of her.

". . . Though we see you haven't forgotten your old home altogether. We are very pleased that you remember us, and we wonder what your plans are. Are you coming to live here with us? For ten years you've been as silent as the dead. Perhaps when you take off your raccoon coat and put on a hemp one, you'd like to smell the plowed fields again. Then sell your skin and keep the money for it instead. Here people won't understand your raccoon coat, people are very uneducated here.

"Don't suppose that I'm making fun of you. I respect you, honored brother, and think of you always. And we assure you that our feelings for you will never be quenched, but will continue to grow. I beg you to reply to me, and tell me what you think of my suggestion about the raccoon coat. I can't say how pleased I should be. . . . Father was very pleased with your sending the money. You can't get as much pleasure for a thousand roubles as we for five. If you should write to us, stick a stamp on, for you appear to have the habit of sending letters without stamps. I remain, your honored Leonty, the surviving Vekshin."

The hand in which Mitka held the crumpled letter trembled. His imagination was tortured by the stiff, affected words. Yes, now he remembered the surviving Leonty, that soundless creeper who had thrust him from Yegor's arms to a living crucifixion. Was it mockery? Was it scorn? . . . No, he was simply the surviving one, and warmed old Yegor with the warmth of his impure heart. "How stupid and toothless you've grown, Yegor!" He hid his face in his hands, as if someone might spy on his sorrow. "I came here to boast to Masha of my joy, but it's left a bad taste. In the long years of separation the joys of childhood have gone rotten."

At this terrible moment the demon whispered in his ear that Donka was not asleep, that he knew everything and gloried in the torments of his enemy.

"What time is it?" Mitka asked the sleeper suspiciously.

"Be quiet and sit still. She'll come toward evening," he answered softly.

"I'm asking you what time it is." Mitka's glance was cold and angry.

Donka gave in. "Look there!" He pointed with his finger at a crack in the beams, across which there crept a patch of light. "When the sun's there, it's five o'clock."

Mitka felt that he could not face Dolomanova now, but before he took his leave, he told Donka once more to seek out some "moles" for the undertaking they had decided on. Sanka's wife, who was above suspicion, was to rent the house next to Pirman's business. Donka wrote his best poem immediately after Mitka's departure. "The chained dog recks not the shame. . . . Do not condemn . . . his wagging tail!" Meanwhile Mitka stood in the doorway, unfolded Leonty's letter again, and read the following postscript:

"And tell us why you are called Korolyov now. We racked our brains over it, but couldn't make it out. Mother thinks you've been given it as an honor for distinguished services. Somebody has changed his name in Predotecha, too. He had such a name that no girl would marry him. Tell us about it. It interests us very much, and also what color the aforementioned raccoon coat is."

Mitka read this trivial postscript several times as he searched for the reasons for Leonty's cunning digs. He started, for someone had called his name. On the empty street a gleaming car turned noisily; and Dolomanova stood beside him.

"Have you been to see me?" she asked. Her sorrowing eyes searched for the Mitka she knew in this worn, disreputable shell; but he eluded her. Pity did not suit her face; in the drawing of her ardent brows and her thin imperious lips there was no place for sympathy. Mitka did not like being surprised.

"No, I was looking for Donka," he said abruptly. His hostile eyes reflected the cold autumn evening in which there was not a trace of comforting golden sunlight. He guessed that she pitied him for his unshaven cheeks and his ill-fitting canvas coat (Mitka's predecessor in Zinka's affections had been bigger and broader over the shoulders). Never had he hated Masha Dolomanova so much as now, but never had she been so indispensable to him. The sad smile on her faintly painted lips did its work; he went away without regret at the very moment when she had decided to tell him something simple and important.

THE technique of housebreaking by means of the "Kabur" is as old-established on the earth as man himself, and in housebreaking jargon means a robbery that is carried out by a tunnel from an adjacent house that has been rented for the purpose. If all looks promising, the "moles" burrow into the earth and tunnel out a passage energetically to the coveted treasure. The passage must be sufficiently wide for a man to be able to get through with his plunder. The time such an undertaking takes to execute may last three to ten days, and depends upon the skill of the participants and the size of the obstacles. If there is a single spark of real enthusiasm for the affair, it acquires the glamor of a game, and every new obstacle only increases the joy of achievement.

In the concluding chapter of the second part of his work, Firsov, in his wish to distract the reader's attention and keep him from guessing the truth till the very end, introduced a great number of superfluous details. In his version Alyosha, "a famous crook from Kiev," took part in the enterprise. That, however, was all nonsense. Alyosha was a mere tramp, for whom no job was too mean, who was merely employed to keep a lookout when better men were at work. Firsov asserted that Alyosha began to drink on the very first day of the job, and got a beating duly from Shchekutin, who had no patience with disorderly conduct during work hours. Then Alyosha was said to have disappeared, and after a couple of days the inglorious collapse ensued.

Firsov's deductions were valid, but then his literary invention began (the paper money soaked in ink and all the rest of it). Firsov was quite aware in any case of the real reasons for the failure of the robbery at Yefim Pirman's; he had even foreseen it. Two holidays in succession made the work of the "moles" easier, and immediately after them the "safe man" got to work. Sanka stood at his post at the corner opposite, and his watchful figure reassured the workers in the shop. The work went on gaily, for everybody knew that Pirman could not inform against them, but would have to compromise. Even the most unscrupulous illdoer does not shear the same sheep twice. Besides, Pirman had a boundless spirit of enterprise, and the world was, after all, big and stupid.

They were attacking the fire-proof safe in the corner when Curly Donka came up to Mitka. His ashen face announced immediate danger, but in his eyes Mitka saw a malicious gloating.

"Where's Sanka? Has he bolted?" he whispered, and pointed to the window, in front of which Sanka was no longer to be seen. Then he struck Shchekutin on the hand in which he held his three-legged, clawlike instrument, and, quivering with excitement, cried out: "Treachery!"

Now they all saw it. A squat man, who was well known for his skill and fearlessness, passed the window, and, at the same time, someone whose face was half concealed by the peak of his cap opened the door. The whole scene was played in silence like a pantomime. Shchekutin, who in such cases was in the habit of firing, fumbled calmly in his pocket without shifting his eyes from the glass door through which the warning sounds came.

Mitka caught sight of Donka's legs disappearing through the hole in the wall, and the next moment he had crept in, too, legs foremost, so as not to strike his head on Donka's boots. His hands were still outside when Shchekutin fired a shot, which was returned by a volley from the opposing side. Mitka felt a piercing, burning pain in the thumb of his left hand, and drew it back and vanished into the protecting darkness. He blocked up the exit with the bricks that had been set ready, ran into the backyard, and as he ran, bound up his injured finger with his handkerchief, which immediately turned red. An armed man in the yard commanded him to hold up his hands, and his bloody handkerchief betrayed him, but he struck the man a blow on the hand, made a breakneck leap, and vanished. There were no police pickets in the street.

He found Zinka entertaining his sister with tea and cheese cakes—she observed all church festivals strictly because there were no others in her life. Klavdya was sitting with them and blowing noisily into her little cup. Mitka's sudden appearance terrified them all; from his haggard face Zinka read what had happened and got up with a despairing gesture.

"Tie it up," said Mitka softly, stretching out his wounded hand. "Quickly!" he shouted.

Zinka asked no questions: it was clear to her that Mitka must now leave her forever. She washed his hand, and, while it was still damp, bound it tightly with strips of linen torn from a shirt. Her fingers grasped the situation before she did herself; they moved deftly and skillfully.

The sun had sunk behind the houses, but the teapot was covered with splashes of orange light. Tanya looked at her brother with sad eyes and went up to him. Mitka had already taken his cap in his hand.

"Mitka, what's that?" and she pointed with childish confusion at the dark stain on the bandage.

"It's only iodine." He smiled at her as if she were a child, and, noticing her terror, drew her comfortingly to him. "Try to be happy. I never knew you when you were my little sister, and all at once you became my big sister. You should never marry, for I don't believe you'll be happy. . . . You should never love, sister, for nothing good ever comes of it." All his tenderness had been exhausted in these words.

"And where will you live now?" These were the only words Tanya could find.

"I'll live somewhere," said Mitka, pushing Tanya abruptly to one side. "There's always room for a thief."

Zinka stood with her head lowered, and did not raise her eyes to Mitka's angry, pitiable face. It was as if she wished to preserve him as he had been forever in her memory.

"I must go now," he said. "Forgive me, if you can." He gave her one more look and went away.

It was a long time before Zinka came to herself.

"His linen . . . the linen!" she screamed, and ran into the passage, where just at that moment Chikelyov had felt an urgent call to hammer in an indispensable nail. Mitka was already far on his way. "Mitka . . . I've washed your linen! . . ." she screamed dully down into the dark well. "Write to me, Mitka, even if it's only once a year!" But the stairs only rang dully like a distant echo. . . .

Neither her tears nor her appeals for pity could overtake Mitka. When Tanya went out onto the staircase, Zinka was standing leaning against the wall, in her eyes a look of utter vacancy.

"One doesn't say good-by to women like me," said Zinka bitterly, and now for the first time she began to cry.

They went into the room, sat down, and did not speak —an empty silence reigned as in a house of death. They embraced each other and watched how the western sky mirrored itself in lilac colors on the coffee pot, and gradually grew darker.

BOOK

3

IT IS a flat, well-wooded province and lies apart from the great new highways that have replaced the crumbling roads of long ago. The sun rises early over it, but its glory is departed and its lot is as bitter as gall, for, though once upon a time it was famed for its men and its churches, now its only boast is that the great river draws its tributaries from it. In the spring men drift timber between its blue and yellow banks, and in the summer small steamers crawl up and down it with bored passengers. The banks are thick with hare bells—hare bells that toll the knell of its past glory.

Long-bearded men live on the banks, no one knows how, and their flaxen-haired children sell strawberries at the landing stages. "Here, boy, why are the strawberries so sour?" shouts a traveler facetiously: "are they wolf berries?" The children giggle and cast down their eyes. The hare bells tinkle calmly and noiselessly.

The grandfathers who had borne the fame of the province on their shoulders used to say: "We live content without cemeteries, for our cemeteries are in Siberia." And in actual fact all the winding roads of Russia lead to Siberia, and find there their melancholy end, and for this there are many reasons. The rivers suck busily at the soil, but cannot make headway against the marshy plain. If, out of curiosity, a traveler were to leave his little steamer, he would find marshes everywhere, covered with ferns and interspersed with pools, and surrounded by soft-skinned, resinless birches. The water in the pools is red and stagnant, although it breeds carp.

The fields are covered with coarse grass, the soil is swampy, and in spring, before the moisture has dried from the fields, the people have to tear up the quickly hardening soil with hook harrows. All the same, there were once flourishing villages here, whose inhabitants managed to live somehow.

Demyatino is the richest village in the neighborhood, and celebrated through the centuries for its trading, and the sturdy, enterprising stock it has sent out into the world. The streets are cheerful and spacious, and as for the houses, it would take a cannon ball to break through their gloomy, moss-grown walls. The ponderous buildings are decorated with carvings a hundred years old. The floors are uneven, and the windows have a senile squint, but for all their age their loveliness remains bewitching and perennial, and conceals cunningly their poverty and darkness.

Somewhere in the neighborhood they are bridling the wild energy of the Kudema, like a young bucking filly, with electric tackle. The older generation view the scheme with characteristic disapproval and distrust, for it is a period of transition, and such periods are always fraught with pain and discomfort. The descendants of the rich graze their sheep on the meadows by the Kudema, and nameless people live upon its shores.

A rutty road leads from Rogovo to Demyatino, and parallel to it runs a clean footpath through the aspen wood. It bends at the railway embankment, and leaps gaily over canals and ditches. If a traveler had taken this path, he might have met Mitka returning after all his years of separation. How changed everything was! The distances of his childhood had grown shorter; space had shrunk, and his jaded eyes had forgotten their old joy at the sight of green meadows.

The August noon was full of an exultant humming. Restless, hurrying clouds passed across the fields, and waves of wind broke against the mighty trees. A bird rose in the sky, sank again, and once more soared aloft, abandoning itself joyously to the stream of life, and losing itself in it without a trace. The bright ribbon of the Kudema came in sight, and Mitka's heart felt a foreboding of sorrow.

He did not cross the bridge, but turned aside and sat

down on the bank. He did not recognize the place, nor did the place recognize him. From the meadow came a sound of tiny creatures buzzing and humming; and yet it was still, for there was nothing out of tune with the general harmony.

The noonday hours in August are clear and transparent. A sweet oblivion overpowered Mitka; he dipped his injured hand in the dark, uncanny water, and all at once everything had vanished: the pain, the tormenting thoughts, the unrest. . . . He lay down in the grass, and felt the calming coolness of the earth. It seemed to him as if someone were calling him by name, but he did not answer, though he still saw through his lashes the flicker of the thick and shaggy grass.

He was awakened by a feeling of discomfort. His face had been scorched by the sun and was smarting: a storm wind was blowing across from the river, and a dark blue, black-rimmed cloud overshadowed the meadow. In the storm the Kudema altered her face, she became pockmarked and old, and raged and splashed Mitka, as if it were he who had forced her to drag down stinking human cargoes, and now was making ready to bridle her with thin silvery wires. Lashed by the wind, the grass bristled and flattened itself to the earth. Mitka left the spot indifferently. Soon he caught sight of his father's cottage.

Except for the fresh stump of a tree that had been cut down, everything was the same. The gate whined in the wind almost like a man's voice. Without realizing his own excitement, Mitka buttoned up his shirt, smoothed his hair under his cap, and opened the door. No one appeared. Yegor Vekshin was not sitting on his chair as Mitka had pictured him a moment before. The hut was empty, even the chair was ominously empty. On the window ledges, which used to be so untidy, stood pots with flowering balsams. Outside, the wind tossed the gray tresses of the birch trees. In the heavy air of the hut, drenched in medicinal smells, there was a homely buzzing of flies.

"Is anyone at home?" called Mitka, bending forward and noticing with surprise that his hands were trembling.

There was a creak from the stove, something was moving there; then two naked, sinewy legs were thrust down.

(Mitka had the strange hallucination that the legs sighed.) After them followed a dirty, tousled beard and a bloated face.

"I'm at home!" growled the beard. The old man scared away with his arms the swarms of flies, some of which had even lodged themselves in his beard.

If his father had worn a dozen wild beards, yet Mitka would have recognized him, but this was not Yegor nor even his shadow. The bandy-legged old stranger straddled up to Mitka, delighted with the prospect of this free entertainment.

"Oh, you're from Moscow?" crooned the old man, abandoning the stove. "How are things with the orthodox there?"

"Oh, the orthodox are on the run," said Mitka, altering his expression, and he sat down, streaming with sweat, on the bench, where the old man offered him a place.

"And the flies are eating me up here. I can't close an eye but they start on me. I reckon they'll eat me up before they're done." The old man caught a few flies and tried to squeeze them in his fist, but they immediately slipped away from his nerveless grasp. "There they are again! Why are you looking at my legs?" asked the old man, catching flies in his beard and throwing them on the ground. "They've walked a lot, my old shanks. Walked over a great many stones, too. I was a stonebreaker in Perim. Do you know the pier at Yarlaburg on the Kama? In fifty-two years I reckon I've cracked up a couple of mountains. They photographed me and gave me a rouble. It was all solid stone, and in the middle of it was a church like a little gas station. They say the bad spirits built it, and I reckon they did."

"Hold your tongue, old man." Mitka swung his hand contemptuously and felt the pain again in his finger. "Do you know where the Vekshins live now?" Mitka stared fixedly into the old man's eyes, in which the window and he himself were reflected, senselessly distorted and reduced.

"No, I don't know them," answered the old man, deliberating. "Seryozha, the miller, now, who works on the Kudema, I know him." He began to talk of the electric powerhouses on the river. "Nothing'll come of it, I reckon." The old man cunningly changed the subject, for he was afraid that his guest would go away and leave him behind in his loneliness to be eaten up by the flies. When Mitka got up, he blocked his way. "Wait a bit: my daughter-in-law'll be in in a moment, and she'll give you some tea." And with an old man's shamelessness he whispered into his ear that the young widow could entertain him in other ways, too.

Mitka pushed the old man back roughly and ran from the house. Behind him the gate whimpered like a man once more. It was still raining, and the wind was driving the clouds towards the southeast. The evening came on cold, and Mitka was soaked through and shivering long before he reached Demyatino.

THE blue slowly faded from the sky, and in the cool west the sun stood flushed red as if from a bath, when Mitka approached the village of Demyatino. The wind had died, and a dense, moist silence enveloped the village. In the rising mist the church tower appeared like a purple ghost; then the sun sank behind the ragged outline of a wood nearby and the glamor vanished. Mitka went into the village to find a night's lodging.

The first sound to meet his ears was the bored bellowing of a calf. The night had brought to the village rest and peace after the troubles of the day. Then suddenly under Mitka's nose two women in mummer's dress and a man rushed out of a ruined corn kiln—the man seemed, from the high ring of his voice, to be a woman in disguise. They waved handkerchiefs, and sang an indecent song. Not even a dog yapped at Mitka, but from the houses above there came the gay demoniacal music of a harmonica. Shouting and bumping into each other, a crowd of boys ran across the street. The last of them, the smallest, stumbled along valiantly in boots many sizes too large for him. He tripped up at every step, but did not seem to mind.

"Have you all gone out of your minds?" asked Mitka, seizing the boy by the shoulders and holding him fast.

"No, there's a wedding," screamed the boy excitedly, and ran after his friends, holding his boots by the laces.

His goal was the third house from the edge of the village. It had a dark, old straw roof, but in other respects looked solid and durable. The pillars above the steps were decorated with gay ribbons, and the high, closed win-

dows were lighted festively. The dull stamping of countless feet, the shouting and singing from the house, disturbed the peace of the oncoming night. Driven by the
fleeting curiosity of a traveler, Mitka entered.

At the very door men were standing tightly pressed together, but they made way for Mitka, supposing that he
was also invited. Soon he was standing in the front row
of the onlookers and drawing upon himself the attention
of the whole company. Here and there in the crowd dis-
approving words came to his ears, but all at once through
the din of the feast he heard himself called by his name.

The first half of the banquet had just reached its conclusion. Filled with well-being after their food and home-
brewed drinks, the guests sat on the benches, upright and
proud, and followed attentively the nimbly moving legs of
a dancing countryman. The dancer, a sturdy fellow whose
expression suggested that he was doing convict labor,
danced a succession of dances in the center of the large
room. Sometimes one might have thought that he himself was already dead, and only his boots with their new
galoshes lived on for the general entertainment. The harmonica players sat on the stove, and a boy, specially given
the job, assiduously fortified them with home-brewed
schnapps.

Mitka soon discovered the bridegroom. He was of me-
dium height and good features—there was nothing of the
peasant about him, and beside him sat a beautiful girl, no
rarity in Demyatino. Mitka thought he caught a strange
expression in the bridegroom's face—some evil, hidden
thought. He noticed Mitka, and looked at him sternly
with eyes as hard as though they were chiseled from black
stone. All at once he bowed his head and got up from his
seat. The music ceased, but the dancer went on as though
he no longer had the power to tell his legs to stop. The
bridegroom was forced to go around the room to avoid
him.

"Please come and sit down at the table, Mitri Yegorich," said the bridegroom in a low voice. "We're always
glad to see our benefactors."

Mitka glanced quickly at his clear, fresh brow, but did
not recognize in him the repulsive creature he had pictured from the letter. This confused him, and gave Leonty

his opportunity to lead him without resistance to the table. The bride's father, an insignificant old man whose only claim to distinction was his luxuriant beard, gave Mitka an unfriendly stare and edged to one side to make room for him on the rug of honor.

"Give a welcome to my little brother Mitri!" called out Leonty loudly and imperiously to the half-circle of unmarried women who stood in the corner. The women began to sing in pleasant, lingering tones, and Leonty filled a glass with thick, fragrant yellow liquid. "Drink, little brother! You must drink our healths. I've brewed the drink myself. You can make twelve bottles of it with two pounds of meal, ten pounds of sugar, and half a pound of yeast—try some and see what you think of it." To Mitka's ears the scraping of the glass that was pushed toward him had a sound of concealed mockery.

"Are you getting married?" asked Mitka vaguely, instead of congratulating him. "But why in the harvest time?"

"I was impatient, little brother," Leonty confided, as if it were a delightful secret, and filled the second glass. "Look, this is an entertainment if you like! . . . It's my belief, little brother, that three generations will pass away before people really learn to enjoy themselves properly. . . . If that dancer didn't know how to dance, he'd have hanged himself long ago; his house was burned down, together with his wife and his cow . . . it's his misery that's dancing. . . . Keep the ball rolling! Everybody must have a good time!" he called out to the best man, who was entertaining the guests with his jokes and his grimaces.

Mitka was no longer looking at his brother. Half intoxicated, he observed the rows of guests and looked around for his father, but Yegor Vekshin, drunk or sober, was nowhere to be seen.

"Have another drink, little brother! I want you to enjoy yourself. But look, there they are calling 'Gorko' again! I'll have to kiss the bride." Leonty turned to kiss his bride, but first he prudently turned down the wick of the smoking lamp. He behaved without in any way compromising the dignity of a bridegroom. "Have another one, brother! It's real good stuff! Do!" he repeated, and listened to the best man, who, at the desire of the guests, was recalling some of Mitka's forgotten deeds of valor.

"You'll go far, Leonty," murmured Mitka drunkenly. The relatives listened attentively to the conversation of the brothers.

"With God's help, Mitri Yegorich!" repeated Leonty several times, and closed his laughing eyes, whose lashes were quivering. "For the time being the saints protect us, but the time is coming when we'll be able to get along without even them. . . . But the time hasn't come yet. . . . Have another drink, little brother!" Then they were both silent, as if they were collecting their strength for the coming battle.

Intoxicated by the schnapps he had drunk upon an empty stomach, Mitka surveyed the feast as if it were the funeral feast of all he loved. He clenched his teeth, and despite Leonty's exhortations, not a drop more passed his lips. He stroked his cheeks with his unsteady hand, and as he did so, Puchov's words occurred to him: "Your father'll tell you to shave off your side whiskers. . . ." He was certain that at this very moment, unless he could divert his gathered strength into some other channel, he would commit some abominable act.

At this moment a well-built peasant got up, and the onlookers made way for him.

"It seems to me that the room has become smaller," he said affectedly, and passed his hand across his already smooth-brushed hair. They all began to laugh and cheer, for he was a well-known dancer. The harmonica players tuned their instruments.

"Now, who's my partner?" asked the dancer, smiling, and waited, with his hands on his hips, as if it were a Sunday boxing match.

Mitka panted, and as if some spring in his body had been strained to its uttermost and broken, he leaped from his seat. He could see nothing but that empty chair and the flowering balsams in the window.

"I'll dance . . ." he stammered, reeling and clutching at a fat, pockmarked woman. She pushed him away furiously. "Allow me . . . it's a wedding . . . allow me!"

he shouted at Leonty, who was trying to hold him back.
And so he stood opposite the well-built dancer and listened with a perplexed ear to the fitful wheezings of the
harmonica.

Mitka had never danced in his life. His childhood and
his home had been destroyed, so now he stamped with his
feet on the ruins of their loveliness. Awkwardly moving
his arms, half amusing, half alarming the onlookers, he
danced a wild, unholy dance. His despair guided his feet,
and he felt a real kinship with the soul of the dancing
peasant. The floorboards danced, too, creaking and tittering, and one near the stove kept sobbing: "Mitka,
Mitka, Mitka. . . ."

"He'll stamp your house down for you that way," said
the boy in the big boots disapprovingly. It was the same
boy whom Mitka had stopped in the street and who was
now lying on the stove. He let his legs hang down, and
stiffly and gravely observed the course of the feast, while
on his nose he wore a pair of spectacles he himself had
made of wire. Mitka slowly raised his eyes to him; there
seemed at once mockery and a grim meaning in the boy's
jest.

Mitka could not recollect how he came to be sitting in
someone's lap while his rival took his place and displayed
the marvellous suppleness of his powerful legs. Mitka sat
in a corner, with his head against a patriarchal chest of
drawers, and saw nothing. When he came to himself, it
was dark outside, the lamp swayed and smoked, and a
clatter of china announced the approach of tea. The
dancer was carrying a samovar through the company.
Then Leonty went up to his brother.

"Let's go out and have a talk, little brother." He looked
hard into his drunken brother's bloodshot eyes.

"But you're the bridegroom: people will be offended
by you . . ." said Mitka, and felt boundless shame for
what had happened.

"No one will take offense at anything I do . . . they
won't dare. We're going outside," he said to the peevish
old woman, in whom till now Mitka had not recognized
his stepmother.

Many guests had already left. Only one musician still

played on the stove, and all that one could see of the other was his boots with the toes turned upward. His harmonica lay beside him and seemed to be sleeping under a striped rug.

"THERE's not a soul here . . . it's the back of beyond," Leonty said as he climbed nimbly over the fence and waited for Mitka.

"Forgive me, Leonty, for letting myself go like that . . ." began Mitka awkwardly.

"I forgive you, little brother," Leonty interrupted, and added in a businesslike way: "Your forty roubles came at a good time, and we thank you . . . very much so."

The fog lifted and the night became beautiful. Dark masses of wandering clouds bivouacked over Demyatino, and in the distance the double screech of the landrail broke through the stillness of the night. The leaves of the birch tree near the corn kiln were asleep, only a few stirred drowsily and whispered of the cool breezes of the day. The humid, majestic silence of the night was as exciting as a secret.

Mitka asked how the harvest had turned out and, with exasperation, caught himself copying the peasant talk.

"The harvest's good," said Leonty casually. "What wasn't injured by the rain is doing fine. We've sown nineteen measures." He added this slyly, and it succeeded in embarrassing Mitka. Is nineteen measures much or little? he wondered.

"Sit down, little brother, here on the steps." With a polite but firm gesture Leonty pointed to a place on the steps outside the corn kiln; he himself lay on the straw with which the threshing floor stayed covered till the autumn.

"Tell me, Leonty, about your life . . . about everything . . ." began Mitka cautiously, playing with a bit of
straw.

"You're asking me for a reckoning, little brother."
Leonty laughed noiselessly. "Well, I'm marrying an orphan. I have a farmyard now, four head of cattle, a
cornfield, a head screwed on the right way, a wife, a
house . . ."

"But it's hedged all around with nettles . . . one can
barely get in," said Mitka, and again he caught himself
fearing Leonty.

"Yes, I'm a proper farmer now," said Leonty, who had
not paid any attention to his brother's remark. "And yet
it's not going well with us. One oughtn't to judge a peasant just by what he brews. The soil gets exhausted and the
peasants are discontented. People turn up their noses at
the peasants and say they're ignorant and dull and like
beasts, and that they can't even build a road. . . . Folks
like that are like dogs barking at a rickety wheel; it's easy
enough for them, they don't have to go bumping along
the ruts."

"What do you mean by that?" asked Mitka curiously.

"What I want to say is . . . the peasant waggon has
to roll over every road, bad or good . . . and we don't
bother our heads about you. I don't say things aren't bad
with you in the town: you've gone to the dogs, too. Things
are going badly with everyone nowadays. You'd think that
all the blood that has been shed had turned the air bad.
And we'll have to go on breathing it a long time yet, till a
breeze comes. The armies were too keen by half. . . .
The peasants aren't to blame: I tell you that on my word
of honor." He was silent; he was probably thinking of
something else. . . .

Mitka listened thoughtfully, his brows raised high in
astonishment. His brother's words irritated him, though
he did not understand them. At times it seemed to him
that he had grasped the sense of them, but immediately
the meaning hid itself again, and slyly wagged its little
tail in the darkness.

"I don't know what you're talking about," he admitted
frankly.

"And you needn't, either, I'm only joking. Don't let me pull your leg, Mitri Yegorich. You should keep me in order, you know: you're the elder brother."

The moon had not yet risen. The landrail had withdrawn into the depths of the night, and in the stillness a fly buzzed gently and persistently, or perhaps it was the silence itself that hummed in the brothers' ears.

"Are you the secretary of the executive committee?" asked Mitka, recollecting the best man's facetious eulogy.

"Yes, thirty villages . . . fifteen roubles. And the rouble is a tiny thing nowadays," answered Leonty softly, pointing into the darkness where scattered trees stood and listened to the midnight talk of the brothers. "Do you want to stay here long, little brother?"

"Is anyone listening to us?"

"Only me, little brother."

"Well, I've got something to say to you. I'm on the run."

"I'm in hiding, too, Mitri Yegorich, but we'll speak about that another time." (Mitka began to light a cigarette, but while he was reflecting over his brother's confession, the match went out and the glowing head fell on his knee.)

"Take care, or you'll burn your pants, little brother! And by the way, you've got some mud on your coat, too— why don't you wipe it with a wisp of grass? How one can get carried away by an idea! Do you know I was silly enough to think you had a fine raccoon coat. It almost frightened me to think of it, but now it looks to me more like a dogskin. And we used to brag everywhere about your luxury! Fedossey Kuzmich from Predotecha said straight off: 'If Mitri has a raccoon skin, then sure enough he's got a bicycle, too!'" Leonty smiled bitterly, and Mitka felt his smile in the darkness.

"It's odd now, isn't it, that a sensible chap like Fedossey—he's no longer young, either—should take it into his head to make a wooden bicycle. He sweated away at it for two years—he got it out of a little book—but he finished it in the end. He took a ride on it, too: he rode almost half a mile to the bridge near the wood, you know, but then his bicycle caught fire . . . it went up in a sheet of flame, and the whole village was looking on. A funny story! Really funny!"

"Hm!" As if he were spellbound by Leonty's spiteful chatter, Mitka edged nearer to him.

"It was a dream of his, you see—we've got as funny chaps here in the country as you have in the town, I always say."

"I believe you invented the story of the bicycle yourself," Mitka laughed nervously. "I see you're very inventive, but I'm no calf, either. I can invent, too, and I can tell you it was a fool who built it and that's why it went on fire."

Behind the wood the half-moon, whose dim light scarcely served to illuminate itself, rose red and terrifying. Fog hung over the ravine.

"But if one can invent well, why bother about the truth? Hasn't everything in the world been invented by men, little brother? There wouldn't be any nature otherwise: things didn't begin to exist till men invented them." Leonty became embarrassed, as if he felt he had given himself away, and suddenly changed the conversation. "Fedossey lives in the end house on the edge of Predotecha. You ought to visit him, and he'll tell you about the bicycle. He says that from his childhood he always had an interest in those things and didn't suddenly get interested. He's a cute old bird and he's fifty-eight now."

"No, you invent everything and use such funny words." Mitka gave a forced laugh, and for the first time felt the damp morning air. "You're trying to scare me, Leonty! Who would ever make a bicycle out of wood?"

"You're wrong. Fedossey Kuzmich made his machine of wood because he hadn't any other material at hand. And I only use what lies before my eyes for my inventions."

"And why do you have to hide yourself? Why? You till your fields and pay your debts. . . ."

"I do," answered Leonty calmly.

"What's the matter, then? What's the skeleton in the closet?"

"Do you mind if I don't tell you?" asked Leonty softly.

"Just as you like."

"Thank you very much, little brother," said Leonty dryly, and got up. Mitka got up, too, as if he had recollected the wedding in the house. Exasperated with their conversation, which had interested them but put them out of humor, they both went back. Leonty whistled as he walked, and the moon, which was high in the heavens, showed clearly the coarse material of his coat. The brothers were silent as side by side they walked across the field . . . both were spiritual outlaws, yet no two men were more dissimilar . . . they were reserving the strength that welled up in them for the future.

"Brother!" said Leonty finally, in a friendly but scarcely audible voice that made Mitka assume he was now going to hear the solution of his brother's riddle. "Don't think that I don't believe in your raccoon coat. I believe in it—very much so . . . but I wanted to ask you . . ."

"Ask, brother!" Mitka met him honorably and directly. For a time they walked on in silence.

"Have you ever eaten oysters, brother?" asked Leonty suddenly.

"Oysters?" Mitka recoiled and stood still. "No, I've never eaten any. But why do you ask?"

"I've never eaten any yet, either, but I've got the notion into my head and I can't get it out again. I can't explain it, for one doesn't think in words, but I read once in a book about a gay chap eating oysters, and it went to my head. Here am I celebrating my wedding, the only feast in my life, and I haven't any oysters! And yet there are oysters in the world, I know there are! . . . I'm not so set on eating them alone as on hearing them whimper. That's the main thing about them, the whimper. A notion like that would make the whole revolution worth while. What do you think, should a man sacrifice his soul for oysters?"

Mitka preserved an offended silence. He went a little behind Leonty, clenching his fists, and the pain in his bandaged finger was sweet to him. At that moment he felt Leonty's hospitality, his welcome, and his words as the cruellest humiliation.

"It's so many years since we've seen each other, Mitri, or rather we've never really seen each other . . ." Leonty went on, fearlessly walking in front of him. "We don't even exactly know that we're physical brothers. Do you know Manyukin?" he asked, as if incidentally, in a voice in which there was a ring of pain. In a flash Mitka understood everything. "We write to each other now and then. Are things going badly with him? You and I, we're different. I'm spiteful, I know . . . I'm spiteful because of all the things I can't do. I wanted to study, I used always to read little books in the attic—books, books without beginning or end. . . . I admit it, I'm spiteful . . . very much so! I admit I laughed at your letter. When a man has a raccoon skin, there's no need for him to confess to his father, little brother. I saw through you, little brother, and didn't like you as soon as I read the first lines of your letter. I can't endure muddle . . . spiritual muddle any more than the other kind. I haven't any power over you, but I think it my right only to respect those whom I want to respect. There's no law that could make me respect you. . . I wrote my letter frankly, frankly in the good Russian sense: I wanted to scare you." His deep, penetrating voice suddenly became hard. "And, you know, I'm very fond of speaking with anyone, man to man: it puts one in a strange, alarming, excited mood."

"Well, go on singing your own praises, Leonty: you stand on firm ground while I'm all at sea," said Mitka bitterly, his lips twitching with contempt.

Leonty did not invite his guest to pass the night with him, nor would Mitka have accepted the invitation, for the thought of passing the night under the same roof as Leonty revolted him. They went back silently. Only when he was fixing a pole across the gateway into the field did Leonty look challengingly into Mitka's scowling eyes.

"I suppose you want to know about Father. Don't worry yourself about that, I've put up a little cross on his grave, and done what's usual in every other way. I don't despise order and custom. Tomorrow morning people will break pots outside my door to wake us, the bridal pair. Let them, I shan't stop them. I'm a *mouzhik* and as such I must respect the routine of life"—he was bent on infuriating Mitka—"and till I'm tired of all that, there's no need for you to gloat over me." Scarcely flinching, he made a scornful gesture at Mitka's clenched fist.

"Take shame, little brother! It's a good thing nobody

saw that. They'd have thrashed you for insulting the bridegroom, and that would have fixed you up till kingdom come. Come early tomorrow morning and I'll take you to Father's grave. Pleasant dreams, little brother!"

He disappeared, and Mitka remained alone. His soul was in pain, and so great was his suffering that he could almost have screamed aloud. Something black, perhaps a bat, fluttered over his head. Something hoarse, probably a night bird, screamed near him. Tortured and frozen, Mitka looked into the distant misty fields, where the enchantment of the night still lingered. He heard something move behind him, and, turning around, saw a little girl, who offered him an apple in her open hand.

"Uncle Leon told me to give you the apple . . . to the prodigal son," said the little girl. She said the words she had learned with the singsong accent of her province without understanding their meaning.

"Wait, little girl." Mitka seized the child by the arm. In the hope of finding a small coin, he rummaged in his pocket till he found something with a sharp point. It was a heavy gold brooch he had taken with him in his haste from Pirman's shop. He pinned it onto the child's breast, and, blinded by the gleam of the cheap gold, she stood scared and silent. "Wear it . . . it belongs to you."

And he went quickly through the wet night fields, as if he were frightened that the child might overtake him and forcibly return to him his sinister gift.

THE two days Mitka spent alone in the midst of nature brought unexpected peace to the turmoil of his mind. In these fields over which the winds howled there rang in his ears a still more imploring cry, but Mitka did not hear it. He wandered through villages of whose existence he learned now for the first time; he saw unfriendly men, and houses with straw roofs that were as torn and ragged as though crows had clawed at them; he saw misery, he saw life at its most primitive. It was the same earth that allowed the thistle and the crab apple and the mighty oak to grow up impartially, unplowed, unsown.

All at once he began to understand with his heart what before he had tried to grasp with his mind. The unsown earth, the starless sky that reddened to the glow of distant fires and is cleft by sudden meteors; they must be yoked to electricity! The meaningless human river that was history must be converted by the universal turbine of the intelligence, which can purify the energy of man. A new humanity would arise when the turbine had done its work. And if it cheated men's hopes? Then let it be burned up and consumed.

These thoughts occurred to him as he sat one evening in a gloomy peasant's cottage, where he was given the black bread of charity and the soup left over by the shepherds. The Mother did not welcome her prodigal son as in the parable.

The second night Mitka slept in a field among some oat sheaves. The whole night the owls hooted, and now and then there was a crackling sound of branches falling in the wood, and then it became quiet again. The Mother bared her predatory teeth in the woods, she terrified her son, and tested him to see if he had already spent all his heroic spirit. He did not get to sleep till dawn broke, and he woke when the sun stood on the horizon, peeled from its clouds like an egg from its shell. In its red light every hair of the brown, club-footed animal that stood by Mikta could be distinctly seen. The beast blocked out the sun and looked blacker and bigger than reality. Its suspicious, snorting breath bent the grass stalks on the edge of the field. Suddenly the beast growled and went away. The Mother had sent a bear to terrify her son.

A breath of coolness rising from his sense of victory, or at least his knowledge that he had not met his master, crept over his body. Mitka rose from the oat sheaves, feeling a new man. The world was new to him, and the fragrant morning air, not yet poisoned by the midday heat, filled his lungs. A wood path led through marshes to the backyards of the village of Demyatino. . . .

Leonty was just putting on his boots when Mitka arrived, and there was no one else in the room. With a nod of his head Leonty indicated that his two days' absence had not surprised him. Mitka went out to the front steps and waited for him there. The cocks crowed, a small calf mooed by the well, and a cart creaked past to fetch in the sheaves. Leonty's boots clattered solemnly and noisily behind him, and Mitka rose up from the steps to go.

"Do you smell the air? It smells of fruit," said Leonty. There was a ring in his voice that implied: "I'm contented with everything, very much so. . . . Are you contented with yourself?"

"Where's your young woman?" asked Mitka.

"She's gone to get yeast from a neighbor," said Leonty in a tone that seemed to say: "You've squandered your strength, but I've preserved mine."

"Let's go! What are we waiting for here?" said Mitka abruptly.

The whole way he scanned his companion secretly and searchingly, for he did not recognize in him the Leonty who had laughed at him on the wedding night. This man was a reserved, dignified, self-respecting peasant, but in the other he had only felt the surge of something evil and elemental. Leonty felt Mitka's dumb questioning and confessed: "Mitri Yegorich, I was drunk then, very much so, and I may have said a great deal I oughtn't to . . . but I don't want to quarrel with you, so don't bear a grudge."

"I've got nothing against you," said Mitka coolly. "It's your own lookout, but mind you don't burn your fingers someday!"

He stood still and listened to a slight rustling in the thick undergrowth on the edge of the track. They went toward the main road.

"That's a hare," said Leonty. Soon the little beast leaped in terror across the track and hid itself in the scrub. Then they came to the high road.

A crooked shape, which Mitka had taken for a withered tree from the distance, now appeared as a wooden cross. The roughness of its knotted wood made it look as though it were growing. It stood by the road on a sloping bank, which was thickly covered with valerian. Mitka could not make up his mind to kneel down, but something drew him toward the soil in which Yegor Vekshin's soldier bones lay moldering. Leonty turned away and looked at the road, which paved with small cobbles. The sun was already hot, but the grass around the cross was still wet with the dew of the night.

"Don't grieve too much, little brother!" said Leonty. "Practically nothing of him lies there now." In Leonty's voice there was now not a trace of mockery.

"You see, there was nothing to bury . . . they had to gather up the fragments somehow or other . . ." he went on, and looked into his brother's tortured, ash-gray face, which was turned to him. "This was where it happened." And he made a gesture as if he were anxious to scatter a handful of earth or of seed corn on Yegor's grave.

Then Mitka sat down on the edge of the road and tugged at the dull purple blossoms of the valerian, and Leonty told him how it had happened. Kolchak's shells had reached this spot, and in those days the hearts of the peasants were afire with hate, and powder magazines were stored in their heads. One day the peasants of Demyatino and Predotecha found a live bomb. (At that time the Vekshin family already owned the house in Demyatino

which Mitka's stepmother had inherited from a childless
aunt.) Long and gloomily had the peasants contemplated
the rusty steel portent. They pushed it about with their
feet, but rain came on and they did not wish to go away
without having satisfied their curiosity. "Let's smash it!"
said one, and immediately they all agreed to the proposal,
to smash the infamous thing on the stony surface of the
road.

They swung the bomb and flung it on the road with
their united strength, without judging the distance.

"Fedossey Kuzmich says that it looked like a mountain
in flames. It was only by a fluke he wasn't killed himself.
His wife had given him too much unfermented kvass, and
he had to run into the bushes." Leonty's voice broke, and
involuntarily the habitual mockery rippled through his
words.

"It wasn't really my father I came to see." Mitka got
up and wiped off the grass that had stuck to his pants.
"And now I've lost something else, too . . ." he said violently, and withdrew from the grave.

"I understand," said Leonty. For a time he walked on
with his eyes almost closed. "Is this Manyukin in beggary?"

"He's got his little job," smiled Mitka.

He turned around. Now one could no longer see the
cross, or even the spot where old Yegor had been launched
into eternity. The piebald ribbon of the road dwindled
and lost itself in the distance together with the telegraph
poles, and together with Mitka's grief for his childhood
and his home. As they said good-by—the brothers, who
were no brothers—they looked into each other's eyes once
more.

"Does he write to you?" Mitka brought himself to ask
about Manyukin.

"Yes, he writes to me," said Leonty, and lowered his
head, "but only out of curiosity. He writes that he'd be
ready to buy death, if death were purchasable, and yet
he's interested in everything. I invited him here, but he
won't come: he's ashamed. He's always comparing you
with me, and me with his son. He calls it blood affinity."

"Who does he compare you with? With Nikolasha?"

"Yes."

"Has he written anything about me?" asked Mitka, and flushed imperceptibly.

"Yes," said Leonty gravely and importantly.

They said good-by, and there was nothing either insincere or unfriendly in their leavetaking.

"If the cross should get rotten, then put it to rights."

"Right you are!" said Leonty, and looked away. "I've a little white lead left and I'll give it a splash of oil now and then."

Soon Leonty's yellow shirt was no longer to be seen in the hot haze. The bushes swallowed Mitka, too; and now he felt that he could never return.

THE distant city drew Mitka to itself as the sea draws a wandering cloud. There were still five hours before the departure of the train, so Mitka took a walk through Rogovo, but he could not make up his mind to go into the old house in which the Dolomanovs had once lived. An unknown young woman stood there on the front steps feeding hens. In the evening Mitka got on to the train without either ticket or passport.

There were not many travelers, and what there were were mainly peasants. In the lugubrious light of the railway carriage lamp, Mitka sat opposite three peasants, who swayed backward and forward in their sleep. Two of them were escorting a young boy with an unpleasant, narrow face, who sat between them, to the town lunatic asylum, but the lad betrayed no outward symptoms of his disorder. He sat calm and well behaved, and only when the station lights passed along the carriage did he stir; and it was possible then to read in his face depths of suffering which made it inhuman.

"It's night outside, but we've got a little lamp with us all the time," said the peasant on the right brightly from time to time. Tall and lean, he resembled the apostle Paul, especially when he turned his head on his proud, straight neck. "And screws everywhere, little screws." He said this softly, abandoning himself with secret rapture to the iron monster that bore him from his home. "What power there! Only think!"

"That's the engine, Pavel Paramonich," said the other who sat in the shadow. Now the half-witted boy began to stir, too, and to inquire after some lame children he knew.

At a station the peasant with the apostle's face grew restless; he looked toward the door and hurriedly left the carriage. Mitka divined the approach of the ticket collector and followed him. They got on to the ledge of the carriage. The lights of a passing station lit up the footboard where the two ticketless passengers stood.

"Now we must get out, and get into the last carriage. Do you see, little son?" The old man turned around hastily and in a flash of light that accidentally fell on him his bright bulging eyes could be seen.

"You're a sly one, Daddy," Mitka laughed, for in this deception he saw the only bond between him and the man in bark shoes. "Have you left your conscience at home?"

"Poverty cripples the conscience," answered the peasant. When they had stepped out of the carriage, he explained. "I'm seeing my nephew off. I have eight mouths of my own to feed. It's terrible to see them all gaping for food, it makes one sweat to think of it. And yet I'd like to help this one, too. His father's my brother."

Soon the darkness parted them.

The end carriage was almost empty. Mitka sat down on a bench in a patch of light and observed the sparks flying outside in the darkness. In a corner of the carriage a woman was drowsing, wrapped in a shawl. She could not get to sleep, for a cold night wind blew through the carriage. Mitka closed his eyes wearily, but knew that he could not sleep, although he felt an overpowering drowsiness overcoming him. Suddenly he felt a timid, apologetic nudge.

"Please be so good as to shut the window," pleaded the old woman. From her tone it was plain that she had already made this request several times. "I can't do it. I'm too weak, and there's such a terrible draft."

"Sit with your back to the engine and then you won't notice it," said Mitka hoarsely. He was cross at his sleep being disturbed.

"I can't sit with my back to the engine. It makes me feel sick. Please be so kind! . . ." It seemed to Mitka that the old woman had sat down beside him on the bench. His drowsy exhaustion prevented him from putting an end to her mumblings. "I can't sleep . . . I think of him, I always think of him," she lowered her voice to a whisper and settled her head kerchief. (It was strange that the rattle of the rolling wheels could not drown her voice.) "And I've just got one other request: allow me just once to look into your eyes, just once. . . . I should love so to see him. . . . Otherwise I always keep thinking. . . ."

"What's the good of thinking?" said Mitka violently, crushing into the shadow from a teasing beam of light. "You must sleep, sleep!"

Mitka was aware of the presence of the old woman with all his senses (she even seemed to smell of strawberry soap), and yet he doubted her existence. Then beyond all doubt he realized that it was only his thoughts that were sitting beside him and mocking him.

"Nonsense, nonsense . . . go away!" he screamed, shaking off his delirious doze.

When he opened his eyes, he was stunned by the clatter of the rushing train and blinded by the light of the ticket collector's lantern.

"Your ticket, please!" said the guard, who accompanied the collector. From his tone it was obvious that he had asked this several times.

The sly, yellow tongue of flame in the sooty lantern finally dispersed the fine-drawn web of hallucination. Quite aware of how this stupid episode would end, Mitka got up, fumbled in his pockets, and looked in alarm at the window, through which nothing but night sky and wood was to be seen.

"We've passed Yergenyevo station already," said the guard in spiteful triumph. The collector looked on with incorruptible dignity.

"Passed Yergenyevo!" exclaimed Mitka hypocritically, and before the arm of authority could catch him, he had run through several carriages and was standing on the footboard.

From the rushing darkness of night there blew a keen and roaring wind that swallowed up the sparks from the engine. The line here took a sharp bend to round a dismal grass-covered swamp. Somebody stepped out behind him, and Mitka would have jumped into the brush along the line if he had not recognized the calm voice. (He actually regretted the next moment that he had not jumped off, so ardently did his muscles clamor for violent movement.)

"That wasn't the collector at all last time: you gave me a shock all for nothing, Daddy." Mitka smiled as he recognized the old man with the apostle's beard, which was waving in the wind.

"We step into the end carriage again at the next station," said the old man calmly and gravely, as if he were reciting aloud the ten commandments. "You can see the lights over there, look!"

"But it's illegal, Daddy," Mitka chaffed the old man good-humoredly, and hung out over the flying darkness into the cleansing wind.

"Yes, my dear!" the old man smiled understandingly. "If we were to start obeying all the laws, then there'd be no time left for living. Just count up: if every person in authority were to make just one law apiece, how many laws would we have to obey then?"

And so they flew from one station to another. The nearer they got to Moscow, the quicker went the train. For the city greedily swallows up everything movable that can produce no patent of stability, whether it be a carriage, or a man, or a grain of dust.

AFTER Mitka's disappearance, a dreary desolation or, as Chikelyov might have expressed it, "perfect order" prevailed in No. 8; and yet life went on. Zinka's indebtedness to Chikelyov grew every day, and she had not yet secured the post of embroideress which had been promised her. Chikelyov felt the day of his triumph approaching, and pictured it to himself in rainbow hues. And now, whenever she visited him, a blush of shame at the thought of her impending surrender colored her cheeks, for, in spite of all her errors and lapses, she had, unknown to herself, preserved a certain shy purity of heart; and she suffered. In the course of the past month Mitka had stood in her memory like a remote and baleful apparition—like the sweetest and last disturbance in her stale existence. She forgot her tears and forgave him his disloyalty, for she knew the face that he hid from the world.

In the early days of autumn, when the first snow was thawing on the streets, Chikelyov boldly opened his campaign. A misfortune that had befallen him fanned his passion to fever pitch. He had been removed from his post at the very moment when he thought success and honor were within his reach. At first he smiled stupidly, and tried to persuade himself that he had been confused with a certain Koshelyov. (This Koshelyov had a screw loose.) He even went on going to the office; but there was no official recantation of this glaring mistake.

He used to come back gloomy and quiet; he was always on the crouch, like a tiger ready to spring. (Bundyukov compared him to a tiger, and this piece of flattery did

something to lessen Chikelyov's despair.) When Zinka
went to him for the rest of the money he had promised
her, Chikelyov angrily announced the melancholy news.
In that brief moment of dismay, Zinka's fate was decided.
The fortress was surrendered, but when Chikelyov entered
it in gloomy pomp, it was already deserted. This pitiable
victory Firsov had prophesied long before.

"And you can be attracted by a person like me?" said
Zinka sadly and reproachfully as she lowered her head in
surrender.

Chikelyov had chosen the right moment. The same
morning Klavdya fell ill. The evening before she had been
playing on the floor, and her mother had watched the
child catching sunbeams and busily putting them in her
pocket. When both lover and success had deserted her,
she had become conscious of her lack of care for her child.
In the evening Klavdya had a high fever. The winds grew
stronger every day and the sky was clouded over. Autumn
was advancing over the land, and Firsov had already taken
his faithful ulster to the tailor to be patched up.

If Klavdya were to die now, Zinka would be like a withered leaf that had lost its place on the branch and fallen
into the whirlpool of life, and Pyotr Gorbidonich's trouble would be in vain. It was because of this that the un-
reformed Chikelyov acted as he did; although he himself
attributed his magnanimity to his fatal partiality for
plump women.

One of those days Firsov looked in on Manyukin in
passing. His story, which was almost finished, centered
now on Maria Fyodorovna Dolomanova, so its author had
little interest in the destinies of the inmates of "Noah's
Ark." So he neither knocked nor waited in front of the
door, but simply flung it open and walked in. A strange
moaning music caught his ear. It reminded him of
Minus's flute playing, but it was more shrill and discordant. (In any case, Minus could no longer be counted
among Firsov's lodgers: at the beginning of summer he
had been taken away, and his room rented to a trader with
the proud title of "The Wax-works King.") The door of
Zinka's room stood open, for she had run to the chemist
for some medicine.

Very softly, and licking his lips—God knows why—

Firsov put his head into the room from which the music came, and listened. Her lean arms outstretched, poor Klavdya was lying like a crushed flower in Mitka's bed. The light of the lamp was cut off from her by a pile of books, and her face was in shadow. Beside the bed the chairman of the house committee was wildly prancing. He was playing a tune on a comb, and dancing about, completely absorbed in his effort to entertain the sick child. Pyotr Gorbidonich had never had much of an ear for music; he was never heard whistling or humming to himself. The sounds he gave out were more animal than human; now it was a mouse squeaking, now a tiger roaring, now a camel snarling. Firsov could see only his puffed-out, quivering cheeks, and the back of his head with its comical little rat's-tail of hair.

All at once Pyotr Gorbidonich interrupted his incredible music.

"Childie!" he said tenderly, for he had not yet remarked the eavesdropper in the checked ulster, who was gazing on as if at a miracle. "Would you like me to turn a somersault?" Klavdya's smile made Chikelyov aware of the presence of a third person. A confusion of emotions passed over his startled face, and then it became wooden and expressionless once more.

"Pyotr Gorbidonich, I've come to ask your forgiveness . . ." murmured Firsov awkwardly, for a heart, even though it was only a professional one, still beat in his breast. "You remember that time at the birthday party . . ."

"You're spoiling our game," Chikelyov said quickly, and wiped his perspiring forehead with his sleeve. He had the guilty look of one who has been caught at something disgraceful. He was visibly ashamed of the humanity that had dictated his antics. Exhausted by calamities and the shipwreck of his career, he now looked upon himself as a failure. His unhappiness had been caused by the following accident:

At the new election of the lodgers' committee which had taken place the previous evening, Pyotr Gorbidonich had suffered a crushing defeat. A citizen from the basement floor had attacked Chikelyov in the presence of all the inmates of the Noah's Ark. He had attacked Chikelyov from the drainage flank, so to speak; the drainage was, however, in splendid order and actually it was only a pretext. His assailant had merely become disgusted with the basement, just as Chikelyov had in his time when he was still a simple tenant. Pyotr Gorbidonich had met all the jeers of his opponent with the greatest restraint, and had proudly left the meeting when his assailant applied the term "Marabu" to him. So, the selection of the tenants' committee was left to the old women, for the younger ones had something more important to do, or were resting from the labors of the day. Chikelyov's opponent exploited the opportunity, and carried a resolution, embellished with the brightest jewels of rhetoric, to the effect that Chikelyov was deposed and the election of his rival proposed and agreed to. From now on this new guardian of the common good would subscribe his name to the various documents regarding drainage, lodgings, and other matters.

Chikelyov had no ground for being particularly cast down; he had now more leisure to brood over his book of anecdotes. But it turned out differently: he did not really enjoy his release from his official duties, for a calamity befell one of the lodgers, so serious that even his marriage had to be postponed.

Eventually, however, the wedding was celebrated, but there was a feeling of constraint at the party. Among the guests were The Wax-works King and Tanya, who, after Mitka's flight, had become close friends with Zinka. The ground for their friendship lay less, however, in their common love for Mitka than in their common suffering. But Tanya was cheerful again; she had become plumper, and, as a result, looked younger: her engagement to Zavarihin had put an end to her midnight terrors. Her future husband arrived just as the party was ending. A strong, prudent, well-washed man of indomitable capacity, there was not a fault to be found in him, and just because of this Zinka disliked him.

The party passed off peacefully and soberly, and did not overstep the bounds imposed by the new chairman of the house committee. Pyotr Gorbidonich himself looked thoughtful and mysterious. He ate little and said less. His expression said: "Enjoy yourselves according to the regulations, but don't forget yourselves." This restrained tone saved the situation, otherwise the wedding feast might have developed into a lecture on the decay of morals. Only at the conclusion of the party, almost mollified by the consciousness of his dignity, did Pyotr Gorbidonich become a little more cheerful, or, more exactly, a little more animated.

"Drink, my friends, try some of this!" Chikelyov's face was almost cut in two by his hospitable smile. . . . "Three and a half roubles a bottle," he added, and Bundyukov furtively put back the apple that he had been going to eat.

"Excellent wine!" said The Wax-works King.

"Why do you talk about the price, Pyotr Gorbidonich?" whispered Zinka to her husband. "After all, the guests know themselves . . ."

"That's typical! I'll beg you, Zinaida Petrovna, not to interfere," murmured Chikelyov forbearingly.

Madame Chikelyov was silent, and did not dare to look at Klavdya, who was sitting at the table. The child had shot up after her illness. A glass of sweet wine stood in front of her, and she ventured now and then to take a sip, for she felt warmed by her stepfather's glance. The bridegroom, true to his habit, drank nothing.

Tanya observed with apprehension all the details of this party that in so many respects resembled a funeral feast. She kept glancing anxiously at Nikolka, wondering if Chikelyov's qualities were latent in him, too; Zinka's gloomy looks were not auspicious for her own family happiness. Then she looked around for Manyukin, and as she did not see him, asked Zinka about him. Her loud inquiry plunged everybody present into profound embarrassment.

CHIKELYOV'S roommate was not present, for recently he had not merely been drinking, but drinking with the determination of a man bent on his own destruction. Even before this happened, there had been nothing left of him except his memories, although he still clung desperately to his old gaiety, and the evening before had remarked jokingly that Zinka would never have married Chikelyov if she had once seen Agarin's eyebrows. During the last few days, however, Sergey Ammonich had stopped going to his usual begging station; he lay all day in bed in a drowsy stupor. As is usual in such cases, his acquaintance began to recollect various particulars about the last few days so as to establish their innocence in bringing about Manyukin's catastrophe.

Above all, the author's constant visits to Manyukin were recalled. They had held whispered conversations together like conspirators, and, despite all his efforts, Pyotr Gorbidonich had not succeeded in overhearing them. Moreover, a postscript had been found on the first page of the diary, which Chikelyov had pulled out of Manyukin's drawer immediately after the disaster. It ran: "After my death I bequeath this diary to my benefactor F. F. Firsov, on the condition that he shall secure me a respectable burial at his expense." (Firsov's address was also given and the postscript was countersigned by himself. The separate letters straggled along like sheep without a shepherd.)

Not even Chikelyov had any desire to find out what had really happened in this sad, dark affair; he set too slight a value on Manyukin's literary effects for that. It may as well be mentioned that for some time Sergey Ammonich had had always enough money for lodging and food and taxes, and that Firsov had played a part in this delicate matter.

From scruples of conscience difficult to explain, Firsov later destroyed Manyukin's diary with his own hands—a significant fact. In his story, which appeared two and a half months later, he quoted not a single passage from the diary, and merely added at the end of an unobtrusive paragraph: "The gradual degeneration of this last nobleman of Russian birth adds no luster to the new sun that is rising over our land." This was not at all in keeping with the author's professional greed for human documents, but, in spite of all Pyotr Gorbidonich's Pinkertonian activities, the secret remained inviolate.

The calamity happened on the second morning after Firsov had surprised Chikelyov in a musical mood. The little girl was convalescent, and Chikelyov was sleeping calmly in his corner of the room, or rather he was not sleeping calmly, but having the most fancifully horrible dreams. Pyotr Gorbidonich wakened before midnight and listened to the unusual silence, for it was quite undisturbed by Manyukin's snoring. He lit a match. Manyukin's bed was empty, but Chikelyov was not particularly alarmed by this; after all, Manyukin was a grown man with a right to do as he pleased. But after midnight Chikelyov wakened a second time, exasperated even in his dreams by the insults of the basement tenant; and in great agitation he crossed the dark room and sat down on the edge of Manyukin's bed. Manyukin was sleeping fully clothed, for he had long ago sold his bedclothes.

"Sergey Ammonich!" Chikelyov roused him, shivering in the cold and darkness, in which even ordinary things took on alarming shapes. Manyukin wakened slowly, mumbling all kinds of things, fragments of the day's happenings. "Sergey Ammonich," Chikelyov whispered imploringly, "the word 'Marabu' came to me while I was dreaming. What does 'Marabu' mean? You're a well-read man."

"Marabu?" asked Manyukin, drunk with sleep and painfully assimilating the word. "Marabu . . . it's the name of a French general." Thereupon he began to snore again.

Chikelyov sat there half naked, thoughtfully clasping his crossed legs.

"Sergey Ammonich!" he began again almost in tears. "When did this general live?"

"What? . . . What general?" Manyukin sat up, rubbed his eyes, and now noticed that his right arm would not obey him. "It's gone to sleep," he thought, and his face clouded. "Why have you wakened me? What general are you talking of?"

"Marabu."

"Hm, Marabu isn't the name of a general, though, Pyotr Gorbidonich. Quite the contrary, it's the name of a bird."

"You'll repent your jeering at me bitterly one day," screamed Chikelyov, and ran back to his corner, where he presently went to sleep.

In spite of all his efforts Manyukin could not get to sleep again. He tried to count to a thousand, but his attention was distracted by his numbed arm. Then he got up and went to the window in the twilight of dawn. Snow was falling hesitatingly on the empty square. With a sigh of inexplicable regret Manyukin sat down at the table, covered the lamp with a sock, and fetched his manuscript book. In the course of the last month the book had noticeably filled, but the handwriting had become less and less legible, and at the end was legible only to its author. Sergey Ammonich began to write on the last page, without reading through what preceded it. The wretched light that filtered through the meshes of the sock cast a network of lines over the page.

"Everything seems to me now so vast and great, Nikolasha: I feel as if I stood on a precipice and could find nothing to rest my eyes on. And the jump down there is terrible! I struggle with myself and overcome myself and lie helpless and forlorn at the edge of this last abyss. From here I see everything and understand everything, but it is all meaningless to me already. In this decisive hour I send you neither blessing nor curse, but only the friendly advice: hold to what you have attained, be strong and firm, not only in your plans, but in your actions. (I shan't be offended at your laughter over my bequests. Laughter is useful to the living: it is a mild purgative like senna tea. I'll laugh with you.)

"While you are taking Russia, and with it the whole world out of my hands, I feel you are asking me silently what my thoughts are. Then listen! The Russians are above all a people who inhabit an indeterminate area in space. It is not the birches, or the ravines, or the white country houses, so often sung by the poets, that are Russia. It doesn't shock me any longer now when a birch tree is cut down, or a country house is enthusiastically set fire to, or a romantic river is harnessed to machinery and made to serve man. Living things are never unchangeably the same, every living thing is a phoenix, it grows and spreads, and bursts the narrow bonds of reality, and flows on forever. May God preserve the soul of the people from evil, but you must help Him, for even the Almighty's arms have grown short. (My little angel, senna tea does no harm, even when the body is working properly.)

"Yes, the time has come when even the people should get a glimpse out of the window that Peter broke open. Perhaps they are ripe for it already, and have already acquired all the vices that are so indispensable for the government of our beloved fatherland. Unconscious of itself, the soul of the people grows up, and suddenly it bursts like a bud, and before the eyes of all appears something that never had existed before. You must pass on our culture to your heirs. The horse takes a great leap—out of the fourteenth century . . . into what? . . . Beware lest the man you despise but whom God has chosen should one day put on a fine waistcoat with a silver chain across his belly! Then you'll be terrified, and in your terror you'll kneel down before this god or this monster. Who can tell? For we have known our people after all only as footmen and bathing attendants, and coachmen and nursemaids.

"But other faces, other things rise before me . . ."

Sergey Ammonich suddenly grew very tired, and, dropping the pen from his hand, began to muse. His musing was like a sleep, and his sleep like the sleep of death. The

lamp was scorching the sock, which began to smoke malo-
dorously. Manyukin leaned back in his armchair (the leg-
acy of a lawyer who had fled the country), and sat on
without thinking. He wanted a smoke, so, with awkward
fingers he scattered tobacco on a piece of cigarette paper,
neatly wrapped it up and gummed it, and was about to
lift the cigarette from the table. Then it seemed to him
that Chikelyov was coming toward him, and his heart contracted and began to beat wildly. He could not reach the
cigarette with his hand, and fell back into his chair, gasp-
ing. The cigarette remained unlit, the page was not written to the end—Sergey Ammonich had had a stroke.

Next morning Chikelyov first of all put out the lamp,
which was smoking badly, and then ran everywhere to
tell the news. He was even more afraid of death than of
dismissal from the office; so he was overwhelmed by this
disaster which had occurred so close to him. The assistance of Madame Bundyukov, a tower of strength in a
crisis, was invoked to restore order after the morning's
confusion.

At Chikelyov's request, Manyukin, in his armchair, was
set with his face to the wall. A doctor, who hurried up
with Zinka from the floor below, administered first aid
and helped to get the sick man to bed. An agreeable
young man, he was pleased at the opportunity of appear-
ing in all the panoply of his wisdom before the ex-chair-
man of the house committee. He immediately made a
sketch of Manyukin's heart, main artery, and head on a
small piece of paper, and showed, by means of dots, the
course of the blood clot that had blocked a vital passage
in Manyukin's brain. Chikelyov murmured approvingly
and passed on the drawing to Klavdya, who immediately
penciled on a mustache and embellished the head with
horns.

"Does he hear what we're saying about him?" whispered Zinka in terror, interrupting the doctor at the most
interesting point in his exposition.

"Not a sound! It's all the same to him now," answered the doctor.

In the anteroom Chikelyov seized the doctor. "A
moment!" He excused himself awkwardly. "Couldn't you,

as a doctor, take him with you?" However, he instantly realized that this was a shocking breach of medical etiquette, and drew back in time.

The whole day Chikelyov dragged Manyukin around from one hospital to another until at one they at last agreed to take in this uninsured patient at their own expense. Firsov melodramatically concluded the chapter on Manyukin's collapse with the following sentence: "The world is not boring, but merely cruel, my masters." (It may be remarked, incidentally, that Firsov did not hear of this sad event—no one knowing where he was—till some two weeks later, by which time Manyukin had been turned out of the hospital.)

But life went on, though so many boots had trampled on it.

Chikelyov's room was rearranged and filled with new furniture, which had the solidity of tombstones. In place of Manyukin's small bed rose a colossal cupboard, and on top of it a clock, Chikelyov's fervent dream for years. The chimes of this clock lasted so long that the second quarter was due to be struck before the first had well stopped sounding. The ticking of the clock was so loud that the springs had to be wrapped up in tow, for Pyotr Gorbidonich himself often leaped up in the night and gazed at the obstreperous dial in helpless fury. But, generally speaking, his secret ambition was gratified.

"It's typical of me," reflected Chikelyov aloud after supper, while Zinka dusted their wooden monster of a cupboard. "If I have something solid and durable of my own, my intentions must be above suspicion. And if my intentions are above suspicion, my hands can be relied on. And if my hands can be relied on, then there can't be anything deceptive in the goodwill my superiors show me. And if that is so, who am I, Zinaida Petrovna?"

"A pillar of strength," supplied Zinka, promptly and obediently, and her face was drawn with boredom.

"Yes, but what sort of a pillar? Please observe that lots of pillars only serve as supports for doors."

"A pillar of the State," completed Zinka yawning, to Chikelyov's immense satisfaction.

Yes, poor Zinka had now completely grown into Madame Chikelyov. Her dreams were smothered and bur-

ied under the petty details of existence, and, as if to grat-
ify Chikelyov's partialities, she was becoming monstrously
fat. Their peaceful married life was more intolerable to
her than convict labor. One autumn day Klavdya was
taken to school. The soft-eyed little creature had shot up
into a thin, tall girl, who had seen a lot of life, but could
be merry at times. Pyotr Gorbidonich indulged her childish tastes for amusement judiciously and in moderation.

Firsov was able to observe all these transformations
with his own eyes when he came to test some deductions
he had made in his story. Always dreading the sudden
appearance of her husband, Zinka treated him capri-
ciously, and at times impatiently; and with a stream of
compliments, Firsov would edge to the door, for he had
neither leisure nor inclination to watch human dreams
being turned to ashes. (Yet he found time to notice that
Zinka's brother Matvey, who had come back again, had
taken up his quarters in Mitka's old room.)

During the last few months a wave of unprecedented
energy had filled Firsov. Every time after he completed
a new piece of his work, he would walk about the city as
if in a trance. He used to talk to himself in the street, and
even aroused the curiosity of the police. When listening
to conversations, he only heard what corresponded to his
own thoughts, and the whole human race existed for him
only as a few tragic masks, the characters of his story. He
was like a factory with its population of many thousand
people. If he had been hindered in his work, all his
stored-up energy would have exploded and shattered him
and his famous ulster to pieces. Firsov was creating.

His creative work was inextricably involved with his
love affair. He visited Dolomanova rarely, but each visit
was an event for both of them. He brought to her shapeless fragments—torn, raw, and bleeding—from his story,
blossoms of his overheated passion. For whole evenings on
end he sat on her sofa and, regardless of Donka's jealous
eavesdropping, told her his plans for the future—plans for
which the whole universe seemed too small and narrow.
She smiled queerly when with the trembling voice of a
wizard he summoned from the darkness the spirit of that
other Manka the Snowstorm—the beautiful, imperish-
able, cloud-capped Manka, who wandered through life

girdled with lightning. One of Firsov's literary devices was to make Dolomanova always appear in his story suddenly and unexpectedly like a clap of thunder.

Dolomanova was pleased to see herself in Firsov's mirror, where everything took on such dazzling and yet disturbing splendor, though sometimes her reflection scared her like a dream apparition. Sometimes they felt cramped by the four walls of the room, and then she would throw on her cape and wander with Firsov through the city. Over the quiet street hung a transparent stillness, in whose depths a sound would rise and swell like a grain of corn and vanish again. Firsov and Dolomanova went side by side without touching each other, stranger to each other now than on that terrible and longed-for night of Agey's death. Both were seeking for something unsubstantial, yet indispensable to them, and, strange as it may sound, they were fortunate in not finding it.

Firsov walked along the edge of the unflagged pavement and poked his stick through the fresh ice crusts on the puddles. He enjoyed this childish amusement and did not notice that he was lagging behind Dolomanova.

"Firsov!" she cried out, and waited. "You're wrong: thought is more important than action, but one must judge a man by his actions only, for his thoughts are always horrible."

"That's the spirit of the time, madame," growled Firsov.

"You always get cross. But you needn't be cross with me: I'll never give in to you," went on Dolomanova. "When you see the earthly part in the man you love (and that's the dirtiest part), it defiles your love. What are you thinking of now?"

"The same as you were, when you said that about *him*." The writer was angry and jealous of the characters in his book, of himself, and of Mitka. "It's the opposite with other people: to them the earthly is most touching, and it's that that they love in the beloved."

It was snowing. The trees stood motionless and sad; the air shimmered blue in the frost. On such evenings the powers of the soul are many times magnified, and one's eyes almost see that for which sight was given them. Firsov understood quite well that Dolomanova was looking for Mitka in the dark night streets. Although she could call him at any moment, for he lived quite near, yet she still strove to find him as he was reflected in Firsov's deceptive mirror. (Firsov started the chapter treating of this as follows: "So the planet, which cannot tear itself away and sink into oblivion, is doomed to revolve forever around the unattainable object of its love.")

And in actual fact Mitka was not far away, and not infrequently a sinister echo of his fame found its way to Masha. His star that had been eclipsed shone once more with unrivaled brilliance. As he worked alone he could, when he liked, so Masha learned, go off on a tour of a month and a half in foreign countries without being caught. No iron safe could boast that next morning its walls might not be found bored through by Mitka's electric drill. The foreign criminal authorities set their most famous detectives on his track, but their efforts ended farcically. Masha was told how Mitka made one of these detectives drunk in a great hotel, put three dollars into his hand, and said: "Go along, old man, go to bed! You're an official, after all, and my society might compromise you." And perhaps his wild head might have been crowned with the glory of a Rocambault, if he had not been a Rocambault with a Russian coefficient (as Firsov said).

A successful safe-breaking coup in a foreign city demonstrated the total failure of the ingenious precautions elaborated by the banks, and amazed even the greatest experts. The guardian angel of thieves hovered invisibly over Mitka's head. Vassily Vassilyevich Panama swore, driveling with delight, that Mitka was going to naturalize himself and settle in South America to live and work there. From other less reliable sources it was heard that Mitka had been invited to a private interview with one of the most influential personalities in Europe. Firsov, who had close ties with the thief world, experimentally circulated the rumor that Mitka had decided to enter a Caucasian monastery, and already had opened negotiations with the abbot. All this merely proved how great was the craving for romance in those unheroic days.

THEN the days of great deeds seemed to have passed forever. A great peace, unusual for the beginning of winter, ensued. The stars of the thief gang withdrew into humble obscurity, but even there the iron arm of the law found them and hauled them out.

Alyosha's dazzling career was brought to an end before everybody's eyes; he was caught while on some trifling undertaking. They had scarcely recovered from the shock of this event when the news of a fresh loss ran through the thinning ranks of the Moscow thieves. Quiet Benchik's "Mill" was closed and Benchik himself consigned to a spot that did not suit either his weak health or his zest for action. Mitka himself was several times within an ace of capture, and wild tales were circulated about him. It was asserted that he had run across a square from his pursuers, and as he ran, a pet greyhound belonging to a profiteer's wife had set its teeth in the seat of his trousers. This stupid tale was immediately refuted by Dolomanova, so did not have a wide circulation.

"He had to run off in his drawers, it appears," Donka gloated; but she ordered him into his little room and commanded him to be silent. She stepped up to the mirror and looked at herself for a long time; she had bitten her lips until they were bleeding, and the muscles of her mouth twitched as if she had swallowed poison.

There was agitation and misgiving among the thieves, for there was only the younger generation, without talent or principle, to replace the old guard. Secret ears and eyes were suspected in the guard itself. When Petya, the

"Baby" (an overgrown, flabby-limbed lad), who was everybody's darling, was nabbed, they had not a doubt but that Comrade Artemy had betrayed him so as not to have to pay his debts. Artemy himself had only just come out of prison, and used to pass the night in empty waggons; yet he was put on his trial before the thieves' court and beaten; they covered his head first with a blanket. They disgraced the old man for nothing, for Artemy, who was of the old school, could hardly know anything about Petya, for he had just spent half a year in prison. The uncertainty tortured and exasperated the thieves and goaded them to senseless measures. Katya, a receiver of stolen goods, who had once been deserted by Petya, was also suspected and could not clear herself so easily, so she resolved on an extraordinary step: she cut off her beautiful hair and brought it wrapped up in newspaper to the thieves' court. Someone was practising treachery with a gusto that amounted to inspiration; someone was taking a cruel vengeance on the gang because it held him, the avenger, in its accursed lap.

These blows were a warning to the stars of the thief world. Now in secret dens they conversed in terrified whispers; the walls had ears; the wine, the very stillness itself, was spying on them. Their hearts grew dark, and dreaded to beat lest they should betray themselves. The fist of the iron arm, once clenched, did not unclench again. One piece of pleasurable news suddenly cheered their lethargic despair—the news of Sanka's escape from prison ran like fire through the thieves, for in his flight they saw an omen of success to come.

Of course this escape was linked with Mitka's name, and Sanka himself, when he appeared again in the dens, took no pains to contradict it. The thieves knew for a fact that during Sanka's absence Mitka had conscientiously supported his bereaved wife. (The woman drank a great deal now, and went the round of the places where her husband had been before.) Alcohol gave a pink flush to her cheeks, but her lungs were too weak for the rough and tumble of existence. Lashed by these new storms and dangers, her features grew strangely keen and beautiful; any return to a peaceful life was cut off for her. Bound together once and for all, Sanka and his wife wandered together through life, made inseparable by shame and despair. They appeared everywhere together, and the legend grew that their appearance brought cheer to the drinker, courage to the fugitive, and luck to the gambler. Sanka's temporary withdrawal from the band was regarded as a sly dodge to cover his traces. He was forgiven his recent treachery, for thieves, too, can be generous in their way.

So it came about that Alexander Babkin's boot-last workshop was never properly set going, for after his arrest Sanka did not return to his beloved cellar. But Fate now smiled on the man she had ruined: he was fortunate in two small undertakings. Donka's affairs were even more of a topic than Sanka's; he still persevered in his role of love-sick flunky, but no one who knew his violent temperament and Dolomanova's indomitable will dared to laugh openly. Donka was silent and tense as a fiddle string, and Dolomanova was now seldom seen among the thieves. At this time she was engaged in a widely discussed film, whose scenario had been written by Firsov.

At the beginning of October, after overcoming all sorts of difficulties, the film was finally produced in the cinemas of the capital. Now all Moscow had the opportunity of seeing Manka the Snowstorm. But the audience, who saw only the play of shadows on the screen, could have no idea of what had taken place behind it in actual fact. (Following a plan of his own, Firsov had put a good half of the characters in his novel into the scenario, simplifying them somewhat for the popular taste, and disguising them a little. In his story Mitka was engaged on deep problems in the sphere of applied mechanics, and at the end invented a kind of flying steamer; Manyukin danced goutily, and expired with a song on his lips; Dolomanova cast her spell upon them both, in the interests of the class war, but drove Donka to his destruction merely from the sensuality characteristic of her class. Soon the blood of suicide stained Donka's officer's tunic. Firsov's experiment was completely successful: the masks conducted themselves according to the formula.)

The fame that had so quickly come to her depressed Dolomanova. At the last rehearsal she gazed despairingly at the screen, where, in the guise of a self-satisfied diva, she went through her various degrading antics. The crude simplifications of the screen disgusted her, and she let her eyes fall on the little bag that lay on her knees.

"Do you like it?" asked Firsov delightedly. "Isn't it a luscious spectacle! Which of the leaders of the revolution could have dreamed of such felicity? To the left virtue, to the right vice, formed up in rows like soldiers in a barracks. . . . It's the petit-bourgeoisie eliminating itself before the just judge. And I am the chief mourner. . . ."

"I want to go home," said Dolomanova dully, and got up.

"Won't you give the chief mourner some coffee?" He did not overtake her till they were in the cloakroom, and then, without waiting for her assent, Firsov took a droshky. She stepped in silently. Firsov squeezed in after her and the drive began.

The weather was abominable. In the foggy streets a universal gray prevailed, and only a single moving red patch, a seller of autumn peonies, gave a splash of color to the dingy scene. Soon electric lamps flashed out with light that fatigued the eye and made one want to yawn. It was about five o'clock.

"If he sees me on the screen like that, what will he think of me?" Dolomanova laughed.

"He won't think anything, he won't even understand it: it will only fan his love for you," said Firsov crossly. "Lord, I'm so hoarse, I might almost qualify to sing in a church choir. . . . Madam, he won't understand anything and he won't suffer, either. He isn't at all the man you think he is. One can't mix with rogues and not pay for it."

"Your wit's wearing rather thin, Firsov, and you're jealous. Take a rest!" said Dolomanova disapprovingly, leaning on his arm as they entered the yard. "It's not you but your ulster that was responsible for that joke."

A big puddle lay right in front of the door and, watchful as a house dog, blocked the passage of pedlars and wandering musicians, should the whim take them to go about their work in such bad weather.

AT THE entrance Donka announced that a strange young
lady was waiting for Dolomanova. There was a note of
anger in his voice beneath his constrained courtesy. He
had already read his poems to Tanya, who had been waiting for a whole hour; he had never before confided so
much in a stranger, and a woman at that, for fortunately
he had not guessed that she was Mitka's sister. A storm
was gathering in Donka's soul; in the dark the raging
winds swelled and sought for an outlet. He was pleased
with Tanya's visit, and she liked his queer poems, in
which there was a sensibility that was new to her: her
pleasure was the pleasure of surprise. . . .

Shivering with cold, for she had been soaked by the
rain, Tanya had wrapped herself in Dolomanova's dressing
gown, and was listening excitedly to the cadence of
Donka's voice when the bell rang. Donka hurried awkwardly into the front room, and Tanya could see through
the half-open door how nimbly his obsequious hands
grasped Firsov's coat, which had been carelessly flung at
him. Dolomanova went up to Tanya with a calm, firm
step. Tanya seemed to ask something with her eyes, which
Dolomanova answered affirmatively. Then they held their
hands out to each other without uttering a word. It was
too much for Firsov, and he turned away from this histri-
onic recognition scene, which lacked the simplicity of the
stage.

"I've put on your dressing gown and slippers, I was
frozen to the bone . . . do you mind?" asked Tanya in a
shy and confiding voice.

"We'll have some tea in a minute. Will you have some brandy with it?" Dolomanova smiled warmly and dropped Tanya's hands.

"Yes, some brandy," Tanya repeated with a bewitching smile. "Do you know I was very much afraid of meeting you. I had heard so much about you."

"From Firsov, I suppose?" Dolomanova gazed at her coldly and penetratingly.

"Yes, from Firsov," admitted Tanya, and a feeling of returning courage flushed her cheeks.

"Firsov told you the truth."

"He said you were bad . . . bad for my brother. And you're so simple and nice! . . ."

"Everyone is simple and nice," said Dolomanova gravely. "But I can be different, too, Tanyechka." She asked Firsov to get the tea ready, and he hurried out so hastily that he broke his cigarette. "So this is what Mitka's sister looks like! I have never managed to see you in the circus."

"And you won't see me there again, either," said Tanya, flushing once more.

"Yes, I heard that, too."

"From Firsov? . . . He told me that he had described me in his book. I read a bit of it . . . it was printed in a magazine. But it isn't true to life. He describes me as a weak girl . . . but I'm not weak and I'm not a girl any longer, either. I'm a circus artist: we never cry . . . or if we do, only from temper." She smiled to show that she was not in earnest. "I'm really very strong."

"I can see that. Is your wedding coming off soon?"

"Next Wednesday . . . if business permits. . . . Nikolka"—Tanya stopped again, as if she were confessing something disagreeable—"Nikolka always has some business or other." (All at once Tanya wondered. Dolomanova did nothing but ask her questions—told her nothing about herself, and Tanya had not the courage to ask.) "Next Wednesday," she repeated wearily.

"And aren't you sorry to be leaving the circus?" Dolomanova wanted to talk to her of the humdrum side of every marriage, but read from Tanya's eyes that she knew all about it already. "The circus is life at top speed. I love the circus because one always sees something extraordinary there. Certainly," she said reflectively, "like every wonderful thing it has its reverse side."

"No, it gives one work, work, work . . . and the possibility of breaking one's leg," Tanya laughed. "I'm not sorry to be leaving. To bring up a child and make a man of him is useful work, too. I don't approve of women who . . . well, don't have children." (She warmly defended her strange opinions, because actually she still felt a yearning she could not stifle for something different. Dolomanova observed that Tanya was still entangled in her own spiritual struggles, and that she spoke of motherhood as if no one had ever sung its praises before.)

Dolomanova became silent, and did not thaw until Tanya, who did not know what else to say, stopped talking.

"Will you invite me to your wedding?"

"But *he* won't be there." Terrified by her own clumsiness, Tanya added quickly: "He wrote to me that it wasn't right that I should keep up relations with a thief, but he's good all the same."

"He isn't good: he's a willful man, a hard man. . . . God preserve you from loving a man of Mitka's stamp. Love means to him at most not despising you, and even so he loves very few people."

"Mitka doesn't despise me." Tanya defended herself, addressing the empty dusk, for Dolomanova had gone behind the screen in the other corner of the room.

"It's quite different with you. You're the screw that keeps him up to the mark, otherwise he'd stop being ashamed. A proud man has nothing to be ashamed of. You are his feeling of shame, Tanyechka." Behind the screen Dolomanova spoke of the beauty of human aspiration, which was only wise, however, if it recognized that earthly influences could impair its strength and faith. It was clear that in this sermon that Dolomanova was thinking of something else.

Tanya suddenly got up cautiously and went to the corner where her hostess was standing. "What are you doing?" she asked softly. "Zinka says you're bad, but you're not, you're only unhappy."

"And you're silly, Tanyechka," answered Dolomanova, coming slowly from behind the screen. "You resent life as it is, and yet how do you propose to live?" (Then she sat down on the sofa near Tanya and told her of an incident in her childhood. As a girl she had seen dark stains on the bed sheet of the pockmarked woman to whom old Dolomanova had sent her for her summer holidays. The only light had been the lamp burning before the holy icon; it was evening. "It's nothing, it's nothing," the woman had comforted Masha as she sat there weeping and terrified. "Even the Mother of God herself had them. They're called the monthlies.")

Tanya violently pushed away Dolomanova's hand, which was stroking hers, and leaned back in disgust.

"You're all of you always educating me. First of all Firsov, then that Chikelyov, and now you. You hate my not wanting to know all that. You think you're developing new thoughts about mankind, and, really, you're just degrading everything. Men are just men, indeed? That's all Chikelyov talk! There was never so much disappointment with mankind as there is today. . . ."

"You've seen your brother seven times altogether, I suppose, Tanyechka, and you've come to love him beyond your strength." Dolomanova brought the conversation nearer home. "Haven't you anything better in life?"

Suddenly the door opened and Firsov's voice asked if they might come in. Then came a whole procession. First came Donka on tiptoe with the samovar, which bubbled and hummed and spread a homely smell of warmth and charcoal. Then followed Firsov, a jug and tea things in his hands, a napkin under his arm, and an obliging smile on his lips. Third came the famished cat, Donka's friend, who lived with him in the little room.

"The great poet's Pegasus," Firsov introduced the cat, but Donka seized the animal and ran away with it.

They drank tea to the sighings of the samovar, and spoke of Mitka. "He's a geyser set spouting by an earthquake," remarked Firsov, busily looking through his notebook. "The sun is passing through a terrible phase. Mitka is plague and anarchy and ignorance and even ruin. He is the lump of wood from which the progenitors of the future man will be carved. But humanity will not go to the dogs all the same. I'm a melancholy fellow, but I maintain that the organ of laughter, the spleen, will scent the danger in time and save the world. If I skip the last few years, I'm forced to admit that man is somehow beautiful and his creation somehow wise. Himself warm and living, he seeks out and creates every moment new idols for himself, and cannot realize that he himself is better than all his creations. Man is alive, but an idol is dead, even when it is obeyed."

Donka interrupted him. "An old man has come to fetch you away," he said to Tanya in an intentionally exaggerated flunky voice.

In the front room Pugel, whom Tanya always told where she was going, was waiting. He was soaked by the rain and excited by pleasant news, and could barely wait on his chair till Donka found a suitable moment to announce him. Tanya absent-mindedly said good-by to Dolomanova: the news that Pugel had brought her had shaken her out of her apparent calm.

"I hopped along the whole way like a poy," whispered Pugel into Tanya's ear. She stood with her eyes closed and swayed imperceptibly. "A great deal of money! I've counted it up . . . if one opens a tobacco business with it one can live to a hundred and two." (Pugel considered a tobacco shop as the only business that Tanya could decently retire to after leaving the circus.)

"See here," said Tanya to Dolomanova as she went away, "I know Mitka better than you, all the same, because I'm a woman and I love him. One can forgive the past if one believes in the future."

Dolomanova did not answer, nor did she invite Tanya to visit her again. She stood at the window and looked at them both as they walked across the yard. Tanya's tall figure, embraced by the wind, walked erectly and slightly bent forward, and beside her flitted the smaller figure of Pugel like a shadow. The twilight had already swallowed them before Donka, rattling angrily at the bolt, had shut the door.

"Is the young man rebelling?" Firsov inquired.

"I enjoy breaking in rebels." The hard electric light accentuated the arrogance of Dolomanova's features.

TANYA heard strange new voices as she walked home. The street lamps winked mysteriously at each other; beneath her feet the slush made little uncanny sounds. The street seemed to her like a magic corridor at whose end a sweet, irresistible temptation was waiting for her. Without admitting it to herself, she had already seen the folly of her flight from the circus into marriage, for though her feelings toward Nikolka remained the same, her faith in his powers to heal her had been shaken. He held himself aloof, as if their kisses were counted, as if he were afraid of taking on himself the burdens of real love. And this was actually the case; but besides this, his consciousness of the debt to Tanya, which he had never repaid, poisoned even the purely physical joys he derived from her frequent visits.

Although Nikolka postponed the marriage from month to month because he wished to celebrate it with pomp and jollity ("A Zavarihin only marries once in his life!" he used to say), all the same he always showed a clumsy solicitude for his betrothed, and even a guilty tenderness, as a compensation for his lack of genuine feeling. Tanya had no whims and caprices; Nikolka himself, therefore, used to invent them so that they might be immediately indulged. His presents to her often revealed his character. In the first months of their engagement he presented her with a thin gold medal with his head on it, as well as half a dozen handsome chairs; one had to be Tanya to find something touching in his clumsy pedlar's souvenirs. They should long ago have parted, but a false delicacy kept them faithful to the decision they had made. Nikolka had, up to now, amassed little wealth but a great deal of experience. His ambition kept him from resting on his laurels, and he dreaded petty commercial complacency as a circus rider dreads superfluous fat. He, who knew when to watch and when to pounce, was aware that a single false step must surely rob him of all the fruits of his exacting toil.

Tanya finally understood what Zavarihin wanted: he wanted, above all, to see her healthy and strong, and capable of striding over all the filth life would strew in their path. She knew in her bones that Nikolka would never really love her until she showed she could do without him. Once he gave himself away and fell into a tiny trap she laid for him. She was jealous of herself, the one-time Hella, and she asked him not to call her Hella any more, for the name was silly and ugly. Nikolka thought a moment, propping his great chin on his hand, and stared at the fire in the stove, then he said: "You'll always be Hella to me. That's when I love you, when you're in danger and snap your fingers at it. Anyone can make soup!"

"The time will come when you'll be sick to death of me and my soup."

"Time! . . . What's time? It's just imagination, a kind of mist. A man who's worth anything won't let mist defeat him. You wait, the men of the future are going to be tough lads." His voice became confident, and it was as though his heart were warmed by old memories. "Between ourselves, I didn't do too badly out of the state forests at home—I used to help myself to firewood and sell it. The way I look at it is this: if your friend has a lot, but you've only a little, take some of his on the sly. If you ask him for it, he'll be sorry, but he won't give it—and that's awkward between friends. But if you take it on the q.t., you're as good friends as ever."

"And your conscience?" asked Tanya, flushing at her capitulation to Nikolka's principles.

"Time shows that conscience is just what suits you. They ate it all up in the hunger years, when they hadn't bread. My brothers plow the fields that belonged to the landowners, but conscience doesn't trouble them. If it did, they'd die of hunger. You won't grow fat on a good conscience, Hella!" He snapped his teeth together as if he had some dainty morsel between them. "Once I was walking in the forest to take a look at something and I stood still by a stream—I was a lazy dog, then, though I'm a first-class champion now—when all at once a funny little old dandy who only reached up to my waist came up to me. 'Why do you walk about in the wood without any arms, you fool?' said he. 'Is this too small a tool?' I answered, and showed him my fist. The little dandy laughed and said to me quite softly: 'Now, my little pigeon, just turn your back to me.' I turned around and . . . smack! . . . He gave me one on the seat that sent me flying like a little bird to the other bank!" Nikolka's voice quivered. "I've never cried in my life, but that time . . . that was a lesson! And I can swing a weight of five *pud* and think nothing of it."

"Well? Go on, Nikolashka!"

". . . Only that we don't like changing often, it disturbs our balance. . . . You've shot me through as if you were an arrow, and you don't know yourself what a hole there is in me. You go on sticking in it and it hurts me terribly, but it would kill me to pull you out." Strangely enough he believed in these lies of his himself.

Scenes like this were usually concluded by the customary kiss, a chaste contact of lips.

Today Nikolka arrived of his own accord, as had happened now and then lately. Pugel escorted him respectfully to Tanya's waiting room and immediately left it on tiptoe and with an exaggerated show of respect; he then sat down in the passage with a ridiculous colored feather brush in his hand, the inseparable badge of his new office. For some time past Pugel had had that frail, unearthly look that comes to old men when they realize that they have no part in the life of the young.

The door stood open, and Nikolka looked around suspiciously when he entered.

"Silence, pleess!" Pugel blocked his way, and, with quite unusual audacity, pressed his finger on his pouting lips. The finger was damp and cold and smelled of kerosene. Then Pugel listened again at the curtain and shook his head. Every time the voices in Tanya's room grew louder, Pugel signed to Nikolka to listen. With a stupid, forced smile Zavarihin complied.

Someone was speaking in a flat but firm voice. He was not speaking Russian, but somebody else was cheerfully interpreting for him; the interpreter spoke in the accent in which funny stories are usually told about Jews. He sounded extremely self-satisfied and undoubtedly smirked as he talked.

"Herr Mangolf is offering you, in consideration of your . . ." (he asked something in German) "qualifications, an amount which in Germany is only paid for exceptional attractions." He named the sum, and Nikolka's ears, which were touching the dusty, rough cloth of the curtain, reddened. He felt the approach of a misfortune.

An amount such as Mangolf now offered Tanya, Nikolka could have earned only by a whole series of risky stratagems. ("There isn't a spot on me," he said once bitterly, "that hasn't been spat upon for every rouble I have.") It seemed to Nikolka that his whole body was covered with a flush of unspeakable embarrassment. ("And I spoke to her about my successes!" he reflected, sick at heart, and remembered Tanya's soft laugh during their last conversation. . . .) The dark power of Mangolf's roubles showed Tanya to him in a dazzling light.

Then Tanya was heard answering; she was declining the offer.

"What are they saying in there?" Nikolka nudged Pugel, although he guessed the drift of the drama behind the curtain. He felt an impulse to go in and order Tanya to refuse the offer and chase all these strangers from the house, these strangers who had tried so severely the tottering power of his love. He waited and clung to Pugel. Pugel parried him, and neither noticed that their struggle made the curtain tremble a little.

"Oh, that Mangolf! He got a head so big as the earth!" Words failed Pugel to express his feelings. "He made the Three Flying Robinsons that do *corde volante* with torches—the whole world know him. And now he offer Tanya a foreign tour!" he said, almost suffocating with rage. "What do you want? Do you want my Tanya to bring a peasant child into the world? I'd go without my coat and . . ." He did succeed in saying what he intended to do without his coat.

In the room they could hear chairs being scraped back; Pugel leaped to the door and opened it with eager obsequiousness, but Nikolka could think of nothing better to do than to hurry out to the staircase and stand there in a stupor of shame, crumpling his new cap. He heard them all stepping into the anteroom and Tanya laughing at a joke from the cultured gentleman. Her laugh seemed to Nikolka sycophantic and full of humble gratitude for so exalted a visit; his ears drank in every sound and syllable. He even listened eagerly to a German sentence of Herr Mangolf. The interpreter immediately translated it.

"Herr Mangolf says that you live too . . . restrictedly." The interpreter smacked his tongue in the agreeable consciousness that he had successfully coped with the problem.

"*Aber ich wollte etwas anderes sagen. Ich wollte sagen. Sie wohnen zu ärmlich!*" corrected the German, laying especial emphasis on the last word. "I understand a leetle Russian," he added, and smiled slyly. "The interpreter say a big lie." (Now an unusual smell reached Nikolka's nose; the German was smoking a cigar.)

Then all of them except Tanya came out onto the landing. The electric light on the staircase was out of order, and Pugel lit their way with a candle. The hot wax dripped onto his hand, but he did not notice it. A cold draft blew up from down below.

"Who's there?" asked Mangolf, using his cigar as if it were a finger to point at Nikolka. He asked only out of interest in Russian customs, and Nikolka was less offended by the German's contemptuous gesture than by the answer that Pugel returned to him.

"Oh, him! . . . he's . . . a   kind   of . . ." Pugel added a few German words and waved his hand contemptuously in the direction of Nikolka, who stood bareheaded against the wall.

Zavarihin approached Pugel, his face distorted with rage. "If you just dare another time, you old cabbage head," he said, extracting every ounce of meaning from the Russian expression, "to point at me with your finger, I'll pound you into a jelly. Do you understand?" Pugel dropped his candle, and Nikolka went downstairs in complete darkness. Mangolf gave a startled exclamation, and in the dusk of the staircase the spark of his cigar had a lonely and questioning gleam.

Tanya came running to her fiancé half an hour later, and found him in an unaccountably cheerful mood. He was sitting on the edge of his bed with his waistcoat open, playing his harmonica. He was completely sober, for his cheerfulness was the outcome of temper, so there was something alarming and menacing about his unalcoholic gaiety. Beating time with his boot (with every blow the dull flame of the small, smoking lamp quivered on the floor) he sang lustily in a high, thin voice:

> "O Moscow, O Moscow!
> City of golden towers!
> There I spent golden hours,
> There I picked poison-flowers."

The superficial veneer that Tanya had tried to impart to Nikolka (Firsov, too, had worked at it, following his notion that "the old culture must be carried on by the rising generation") had been shed like gilt from ironwork, and all that remained was the harmonica, the terrified smoking little lamp on the floor, and a peasant's bared and hairy breast. He gave a sharp glance at her as she came in, and went on singing more gaily and coarsely than before. . . .

"What's the matter with you, Nikolashka?" Tanya cried out for the second time.

"There's a volcano inside me," he said hoarsely, without stirring his hand from the harmonica, which emitted passionate sighs from its gaudy breast.

Tanya sat down beside him and told him of the offer that had been made her. Mangolf, a famous impresario, had prophesied a great success for her in a tour abroad, and had hinted that on her return Tanya would have sufficient funds at her disposal to be able to leave the circus forever. 'Das wird Ihr Schwanengesang sein!' he had said a number of times, drawing in the air with his cigar the eloquent row of ciphers in her salary. (Mangolf took Tanya's refusal as a Russian idiosyncrasy that could be cured without much trouble by a slight appeal to her intelligence.) Without being a great psychologist, Mangolf had not allowed Tanya's refusal to put him out of humor; he had merely pointed out once more the net profit of the "swan song," and given the telephone number of the hotel where he was going to stay for a week.

"On my way to you I decided to accept the offer. I've got back my self-confidence, I think I'm quite well again." She seemed to be appealing for his approval. Nikolka went on playing, but now he played a slow, lingering tune to conceal his embarrassment. "What do you advise me to do, Nikolashka?"

He stared at a spot on the floor and was silent. He did not value work which he did not understand and of which he was incapable himself, and he hated idlers with the bitter hatred of the peasant. (He considered even Firsov a scoundrel because of the cleverness with which he concealed his idleness.)

"Look, there's a bug crawling about: it'll bite you in a moment." He pointed at the floor.

"Let him, as far as I'm concerned . . ." Tanya understood his too transparent ruse. "Should I accept it, Nikolashka?"

"You should refuse it," he murmured gloomily. Yet Tanya saw that his whole soul cried out against his words. He began to play something merry and graceful.

"Nikolashka, think how much money they'll pay me!" she said, and looked at the deep flush on his sunburned face. Trapped, and with his back to the wall, he fidgeted uneasily, and to cover his confusion he drew Tanya to him with the hypocritical tenderness of a shopkeeper. His silence admitted everything, and pleaded for her indulgence.

She noted his embarrassment with delight, because her resolve was already fixed. For the first time she felt well and carefree in the little low room with the arching walls.

In the dim theatrical light shed by the little smoking lamp, the second half of Tanya's life opened, without announcement, before her. It drew her again to the great round house streaming with light and crammed with spectators, the house for which she was born. She had abandoned it, and now it called her back, and tonight she could not muster the strength to resist its appeal.

Firsov's notebook held about forty pages and was grimy with constant handling—deliberately so, perhaps, for he enjoyed disinterring the shapely living body of his future work from the confused chaos of his daily notes. The first two pages were filled with sketches, and everything here was carefully numbered and, in spite of the apparent muddle, in good order. A rigmarole quite unintelligible to the uninitiated began on the third page. First came a verse:

> "Eat with discretion and live on a diet,
> But first have a bottle or two on the quiet."

(It referred to a morose poet, who had no part, however, in the action in the novel. Incidentally, the lack of fools in the story was later deplored by the critics. "Make the reader laugh, and put him for a moment in a superior position to your heroes, and then he'll forgive you a lot." That was literally the sentence in which a critic bewailed the absence of comic relief in the story.)

"Life is everywhere one and the same: the difference between Us and Them lies in the particular incidents you emphasize."

The next was an inscription he had found on a lavatory wall: "Grinka Tuzov sleeps with his stepmother."

Then came various notes:

"Puchov tells me: 'Perhaps the world doesn't exist for men any longer, but only for certain birds and beasts who haven't yet been polluted.' (By what? By thinking? . . . The man's an incorrigible muddle head!) To my question: 'What would happen if mankind were to realize all its dreams?' (a man who has realized all his dreams is a contemptible fellow), he answered: 'Lucifer and Beelzebub fight eternally against each other in the universe' (that's exactly what he said), 'and for a long time there has not been a third. The victor in this struggle continually falls into two halves, and the halves begin the battle against each other afresh. And so it goes on!' 'Till the end?' I inquired. 'No,' he answered, 'till the bitter realization.' "

Here the note broke off and a drawing followed: a fish with an open mouth shaped like a purse, and three letters laboriously marked on it in ink. Real literary mumbo jumbo!

". . . Can the spleen stand such a load or not? And yet, why do a hundred million spleens work more successfully than a single one?"

". . . Dolomanova says: 'I am much too strong to entrust my thoughts to anyone, even if it is only a diary.' "

Under the nineteenth of October was the following entry: "Zavarihin, all the same, won't marry Tanya till he's acquired a great many more advantages. Tanya doesn't realize that by accepting the German's offer she has postponed the wedding, and not brought it nearer, as in her simplicity she imagined. Now they will fight in bitter earnest, and who can tell which of them will gobble the other up when she returns from abroad? Zavarihin has strength behind him, but it isn't altogether pure. He himself said once to me: 'The peasant isn't in any hurry about confession: God knows the peasant's sins well enough anyway. We can settle things up with the dear Lord any time: we can't get out of it because we're nearest to him.' To my question of how he had climbed to such a height, he answered: 'I've got nimble fingers because I play the harmonica.' (He speaks quite frankly to me without any concealment.) 'My dear Firsov, I don't trust the co-operatives: a hired man can't take care of other people's money as faithfully as the owner can himself.' (To my objection that in the co-operatives it isn't a question of other people's money but of one's own, he only laughed and waved his hand.) 'It seems to me, Fyodor Fyodorich, that justice is based on property. A man who hasn't anything (now that they've taken away his soul and his property, they've stripped him of everything but shame), a man like that might easily get a fever in the brain—wait till you've been spat on and you'll understand—and then comes chaos. No, everyone must have something he can lose, that's sure! A man's like a child, one can't look after him carefully enough. He may suddenly get tired of being honest and carrying a soul about with him from which he can expect nothing but misery, and no profit or amusement. Then he'll turn a somersault to make even the dead laugh. That's the way it is.' (A terrible fellow this Nikolka Zavarihin; he's been through the school of experience.)

"Yesterday a writer of my acquaintance asked me whether I had burned Manyukin's notes or not. I replied that I had gone for that very reason into the Urals and burned his book there in a blast furnace. (I couldn't explain to him, though, that it would be a shameful thing to make a public show of the last Russian nobleman in all his nakedness.) Then my friend asked me for fifty roubles, but I declined to give him anything. My friend felt himself insulted by this and warned me that this year they were going to cut me to pieces. 'Whatever you write, we're going to cut it to pieces!' Now this friend is spreading all kinds of slanders about me in Moscow. (He's been caught in the act of writing some filth about me on the wall of a closet in a printing works. It's frightening, what a writer can stoop to!)"

After this came the word "dac-tylo-sco-py" in printed lettering, and then a drawing of a so-called goose's foot, a simple instrument for tearing open fireproof safes. Firsov was here evidently occupied with criminal matters.

"Manyukin replied: 'No, you mustn't speak ill of the thrush. The fat of the thrush is like a bunch of grapes, and very delicious when cooked with cabbage. It's great sport to bring down five birds with one shot.' Then he mentioned the superstition that once a year every hunter must fire off his gun against himself: if he remains alive that means that he has the goodwill of the birds and beasts. The evening before his breakdown he told me some stories in the beer hall about his father, Ammos Petrovich, and

among others how he used to suppress peasant strikes. In
such cases he used to appear before the peasants dressed
up in all his orders. 'Which of you are on strike? Kindly
step forward!' Silence. 'Bring out the ringleaders!' They
were brought out. 'Hang them up, I take the responsibility.' The witnesses turned pale and the peasants knelt
down. Ammos Petrovich immediately forgave the ringleaders. This treatment was called 'paternal and humane.'
The peasants were fond of him, although a stone was
thrown at him once, but without hitting him. (I must
certainly make use of this story in my description of the
nineteenth century: it's slim and graceful like an obelisk.
One should always look at monumental buildings from a
distance. So with regard to our own time, too: one
should merely record the facts and not comment on
them. . . .)"

At this point Firsov had not even the grace to complete
his idea, he merely drew a little house with barred windows. It was clear that his thoughts were traveling in two
directions simultaneously.

"Among the thieves there's someone who's betraying
right and left. They're all in a wild panic."

". . . Yesterday I visited M. F. D. Donka asked me if
I could help him to bring out an edition de luxe of his
poems. Who can have put him on to such a mad notion?
Besides, his poems no longer smack of erotic vulgarity,
but of something quite different. It's interesting—a poster
can be made to look a work of high art by giving it a slight
twist, and vice versa.

"N.B.—I must write my vulgar stories."

Under the twenty-third of October stood the following
entry: "Tanya Vekshina is training in the circus. Yesterday I met Mangolf with her. I had a talk with him while
Tanya was dealing with L. E. about an appearance in Moscow before she starts on her foreign tour. Then Nikolka
and Pugel came, the elephant and the pug: they're always
fighting. I talked to Mangolf in German. I said: '*Deutsch-
land ist nicht von der Niederlage so sehr beleidigt, wie
davon dass es die Maske des Besiegten anzunehmen
gezwungen war.*' I believe firmly in the swift recovery of
Germany.

" 'You dare to say that to me,' he replied, and cast a

side glance at the interpreter. 'You're very bold.' The devil only knows what people imagine our life here is like."

Then some verses:

"The Mathematical Equation
Is a thing I do not like,
But K.P. is a crustacean
And an excoriated pike."

(But these verses clearly were of no importance.)

"How disgusting! Chikelyov has got Zinka to make herself a slit skirt, and now she's bought herself a bag of imitation crocodile skin, but she looks more like a wild boar than a woman. Yet she'll make one more bid for freedom before old age comes on—matter for a special chapter—and then look out for yourself, Chikelyov!"

". . . Yesterday I saw Mitka in the theater, he was sitting in the third row of the pit. We greeted each other politely."

". . . There must be a lyrical chapter in my book: Pyotr Gorbidonich Chikelyov (after reading Gogol's *Coat*) has a talk with Akakey Akakiyevich Bashmachkin about the present time. Chikelyov taps his finger on the leg of the bed and says: 'I'll order myself a coat all the same, little brother!' I must describe the incidents connected with this improbable event. The chapter will be called 'Akakey Akakiyevich turns Savage.' "

" '. . . and even if it's all in vain,' said Manyukin sourly as he took his leave. (The man has sunk into Lethe, and not even bubbles rise to the surface.)"

". . . something lyrical about the impossibility of artificial insemination for the Russian people. . . ."

"Where will the paths of Zavarihin and of Mitka eventually cross?"

"Observations on the theme: 'From dust thou art, to dust shalt thou return.' "

". . . Will Mitka survive? A bridle on himself."

". . . A theme for a story: 'The triumph of Zavarihin, the evildoer, or, The seduction of a girl of twenty-nine.' "

". . . The following scene must be worked in: Zavarihin and Mitka meet in a train. Hate and night. . . . The former says: 'Let's go out, little friend.' They get out and fight their last fight, a decisive scrap with their fists, on

the night-shrouded fields near the railway embankment.
. . . No one hears them or sees them. . . . Blood flows.
The train disappears. . . ."

"Pure lunacy: Donka best friends with M. F. D."

". . . My slanderers are working hard and well: yesterday one of them was seen in five places! . . ."

All this nonsense, not good enough even for a newspaper article, was to be found in Firsov's notebook. The
filthy exercise book lay on a pile of scribbled scraps of paper containing the completed story. Suddenly a new event
compelled the writer to undertake a substantial reconstruction of his work; for Firsov could not resist the cheap
temptation of linking Mitka to Xenka, Sanka's wife, with
the cruel bonds of love. This occurred in the following
way.

I⊤ was the end of October. A raging wind tore through the streets, and the dark evening sky shed a torrent of singing snowflakes over the city. The *izvozchiks* raised the hoods of their cabs, and the few pedestrians, who had to battle with the gusts of wind which met them at the empty street corners, looked upward in alarm toward the spot from which this wild Siberian blast was blowing. The wind whistled through the cracks in the houses. It was amazing that its cheeks did not burst.

Near the beer hall in which a year before Firsov and Manyukin had got to know each other, the lamp swung hopelessly on its iron chain. The wind had blown away the old letters from the signboard and formed new ones, but these had the same meaning in spite of this; they spoke of Beer the Consoler. The wind sang its incoherent songs, but inside in the beer hall there was a clatter of merriment and din, as if the customers defied the wind to daunt their spirits behind closed doors.

In the beer hall the tables were arranged differently. The old African palm had been shriveled by the tobacco smoke, for even the false grows old. The same niches gaped in the walls, though now they were covered with paint. The same ageless pockmarked waiter, Alexey, ran around between the tables, swinging his malodorous napkin; his face was gray and furrowed with care. Where once Zinka's song used to flow like a broad river, there now sat five sulky mandolin players in sweaters, and a piano player without a neck, who stared despairingly at the floor.

The sentimental music was quite inappropriate to the din of the beer hall.

Under the dead African tree with its shaggy tufts the man in the checked ulster was once more sitting. But Firsov was now a regular customer, and no one was surprised when now and then he made notes on the back of a pack of cigarettes. Today the writer was entertaining two guests.

"You oughtn't to drink any more, Xenka," said Sanka severely as he dismembered his boiled crab with a show of indifference. "You mustn't drink any more!"

"It's all the same to me now, darling!" Xenka almost screamed, and lifted a new mug brimming with warm, sour ale to her mouth. "Everything's allowed me now. Isn't it, Fyodor Fyodorich?"

"I really don't know . . ." Firsov shook his head dubiously. He saw that the roses on her cheeks were darker, and ready to fall. He smoked a lot and piled up his cigarette butts untidily beside the overflowing ash tray.

"I read in your book, Fyodor Fyodorich . . . a story of how a wandering sailor in 1918 met a beautiful fairy who fell in love with him. She was fascinated by his wild nature and his restlessness. 'She called the sailor to her and a strong love grew up between them?' . . . something like that." Xenka slowly recollected the words of Firsov's story, and the writer ran his hand through his unkempt little beard, as he had no mind to discuss the matter with her. "The sailor lived with the fairy: he lost his craving for travel, and grew fat with contentment and good living. Do you remember how he drank flower milk with her?" Quiet, gentle Xenka suddenly laughed hysterically, as if there was no one else in the beer hall. "And one fine day when the fairy was expecting him on her downy cloud (on earth called a 'feather bed') the sailor pulled on his faithful top boots, his sailor's jacket, and his oilskins, put his fairy clothes in the corner, and went away again to wander over the hungry, homeless earth. Do you remember how touchingly he described to his friend the failure of his happiness?"

"No, I don't remember . . . it was one of my first stories . . ." murmured Firsov crossly, and glanced sharply around, as people were already beginning to listen. "The story's of no value."

"The sailor said: 'Human happiness isn't decent, you can see through it . . . you can see through to all the shame.' You've written some remarkable things, Firsov. I read it to Sanka, but he didn't understand a word of it. A lot of it's hard to understand, anyway. . . . Why did you spit on human happiness, Fyodor Fyodorich?"

"Petit-bourgeois happiness!" said Firsov rudely and insincerely, drawing at his cigarette.

"Happiness is always petit bourgeois. Happiness begins at the moment when there's nowhere farther to go, when you have achieved everything, everything!" Xenka's face was now almost beautiful in its reproach. Her eyes shone, making Firsov ashamed of the truth of his story. "How I cried as I read your story, Fyodor Fyodorich!"

"Well, even the fairy cried. But the sailor was a good chap: he had preserved in himself the germ of shame."

"Don't lie, Firsov. Happiness isn't given to men to torment them."

"And I suppose that the sailor got fed up with his little happiness, that's all it was," said Sanka. "He knew neither bad luck, nor bitterness, nor bad weather, nor evil. . . ." He suddenly stopped talking. As he turned his glance toward the point at which his drunken wife was looking fixedly, he experienced a strange sensation, almost a shock. Smiling queerly, he got up from his seat and sat down again. But neither his will nor his voice could restrain his wife as she leaped up from her seat.

At the next table sat Mitka, absent-mindedly gazing at Firsov's party. His shirt collar peeped out from under the velvet lapel of his fine coat. His foreign felt hat lay on the edge of the table and, when Mitka moved, fell as softly as a feather on the dirty floor, much to the embarrassment of the horny-handed patrons of the beer hall. Mitka's appearance was like that of a meteor that passes across the heavens at the beginning of a great century, and they were all stunned and speechless at his cool presence here at the very moment when the police were hard upon his track.

Scarcely had Firsov greeted him with a nod than Sanka's wife hurried up to Mitka. With her right hand she fumbled in her blouse, but she did not seem to find what she was looking for. Everyone's eyes were turned in her direction, and a party of railway men, who sat rowdily in a corner, stopped talking and moved to an adjacent table.

"There you are, take it, you swine!" Xenka's lips twitched convulsively. "Take your help back . . . you're a devil!" (She apparently wanted to fling in his face the money he had given her during Sanka's imprisonment; Firsov had not been mistaken.) Xenka could not find the money. Her face grew pathetic and tiny, and she bent her head in humiliation. "Sanka!" she screamed suddenly in abject dismay. "Sanka, I've lost his money."

"Be quiet, you silly . . ." Sanka replied in embarrassment, shaking her by the shoulders. "Calm yourself, Xenka!"

"Tell him I'll give it back to him again," she murmured in confusion without listening.

"Fyodor Fyodorich, I swear to God I had the money here the day before yesterday." She pressed Firsov's reluctant hand to her blouse. "Fyodor Fyodorich, you don't know how hard it is for me, and how ashamed of myself I am!" She did not scream any more, and Alexey no longer thought it necessary to hover around the table.

The inner meaning of this painful incident was not revealed till later. With his teeth clenched, Firsov sat at Mitka's table and tried to joke, but it was no use. Sanka stood by, stiff and smiling, and the strangest thing about him was his hands, which clutched the air despairingly with a hint of abject entreaty. He ran to Mitka as if he intended to strike him, but then with unconscious servility he picked up his hat instead.

"You mustn't be angry, master," said Sanka imploringly, and bowed his lean body before Mitka, who sat unmoved with an expression of concentrated thought on his face. "She's gone quite mad . . . in the night she wakes up and speaks of you, by God! Don't be angry, she's got a . . ." He winked and pointed swiftly to his chest, so that his weeping wife should not observe his gesture. "The doctor says it's bad. . . . It won't last much longer. She's raving mad. . . . She tried to make me kill you, master! She doesn't want to die." Suddenly he gave an ugly laugh and said: "And it seems to me that she loves you on the sly, master. That's it . . ." He was struggling to waken Mitka from his torpor, but he did not succeed.

"That's all nonsense," said Mitka patronizingly, grasping the jug, in which the froth had changed to a thin, unappetizing film.

Sanka got up and stood still for a moment brooding over the master's careless words. Firsov would not have been Firsov if he had not noticed the grimace that for a moment lit up the gloom of Sanka's face. Firsov went up to Xenka and led her into the back room. Sanka looked around triumphantly, as if he wished to call everyone to witness his daring, and sat down without more ado at Mitka's table.

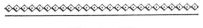

"AND Donka . . ." began Sanka as he filled his glass from the master's bottle with an impudent smile. Some baleful power held him fast to the table. "I could tell you a great deal about Donka, master. It can't be concealed any longer: he's quite gone to the dogs. Even Xenka owes her consumption to him, although she had a . . . a . . . *tensioncy* to it before. Have you noticed her cheeks? I tell you straight: Donka's been asking Xenka to love him, if you please, yes, as a bribe. To keep his mouth shut."

"Say what you've got to say, and then get out. You're a bore today, Alexander." (At this moment Sanka was saved by an odd chance: he sneezed and covered his face with both hands. His cheeks, which had grown fat and coarse in the last few months, flushed consciously. Mitka's features sharpened, and his face looked leaner than ever.) "A stupid fellow, Sanka," he thought, "but he's straight, he has an inflexible conscience. He never avoids a trap, he goes right in. But even then he keeps straight, good old Sanka."

"I'll tell you everything on the square, master. The evening before the Pirman affair, Donka comes and says to me that we should do away with you on the quiet. He said that you despise us both, master. 'Don't trust him,' says he, 'not even when he's down and out! He's always "quite the gentleman," he looks down his nose at us.' You don't believe me, but I'm not lying. Strike me dead, if I am! Donka begged me with tears in his eyes."

A new customer, burly and apoplectic, came into the beer hall. He was so drunk that he seemed completely oblivious not only of his fellow men but of himself. On the doorstep he recited a poem about earth bubbles, whatever they were, to an accompaniment of majestic gestures. Everyone in the beer hall knew him and enjoyed laughing at him. Spotty Alexey waved the napkin at him as if he wished to chase away a troublesome moth. "Alexey, don't pester me, but do me a kindness. I've ten kopeks in my pocket and the Republicans here will make up the rest." But nobody showed any desire to treat him, and for a long time he walked with a humble and comical air around the tables, but had no success, and finally sat down on a chest near the buffet. In the pauses of the music his voice could be heard gobbling like a turkey.

"You've let yourself down, Alexander. I can't get to the bottom of you at all," said Mitka severely.

"Let me explain, master. . . . You never listen to me and that's why our friendship is broken. I'm warning you now against Donka, but you won't believe me." (Firsov paid the bill, and nodded to Sanka to come across to him. Xenka turned her face away, sank her head, and made a detour to avoid Mitka's table.) "I must go, but let me come and see you and talk it all over, master. What things we've done together, master! We wanted once to conquer the whole world so that everyone should be happy, but look at the muck we've fallen into! It isn't bluebirds who are waiting for us, but bullets in somebody's pocket."

"Now go, they're calling for you." Mitka pushed him away and turned to his glass. He seemed quite apathetic again.

Firsov had his hand already on the latch of the door when something happened which made it possible for him to introduce Stassik into his story, hitherto an unregarded figure. Amid the cheerful music a scream was heard, and immediately a crowd collected around the spot from which it had come. Firsov pushed his way to the center of the group, and found a woman rolling on the floor in a fit. She was no longer young, and wasted by drink and poverty. There was a swelling in her woollen stocking; it was where she kept her money. Near her lay a bunch of brass keys.

"Oh, you've made me quite giddy . . ." (She had a Polish accent, which distorted her words.) "Why do you stupefy me like this? Dear God, what I've suffered. My child, I reared you, why don't you stand up for me? Stas-sinyok . . . Stassinyechok! Anna Vassilna, they'll shoot him yet . . . he's fallen . . . I forgive you, I forgive you, Stassinyok!" (She was evidently the mother of a thief.) Anna Vassilna, painted up to the nines, tried to cover the woman's face with a newspaper, but she did not succeed, and she began to curse the people standing around:

"A poor woman's rolling here in the dirt and you just gape at her. You're not men. You're just stocks of wood, you rabble!"

The incident was quickly closed by the intervention of Alexey. Firsov and his guests were no more to be seen; even the railway men had gone away. Mitka ordered Alexey to carry his bottle to the quiet, clean, vaulted back-room. There he filled his glass and sat on, sunk in thought.

During the last month he had often been near Masha's house. An irresistible impulse drew him there; he wished to make his peace with her, but some hostile power pre-vented him from entering the house. One day he over-came his reluctance and went in. He was dressed in the height of fashion—almost insolently well dressed—and, in spite of his childish shyness of Masha, he took off his glacé kid gloves slowly and carelessly (as if he had a hun-dred fingers on every hand) with a self-confident smile on his lips. His restlessly roving eyes sought out the changes in the room, due to Dolomanova's altered circumstances. Donka entered behind him, and Mitka felt his hatred like a rude slap upon the back. (When Mitka later recollected this moment, he blushed with anger at himself. He could remember everything, even the smell of the Antonovsky apples that lay on the table.)

"You haven't been very nice to me, Mitka." Dolo-manova, who remained seated in her armchair, welcomed him with those words. "But what a dandy you are . . . just turn around!" She laughed discreetly so as not to of-fend her visitor.

"I have come to wish . . . you and Donka happiness, as a return for your congratulations," said Mitka lightly, and sat down without waiting for an invitation. He fum-bled in his pocket for the fat cigar he had bought half an hour before, but did not venture to light it. Suddenly he felt impelled to say something outrageous. "I'm sorry you weren't there, Masha, when I was sweeping up all the rubbish." He smiled and began to crumble the ill-fated cigar in his pocket.

Masha did not answer, but her face grew cold and indifferent. Mitka felt that he was losing ground every moment, and that it was only his despair that kept him to the path he had chosen. His presence did not seem to excite her at all; he could not detect a trace of agitation, however attentively and maliciously he observed her movements. She took up an apple and bit into it.

"What sour apples you've bought!" she said, turning on Donka and throwing the nibbled apple at him. Donka instantly ate it with exaggerated relish. "Do you want me to throw you out, Mitka?"

"You . . . you're a magnet that attracts the iron in men!" shouted Mitka, losing control of himself. "That chap there's brass . . . samovar gold!" He pointed at Donka.

In the silence his laughter rang false like breaking glass. Donka leaped to his feet.

"Will you allow me, Marusya?" said he, so pale that his face had a sort of beauty. "Will you allow me to give this gentleman a lesson?"

"Go to your room, Donka," said Masha after a while. "Go for the moment. Don't you see that he's suffering? He doesn't often come, and you're always with me. Go, or he might shoot you yet."

Donka obeyed readily, for by his obedience he wanted to show his superiority to Mitka.

"How can you love a man like that, Masha? You're so proud and high-spirited, and you're not a fool. You never complain or cry." He thought of all the qualities for which he loved her.

Masha took up another apple and ate it. But this subterfuge could no longer hide her agitation.

"What a fool you are, Mitka! Why shouldn't I love Donka? Hasn't he given me a pair of stolen Persian wool stockings? No, don't touch me!" she said in the same tone of mockery when Mitka went up to her. "You should have come to me that time I found you at the gate in a filthy coat belonging to someone else . . . when you were so pitiable. But now I'm ashamed of feeling pity for any-one so smart!"

He was sitting quite close to her, and he stared at her as if she were an enemy. She went on eating the apple, and he gazed at her lashes, which were so long that he al-most imagined he felt a breath of cold when they moved.

"Long ago I wanted to ask you," he said in a strange, cold voice, "how it was that Agey was caught that time. I know it wasn't through Artemy, he was as sly as a fox."

"You can't guess?" Their glances crossed and avoided each other. "And do you remember the notes that got soaked with ink?"

Mitka laughed. "Firsov invented that for his book. Agey couldn't be tracked down through them. No, Shchekutin, who's dead now, took the damaged packet of notes with him to Irkutsk. I left my money with Pirman, so that Agey had clean money. No, I was thinking of something else." He looked at the door through which Donka had gone.

"Do you think that that fool would be capable of—? No, even Firsov couldn't beat that. And did it never occur to you that I had a right to get rid of Agey myself, so as to be free for you? People can discover everything about each other but the obvious. Now you come to me and start a scene: perhaps you've excellent motives, all the same I can't see why you're more to be pitied than, say, the man without any legs who sits at our gate. . . ."

. . . So Mitka sat in front of his beer and remembered his stupid visit to Dolomanova. He felt a pain at his heart, and this dull ache did not cease even when a big black kitchen cockroach crawling along the blue wall caught his attention. Some inscrutable reason had induced the cockroach to leave the sweet kitchen smoke to explore the unknown wall. From time to time it stood still and moved its feelers, as if it wished to spy on the neighborhood.

A hand with swollen fingers reached out after the cock-roach, flung it down, and the scraping of a boot sole an-nounced the insect's end.

"It's too funny! One has God knows how many friends, but one can't get a dinner anywhere!" someone roared out just behind Mitka.

He turned around and saw the drunk, who was casting longing glances at Mitka's little bottle; his hands trembled guiltily, and in his drunken, cheeky face one could still see the traces of former good nature. Mitka filled his glass with insulting leisureliness.

"Too rich! Tolya stands up on his hind legs like a dog in front of any stranger's table!" he grumbled patiently while he allowed Mitka's silent contempt to pass over him. Mitka seemed to him a rich man, who had come here in quest of a little spicy diversion. "It's a shame you weren't here yesterday. I beat up a Negro," he added with a forced laugh.

"Sit down!" Mitka invited him.

"My name's Tolya. I don't want to eat anything, but you can order me some boiled eggs with my beer. Confounded fellows! They won't even lend a chap an egg! Nowadays one can buy a man for an egg. Confound them!" He looked gloomily at the walls. "Well, then, I'll have some beer. Do you know Alyosha?" he asked, after draining Mitka's mug at a draught.

"Not run up against him yet," said Mitka, looking at him curiously.

"Alyosha's my friend, a smart chap, but I'm three numbers up on him." He sighed, and assumed a mask of deep scorn. "Would you believe it, Alyosha called me a good-for-nothing . . . that's a nice thing to say, what? He's a wag, that Alyosha. Let me have twenty kopeks."

"What for?" asked Mitka curiously.

"I'll eat the egg up, shell and all, and you'll get a laugh."

"Why do you drink?" asked Mitka indifferently.

"I drink for noble and obscure reasons," answered Tolya mildly, raising his pudgy finger. "Heavily sank my golden head . . ." he proclaimed with unctuous pathos, obviously charmed by the decadent glitter of the poem. "No, if I've achieved anything, I'll bury it myself," he shouted lugubriously, returning to his tormenting thoughts.

"Get on with your beer and stop talking," Mitka interrupted him. "I can't stand this bawling."

"Yes, I drink to justify my existence. You think, no doubt, that I'm just a cad? Is there anything more disgusting in the world than a sponging cad? But it's a lie!"

He tapped softly on the table, "I'm not a man, I'm a meridian," he said, and poked at something imaginary with his outstretched finger. "The south and the north— got me? The west and the east. The united proletariat . . . and all the rest of it! That's me and that's why I drink." He drank, pulling faces; he drank and could not quench his burning thirst. He obviously despised Mitka for being well dressed like a trader and sitting so calmly in this den. "A meridian! Can a meridian be steadied up and stop being a meridian? That's too funny. Take a good look at yourself, man, and you'll always have something to laugh at! Well, then, I bought myself a calculating machine at the pedlars' market (it was more like a piano than a calculating machine), and I began to count up other people's kopeks (everything that doesn't belong to me is other people's). What sort of work was that for a meridian, I ask you, after all he'd done? Wasn't it a come-down? And so I blew the reckoning machine for fifty kopeks. It's a shame that I didn't meet you, I'd have given you the machine for nothing. You could count away on it, and exercise your fingers, you bourgeois." The beer was fizzing in his inside and making him eloquent.

At this moment Alexey brought the eggs that had been ordered for Tolya and took away the empty bottle.

"Why's your face gone mildewed, Alyosha?" asked Tolya in revenge for former insults, plucking at his sleeve.

"The human spirit, that's what did it," said Alexey, smiling wearily at his persecutor. "Look at that picture, how it's faded, and even silver spoons grow rusty." He gave another whisk of his napkin and disappeared.

Tolya laughed comfortably and contentedly. It was impossible to tell now whether he bragged of his depravity to make himself interesting, or whether it satisfied some need of his great bloated body. Mitka looked into the drunkard's blue eyes as into a mirror, and hated him.

"You drink all the time, what more do you want?" asked Mitka, gazing at him fixedly.

"I want everything . . . women, wine, fame! The world's a forsaken hole without them," went on Tolya gloomily. Suddenly he began to shout. "To hell with it! I would like to discover new lands, conquer new islands . . . Tabu, Madagascar, Tomahawk . . . but could you beat it? . . . everything's been discovered by damned nobodies, and Tolya has to sit here kicking his heels and thankful to be given a herring. I was meant to blast rocks and move mountains, and someone dumps a reckoning machine on me! . . . There are no more mountains, there's nothing big left in the world. The world's crumbling away. . . . Are you a writer?" he asked suddenly, and his face clouded over.

"No," answered Mitka shortly, stroking his side whiskers.

"I despise writers, I don't know why. It's just instinct." He stared at Mitka and nodded his head condescendingly. "Well, then, I'll tell you your future, free of charge. 'Speculator, avoid cats, mountains, and fire.' That's rich, isn't it? That's my game now, fortune telling. I've told all the old women on the Smolensky Place their future for ten kopeks. That's fine work for Anatoly Mashlykin, the old Balt! . . . I stormed Ararat and I've seven bullet holes in me . . . with these very hands have I killed seven Hetmans in the Ukraine . . . and now I've sunk to this. . . . Give me a rouble and I'll bite that respectable party in the corner. I know him, he deals in woven goods on the market. Now, humiliate me, speculator, humiliate me! Anatoly of Ararat going for a rouble! What offers? Don't all speak at once! . . . I suppose I've asked too much, but I'm ashamed of begging from you, you know. . . ." He twisted a match between his quivering fingers and snapped it without knowing what he was doing. "Very well! If you like, I'll tell you for eight kopeks how I built a coronation pavilion out of rubbish."

"I know that story. But it's a lie, I suppose, isn't it?" said Mitka.

"Yes, it's a lie," admitted Tolya shortly. "But do you know why I lie?"

Mitka's silence provoked him to further admissions. Tolya's face was swollen and twitching, but Mitka's remained sculpturally impassive. Tolya was on the verge of tears, for no one in the world believed any longer in his exploits. Mitka understood now why the rabble of speculators took a pleasure in laughing at what remained of Anatoly of Ararat.

"Yes, the revolution has failed!" The drunkard was suddenly shaken by a profound sob, and in despair he laid down his head on the table.

Mitka stretched out his hand deliberately and, seizing Tolya with two fingers by the nose, flung back his head. "You can cut out that about the revolution when you're drinking with me," he said sternly, lifting his mug.

The moment that followed was like the flash of a knife. Tolya's head swayed, as if it had lost its equilibrium. Full of hatred and terror, each recognized himself in the man who sat opposite. Mitka's high forehead gleamed, and his pupils flashed gloomily in their deep sockets; in their fire, Tolya's tears were dried up. A flash of surprise lit up his face.

"You? . . ." This was the only word he managed to utter, and his eyes blinked with astonishment. "You dared . . . to take me by the nose. . . . That's rich! But do you know, speculator, I respect you. I won't touch you. When Alyosha said to me I was a good-for-nothing, I flung him up into the air three meters and hurled him on the ground . . . like an egg—got me?" His tipsy dejection gave place to exaggerated raptures, he wept and tried to kiss Mitka, and for a moment his burning resentment against the world was quenched.

"I tell you again, you're a fool," said Mitka, and, in irritation, pushed away the empty jug. "You're as stupid and hollow as an egg shell. I'm Mitka . . . have you heard of me by any chance?" he said with an angry laugh. "I won't forgive what you've said. I'd shoot you down if we weren't sitting in this vile hole." Mitka spoke calmly and collectedly, but his angry words scorched and pierced through Tolya's puffy softness, so that his very face seemed seared with fiery spots. "You dare to raise your bragging horns against the revolution! What rascal can brag that he has sacrificed too much to the revolution, and that it was all his doing? Its source is in the hearts of millions who can't even give it a name. . . . The revolution overthrows mountains, and levels abysses. You've got flabby with whining, but the revolution is the impulse forward and upward, forward and upward . . ." Mitka spoke in an urgent, low voice.

"Go on!" whispered Tolya, fidgeting on his chair with confusion. "I'll answer you."

The noise from the beer hall did not reach the room in which they were sitting. Only a low murmur, like the humming in a shell, came to their ears, disturbing them in their thoughts no more than the thick smell of food from the kitchen.

"The revolution isn't even anyone's doing . . ." Mitka began to say, but suddenly stopped to listen to Tolya's muttering.

"And if it isn't true, and if that sort of talk has let me down once already?" Tolya's whisper was ferocious, but his face remained expressionless as before.

"All right—drink your beer," said Mitka. A film of apathy gathered over his senses as his feverish thoughts died down. The touch of the glass mug upon his teeth was cold and sobering.

"To hell with beer! You want to waken me to life again, do you?" Tolya turned upon Mitka in hostility, fixing his eyes upon his turquoise ring. "Yes, the revolution's marching, all right . . . she's marching along. She's scattering flowers. Her eyes are two suns. . . . Poetry! That's why I hate writers. The revolution's got a heavy heel, and I suppose you'll say a man's got no right to squirm when he's under it, however much he's hurt. There's the music now to drown my shouts . . ." And actually Tolya was almost shouting, and Mitka had no power to restrain him. "Nobody hears me!" He put on a stupid expression and suddenly burst out laughing. "That's rich! Anatoly of Ararat begs pardon and gets his nose pulled for a couple of eggs and a glass of beer. You've bought me cheap, even if you are only a speculator or a poet!"

"Why did you kill the cockroach?" asked Mitka with a feeling of nausea; he was tired of Tolya's great fleshy carcass.

"It's only vermin, and aren't I the king of creation?" said Tolya with his mouth full to bursting. He made haste now to eat up the eggs and, as he crammed them in half shelled, they cracked in his mouth. "Devil take it, hasn't Tolya a heel, too? Besides, we won't have vermin and speculators in human flesh in the future state. It'll all be lovely and bright, like . . . a polished door handle. Ha! Ha! Peace, perfect peace!" He was teasing Mitka, and Mitka knew it. "But what about the vermin? Vermin's one in the eye for the new man! It's not in the picture, eh? If you ask me, the world ought to be put in the pot and stewed. That's rich, little friend! Amid all the glamor of collective intelligence . . . amid the roses and tulips . . . suddenly a cockroach!"

"Well, and what if man? . . ." Mitka bit his lip.

"Are you speaking of me?" asked Tolya raising his eyebrows. He spat a piece of half-chewed egg into his hand and threw it on the ground. "I'm full," he said.

"No, I'm speaking in general . . . about vermin . . ." said Mitka evasively, playing with him.

"Ah, I see! Then crush it with your fingernail!" Tolya grew embarrassed, for he had caught himself in self-contradiction. "All the same, under the heel it's . . . mighty painful."

"Well, and could you crush it?" asked Mitka, trying to appear unconcerned.

"Crush what? You?" Tolya flushed deep red and looked at Mitka maliciously.

"I'm saying: vermin among men."

"So you're thinking of me?" said Tolya defiantly.

"No, I'm thinking of someone else."

"Oh, with the greatest pleasure and in full consciousness of doing my duty." He blurted it out without thinking of the bearing of his words. "It's the duty of Anatoly of Ararat to root out all vermin. And if ever I should recognize myself as one, I shall eradicate Anatoly Mashlykin out of existence."

Spotty Alexey called out that it was closing time. Mitka paid the bill, looked once more at Tolya, who was eating up a herring, and went out into the street, where the wind caught hold of him and bore him away finally to a thieves' den. (That night there was a hurricane and Firsov entered in his notebook: "You'd almost think the wind was out of its mind and trying to catch its tail.")

At dawn the storm had passed, and it began to snow. In the morning the sledges were out, and the unaccustomed eye was blinded by the gleaming streets. Mitka drove to his sister at the circus, and as the sledge raced along, he hung down his hand and scooped up the clean, gay, laughing snow.

TANYA had agreed before her departure abroad to appear
at several special performances in Moscow. The tour was
to begin in November, and in the meantime she trained
energetically and spent several hours every day in the cold,
empty circus. The dome, half illuminated by a single lamp
and the faint blue light streaming in from the exits,
seemed strangely large and shapeless in the daytime.
Voices soared and sank in the dim light, drowning each
other and dying away into vague echoes in the corners.
Tanya finished her exercises and, sitting on the trapeze
with her legs hanging down, looked below her.

The Belgian acrobats were practising silently in the
arena, now and then encouraging each other with unintelligible noises. The cleaners were sweeping from the
stalls scraps of paper, dust, and orange peel, and all other
trace of yesterday's audience. A ringing, well-fed neigh
came from a horse whose legs had grown stiff with standing, and a cleaner with his shirt sleeves rolled up shouted
into space: "Semyon Ivanich, bring along the pitchfork!"

Tanya tested the rope and her muscles several times—
everything was in order—then she took her seat again and
waited. . . .

She smiled, for she was thinking of the miracle that
would happen that evening. She pictured the walls of electric light which would cut off her retreat, and the thousands of eyes in exquisite, anxious yearning which would
gaze at a single point, at her body condemned to self-dis-
cipline. Now she was no longer scared by the consequences of her fame; the thought of Nikolka's help no

longer accompanied her as she "took the air"; with her woman's instinct she perceived that Nikolka, now as never before, depended on her. Her body had become strong and rid of all superfluous flesh, and after a few exercises her gait had become elastic as before: she placed her foot on the floor as a card player places his highest trump on the table.

In secret she blessed the moment when Mangolf had entered her lonely room, for the circus had not relaxed its hold on her. Everything had not yet been accomplished which her body, with its expert training, had power to achieve, and her whole soul thirsted for that final leap, after which she might relapse into peace. The pause in her artistic activity had given her courage for new and more daring feats. The "shtrabat," or leap in the air, of which she was the only exponent, signified to her something more than a professional leap into danger; it had become the acid test of a power and talent which doubt and misgiving had undermined. (After a great struggle the management had secured permission for Tanya's foreign tour: it supported its claim with the argument that Tanya would display her art abroad, and so provide personal propaganda for the progress of the Soviet Union in circus art.)

Her eyes searched for Pugel in the dim depths of the arena and found the vague spot of his face, upturned toward her from a side box. She took him with her to rehearsals, for his presence fortified her self-confidence and put a check on her occasional attacks of recklessness.

"Pugel, let's begin!" she shouted down. She stood up on the trapeze and buckled on her shoes.

She saw Pugel getting up hurriedly and raising his arm imperiously. Tanya was about to start when someone shouted up something to her and called her by name.

"Someone's waiting for you," shouted the cleaner, making a trumpet of his hands.

Tanya suddenly felt an agreeable sensation of fatigue and let herself drop quickly down the rope.

Her face was radiant as she passed the Belgian acrobats. There were five men and a boy. They lined up and greeted her with foreign words and gestures. She did not understand what they said, but knew that she deserved their homage. She laughed, and nodded her thanks to them. But her riotous good humor gave place to a feeling of hostility when she saw her brother in the dressing room. He had come to her again with news of the unrest of the world. In her thoughts he appeared to her a messenger of evil who could not be avoided; his unhappiness was strange and unintelligible to her. His visits oppressed her, his appeals were threats, and under his glances she, who had committed no crime, had to cast down her eyes. Even now she stood with her head lowered, and stretched out her hand submissively to her brother. Suddenly Pugel ran up from behind and flung a black shawl across her shoulders.

"Well, let's go somewhere." She drew away her hand and made to take his arm, but caught herself behaving insincerely and blushed.

"What's the matter?" Mitka cast a side glance at her.

"It's just that I always get embarrassed when anyone sees me without my shawl."

"But you're dressed!"

"Yes, but you look at me as if . . ." She became still more embarrassed, and ran quickly up the stairs into a box, where she sat down and wrapped herself closely in her shawl. "Your face looks terribly puffy. Oh, by the way, someone came to me and asked me if you ever visited me."

"Yes, I'm being shadowed," he admitted simply. "I hear that Zinka is married."

"Well, is that a shock for you?" Tanya could not resist a smile, and yet her brother's happiness was very dear to her.

"No . . . It was the best thing she could do," he answered indifferently, glancing into the arena, in which the circus apparatus was being put up.

"Those are the parterre gymnasts," said Tanya, following her brother's glance. In his eyes there was an expression of curiosity until now unfamiliar to her. "And what are you doing? Is everything going on as usual?"

"You mean, if I'm stealing?" He pursed his lips. "I'm stealing a little. I'm working in the sweat of my brow."

"Well, one doesn't see much sweat," Tanya jested, but she had an uncomfortable feeling.

"We only sweat once in our lives, but that time thoroughly," he said with meaning, and looked challengingly at his sister.

"You talk as if I was to blame for it, Mitka!" she said in an angry, trembling voice. "Perhaps you want me to be in the same boat, too!" She had been wounded and now she struck back. "Some people would find that a great relief!"

He seemed now to realize himself the brazen impudence of what he had said.

"I'm not in a sociable mood today, I know. And my face is puffy, too. . . . I'm in a bad way, sister. I'm lonely and without light or friends. People curse me, and everyone will curse me till they get tired of it—but the worst is that I'm beginning to lose my self-respect. Perhaps you think I'm an ideal figure, a fallen archangel. . . ."

"No, I don't think that," said Tanya softly.

"Well, well, Tanya! I'm just a common thief, who ought to be put away. I live from one robbery to another. I'm not ashamed of myself, but I feel sick and disgusted. I suppose I've got tired. . . . If you want to know the truth, I tell you that I'm sometimes ashamed to look myself in the face."

"It's a pity that it's only sometimes," said Tanya, rising.

Mitka sat with his eyes half closed, as if he were listening to a dialogue in his mind. Tanya's remark made no impression on him. Suddenly a thought flashed like lightning across his face.

"If you like, Tanyushka, I'll give you some money . . . a great deal, too. Take it and run away from Zavarihin and your life here and . . . me! You'll live happily somewhere far away from here, and nobody will ever know anything."

"I won't take your money, Mitka. Now I must go home, the old man's waiting. Besides, I've nothing else to say to you."

"No, sit where you are, sit where you are!" said Mitka imperiously, and pushed her back into her seat. "I'm telling you the truth. I've found out all I can about your Nikolka, for I've got to know the chap my sister, my own sister, is going to ruin herself for," he added crossly. "Nikolka is a thief, Tanyushka, but a very circumspect thief, and they're the most dangerous. He's piling up money and gold and jewelry, but they're all smuggled or stolen . . . it makes me sick to think of it. Human nature is still just the same as it always was, the leopard can't change its spots." Mitka twisted his glove around his hand. "Forgive me, sister, my brain's working badly today: I didn't sleep a wink the whole night." He looked around the circus with dull eyes without grasping what he saw.

"Are you drinking?"

"Not a drop. Will you take the money?"

"You're trying to get a hold over me, Mitka."

"Hold over you? I'm only thinking of your happiness."

"Don't bother about my happiness. We've each of us got to shift for ourselves, Mitka."

The rehearsal had come to an end. The winter day, hardly begun, was already on the decline. The dome of the circus grew dark . . . great spaces have a terrifying effect on us at the moment when the light surrenders hopelessly to the darkness of night. The dome, filled with danger and enchantment, opened once more its insatiable jaws.

"Sister!" whispered Mitka, while Tanya wrapped her legs in her shawl and shielded them from her brother's wandering glance. "Sister! Mankind can't do without a shepherd. In one of his poems Donka says: 'Behind the mountain peaks the sun shines, but the road over the mountain is dangerous. . . .' There's sense in that, I tell you! You won't lead men to the light unless you harness them with an iron yoke. I've been living with the *mouzhiks* this summer, and, take my word for it, they need a kind father, but a father with a rod. They'll remain as they are for another five hundred years, like an undiscovered vein of ore."

"And then it'll be discovered and made into pocket knives," said Tanya acidly.

"Without shepherds men will cut each other's throats, they'll become like beasts, they'll raise their snouts to the sky and howl to God, and the darkness will resume its power. The human race is in its dotage. All the grain has been threshed from the sheaves, and they should be thrown into the fire, sister . . . we must wait for the new ones to come."

"Nikolka is the new one."

"Nikolka is the blight," Mitka laughed, and squeezed his sister's hand tightly. "The little black fungus on the ears of corn—it must be stamped out. I've got a plan already."

"That's quite enough, Mitka. I've got a performance today. Come another time." She got up, ready for anything, even for a breach with her brother. "You're a nuisance today, like Chikelyov. You've become as fussy and pedantic as he is." She left the box without saying good-by.

"And yet I wish you happiness, sister, as I understand it. I wish it with all the good that still remains in me," whispered Mitka, and he went quickly down the stairs.

Tanya did not call him back. She stood staring motionlessly into the darkness of the empty circus, where her jagged and grotesque shadow lost itself. Her anger made her almost beautiful. On her half-bared shoulder the tinsel gleamed, and her light, loosened hair was like a halo. The warlike maid herself would have envied her her figure and the straightness of her knit eyebrows.

"What did he come for, and why did he want to palm off his dirty money on me? Why did he flatter me, and why was he pitiable in spite of all his threatening talk?" A cleaner with a ladder in his hand ran past, and a whiff of sweat rose into her nostrils. She turned around slowly to Pugel, who was sitting on a step and had not dared to disturb her agitated reflections.

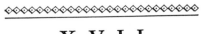
In the fifth chapter of his book Firsov singled out a murderous sword stroke as the turning point in Mitka's destiny and the beginning of his sufferings, but he offended against the truth in a particularly sacrilegious way when he told that Mitka had only hacked off the captain's arm and then flung his body into a ditch. This was, of course, far more picturesque and even artistic than the simple murder that actually occurred, and far more suitable for an elegant little story about the civil war. That war, which was the most important in history and to which thousands of men sacrificed the flower of their strength, Firsov regarded as something florid and unreal, which might offend the fastidious by its senseless squandering of colors.

As Firsov had no liking for the themes that were presented to the writer in those years, he had not the courage to grapple seriously with Mitka, to present him as a dark, subterranean power, or as a fire that, once started, sinks and flares up alternately and every moment changes its shape and its hue. The writer could not endure disorder. (He actually rented in a remote street a room that looked out on a garden, a measure that considerably quickened his inspiration.) Firsov, indeed, could not summon sufficient affection for Mitka to tell the truth about him. For why was it that Mitka had fallen away from the position in life that he had won for himself with such pain and effort? Why at the break of day (as the critics put it) was he overtaken by the impenetrable darkness of night? What were the real causes of his struggles? (Firsov's elegant phrase-making about Mitka having "graduated as a proletarian" by leaving his home and his relations was far too obscure. He evidently considered Mitka's first crime as the last convulsions of a new spiritual rebirth.)

Firsov described romantically the murder of the captain by night, and laid special emphasis on Mitka's age. "Young songs are sung only in the red glow of dawn, before the midday heat has set in and the natural doubts of youth have assailed the mind." ("What song is the author talking about?" asked a critic acidly. "Is it, perhaps, the revolution that he has in mind? We know what the writer means when he says that 'the great deeds of men only appear in their true light before the eyes of their descendants.'" The most esteemed critic of the age, in his observations on the unreliability of any esthetic judgment on the revolution, declared in tones of thunder that the age needed a serious and truthful language. "We allow anyone to utter those truths which we have all experienced in common, and which are dictated by a firm confidence in our final victory, but not those which are motivated by a malevolent and prejudicial skepticism.")

Well, the truth is that Mitka put an end to the young captain's life that night with a blow on the skull. ("What of it?" asked another esteemed critic. "He was loved in the division just because his will was as bright and flashing as his sword. And even if twenty captains had been there, Mitka's hand would not have wearied.") It happened at the time of Mitka's mysterious rebirth. When the fire leaps up, who will direct it or bend its flaming spire? ("What will you have? The twisted stove pipe, the tiled stove, the storm wind, or fate?" asked Donka in one of his poems which Firsov had printed in a weekly.) The living, flowing fire went its way with nothing to guide it but its consciousness that it was a liberating fire. Firsov was reproached with lack of principle, but unjustly.

To diversify the plot of his work the novelist created some very ingeniously contrived situations. Masha, in a critical moment, was supposed to have said to Mitka: "Yes, you murdered him, but not in anger, but from jealousy, because you couldn't possess yourself of the last and greatest of his qualities, something which could be neither weighed nor measured." And she was made to bring in Agey's name here. (But this is in complete contradiction to Firsov's own statement that Dolomanova wanted to erase this accursed name from her memory. Firsov employed Agey as a dark screen that cast a grim and baleful shadow over Mitka's relations with Masha.) This particular passage was attacked by one of the most eminent critics. "We must learn to fight . . . not with mere words, but with courage and daring, as our fathers and elder brothers fought on the battlefields of socialistic glory. We must not rest till we have unfurled the flag of triumphant Labor on the topmost citadel commanding earth and sky —we must gain possession of it with our own hands." (The critic overlooked the fact that if Firsov's story roused him to these pronouncements, it was at any rate a good picture of the times through which the land was passing.)

At the conclusion of his unfortunate fifth chapter Firsov said much the same himself. . . . "All this coincided with the happy moment when the Commission for Popular Education ranked in importance with the Supreme Economic Council, and thousands of young people hurried to the new high schools, which had supplanted the moldering institutions of former days, and old people learned at last why water boils, why a river flows downward, and why the sky is blue." By using the slogan "The Conquest of Culture," Firsov ran the risk of simplifying the personal fate of his hero until it became a diagram, but no one appreciated this. Mitka was regarded as the antitype of the men of the postrevolutionary period. Mitka suffered and struggled, but no one saw this. The moribund remnant (fortunately small) of the Russian intelligentsia jeered at him to their hearts' content.

Mitka had been interred with Firsov's story, but Mitka still lived to spite the writer's assertions. He had not been drinking lately: his very being had become parched and arid. A new sorrow lay in wait for him, and with roving eyes he searched for someone fixed and steadfast, by whose side he might wait until the storm had passed. He transferred to his sister his whole store of tenderness which had been spurned by others. It was a momentary weakness; her pathetic little happiness seemed to him like a tiny fire by which he might sit through the interminable loneliness of his nights. His mental sickness continued, although the old woman no longer haunted him. But once he went to sleep in the cinema, and when an attendant shook him awake, the auditorium was empty. The stuffy air of the hall was dust-filled and poisoned by human breath. Mitka went out to the steps, which were covered with the torn halves of admission tickets, and there in the half-darkness the thought shot through his brain that the old woman was waiting for him behind a pillar. Beside himself with terror, Mitka ran behind the pillar, but he found nobody there. Yet he was convinced that the old woman must be somewhere, and he ran through the cloakroom, through the foyer, and looked into the operator's room; but everything was empty.

Then Mitka resolved on an extraordinary step. The idea of consulting a psychiatrist had been growing on him ever since he had read in a paper a review of a book on medico-legal judgments. In a week Mitka discovered the professor's name, address, and consulting hours. The professor usually returned from his office about five o'clock, sitting in a droshky with a well-worn portfolio on his knee, a stout, puffy figure. Mitka already knew other things about him, for he had stood daily watching in the park near the house, but had always been afraid of knocking during the consulting hours.

Finally he made up his mind that if the number of paces between two trees should be even he would go. The number of the paces was forty-eight, a number of peremptory command; Mitka leaned with all his force against the knob of the electric bell and rang.

The visit to the doctor did not last more than four minutes. In the large, untidy consulting room stood a table covered with books, the most solid object in the room. A small cat was sitting on the books; it stared at Mitka inquiringly. He stood in his coat in the middle of the floor, and swung his stick with the ivory top. Then the famous doctor appeared, still chewing his interrupted lunch. He turned on Mitka his half-closed, smiling eyes, which had probed so many secrets, and indicated two chairs. Mitka shook his head impatiently.

"Take a seat," said the doctor, and pushed back his cuff into the sleeve of his worn indoor coat. "Sit down! What can I do for you?"

"Sit!" repeated Mitka, gazing at the rolls of fat on the psychiatrist's smiling face. His mind remained fixed on the two chairs, although they were quite ordinary chairs with straw bottoms. "I can sit down either on this one or on that one," said Mitka reflectively. "When I think back, it seems to me that I've already sat on one of them. Will you please listen to me?" he said seriously, laying his finger on his lips. "Therefore I must sit down on that one again. . . . I can't afford to make a mistake. On which of them am I to sit?"

"On whichever you like," the analyst said smiling, and went up a little closer to Mitka. "The one on the left has a nail sticking out, but the one on the right is quite safe, please note that." He went on chewing the morsel he had in his mouth.

"No, it isn't a question of that," said Mitka crossly. "It's a question of a law . . . one of two things: either I remain alive or I don't . . . Wait! . . ." Before the analyst had time to say anything to reassure his patient, Mitka had gone. His eyes wandered, and on his face there was an expression of exhaustion and sickly apprehension. With his hat in his hand he walked across the boulevard; then he recollected that Zavarihin must certainly have been waiting for him a long time at Batashiha's. Then he put on his hat again.

It was twilight, and the naked poplar twigs swung like rats' tails. Mitka raised his head and noticed that snow-flakes were falling from the dull gray sky. He turned around and set off in the opposite direction, and there, on the road that branched off to Batashiha's mill, he met Curly Donka.

Donka was strolling the pavement slightly intoxicated and singing as he went: he was making for the same goal as Mitka. His leather jacket was flung wide open, and his blue-crowned cossack cap was perched on the back of his head with an air of jaunty devilry. Mitka walked beside him in silence, and Donka became silent, too, and stopped his singing. In any case, the narrow street, which wound like a worm hole in a nut, was not suited to intimate conversation.

"How's life, Donka? You've no reason to complain, anyway," said Mitka at last, banteringly. He had now completely recovered from his ridiculous adventure with the psychiatrist. "You're young, you have talent, you have a woman . . . and a fine woman, too!"

Donka went on in silence, but his boots scraped noisily on the asphalt. Suddenly he stood still.

"I'm going to be even with Sanka!" he flung out defiantly, and his voice throbbed with the hate that had gathered in him in the last few months. "The fellow's given us the slip, and you've helped him, too. I'm going to show him up . . ." He did not finish speaking, and Mitka fancied that he was confused by his straight, sobering glance.

"Why are you so sure it was Sanka? Perhaps it was you," said Mitka's eyes.

Mitka, who did not suspect how cunningly the cards had been shuffled for the game that was to ensue, thought he had seen through Donka's stratagems. "I'll get Tolya to help me, and I'll prove my mettle on this man—I know he's guilty," he thought, and blushed at the thought of the psychiatrist. Why had he taken to his heels so contemptibly? Was it that he did not want to face his fate? or was he so weak that he did not believe any longer in the power of his own will over the future? A secret desire to turn back again brought Mitka to a standstill in the middle of the pavement. What would he have had to discuss with the psychiatrist except the things he was straining every nerve to forget? "Show me your tongue, most honored sir." No, no, why the tongue? What nonsense! He would speak of other things, he would state in advance that for science there are neither good deeds nor bad deeds, but simply the formulas of cause and effect. Suddenly Mitka was convinced that a servant would stop him on the threshold and say that the professor was out. "What? Out!" "Yes. On a bus. He can't sit and wait the whole evening till the celebrated thief visits him. . . ."

Suddenly Mitka realized what it was that held him to the spot: on the fence in front of him hung a great colored poster announcing Tanya's fourth and last but one appearance in Moscow. A huge exclamation mark was drawn inside a black, slightly improbable noose. Mitka frowned irritably and hastened to overtake Donka. Donka looked around and slowed down with a forced smile that seemed to Mitka insulting and shameless. He struck Donka on the shoulder, and Donka stood still, and suddenly turned pale. The light of a lamp screwed in over the door fell vertically down on them. They were standing in front of the entrance to Batashiha's mill.

"How's life, Donka?" said Mitka facetiously, without shifting his eyes from his rival.

"I love Manka: for her sake I'd lay hands on my own father. Why don't you come to the point? Shall we fight? Then let's go beyond the turnpike and put an end to it there. . . . Well?" Donka's voice was quiet, but Mitka heard in it a ring of anger.

"A duel?" laughed Mitka. "If I should think it necessary I shall always know where to find you." His icy tone struck a chill to Donka's heart.

Donka sank his head dispiritedly. "I'm with you about Sanka, all the same. To test him, ask him to join in some other job, and then we'll just see." He stopped talking, but did not let Donka escape yet. "You don't know the meaning of discipline." (But he thought to himself: "And yet I despise the ones that do.")

The wire cage that protected the lamp from thieves checkered the darkness of the staircase with faint squares. This gave it a squalid look, although it was kept spotlessly clean; the houses next door to the thieves' den were inhabited by the families of highly placed civil servants. An almost mysterious peace reigned here. The highly respectable exterior of the saloon, into which spendthrifts had access only on special recommendation, was mainly to be traced to the personal qualities of Batashiha herself. Once an autocratic landowner, she was now an old woman with owl's eyes and a voice of thunder, and she lived a life crammed with adventure. The peasants in her neighborhood remembered her as a childless widow, who, in some ways, had been even more dashing than Saltichiha. They used to speak of her wild pranks, and how she went out driving by preference during thunder storms; she always had the horses yoked at the first clap of thunder. During the revolution her horse, "Flea," a black mare, famed through the whole district, had been commandeered and used as a carriage horse by the puny local Prodkommissar. Once she came to him during office hours, struck him on the forehead with her ringed hand, and said: "You shan't drive my Flea, not you, you wretch!" Then she went away, and no one dared to detain her. On account of a rebellion she plotted a week later, she was condemned to death. As she was driven half undressed to the place of execution to be shot, she suddenly jumped onto her mare, which happened to be passing, and dashed away for six versts, nimbly eluding her pursuers. In a cellar that she used as a hiding place she escaped the fate of her fellow culprits, though her breast and shoulder were frozen and the cold terror of the cellar had sprinkled her dark locks with white. A year later she appeared in the capital as proprietress of a gambling hall called "The Windmill." All who were hiding from the iron arm of justice found with her a safe refuge for which no rent was asked, but although she behaved honorably and justly to her protégés, she was disliked.

In contrast to Artemy's den, everything here was in the best of order, almost stylish. In a corner a lean young lady was playing the piano, while a keen game of hazard was being played at the tables. In her own house Batashiha was treated with great respect. She herself opened the door for Mitka and immediately handed him a note.

"Someone was here asking for you, but he hadn't time to wait any longer, so he went away," she said, as she locked the door. "A big, stout chap . . . he sat there the whole time and looked around him."

"One of my lads," answered Mitka, and began to read Zavarihin's missive by the light through the crack in the door, a light that streamed into the hall. A low whispering buzzed the whole time in his ears; two boys were practising card sharping. . . . "A pack of fifty-two cards should be shuffled eight times. If it's cut wedge-shaped, you can tickle all the fat out of the pack any moment you like. But you must look into his eyes as you do it! . . . You must play with your eyes!" "Right you are!" answered the other humbly. Both became suddenly silent when Mitka began to curse Zavarihin in an undertone.

Nikolka wrote that he was going to the circus for half an hour to "get a look at little Hella." At the end of the note he informed Mitka that he would bring Tanya along after her turn, to show her "what some of your lot look like." He had even added: "Just you have a look at the lout by the window . . . full to busting on other people's bread, you bet!" He evidently referred to Tolya; the futile old good-for-nothing was sitting by the window at a little table with his head propped on his hand. His left leg was stretched out on the carpet, a dignified leg in green gaiters. Mitka understood: Tolya had at last found his vocation and a use for his strength. Batashiha had taken him into her service in case of emergencies, for from time to time spendthrifts get out of hand.

The game went on with the three famous cards. Mitka sat on a chair close by the table, lit a cigarette, and watched. He did not know the players; some sat with eyebrows raised, others bit their lips, all alike silent and withdrawn into themselves.

Among them sat Donka with a pale brow and moist hands, feverish with excitement: he had lost against five players straight off, and the game was for high stakes. A little old man, dressed like an Old Believer, had heaped up Donka's money beside him against a beer bottle. The young lady at the piano played on gaily and unconcernedly.

Mitka felt in his pocket. The money he had brought with him for Zavarihin was there, none of it was missing. Suddenly Donka called out a high stake and immediately the young lady struck a false note; she had been appalled at the sum. The old man rapped his fingers on the table top. "But you're lucky in love, Donka," said Mitka teasingly as the old man busily clawed in Donka's money.

"Exactly . . . Mitka!" answered Donka, baring his teeth in an insulting laugh.

The stillness and the music plunged Mitka into a sort of stupor. He barely heard Donka's words, for in his drowsy consciousness everything appeared in vague and ragged shapes. Later he could scarcely recollect that Tolya had stepped up to the table, a glass of beer in his hand. He seemed to be saying something, and someone was answering him. When Mitka raised his heavy lids for the last time, he saw that in the room next door, which in the daytime bore the title of "Dental Consulting-Room," Batashiha, who was half asleep, too, was knitting a stocking and nodding her shaggy head.

His dream was chaotic and disturbing, and scarcely to be translated into words. (The critic reproached Firsov vigorously for his rhetorical description of Mitka's visit to the "House of Union" where Lenin's coffin stood, but it was no exaggeration, for Mitka had gone past the leader's coffin groaning and reeling. The chapter ended with one of Mitka's fellow visitors whispering severely in his ear: "Groaning is forbidden here, citizen!" Through his darkest days Mitka had always cherished the hope of speaking someday with Lenin, intimately as man to man, the only man in whom he could utterly have put his trust.) This was his dream: in a large, dimly lighted room Mitka was waiting for Lenin. Lenin was not there yet, but one could feel in the air the imminence of his approach. Then there was a strange gap in the dream . . . and Mitka felt that he ran to the door, opened it, and saw the familiar face of the psychiatrist, in whose eyes there was an icy majesty and wisdom, multiplied a thousandfold by the fantasy of sleep. And suddenly the psychiatrist shouted loudly and coarsely: "He's spat into my beer!"

Mitka opened his eyes and stared at the scene without understanding. It was Tolya who, scarlet with rage and drink, had shouted the words about the beer. With quivering fingers he pointed to his glass, in which bubbles of froth were swimming. Evidently it was Donka who had spat in it, and he had done it because Tolya had been forcing his advice on him and bragging insolently. Donka sat with his arms crossed at the corner of the table and laughed at Batashiha, who was making an effort to snatch away Tolya's polluted glass. The gamblers laughed, and there was a horrible uproar.

Suddenly (and from that moment Mitka could remember clearly) knocks resounded in the anteroom; someone was banging furiously on the door. The old woman rushed toward it, commanding silence with an imperious gesture. The young lady disappeared. Mitka listened with a foreboding heart: at first they heard the iron creaking of innumerable bars, then there was a short moment of complete silence, and suddenly it seemed as if a wind rushed in and flung Batashiha screaming to the ground. The gamblers got up in silence and the Old Believer tugged at his beard. On the doorstep stood Zavarihin.

His corpse-pale face was featureless and blank, as if he had neither nose nor mouth; his eyes roamed around in quest of Mitka, who was sitting at the table, and not till he saw him did his mouth open like a great black patch in his face. He did not shout, but Mitka stepped toward him rigid as steel. His throat hurt him unbearably.

THE accident had happened at half-past ten, and more or less as follows. At the appointed time the circus was full to overflowing, and the carpetman had already spread out the carpet to sharpen the appetite of the spectators for what was to come. A whisper went around that members of the government were sitting in the stage box, and their presence turned the evening's entertainment into a special occasion.

Tanya had arrived toward the end of the first half of the performance. Two spoof musicians, both of them of considerable talent, were playing a mazurka of Godard's on kitchen utensils. In the lower rows the audience were eating oranges, in the middle apples, and higher up still they were sucking peppermints; the gallery contented itself with just being there. A carpetman looked spellbound at the blinding lights between which a scarcely visible black noose hung down. In the government box newspapers were being unfolded; they were full of details of an astonishing robbery. Tanya peeped out from behind the row of stagehands into the arena to satisfy herself that everything was in perfect order. There were still two more items in the first half of the program: "The Flying Fountains," and the comic bicyclist Blumenhaff.

Tanya was this evening, too, the main attraction, more on account of her personality than the mysterious title of her sensational turn. The evening before, a tactless article on circus artists had appeared in the newspapers in which Hella Velton was referred to by her initials, an utterly transparent disguise. The subject of the article was the vicissitudes in the careers of circus artists and the tragic end of many. The public had been attracted by the chance of being present at a possibly tragical fiasco. Besides this, in the government box it was known that the artist was closely related to another celebrity whose activities had from time to time been chronicled among events of the day.

Pugel had arrived half an hour earlier with the requisite circus equipment, and Tanya found him sitting in a corner, his hands folded calmly on his knees, the embodiment of perfect peace. His face was lit up now by a smile, now overcast by a shadow of anxiety: this was the way he used to listen to some inner conversation with himself. Near the small open trunk on the little dressing table lay a twig of hothouse jasmine. It was Pugel's surprise.

He instantly jumped up and began to bustle. "Ah, my bad girl!" he whispered into Tanya's ear as she sat down at the mirror.

"I'm not your girl," she answered him laughingly, and struck him with the jasmine twig on his withered old hand.

"Ah, Tanya, how could you think to leave the circus? A soldier he must not run from the battle. Ah, I know you so well as the two kopeks in my pocket!" He got excited, for he was the prey of forebodings he could not understand.

"And do you know"—she turned to him with childlike tenderness—"I haven't yet got used to the thought that I'm a real circus artist. My whole life seems to me to have been just one long effort to do what one can't. I love my art, Pugel, because I know what a struggle it cost me at first. How I used to cry if I didn't succeed in anything! . . . Do you remember that time in Volhynia? You flung that rope to me. . . ."

"Yes, yes . . . the rope which hold the tent," repeated Pugel like an echo . . .

". . . Suddenly I became happy and gay, and instantly everything went well with me. And do you remember how we gave the third bell signal eight times because the fools never turned up? But I was happy. Any work gives one pleasure if one loves it: even one's failures are fun."

For the first time in all the years they had spent to-

gether they thought of all the tiny happenings of the past,
which were dear to them both. It was amazing that all the
humdrum occurrences of every day had not been shaken
out of Pugel's head by his journeying from place to place.
Then the first signal bell rang, its long-drawn clang rolled
through the building. The interval came to an end, and
in the distance the band blared a muffled tune. Pugel sat
with his back to Tanya, who began to dress quickly.

"It's possible that I won't marry Nikolka after all," she
said. "I don't need anyone's help any more, now I can
stand on my own feet. It's odd, you know: I hurried to him
then, when that German . . . do you remember that evening? . . ."

"Herr Mangolf," completed Pugel, and gave a small,
respectful cough.

"Yes, I thought he'd take a strong line and scold me
and beat me, perhaps." She laughed. "No, it wouldn't
have got as far as that, I know! He didn't make any use
of his strength: it would have helped me to make up my
mind if he had. Then I got ashamed. But you'll never understand how we Russians live through every tiny detail
of our troubles."

"*Ach*, so!" In broken Russian he told her that a Russian is always a little ashamed of his goodness, and on
that account everything takes a topsy-turvy course with
him. "This *mouzhik* of yours, Nikolka, is vairy, vairy honorable: how much have I wept on his account! I felt myself not wanted, I wished to run away. But then I think
who else is there who could understand your fame?" He
listened. "They're playing . . . they're playing. They're
waiting: it's time, Tanya!" And then an individual with
a close-cropped head appeared in the doorway and announced that it was time to appear.

"Knock before you come in!" said Tanya sharply. "Shut
the door. There's a draft."

The door shut again, the music grew fainter, but it
played on continuously. Standing in the middle of the
room, Tanya massaged her neck and twisted her head to
test the suppleness of her muscles for the strain they were
to undergo.

"You can turn around now, Pugel. I'm ready. . . . Listen—I don't suppose you noticed, though—side whiskers

suit Mitka awfully well, don't you think? He's very handsome now, or is he just proud?"

"I had side whiskers once, too," recollected the old man
vaguely, and noticed now for the first time that there was
a small hole in her tights at the hip, the size of a silver
coin, a little below the flashing blue belt. The next instant
the old man was deftly plying a needle with thread the
color of the tights, but his old hands shook with excitement, which his enfeebled will could no longer restrain.

"You're pricking me, Pugel."

"Focht, who was a vairy, vairy big man, was killed
through a leetle hole like that: he got confuse and fell."

The door flew open and the individual with the cropped
head stepped in again.

"It's time, Velton . . . high time!" he cried, and
added something irrelevant about the government box.

"Out with you . . . I'm not dressed yet!" answered
Tanya crossly. A moment later she stepped into the corridor and met Nikolka there.

"Have you come to see me?" she asked rapidly.

"Yes, I'm bringing you the money you gave me. I
wanted to come before this, but I always had something
to do. . . ."

"You always have something to do," laughed Tanya
coolly. "No, I've got nowhere to put your money at the
moment. Keep it a bit: the interest on it for an hour
won't come to much, you know!"

Zavarihin disappeared into the crowd once more. He
deliberately did not hurry himself and made himself uni-
versally unpopular by the inconsiderate way in which he
shoved in without apology. His half-closed eyes glowered
defiantly. There was a burst of applause and the public
stopped chewing. In the government box the newspapers
were folded up. Tanya stood on the trapeze and let her
eyes travel over the innumerable tiny details of the scene.
Everything was in order: her body was poised forward,
eager for flight. The band played a sentimental tune, and
Tanya fastened herself with strap nooses to the trapeze.

In the first row from the stage Nikolka sat biting his
lips and glowering: the lines of his face were calm and
proud. "Oh, butterfly!" whispered his lips to shake off the
bewitching spell of the moment. The features of Pugel,

who sat on a small sofa in the cloakroom, were tense and drawn. "Oh, sun!" he muttered, as if he himself were soaring in the cupola above the evil-smelling sand. The music stopped.

With his whole being he felt time passing, it trickled through his fingers like an electric current. Suddenly he leaped up: it seemed to him that he had left one of Tanya's tights at home lying on her bed—in circus superstition an omen of disaster. Gnawing at his fingernails, he rushed to the door, but drew back; from inside there came the sinister throbbing of the drum. "Too late!" he murmured feebly, sat down, and watched the blood flowing from under his bitten nail. Without knowing it he sat on the branch of jasmine. He had neither sight nor feeling, his whole soul was centered in his alert and straining ears. The stillness calmed him, he half smiled. Then, suddenly, a terrible cry (that seemed close beside his ear) drew him from his seat.

The accident had happened a few seconds before. Straining every nerve, Tanya had measured the farthest distance to which the noose would carry her. A mad daring came over her as she looked across the ranks in which human faces lay like a mountain of apples. A breath of icy terror came out from them. The seconds divided themselves into thousandths of seconds, and these divided again into new, tiny moments the mind could no longer grasp: Tanya swung down, and time seemed to stand still. Then they all saw a blue, rigid body that hung there like a faded flower, but it made no deep impression on their minds. Tanya hung there; she was dead and seemed to be gazing into the dead light. The noose had caught her chin. "She's an artful one, the way she keeps up the suspense!" said the carpetman, for his admiration was greater than his envy. But then the woollen cap that held together Tanya's hair began with a deadly slowness to drop into the sand.

Nikolka jumped over the front rows, trod on backs and hands, and came crashing down. He stood in the arena, waving his arms and looking like a tree that had gone mad. The liveried attendants gazed distractedly at the wild brandishing of his fists. The audience streamed from their places, glittering in their gay clothes. Time flowed on again at its normal speed. The gallery raged and moaned like a beast that has swallowed a needle in its food.

They carried Tanya first of all into her dressing room for the necessary depositions to be taken. Death had been caused by a jerk of the rope, which had broken her spine. But no one guessed that this had been due to a very slight twist in the rope. In the corridors the accident was being discussed. A man with an unbuttoned fur coat was gabbling excitedly in the center of a group of people about the carelessness of the management, and his wife was whispering to him every other moment: "Petya, feel if your pocketbook is still there. . . ."

Then Tanya was carried away.

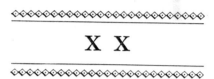
"It's heavy," said Mitka.

"Oak," answered Zavarihin, and lowered his flushed face.

The circus artists, Tanya's colleagues, were helping to carry out the coffin. The narrow staircase, with its stale smell of cats, squeezed them together. Tanya was to be buried in the new "Red" way, without incense or song. While the open coffin was put on the catafalque, Firsov stepped up with a mourning band on his sleeve. His eyes were blinking and streaming, for he had spent the whole night revising his story. Not far from him stood Puchov, in stony gloom. Mitka did not leave Nikolka's side the whole morning.

A crowd of sensation hunters attracted by the tragic accident mingled, in the soaking rain, with the mourners. Then the wheels creaked on. . . .

A glint of purple shot through the hoar frost that crisped gaily on the trees, and a blue shadow slid across the snow beside the procession. It was a bright morning with a sting of frost in the air. Over the roofs hovered tiny clouds of smoke. The acrobats had brought a small wreath, which looked touchingly fragile in the frost. The sudden sting of death had not disfigured Tanya's face, but Firsov saw a new sternness and solemnity in her features. (Even here his imaginary pencil was scribbling on imaginary paper.) Pugel kept close to the edge of the hearse, and strode beside it with bared head. On the way someone put on his fur cap for him, but the old man did not noitce it; with Tanya he had lost his last link with life. At a cross-

roads where the snow shimmered blue like glass Pugel fell
to the ground and remained lying there; but he was picked
up and put on his legs, his cap was set on his head, and
he was able again to follow in the procession. In spite of
his small stature the eyes of all were on him. Behind him
the Belgian acrobats walked in a row: in the sunlit snow
the conquerors and flyers and supermen of the day before
looked bowed and tired.

Oh, what a blessed reprieve that sunrise was to the
three watchers by the coffin—Mitka, Nikolka, and Pugel.
Pugel had sat the night through at the door, for his weakness gave him the right to sit, but toward sunrise he collected himself and began with an almost incongruous zeal
to tidy himself. By the coffin Zavarihin stood watching,
stiff and tireless as a post. His eyes remained fixed, as if
mesmerized, on the flashing metal handles of the coffin.
The lamp was covered with a yellow cloth, and its light
seemed in keeping with the feeling of the night. Zinka and
her aunt had washed Tanya and dressed her the evening
before. Zinka was not there on the last night, for she had
succumbed to an irresistible craving for sleep.

Mitka sat in the front room; a child could have caught
him now. His clothes, which had been neglected for three
days, looked as though he had spent a month in a filthy
railway waggon. Although he was awake, yet he felt, as
in a dream, that he was telling Puchov something about
himself, but could find no words except the invariable
complaint: "Ah, old Primus, I'm pretty well done for
now!" It was as if he were sliding down a high mountain
into a dark and lifeless abyss.

"Mitka . . . but that isn't right, is it? Eh?"

"What isn't right?" asked Mitka without stirring.

"But look here—she's lying there . . . alone. They
ought to read a psalm surely! I don't know what the custom is today." Nikolka's words sounded shy, and were interrupted every moment by yawns.

"You think it's boring for her?" Mitka raised his eyes
and finally shook off his lethargy.

"Not boring, but hard. What's boredom, anyway? It's
all nonsense! Should I run over to my uncle for a psalter?
Shall I? I read it over my father, I'm a good hand at psalm
chanting. It won't do her any harm, and she'd like it. It

won't be so bad if there are people who are trying, reading . . . as it ought to be . . . well?"

Mitka did not answer, but looked again into Zavarihin's
lowered face. He had evidently found time to shave himself. There was a cut on his cheek, covered by a piece of
paper.

"You won't wake her up to life again, though," said
Mitka roughly, swaying on his feet.

"We haven't enough faith . . . but if we had the faith,
then we could go up to her and call out the right word and
she'd get up," whispered Nikolka mysteriously. There was
deep defiance in his wide-open eyes. "My uncle told me,
there was once a saint called Ivan the Post. He struck an
aspen post into the ground and prayed over it till it began to flower. If all men had faith, even mountains might
get up and move about. We need faith!"

"It isn't faith, but will, Nikolka," Mitka interrupted
him.

"No, faith . . ." insisted Zavarihin, and there was an
angry gleam in his eyes.

"Will," said Mitka again, yet already more feebly. Suddenly he raised his head. "You've nobody now, Nikolka.
You're burying your Tatyanka . . ."

"Hella . . ." said Zavarihin roughly and seriously.

"It's a lie! Tanya!" Mitka angrily thrust away the hand
that touched his shoulder.

"Hella . . ." whispered Zavarihin softly, almost as if
he were drunk.

Then Mitka's face seemed to crumple up, and his eyes
became dead with exhaustion. "Run for your psalter, get
along quick!" said he in disgust, and waved his hand.

The door was open, and into the dim stuffiness of the
front room a faint breath of musty coolness made its way.
It seemed to Mitka as if he were quite alone. Down below,
the door slammed on Nikolka. At the other side of the
curtain he thought he heard a whispering; he remembered
Pugel, and stepped into the room in which Tanya lay.

The old man was sitting in the same position as on the
day before; he looked respectable, almost refined; his
tight-closed lips betrayed his inward emotion.

"My bad girl!" he repeated in a singsong voice. It
sounded almost like the reproach of a lover.

"What are you mumbling about?" asked Mitka, bending over him.

The other did not understand him.

"The biggest sleep a man ever sleeps is when he dies," he said shyly. He recognized Mitka and leaned toward him confidingly. "She liked vairy, vairy moch . . . jasmine."

The yellow light was a torment.

"Jasmine, do you say?" Mitka asked him with strange harshness. "And you like jasmine yourself?"

"I liked . . . vairy, vairy moch . . . roses . . ." confessed the other guiltily, but Mitka was already out on the stairs; he had a headache. The minutes dragged on endlessly.

The Zavarihin came back with Puchov's psalter under his arm, but he did not succeed in reading it; the dawn was breaking. Preparations had still to be made, although most of them had been made already. The room had grown cold . . . with the shivery feeling that follows a sleepless night.

"It's freezing," said Nikolka, without trying to subdue his powerful voice to the stillness. "I took some bread with me from my uncle . . . There is is, eat it! And do you know, Mitka, I got terrified before, when you screamed at me. I thought you'd begin fighting . . . but I can't fight with you here, so near her!"

"All the strength has gone from my hands. Give Pugel the bread," answered Mitka wearily.

So they waited till sunrise.

Nikolka did not stint the expense. "If the wedding wasn't a success, well, the funeral will be!" The small number of people and the absence of the wretched Trade Union band increased the solemnity of the occasion. They had already walked half the way when Donka stepped up to Mitka and drew his attention to the risk he ran of being ambushed and arrested. He hinted repeatedly at Sanka's double dealing; he was a dirty hound. Mitka's disappearance roused no particular attention; no one noticed it but Zinka, who was on her husband's arm.

Presently Pyotr Gorbidonich hired a sledge. "Tell me, honored sir," he asked Puchov importunately but impressively as he bowed to him from the sledge, "what details of this sad occurrence have come to your hearing? It's really typical: I always feel a shudder down my spine whenever I pass a circus."

With head sunk and struggling not to get left behind by the sledge, Puchov told everything he had heard from his nephew. Pyotr Gorbidonich shook his head, and often, turning to his wife, invoked her sympathy by a movement of his eyebrows. Suddenly he noticed that they had remained behind the procession.

"On, on, my good fellow!" he ordered the coachman. Puchov got left behind, and so the most important part of the story remained untold.

AT THE corner stood a taxi. The chauffeur, a traditional, sharp-witted Moscow Vanka, dressed in a skin coat and enrolled as a member of the Union, looked at Mitka nonchalantly. Mitka crept into the old box, and, waving his arms as if he were still flogging a nag, the chauffeur heaved at the crank, and the car started to rattle through the snow.

"Slowly, you road hog! I'm going to my sister's funeral," shouted Mitka through the little window.

Chikelyov's shadow flashed past, and the silly feathers on Zinka's hat fluttered backward and forward. Firsov was walking beside Puchov and talking excitedly, gesticulating with an ungloved hand, while Puchov smiled as a mountain smiles at the wind that races past it.

"They're making enough row, anyway!" thought Mitka resentfully. A few more circus people flashed past the car window—Stassik, Pugel, and Nikolka, who was surreptitiously gnawing a piece of bread.

The hearse was sumptuously decorated, and two stout fellows in caps with ear flaps drove the horses. Mitka ordered the chauffeur to drive ahead.

Clouds gathered—the provision of fine weather was not one of the functions of the undertaking establishment—and suddenly it began to snow heavily. The streets grew more and more deserted; soon there was nobody stirring but a small boy racing about on a single rollerskate. Then Mitka saw at a street corner a man in a black tunic, whom he instantly recognized. He was the man who had come first into Pirman's shop. So they were watching out for him, then. Donka had been right. The emptiness of the street was very favorable for an arrest. Snorting like a superannuated cab horse, the car slid past.

"He betrayed me himself, and now he's warned me himself!" thought Mitka, smoking one cigarette after another; the smoke sickened him, but at least it stifled the pangs of hunger. "I must get to the bottom of this, and then we'll have a court martial." The old ones were passing, and he himself was already stepping into their shoes; on him now fell the responsibility of holding high the tarnished tradition of the thief world. "Yes, a thieves' court martial!" And scarcely had his resolve to hold a court martial on Donka taken firm root than Tolya came into his mind. "Was that why I lectured him and pulled his boozy old nose for him? So you say that you can get rid of all vermin from a cockroach to a man? . . . And then they try and throw all the blame on to Sanka! It's all a put-up job: they're all out to do each other down nowadays. One might as well try to keep a pigsty clean. . . ."

The car had reached the cemetery.

"Where now?" The chauffeur turned around.

"Go in at the gate," Mitka ordered.

"Can't be done, I can't turn around there," answered the chauffeur, fiddling with the gears. But all the same the car squeezed through the narrow gate and jammed against a pile of snow. Farther on, the road divided into small paths, which were covered with a thin, wind-blown film of snow.

Mitka let the chauffeur wait, and made for the left corner of the cemetery where he had ordered the grave the evening before. Hewn stone and planed wood rose out of the snow, and both alike spread out their arms in a cruciform embrace to meet him. The wind was feebler here, but when it tore down in a mighty gust, the trees twanged like fiddle strings; in frost, wood has the ringing note of iron. Mitka stumbled up to the grave, stood on the outermost edge of it, and looked into its depths. Loose clay, mixed with snow, trickled down under his feet. He stood like this a long time till he heard the hoot of the car. As he went away, he did not notice that he had flung an empty cigarette pack into Tanya's grave.

A gloomy December day is the best for burials, and it

was already dusk when they lowered Tanya into the ground. Mitka, as he flew past the funeral procession in the car, could still clearly see Tanya's profile, though it was half covered with snow. The number of mourners had decreased, and those who remained could barely be seen for the blizzard. The snow as falling effortlessly, covering many thousands of kilometers with its impalpable shroud. Mitka could have sat an eternity on the bouncing leather cushions of the taxi. In Grusiny he got out and paid his fare with some thick paper notes that were immediately soaked. He felt drawn by some strange power toward a place where he had once been a long time ago, when he was still a soldier in the Czar's army.

The zoological gardens were already closed. "Have you come to see them shooting the film, Comrade?" someone asked at the door.

"Yes," answered Mitka mechanically, and he was let through. There behind these impassable drifts of snow shivering beasts sat and waited for Mitka's appearance. There was a swarm of men on the frozen pond. Two searchlights dispersed the gathering dusk; they were shooting the film. An elk lay in the snow with legs tied together, and two stage *mouzhiks* in improbable fur caps screamed over the animal and fumbled with knives. The beast lay quietly and, baring its teeth, stretched its muzzle into the snow. The heavy shadows of the assassins moved clumsily across the surface of the snow, and made the beams of the searchlight appear like the moon.

"Stab it dead, stab . . . tread on it with your boots!" screamed a creature in a sweater.

"They've been torturing that animal for four hours," said a man in a wolfskin cap who stood at the edge of the pond. "They've got their regulations: any animal you like, but you can't kill it. And they've sought out the gentlest creature of all for it, these swine."

Mitka went on at random, turned around a corner, and came to a building where the dark, motionless forms of beasts were silhouetted behind countless upright iron posts. The warm, pungent smell of the animals steamed up into the dusky evening. The beasts seemed to be sleeping, and in the dark they all looked alike, only one of them went up and down tirelessly, full of yearning for his hot, sunny home, and filled the surrounding air with his hopeless lamentations.

In a cage in the right-hand corner lay a bear. His great head rested on one of his paws, for he had made his peace with the iron bars. Mitka stepped closer, and though someone was walking behind him, he did not turn around. In the dark eye of the beast there was indulgence, and even forgiveness toward men, who from time immemorial have robbed the weakest of their freedom. We can all of us read our own sufferings in a beast's eye.

"You've given up bothering now!" said Mitka under his breath. "And no wonder—the bars are strong. But perhaps you were born in captivity and haven't any use for freedom. You lay like this before I came, and you'll still be lying when I'm gone. It's quiet in the forest now, and everything's covered with snow, but I suppose you've forgotten it all—or do you still hanker after it? Oh, Lord, but you're a stupid lump!" It was hard to say whether he was teasing the brown bear or offering him friendship. But when he thrust his hand into the cage, the beast contented itself with a mere sniff at it; its moist breath was almost like a lick.

"He'll pounce on your hand and then you'll change your mind about the stupid lump!" sounded a voice behind Mitka's back. There on the bench sat a man in shiny boots.

"He won't pounce on me," said Mitka with conviction, suppressing a fit of anger which suddenly surged up in him.

He stepped closer and recognized Atashez, the friend of past years.

"So here you are! You've come to take me, I suppose?"

"No, it's just . . . I wanted to have a talk with you," smiled the other. "I hear your sister's dead. I'm sure it was a great shock to you."

"I'd sooner not talk about it. Well, did Donka tip you off about me?" he asked straight out, but did not attempt to read Atashez's expression.

"I'm interested in you myself, Dmitri—I always have been. Do you think I didn't know how you felt—in the old days? But to us a good man who sticks to us is worth more than gold, you know, Dmitri."

"I don't quite know what you're talking about," said Mitka, "but go ahead all the same."

"Listen, Dmitri: things can't go on like this."

"If you want to preach to me, I'm off."

"But what if I shoot you, in that case?"

"I can shoot, too. But what do you want with me?"

"Why did you go to the doctor?"

"He wasn't a doctor, he was a psychoanalyst," explained Dmitri with strange importance. "I went to him because it was necessary. Were you peeping at me from behind a tree?"

"Yes, and then I went on after you." In Atashez's voice there was a ring of real friendship, but a friendship that had already passed into protest. "I know everything about you. With any man, one has only got to get the key to him and then you know everything."

"That isn't true!" said Mitka with conviction.

"All the same, I guessed you'd come here. You're an odd chap, Dmitri."

"It was just a coincidence . . . or you simply followed me. You can no more guess a man's thoughts than you can manufacture sunbeams."

"As you please," said the other, "but anyway, you must admit that you were going to look for Zavarihin after you'd been to the zoo."

"Well, I won't go now," answered Mitka, slightly bemused. He wanted to get up. "I feel uncomfortable sitting beside you. You're an important person with a telephone on your desk and I'm a thief. I'm ashamed of sitting with you. You know me well enough, though."

"Well, I'm not keeping you, Dmitri." He laid his hand, which was friendly and heavy as iron, on Mitka's knee. "You've had a good run for your money, you know. I was arguing with Firsov about you: he says there's no way out for you."

"Oh, you've smelled out Firsov, too, have you? You've got a good nose, Atashez."

"I can take you at any time . . . and I can also not take you. To put it shortly, does it suit you or doesn't it to leave Moscow within twenty-four hours . . . and take yourself off into some out-of-the-way spot? Well?"

"Atashez, you're a very pleasant fellow! I'm only sorry you've got that mustache."

"It doesn't matter, I can get on even without a mustache. . . . Then listen: I forbid you, as a friend, to loaf around here any longer. At our next meeting, look out! I'll shoot you down, Dmitri. The worst enemies are those who were once friends."

"Well, I won't take myself off into any out-of-the-way spot, Atashez. I won't go away. And as for shooting . . . perhaps you'd like to begin now? I should like a smoke. Are you still a nonsmoker?"

"I knew it," murmured Atashez.

"Knew what? that I want a smoke? Well, you guessed right!"

"No, that you'd refuse to go away. Listen, Dmitri, it's not only yourself you're lowering . . ." He broke off, and Dmitri jumped up.

"Be quiet about that . . . or I'll forget that we ever slept and ate and fought together. I don't allow even Sanka to talk of that, far less you. I know myself what I am . . . and I don't want to be told by other people. . . ." He picked up his hat from the ground. "Well, I've had enough of this hide-and-seek business: who sent you here?"

"I'm sorry, but I've been talking to you simply as a private person, Dmitri." Atashez extended his arms.

Without looking around, Mitka went to the exit. But suddenly he turned back and seized the man he had left by the shoulder. "What are you after? Speak, you devil!" he said softly, and he shook his friend with all his might.

Atashez did not defend himself.

"I think that you're worth more than forty thousand, Dmitri. A great deal has been given to you, and you've flung it all away for nothing. . . . Go away, go away!"

He sat on where he was.

Mitka went outside. From the star-sown heavens fresh veils of snow were being blown. The men on the pond were still eagerly at work in the blue beams of the searchlight. Suddenly a tired, exasperated voice cut through the starry stillness:

"Shimkevich! Stab him!"

WHEN Tanya's burial was over, Zavarihin stayed behind a short time at the cemetery; it did not seem to him right to go away immediately, although he was tormented by hunger. He took a handful of snow to lick, but, remembering the graves, he dropped it with a feeling of disgust.

"Here you . . . Ivan Ivanich, it's time to go away!" he cried out to Pugel, who, with lowered head, stood by a tree. (All pathetic creatures seemed to Zavarihin to be symbolized in Ivan Ivanich.)

"Pardon, I am not Ivan Ivanich," answered Pugel angrily, and withdrew for a moment from the dark mound.

Then Zavarihin walked up to him and took the old man by the shoulder with a rough tenderness.

"All right, old man, let's go. Hella's sleeping soundly. We can't spend the night here. Let's go, or the wolves will eat us."

The old man kept an offended silence.

"I'm not joking, Daddy," said Zavarihin seriously, and pressed his fingers into Pugel's shoulder. But immediately he relaxed his grip again, for he remembered that in Tanya's presence such a liberty would not have been seemly.

"She isn't used to there yet . . . Tanya," said Pugel timidly. "I understand vairy well she is dead now, and the living must eat and drink. When my children fell down, I could not eat anything for two days. Then I ate a slice of bread and butter and it had a vairy good taste."

Finally Zavarihin succeeded in tearing the old man away from the grave; Pugel did not resist, for he was

resolved to come here often. He walked without Zavarihin's help; then suddenly he turned around and, in a
quiet voice, asked his companion to look after him henceforward. Zavarihin took over this burden as a matter of
course, and from that hour his guardianship began; he led
Pugel to Blagusha and handed him over to the care of
his uncle with the promise to pay punctually for the old
man's maintenance. Puchov listened to him silently, and
immediately made a bed for the old man out of boxes.
Next day he brought over Pugel's belongings.

"But I snore at night," Puchov confessed to him guiltily.

"I do . . . a leetle, too," nodded Puchov's new
boarder.

So it was that Pugel entered the master's household;
he lived and ate with him, and met Puchov's rough kindness with the submissiveness of a broken man. The
nephew kept his promise: after a week Puchov received
by a mesenger the sum they had agreed on, but he sent it
back. Everything went on again as before: early in the
morning Pugel went to the market for the bread, at midday he cooked the soup, in the evening he listened eagerly
to the locksmith's strange thoughts as he rummaged
among his scraps of wood. The broken threads grew together again, as well as they could, and perhaps they were
woven more tightly than ever before to their new attachments. Life seethed around them and the seeds of future
events germinated. Strangled in Xenka's embrace, Sanka
the Bicycle sank deeper and deeper, while Donka's thorny
tree of fate blossomed and Zavarihin dug his subterranean
burrows. (Nikolka's heart was dried up by Tanya's death.
To the dead a great power is given, and since then no
woman could boast that she had endured his violent caresses.) Firsov brought out his book about Mitka, while
its hero roamed around somewhere in the secret hiding
places of the city. Meanwhile the two old men sat quietly
in Blagusha, taking life simply, as it came, a life that neither kills nor ages. The words they exchanged in the evening grew fewer and fewer, but old men know everything
about each other.

Puchov had not seen Mitka since the day of the burial,
but from time to time some sinister report about him was

borne upon the wind. They heard that Mitka was just a battered semblance of himself and that the end was not far off. The lamp was spluttering on the evening when the last conversation took place between Puchov and the friend of his heart.

"Mark my words, Fritz," said Puchov, bending over his wood. (The little box he had decided to make at the beginning of our story was finished, except for the lid.) "You'd think some Juggernaut had flung us all down anyhow, and yet we can't get on without each other, any of us. Some of us are sitting and some running, but there's a nice balance all the same. In a thousand years men will be run off their legs, but even though they can't see where they're going, they'll keep cheerful. They'll never notice that they're gagged and bound and helpless." Pugel looked attentively into the flame of the lamp. Suddenly he said a few words in German. "Speak in Russian, old man. I don't understand German," answered Puchov.

"I said, do you know that vairy big men must die, too?" Evidently he was still seeking for a formula to console himself for Tanya's loss.

At the same moment there was a sharp rap on the windowpane, not the first in the course of the last hour. Puchov got up and pushed Pugel softly behind the curtain. "Go, I'll answer it myself. Go and get into bed now," he said in a muffled voice. Then he opened the door.

THE winter darkness struck him in the face, and he felt the cold air around his feet. There was no one in the yard, but Puchov did not go away. He cast a searching glance into the corner of the yard, where there was a pile of logs. A clothesline hung between the lilac bush and the fence.

"Mitka!" he called softly, but no one replied. Then he walked around the corner, where the previous owners had piled up all kinds of refuse. But even in the darkness under the eaves there was no one to be seen.

"What have you to be ashamed of before me?" he said into the darkness, without the slightest sign of anger or surprise. "Come in and have some tea."

"There was something I wanted to do here," answered a hoarse voice after a pause, and Puchov could scarcely recognize in it the old metallic ring. "You needn't think I came here to set the house on fire."

"I don't think it, Mitka," said Puchov behind him. "I don't think at all . . . I just see. . . . Bless you, Mitka!" he said with feeling as Mitka came in and turned to him.

"I was passing by and came in," Mitka lied, lowering his eyes. "Once you said to me that if things went badly with me I might come to you. Well, here I am, old Primus!"

The stains and the dirt on Mitka's clothes told of many adventures, and he fidgeted nervously with his hands as he smoked.

"It's no good expecting you, because you always come when you're not expected," mumbled Puchov, studying

Mitka's face. "Have some tea with me, and warm yourself. Tea will do you good. . . ."

"Yes, you've good tea, old Primus," said Mitka, almost burning his hands on the glass.

"The very best . . . a rouble the pound. Drink, Mitka!"

Mitka drank greedily; his ears and nose were flushed with weariness.

"How are you, Mitka? . . . You look worn-out."

"I'm wretched and disheartened, Primus," said Mitka, passing his hand over his face.

"You're ill, are you? Well, your mind can help you there. If you like, I can cure you. Not long ago I saved a man's life . . . although his ribs were rotten."

"What's your cure, Puchov?" asked Mitka with a short, quick glance.

"The same cure that He used."

Both stiffened and edged away from each other. The Master of Blagusha had revealed his cards at last.

"An eye keeps looking at me—a yellow, lusterless, unblinking eye. Wherever I turn, it's always looking at me. I remember during the war a cloud of gas was coming toward us, and even from the gas an eye seemed to be gazing at me."

"A yellow one?" Puchov marveled as he rolled a bread pellet in his fingers. "A spy, was it?"

"No, my own eye . . . the reflection, do you see?"

"Your eyes aren't yellow, but they're dull, Mitka. You need sleep."

"Perhaps they're dull, too," smiled Mitka, leaning back with his head against the wall. "You're a real gravedigger, Puchov."

The conversation was moving on two different planes. Each of them had no intention of granting what the other demanded. Each of them treated as a joke what was for the other the most important thing of all.

"If God hadn't forbidden it, I'd sooner spit on you than tell you."

"No, tell me," answered Mitka eagerly. "You've got your thoughts and I've got mine. There's no one like you, Puchov—at times I feel I could almost fall down and worship you . . . but I know what you're up to, Primus.

You're trying to trap me with kindness. The whole world's like that—you can never get free, however hard you struggle."

"Free . . . for what, Mitka?" But he got no reply. "You're an unfriendly person yourself, so you can't believe in anyone else's friendship, either."

"It's amazing! I'm bored to death sitting here with you, and yet I can't tear myself away."

Both were thinking of different things, but often, when their hidden thoughts met, they glanced at each other, searching for some confirmation in their glances. The clock ticked, and the cat rubbed itself on the doorpost.

"You ought to open a home for failures," said Mitka; but the other was silent. "Everything in your house is tattered and broken. . . . Now Pugel's here. Will you put me up in a corner, too? Will you give me a crust of bread if I ask for it?"

The real battle was being fought deep in their hearts; on the surface there was only the play of words. "For men are only shadows of what they carry in themselves," thought Puchov.

"You're dying, Mitka," said Master Puchov. "Every day you're sinking deeper into the darkness, and soon you'll be darkness yourself. My dear boy, in a steamer a little crack that size" (he pointed to the blade of the knife which stuck in the round loaf) "would be enough to send the whole boat to the bottom. But I love you, and I love your soul. It's tender as a girl's, and sick from always searching and never finding another like itself. Men always idolize their opposites, and that's why the world's full of souls looking for one another."

"Well, I'm a fine sort of a girl!" Mitka made a gesture of protest.

"Go to Communion, Mitka," said Puchov softly, but to Mitka it was like a stab with a knife.

"And if it should make me sick?"

"It won't make you sick. It's sweet," answered Master Puchov, and in that single word laid bare his whole soul.

Mitka stood up, excited and fired by an inward resolve.

"Thank you, Puchov." His eyes were bitter and red. "Thank you, Primus. You take pity on me. . . . I won't do what you want. . . . I don't want to . . . Let's forget we ever had this conversation. . . ." He bowed down in violent emotion to the old man, and kissed him on his faded, prickly cheeks. "I'll tear myself free, even if it kills me. . . . I'm going, Primus."

"Where? To your ruin?" asked Puchov sadly. "What's once been broken never grows straight again."

"Forward and upward, Primus!" murmured Mitka, and went to the door.

At the door they remained standing.

"I don't know how to pray, but I shall think of you always, Dmitri, though you're going willfully and headlong to your ruin. . . ." Puchov's face looked pale, and his arms hung limply down; a look of helplessness and feebleness came over him, for he had given all that he had.

Mitka disappeared in the darkness across the yard, and soon the creaking of his boots could be no longer heard. The stars clustered together and peered secretly at Puchov in his yard. "A fine fellow," his lips repeated several times aloud. He reflected and said once more: "A fine fellow." It was time to return to Pugel, but he continued to stand outside, and gazed into the starry darkness, and saw already in his mind the rising sun.

BOOK

4

THE day on which Firsov first sauntered around Blagusha had now become a dim, insubstantial memory. The distant goal he had set himself had been attained, but the fire that had blazed up and then died down had left desolation in its wake. He had not yet completely recovered from his first visitation, but he already felt the familiar spasms of a new one, as if in elemental chaos a nucleus were being formed, around which inchoate wisps of creative fire fused and circled. At the beginning of January, Firsov sold his gallant old ulster to an old-clothes dealer, and with the money he had his beard trimmed and his hair cut ridiculously short: all this was part of his pathetic efforts to disguise from himself his literary bondage.

He set his desk like a barricade between himself and the world, and drew a balance of the past. He had touched pitch and been defiled; he had exposed a man nakedly to the world, and then taken to his heels. The book appeared in December, but till January the world preserved an astonished silence. It was not till the early days of February that the storm broke; the world, which had expected some exquisite bouquet, had a cesspool stuck under its nose. In one of the thick quarterlies an article appeared by one of the most eminent contemporary critics on *The Misfortunes of Mitka Smurov*. The distinguished man praised the writer's art as it deserved, but stormed against his ideological pessimism (he was referring to Smurov's death).

On the heels of the great critic the rank and file immediately took the field and delightedly followed the lead he had given them. (They had been offended, and with reason, by Firsov's insulting remark that Russian criticism meant nothing to them but bread and butter—it was his revenge for past injustices.)

With one accord they all demanded from Firsov more red-cheeked reality, but in their haste forgot where the red cheeks end and the rouged ones begin. (They spoke of the political unsoundness of the work, but disregarded its artistic failings, which were many, and did not realize that an artistically honest work can scarcely ever be ideologically false.) In any case, there was an extraordinary diversity in the faults found by the critics. Some censured the book because the mysterious Nikolasha Manyukin never appeared in it. Others lamented that it was not clear in what year the action took place. A third reproached the author with sentimentality in his handling of the Russified German, a stock character! (In fact, they reproached him for drawing Pugel from life.) The fourth asked if the author did not overwork the psychological pedal. The fifth ridiculed him for his imitations of the classical writers, evidently including the rudiments of literary technique under that most heinous of all charges. The sixth observed and emphasized. . . . The seventh perceived and maintained. . . . Then suddenly came a deliberate attack.

A private dealer in manufactured articles, by the name of Garmoshkin, used to devote his spare time passionately to criticism. He was furious with the writer for his unseasonable exposure of Zavarihin and the wiles of shopkeepers; so he collected all the articles on Firsov into a book, which he launched on the market at his own expense. But even the professional men of letters did their bit; one wrote a verse criticism and actually found a periodical to print it. Then suddenly they all became ashamed and were silent. The book roused a storm of excitement, and had a wild success, but when Firsov recalled the consequences of his visit to Blagusha, he shivered with disgust. He had his wellwishers, too, but not many, and their praise took the form of an indulgent pat on the shoulder. What was most important, though, was that there were some clever men among his patrons. One of them, a young

man, devoted a page and a half to an article on the cinematographical tendencies in belles-lettres, which were
what the present day needed. He demanded of the writer
the most compact use of literary material; everything
should be treated in its broadest essentials. ("Every figure ought at least to serve as a frame for a film figure,"
he exclaimed, as loudly as he could, and simultaneously
pointed to the noble simplification of drawing and its
poster genius.") After reading this article, Firsov sat
brooding and picking his teeth for more than half an hour;
in any case, he had compressed his characters so tightly
and so much simplified his treatment that the tragedy
had in places been transformed into comedy. Suddenly
he resolved to write to the author of the article under
cover of the publisher, and ask him to visit him.

On that day there was a spell of thaw. Firsov stood
by the window and looked out at the frost-sprinkled
trees. Behind him the spirit lamp hummed genially, the
lofty symbol and also the loyal friend of the postrevolutionary man. Everything, even the smell of the frying cutlet, corresponded to Firsov's prevailing mood. He had a
single room, containing a shelf with a great many books,
though not so many as to rouse the interest of the inspec-
tor of taxes. There was a writing desk, which was also used
as a dinner table, at the window, and on the wall hung
skin coats, covered with a sheet for the sake of tidiness. A
screen along the wall partitioned off three square meters,
the domain of Firsov's wife. She had just concluded an
entomological chat with the chairman of the house committee. . . .

Firsov supposed that the young man from the magazine would shortly arrive (his name was something like
Sturm or Stern), but out of malice he did not tidy up the
room for the visit; there was a basin full of soapy water
on the stove, for his wife had been washing her hair. But
no one came. He sat down at the table on which notes for
a new book were lying, and suddenly on the staircase the
bell rang the concerted five times. Cursing the smell of
cooking, Firsov hurried to the door. Sarcastic words were
on the top of his tongue. "Ha, ha, ha! it needs to be given
a definite shape, does it? Introduction of comic episodes

about the Chikelyov set? Are you on bad terms with your muse that she never pays you a visit? . . ."

"But you simply haven't understood my article," Sturm would reply to him in consternation, "but just . . ."

He opened the door and fell back in amazement.

"May I come in?" she asked, laughing at Firsov's confusion.

Firsov broke into a sudden sweat and, in the words of a character in his novel, answered quickly: "Yes . . . very much so! Take your coat off, do," he went on, and rushed forward to the newcomer.

"Let me in first, though," she laughed, and the half-forgotten rustling of her clothes and her elusive fragrance cast their usual spell.

Her clothes were soaked through; for a whole week the sky had dripped like a leaky roof. Firsov smiled weakly while Dolomanova took off her coat and cast a glance into the mirror.

"Is it boiling?" she said, pointing to the open door behind which the spirit lamp hissed and bubbled.

"Yes, it's boiling," said Firsov dully, and made an agitated gesture at the dim confusion behind him. "Come in!"

"I hunted you up in the address office," said Dolomanova, pressing past him. She wore a rustling green dress. "Have you forgotten me altogether? And what sort of language was it I heard from you last time? You don't seem to be very pleased. . . . Look, pull this nail out of the wall, or you'll tear your coat again. So this is where you live! That's interesting. This is the house where Firsov lives, 'who knows all the souls in the Union of Soviets!'" She laughed heartily as she quoted this ironical sentence from a review.

"Do sit down!" said Firsov weakly and, with heroic un-

concern, called out to his wife: "Katya, come out and
be introduced! Marya Fyodorovna has come . . . do you
remember? I've told you about her."

"I'm dressing," an irritated voice came from behind
the swaying screen.

"All right . . . later, then," agreed Firsov, and bus-
tled about. "Yes, I live here."

Dolomanova sat on his bed; the chairs were covered
with books and domestic objects.

"Don't be embarrassed, Firsov! People like us often
come to see writers. Give me a sweet or an apple. . . .
I'd like something nice to eat. . . ."

"Hang it all!" Firsov got into a temper. "People must
take me as I am! Here I am and this is my burrow. . . .
Why the devil am I rampaging around like this?"

He turned down the spirit lamp a little, and the silence
that ensued was even more embarrassing.

"And talking of that Sturm fellow, it's all rot that he
says! I breathe the air of my own age, too—very much
so!"

"Who's Sturm?" asked Dolomanova calmly. "There's
a Sturm working with us."

"That's him," said Firsov, spluttering out the words
hastily. "Katya, the cutlet's burned!"

"To hell with the cutlet!" came the gloomy answer
from behind the screen.

Firsov got up in a rage. "Hell and Satan take it!" he began in smothered tones. "Why do you come creeping to
me?"

"You told me yourself that you were in love with me,"
smiled Dolomanova frankly.

"Listen, Marya Fyodorovna, you're a clever woman
. . . so don't let's beat about the bush! You were nothing but a turnip that I hollowed out and filled with my
own imaginings! Now I haven't any particular use for you.
Do you understand?"

"You're very unkind, Firsov!"

"I called you up like a subterranean spirit with incanta-
tions, and now I can't chase you back again." He was act-
ing the buffoon, but was in reality deeply serious. "I can't
bear having you all on top of me. Yesterday that Sanka
was here . . ."

"What did he want from you?" inquired Dolomanova, as if nothing at all had happened.

"He wants me to make his peace with Mitka . . . ha, ha! . . . the great expiation!"

"And Mitka wants to speak to you himself. He said: 'I want to convey my respects to the writer.' What a frightful death you've invented for him!"

"Well, I'll prove to the fool that he's dead," answered Firsov in confusion.

"But for the time being he's still alive."

"That's beside the point: even a dead man can walk. . . . Nowadays quite a number of them go walking about."

"Well, that's your affair. What are you doing now?"

"Oh, breathing."

"And when you've breathed your full?"

"Then I'll write a novel about the emancipated Martians."

"Why are you angry? the same old reason? Well, you have my sympathy. But I still remain faithful to him."

"Well, all I can say is, women have very bad taste." He glanced across at the screen. "And what about Donka?"

"Donka's going to the dogs, but that's his own affair. . . . By the way, I don't like your book. I only read bits of it before. Mitka's in a great state about it, too, he can't make out why you don't describe ordinary people: there are lots about still. He was quite angry about it."

"Angry?" Firsov screwed up his eyes.

"Very."

"Where did you see him?"

"He's lying in my little room at this moment. Come and see him if you like."

"Well, that means he's probably not oversober." Firsov shrugged his shoulders. "Why are you looking at me like that?"

"Well, it's odd, but I don't really know you properly yet. I thought I could read you like a book, and now it's like suddenly finding a page in a foreign language. You've become so terribly savage-looking since you cropped your hair."

"Thank you. Do you know a great many foreign languages?"

"I'm learning the third now. I do a lot of work, Firsov." And then Firsov felt that with the appearance of his book the old ties had not all been severed. Only a single bird had flown up and away and had torn itself free for ever from its dwelling of the day before, without regrets for what it had lost. He felt ill at ease. All thought of his story had vanished from his mind; he only knew that Dolomanova sat opposite and called to him, and he was powerless to resist, though she offered him nothing but fruitless torment. She was a spirit that could not be exorcised, a rebellious character out of his own work. They heard the click of a switch in the twilight, a stream of light poured down from the ceiling, and at the same moment Firsov's wife appeared from behind the screen. Tall, with deep-set, expressionless eyes full of unshed tears, half dressed, her slippers on her bare feet, she seemed the most pitiable and wretched of all authors' wives.

"Fyodor!" she cried, coming between them. "For God's sake tell me why my dress is so tight!"

"You're pregnant, Katya!" said Firsov softly, and got up, ready for the storm to break.

But the storm did not break at once; his wife turned to Dolomanova, as if she had not noticed her till now, smiled disagreeably, and scanned her from head to foot. She critically examined every seam and every crease in Dolomanova's dress. Apparently she felt her splendid clothes as a personal insult, and when Dolomanova stretched out her hand to help her, she suddenly lost control over herself. With his head bowed, Firsov waited till her screaming fit had abated. With an insolent smile on her lips, Dolomanova went to the door, and Firsov got up to show her out.

"So you've brought your wife to this," she said with an expression of disgust as she took her leave. "Well, come and see me."

A moist wind raced through the line of trees along the street, and their branches moved with a whistling sound. A cold draft swirling around him, Firsov looked at his wedding ring, which was so deeply embedded in his finger that it could never be removed again. His look was thoughtful, as if he were gazing a thousand versts away. . . . A sudden fury seized him.

"You're wrong!" he roared, and shook his fist after Dolomanova. "I'm damned if I'll come!"

She turned around to give him a friendly wave, and a breath of wind blew across from her to him.

In her conversation with Firsov she had told the truth
when she said that Mitka was living with her, for after his
sister's death he had idled away a great deal of time in
Dolomanova's little room. Firsov did not believe this
derogatory tale. All the same, Donka's room could be
heated and was quite large enough for two people, provided that they neither of them did anything but lie down
or perhaps play chess. The absence of a proper window
even made the room warmer, for the stove was only an
iron box with holes in it. In this room Mitka spent a considerable part of his checkered life.

Shortly after Dolomanova had gone, Mitka got up and
looked for his boots in the dark. His appearance had
changed startlingly. His boots, which had got soaked
the evening before, could only be pulled on with difficulty.
There was a swirl of confused thoughts in his head, jetsam
from the wreckage of an evening in a thieves' den. He
was going to Nikolka's, and was sauntering along without
hurrying himself, when suddenly a carriage crossed the
road. The horse was frantically struggling for a foothold
on the frozen stones in terror of the lifted whip, and side-
ways in the carriage sat the well-known psychiatrist with
a rain-soaked parcel on his knees. Mitka jumped into the
carriage.

"Drive on!" he shouted to the driver, who turned
around, and then without any ceremony he made room
for himself on the seat.

"You're mad . . ." said the professor when he had

recovered his speech. He edged away from Mitka and held fast to the side of the carriage so as not to fall into the mud.

"A little," admitted Mitka, and made a few apologies. "That evening—when I ran away—my sister broke her neck . . . please forgive me!"

"All the same, I'm extremely astonished. . . . We're not still in the year 1919," grumbled the psychiatrist, but his astonishment was already passing into blank alarm. "You ought at least to introduce yourself, damn you!"

"Why should I? If a man wants to speak to another man, to speak seriously, he's got a right to. One can't insult an intelligent man. . . . Drive on!" he shouted again to the driver. "I shan't stay long, for I'm going in the opposite direction. Only one question—is it wrong to kill a man . . . an unarmed man?" He had now completely lost his self-control.

"An odd question to ask at a first meeting! Of course it is . . . need one even discuss it?"

Mitka did not take his gaze for an instant from the sly, sleepy, clever eyes of the other. "Why the devil do you bother me?" said the psychiatrist, and suddenly pushed Mitka away from him.

"I'm curious to hear your answer," said Mitka politely.

"Well, there are various circumstances which might be important: the object, the where, the how . . . but no, damn it all, that's not what I mean. I'm a man. You're a man, too. So I am you. In so far as I kill you, I kill myself. So it may happen that this man, your . . . patient, let's say, is still alive, but you yourself are already done for. It's the intention that matters. Excuse me, I've just come from the lunatic asylum, and I'm a little tired. Visit me in the evening, and then we can discuss it . . ."

"Good, and what will you tell me then?" Mitka still waited tensely, and the psychiatrist's eyes bored painfully into his mind. The carriage plunged into ruts and puddles.

"I'll tell you you shouldn't jump into someone's carriage and ride with him without being asked," said the psychiatrist sulkily, and went on: "Don't worry yourself. The criminal is a man rejected by society. The nature of the punishment determines the importance of the crime. It's a relative conception because it depends on standards of culture, and they vary."

"I wasn't asking you from that point of view," answered Mitka falteringly.

"Why were you asking, then? Was it out of scientific interest? But science can only put a new . . . well, law, if you like . . . in its place among the existing ones." The psychiatrist's eyes smiled through thin cracks and seemed to say: "You're mistaken, you won't find me out!"

"Why do you wear that cap?" asked Mitka.

"For the convenience of the public—another relative conception."

"There's only one thing I can't grasp. Agey killed, and I have killed. The difference between us is clear, and yet we've done one and the same thing. Do you understand what I mean? I'll explain it to you. I had a horse, Sulim, at the front, and it was killed. . . ." While Mitka told his story, he put his cap on the back of his head, and now the old Mitka sat before the psychiatrist, the daredevil boy, the darling of the division.

He edged closer, almost sitting on the analyst's coat, and whispered into his companion's ear the secret that obsessed him. He remembered all the tiny details, which had long ago been covered with the mud of time, and uttered not a single false word. The driver had let the reins hang right down into the puddles, and was singing at the top of his voice, for he despaired of overhearing the conversation.

"Tell me, do you suffer from sleeplessness?"

"Sometimes. . . ."

"And one more question: did this horse not belong previously to the same man you? . . ."

The professor had made a good shot. Mitka had killed the officer just because he had taken everything from another man, even his horse, but had not been able to rob him of his greatest treasure.

At that moment the right wheel sank into a puddle and splashed Dolomanova, who was passing. The professor growled, for Mitka had lurched over on top of him, but neither of them noticed her. The carriage went on smoothly again, but Dolomanova caught another exclamation from Mitka, which he accompanied with a violent gesture. She looked after them in astonishment, and continued to gaze, till they disappeared, at the two heads swaying over the edge of the carriage. A tram car blocked her view, and when it had passed, the carriage was out of sight. All this was very strange; Mitka was to have been that evening at Zinka's, where a sort of memorial party for Tanya was to be held, for it was Tanya's birthday.

Dolomanova turned down a side street and met Sturm, who was on his way to his duel with Firsov. He looked smart, and almost indecently glossy. When he raised his hat and revealed his part, it was evident that he bestowed as much attention on it as on the problem of the cinematographical recasting of literature.

THE guests were late. Pyotr Gorbidonich walked up and down the room, while Zinka powdered her nose in front of the mirror. It was cold in the room, for Pyotr Gorbidonich had had the double windows taken out earlier than anyone else in the town. "Semashko, the Minister of Health, says: 'Don't be frightened of oxygen!'" He raised his forefinger with ineffable dignity. Since he had married and obtained an important post again, his face had always been redolent of the most pensive melancholy, subtle as a spray of eau-de-Cologne, although this was in conflict with the official striving for robust efficiency. Chikelyov was developing liberal tendencies. All the same, his melancholy was so discreet that it in no way impugned the soundness of his convictions and motives.

"A woman who powders her nose," he explained, walking up and down, "may be compared to a neglectful house committee that concerns itself with the outward appearance of the building in its charge, but pays no attention to its inside. Yet it is the inside that is the most important, for without an inside a man cannot live, please note." Then with a fork he casually fished out a preserved cherry from the jar. "How much do they cost?" he asked, and scanned the well-spread table severely.

"Fifty kopeks, Pyotr Gorbidonich."

"Rather sour," remarked Chikelyov imperturbably, and began to walk up and down the room. "Now tell me, why have I been expatiating about all this? It's typical, don't you think?"

"I don't know, Petya," admitted Zinka good-humoredly,

and powdered the rings under her eyes. "You ought to have had the double window put back: you'll get a chill again."

"You don't know? although you've been living with me nearly six months already!" Chikelyov reproached her, and he started on a jar of mushrooms. "It's typical of you: you're not interested in your husband, and I suppose you weren't interested in your former husband, either. Spiritual needs have no value for you. I note, you're not even jealous of me? Pobyedonostsev, in the time of the old régime, used to compare a woman to Fortune, which only cleaves to fools and avoids the wise. Dmitri was a thief, but you had a weak side for him . . ."

"I was sorry for him," answered Zinka in a faint voice.

"I say that he was a thief!" Chikelyov spat out. "If I was a member of the government I'd have people like that boiled down for soap . . . They . . . they just stand in the way of the creation of a new life."

"You're like a yard dog, Pyotr Gorbidonich. . . . You bark at everything," shouted Zinka in a fury, spilling powder on the little dish under her looking glass; but she yawned again immediately.

"I don't pay any attention to what you say or hold you responsible for it, for at the moment you're a pregnant woman," replied Chikelyov weightily. He tapped his finger on the sausage and sniffed at it to ascertain its quality. "I will now return to the train of argument in which you interrupted me. Why did I speak of these things? Because I'm an accurate man. At committee meetings I approve and support various proposals, I never misuse my right of voting, I honor labor, pay all my membership fees without protest, I don't make any claims on my subordinates beyond what is legitimate, and keep my thoughts within definite limits. There, for example, is a cupboard for which I have paid cash . . . if suddenly tomorrow a decree should be issued: 'All cupboards must be given over to the State,' I would carry it there myself and deliver it to the clerk in charge. And even if they were to make a thousand regulations, I myself would think out the thousand and first, and carry it out with ruthless exactitude."

"Yes, but the cupboard isn't worth a scrap . . . you wanted to split it up yourself for firewood," Zinka answered, getting up noisily. In the front room the bell, which had been muffled with a rag, was ringing.

It was as if all the guests had conspired to meet in front of the door. They all thronged in at once. Puchov came with Pugel, the Bundyukovs crept in, and from Mitka's old room appeared Zinka's brother, Matvey (he sat for only ten minutes and then went off to a meeting). A dark, clean-shaven man, one of Chikelyov's superiors, also appeared, and half a minute later came a bowed old man with a beard, a subordinate of Chikelyov's, who instantly met with a reproof for being late; in the front room the bass voice of The Wax-works King was already booming. . . . The party became lively; first of all they had stood around awkwardly and silently, rubbing their hands and looking at the table.

In a gay voice, with an insinuating purr in it, Chikelyov invited the guests to the table and signaled to Zinka that she might start to hand things around. Meanwhile, each guest had drunk up a little glass of "decreed" schnapps, as the high official wittily expressed it.

"Amazin' weather!" said this individual, selecting a specially tender mushroom (Chikelyov was handing him the bowl).

"Yes, the weather's amazing," sighed Pyotr Gorbidonich.

"Yes, rather . . ." the subordinate put in.

"What are talking about?" snarled Chikelyov, treading deftly on the subordinate's toe. "Perhaps it was meant in a completely different sense, and then you push forward with your opinion!"

He was almost sick with worry and anticipation, for he was expecting Dmitri Vekshin, whose appearance promised no good for the success of the evening. Chikelyov had invited the important official to the memorial banquet purely on economic grounds, but now he was suffering indescribable torture. To put his superior officer and Mitka at one table seemed to him a blasphemy, which almost deserved the supreme penalty. Sometimes he saw himself sitting behind a barred window, tortured with remorse and awaiting his end.

"Mahlakov is to be dismissed," announced the superior person ominously.

"I always suspected he wasn't sound. He has a step-father who's . . . a deacon," whispered the master of the house as he poured him a third glass. "An extraordinarily dangerous man. He recited me some verses the other day about the local committee. . . . I was on pins and needles, and he read them out at the top of his voice—yes, with poetic emphasis. 'You mad creature, think of your children,' said I to him, and he answered me: 'I haven't any children.' Such impertinence! . . ."

"Why were you so angry with him?" asked Puchov, poking absent-mindedly at his pilchard.

"Ah . . . er . . . I beg your pardon, Comrade?" said the superior person; and Puchov did not ask again.

Meanwhile, the high official got going on the port wine, and the old man started on an anecdote that was so spicy that The Wax-works King began to bounce on his chair as if someone were tickling him. Pyotr Gorbidonich slipped out during it into the front room. His instinct had not deceived him, for in the half-light Mitka was just taking off his overcoat.

"Good day, Chikelyov," he said nonchalantly. "You've filled out—you've grown fat."

"That's just the light," Chikelyov answered with an acid smile. He was glad all the same that Mitka had not started off straightaway to make a scene. "I'm very delighted, greatly pleased . . . and I feel for you . . . Hella Velton's brother"—he introduced him with a low bow.

". . . and also Dmitri Vekshin, thief," Mitka dryly ended the sentence and walked straight up to the table.

"Ah . . . he's a great joker!" Chikelyov hurried to explain. "Often we laugh ourselves to death, but he keeps as calm as calm can be, as if nothing had happened . . . not a smile!"

"What actually is the reason for the celebration today?" asked the official, tasting the salmon. "It's a real Belshazzar's feast! We'll have to reassess you, Pyotr Gorbidonich!"

"It's a memorial party . . . for a friend of my wife, who died recently." Chikelyov bowed his head. "She was a beautiful woman and died quite young. . . ."

"She would have been thirty today," put in Mitka, letting his glance fall on one of the bottles.

"I mean in spiritual age, citizen," growled the offended voice of the master of the house.

While the guests were chatting, and the old man was again telling such a fruity story that Pyotr Gorbidonich cast a terrified glance at Klavdya, who was eating an apple in the corner, Zinka regaled the guests with a turkey that would have been irresistible to the weakest and fullest of stomachs. It was prepared with Madeira sauce according to a recipe of Madame Bundyukova, and melted crisply and succulently in the mouth.

"Dear Comrades!" said Chikelyov, scarlet in the face and scanning his guests searchingly for unfriendly glances. (Mitka was at the moment talking with Pugel. "Did she remember me before her death?" he asked sadly. "Ah!" answered the old man delightedly. "She praised your side whiskers vairy, vairy moch. She said that your side whiskers are very thick. . . . I spick vary bad Russian!" he excused himself finally with a wry gesture.) Pyotr Gorbidonich glanced across at them disapprovingly. In private he had been preparing an address to a celebrity whom even in his thoughts he would not have dared to invite here. In the office, rumors were circulating that on account of his dignified exterior Chikelyov had been selected to present the address to him. Ever since then Pyotr Gorbidonich had brooded perpetually. He used to jump out of bed in the night to jot down a sudden idea, and learned all sorts of flowers of speech by heart out of the newspaper. He even marked those places in his speech where he would drink out of his glass, in the event of there being a glass there . . . and in society it was his constant craving to make a speech on every possible occasion. He had already started to speak, but interrupted himself again and listened.

"How are you, Zinka?" asked Mitka, and she almost reeled at the tenderness in his eyes. "Are you having a bad time?"

"It's hard, Mitka . . . life is!" she answered.

"But take a pancake in honor of your little sister." Chikelyov slid over to them.

"I've already had one, thank you," Mitka answered.

"Take another one, there's plenty here. We can feed all the lovers full on pancakes and there'd be enough left over for us, too!" Chikelyov blurted this out in an angry whisper, and hurried into the middle of the room. "Citizens, it is already three months since that sad event occurred which we all so deeply deplore, but the recollection of it is still as fresh as the fresh-turned soil. A gifted woman, whom we had all loved for many years, perished —perished in the toils of her labor—the noose I might say—to the accompaniment of the melancholy hand-clapping of the public. Yes, but work demands its heroes, for life is hard, as Comrade Vetchinin aptly says. . . ."

"Oh, you exaggerate," answered the high official, flattered and confused.

"Great words! . . . And it is typical that all thinkers are agreed on this point. And even if hundreds or thousands should perish . . . we will march past her ashes in devoted rows with standards reverently dipped. I see her still" (Chikelyov illustrated his words by gestures), "amid the muted tones of the orchestra she hangs, a smile on her lips, full of strength and hope in her destiny. It is no secret that the deceased lady was to have married. . . . We are petrified with horror: a young maiden in the noose! The purple flames of her attire still gleam before our eyes."

Melting with emotion, he could already hear in his fancy the complacent sighs of the two Bundyukovs and Zinka's suppressed sobs; then suddenly he felt someone firmly gripping the hand he had stretched out in his inspiration, and pulling it down. As he turned his eyes to his assailant he lost his composure, for the very instant before he had seen Pugel calmly sucking a turkey bone.

"No," whispered Pugel beseechingly, and clung to Chikelyov, "she nevair wore purple—always blue."

"Are you positive it was blue?" Pyotr Gorbidonich assumed a contemptuous expression, for somehow or other he had to escape from the disagreeable situation. "And supposing I only meant that in a metaphorical sense . . . well?"

Already the subordinate could be heard tittering, and Chikelyov nodded to him gratefully; but as he did so he saw that the old man's admiration, The Wax-works

King's laughter, and the sudden animation on the face of the high official were not directed at him at all. Pyotr Gorbidonich suspected a conspiracy against his person, and turned slowly to the door, but immediately started back in astonishment. On the threshold stood Sergey Ammonich Manyukin as large as life and bowing facetiously. He shook convulsively as he spoke.

"Three cheers for the noble comp–comp–company!" he stammered with obsequious jauntiness. "I've just run in for an odd half-hour, if you'll p–p–permit me. P–p–pancakes!" he said quietly, as with ill-concealed greed he sniffed up their fragrance.

Pyotr Gorbidonich fell back in dismay against the table.

"How disgusting!" he said finally, and sank limply into his chair.

Zɪɴᴋᴀ screamed and covered her face with her hand as if
Manyukin were a ghost; Bundyukov coughed and took a
small pie, which he had just been going to eat, out of his
mouth, and The Wax-works King scowled disapprovingly. No one availed himself of the melancholy opportunity of laughing at Manyukin's appearance. Sergey
Ammonich had on a vest, and over it a blouse such as
women of the petit-bourgeoisie wear when they go to
market, and, perched on the top of his head, was a
child's little hood, tied on with a piece of yellow string.
He had guessed in advance the consternation that his sudden appearance would cause, so he started deliberately to
behave like a buffoon, and, his body trembling with disease, he shook his sorry jokes over the company like peas
out of a bag.

Before Chikelyov had recovered his composure, Zinka
pointed out an empty seat to Manyukin, smiling self-consciously. (The place had been kept for Nikolka, but he
was evidently going to be late.)

Before he sat down in the seat assigned to him, Manyukin gazed fixedly at Mitka and suddenly went up to him,
undoing his hood.

"Well!" he spat out, and Mitka in this single sound
detected a sorrow that was as venomous as a sting.
"There will always b–be c–c–creat–ures on the earth, who
are d–d–doomed to perdition . . . and so you'll alw–
ways have work," he concluded this sentence, which he
had obviously prepared long before his meeting with
Mitka.

"May I pour you something, Sergey Ammonich?" Zinka interrupted him with a side glance at the high official. That celebrity was negligently chewing a pancake with one side of his mouth, while Chikelyov leaned over and whispered into his ear a glowing account of Manyukin's prowess as a liar.

"I w–w–won't drink!" Manyukin declined, and dropped down into a seat. "One only d–d–drinks when one has s–s–some–thing to drink away."

"A golden thought!" laughed the subordinate, who was already slightly intoxicated and not entirely capable of keeping his thoughts properly in control. "If I'd a hundred roubles, I'd like to give you the whole hundred for thoughts like that, but I haven't even ten. . . ."

"The t–t–tip of your nose is rather red!" Manyukin shook his finger at him. "In any case give me a d–d–drink in the interests of h–h–health, and for the fur –fur–furtherance of high ideals!" he called out pathetically into the void. As he drank on an empty stomach, the schnapps quickly went to his head, and he suddenly confessed that he was living in a cemetery in some family vault or other, together with a cripple who, like him, had lost his hold on life. His ruthless candor sounded like malevolent invention. "I'll get myself a st–t–tarling in the summer. I'll tell him all my s–s–sufferings, and I'll learn how to make f–f–fireworks, and no one shall t–t–touch me. . . . A man can decay even without h–h–help from strangers, gentlemen!" And now, without anyone stopping him, he went on to protest that he was not utterly done for yet, that he had not yet been robbed of laughter. As he said this he glanced across at Mitka, who was fixing the tittering official with a gloomy stare. "M–m–many nights I've listened there: even the c–c–corpses laugh! In b–b–bass and tenor and soprano. . . . They laugh, till you'd think they'd never s–s–stop. . . . The earth q–q–quivers with it. Ha, ha! and you thought it c–came from the tram-lines. G–g–go in and tell them to s–s–stop."

"Don't make a scene!" said Pyotr Gorbidonich abruptly. "You came without an invitation: go and eat a pancake and hold your tongue! But, of course"—he winked at Zinka, and she poured out some schnapps for Manyukin—"if you would tell us a story now! Something in honor of Hella Yegorovna Velton. Yes, we should be obliged if you would," he said, and glanced around questioningly at the high official.

"It certainly takes all sorts to make a world!" piped The Wax-works King in a very high, thin voice, and all were surprised, for up to this time he had always spoken in a deep bass.

Manyukin was not long in acceding to their requests, for he knew that it was the only way in which he could pay for his food and drink at the memorial party. The lights were lit, and Bundyukov brought in a samovar, for the bad weather outside encouraged the guests to stay on. Chikelyov asked permission to open the window for a moment, for the smoke was so thick in the room that it no longer curled up of its own accord from the cigarettes, but had to be blown away at each puff, and there was a suffocating odor of pancake, too. A thin, moist draft rustled the paper flowers on the chest of drawers.

"Listen, everyone!" shouted Chikelyov, clapping his hands. "The International World Actor Manyukin will tell us of his fight with the merchant Pantelyev." He made a bow and pointed to the artist, who coughed gloomily and cavernously, as if he wished to press out his last breath. Strangely enough, he still held the general attention, although he had sunk so far. He ate a lot and bragged of his poverty, so as to hide from the curiosity of strangers the last frayed threads on which what was left of his human dignity depended.

After a short pause the story began:

"In Petersb–b–burg I once got to know this great man in the Christm–m–mas holidays. . . . The merchant Pantelyev, who, to the amazement of the whole w–w–world, invented a process for extracting colors from hens' m–m–manure. . . ." (A pathetic glow of triumph lit up Manyukin's face. "Don't look at me like that, ch–ch–childie," he said to The Wax-works King, who was staring straight into his mouth, "or I'll eat you up!") "He was a famous inventor: in Vyatka he grew oranges in the k–k–kitchen and boiled southern wine in a b–b–barrel."

"I never heard about this," remarked the official, with a long face, and selected the largest apple from the dish. "But go on, please."

"Well, you see, once we fought about which of us would as–s–stonish the world most. Pantelyev said: 'If you beat me, you c–c–can have all my factories, my properties, and all the money I have in s–s–state lottery tickets.' But I said nothing to this. . . ."

"Just notice the sort of things the bourgeois occupied themselves with in those days," said Bundyukov reproachfully.

"In the morning I got up. . . . I disguised myself as the c–c–cathedral of St. Basil and went to Pantelyev's hou–ouse as if nothing had h–h–happened. . . . It was very cleverly done. People even wanted to come into me and have M–M–Mass. I took up my posi–ition at the corner . . . just under Pantelyev's wi–indows and sang the Acathist, ah. . . ."

The storyteller laboriously thought out every sentence of his tale; it was only his craving to stay a little longer in this warm, well-fed circle that induced him to accept the humiliating role of buffoon. Puchov and Pugel had vanished unobserved at the beginning of Manyukin's story. Zinka yawned and poured out tea, while the subordinate nodded drowsily, ready any moment to step into action. Mitka walked to the window, the same one at which Firsov had once stood.

At the corner a gas lamp was burning, and its light made pockmarks in the puddles. The street lay silent and deserted, but over the roofs there hung a glow of light which was as strong as the light of some great fire. In his unconscious yearning to escape from this smoky hole and all its defilement, Mitka leaned out of the window. His head was soaked by the moist wind that masqueraded as rain. Mitka remembered a march at the front, when on both sides of the road dead man lay, naked and gleaming purple in the frosty glare of the December sun. The Republic had not the means to clothe her soldiers, and the living had taken from the dead everything they no longer needed. What a mighty sun had stood over Mitka in those days!

"The scum!" he screamed at them all in his thoughts

as they sat around Manyukin, watching him smolder away like a reeking oil lamp. "Does life need such people? They're only snails that creep along the mildewed road: they're happiest when the sun is hidden behind a cloud. . . ." Suddenly it seemed to him that under the eaves at the outer door a suspicious elbow was protruding. A mad, gloating joy overpowered him; he could scarcely believe that someone had hidden himself there and was spying on him. He heard neither Manyukin's chatter nor the laughter of The Wax-works King; he took a glass from the windowsill and flung it soundlessly against the protruding elbow. He missed his aim, but immediately a face peered out from under the roof—and not without astonishment Mitka recognized Sanka.

"Hi!" he called down. "What are you up to there?"

"I'm waiting for the rain to stop, master!" he called back after a moment's thought, plausibly enough.

"Stay where you are! I'll be down in a moment!" Mitka went to the door. Behind him people exchanged significant and anxious glances. On the threshold he turned around with the intention of expressing in one word the whole measure of his contempt for those who remained behind. His glance fell on Manyukin and a wild scheme shot through his head: should he take Manyukin with him? Manyukin scratched his neck shyly, as if he had guessed Mitka's thoughts and was ready to rise up immediately, although two full glasses of schnapps still stood in front of him.

"My dear Prince . . . Hamlet," he began jestingly and made to get up, but Mitka had already overcome his momentary weakness.

Manyukin was no use now either as shield bearer or as dog.

No ONE answered him when he called out, and Sanka was not around the corner, so Mitka walked away cursing into the thick spring mist. Sanka's disappearance perplexed him, but in a moment his perplexity vanished. He remembered when he called down from the window he had not thought it necessary to wait for Sanka's answer. But what if he had acted on his silly impulse and brought Manyukin along with him? Manyukin would have resisted at first, for a stranger's charity is always humiliating to one in his circumstances. Of course, the whole congregation upstairs sipping wine in honor of the departed would then have united to persuade Manyukin, and they would all have been very generous, because it's nice to be generous on a full stomach. Zinka would have packed him pies in a little bag and Chikelyov would have had to wait, just because Sanka's skin was supposed to be waterproof.

Mitka's heart filled with a fresh tenderness for the friend who from love had become his servant. The remembrance of the forty honorably earned roubles, which had never been repaid, touched his sense of shame. He had no money to pay his debt . . . but friendship must be prepared even for unpaid sacrifice. Friendship? A treacherous word: a wolf, too, may make friends with a lamb. . . . Mitka walked on the roadway, plunging straight through all the puddles; the ice-coated pavements were slippery and shone like glass in the light of the lamps. A damp, cool wind blew across from the houses; he was teased by a strange new bustle of life all around him, by the little newborn streams, by the gentle wind that tenderly wooed the swelling buds of the trees. It must be spring.

"And why does Donka hate Sanka?" He wanted to know that. "Honest men are always hated by cads. Dirt can spread itself over as wide a surface as soap. A single drop can pollute a whole pond. And men like tearing up flowers they don't want. Who said that? Yes, Puchov. Puchov, you're a hermit crab! You don't need anything, for you have everything already. Only he who is thirsty wants to live. He who has everything perishes: he has no need to strive upward and onward. Is it true that I kissed you, as if you were dead, Puchov, when I came into your secret shell to warm myself? You lie on your bed, and you'll lie there immovably for another hundred years. You're like a bark beetle, you've been gnawing out your own entrails for ages and haven't felt it. It's treachery for anyone to lie inactive now . . . treachery . . . what? . . . Where did I get that word from? Ah, Donka!"

With the same indescribable chaos in his thoughts, Mitka turned down the dark boulevard. There he met a woman running toward him. She had screamed till she could scream no longer, and his ear only caught the feverish rasp of her breathing and the rustle of her stumbling feet. She did not notice Mitka, who stood hidden behind a tree, but immediately after her there emerged out of the darkness a second figure running, too. Mitka stood in his way. The man let fly a torrent of oaths as he ran into him. Round about all was deserted; only in the distance loud voices could be heard, which came back in dreadful echoes from the empty street.

"Why are you running after her? Answer me, quick!" asked Mitka in a fresh, clear voice, and remembered the night in the meadow by the birch wood, the night when he had first broken with the past. The other made no reply; his cap was stuck jauntily on his bandaged head and from under the brim a dull rogue's face leered. It was utterly expressionless, and the long thin beam of the distant lamp was broken up on it as on a puddle. Suddenly he plunged his right hand into his pocket and put the fingers of his left into his mouth. A terrifying whistle rent the stillness . . . at the same moment Kitka gave the rogue a smashing blow. Black blood throbbed in his temples when he caught sight of a knife in the fellow's hand.

The phantom of treachery haunted Mitka's mind, and the stillness of the night-shrouded boulevard increased his excitement of fever pitch. He bent over the prostrate figure and struck him in the face, and the bandages, which had been torn from his head and filthied and trodden on, no longer gleamed white in the puddles of melted snow.

"You!" hissed Mitka between his clenched teeth. "What were you doing when the best men died for you? "What have you done for yourself? You traitor, falling on people from behind." The words stuck in Mitka's throat, around him everything was red. The world is always the color the eye gives it.

"Leave me alone," groaned the prostrate figure feebly, and Mitka had no strength to strike him a second time.

The man continued to lie there as if he did not dare get up under Mitka's eyes. Mitka slowly bent down over him, looked into his face, and suddenly ran away from him. The moist stillness behind him re-echoed again with cursing. He ran on, and as he ran, his own shadow that darted before him uncannily across the mud inspired him with terror. Then he noticed that someone was looking at him from around a corner. He rushed there, but there was no longer anyone to be seen. Driven by dark distrust, Mitka ran into the entrance of the house next door and collided with a man in the doorway.

"Who . . . who's that?" he whispered excitedly, clutching in the darkness at the man's trembling hand.

"It's raining . . . I'm waiting for the shower to stop, master," came out of the stillness the soft voice of Sanka, and he released his hand from Mitka's. "Have you made a big haul, master? . . . on the boulevard?" he added, in explanation, as he saw that Mitka did not understand his question.

"What d'you mean? Damn you, no! You're on the wrong track . . . a skunk was chasing a woman out there. Hell, even my knees are wet! . . ." He had a feeling that Sanka was laughing at his impulsive action. "Were you following me?"

"No . . . but I thought you looked out of sorts, master, so I didn't dare come up to you. I walked behind you, and I was frightened that you'd curse me. Then I thought to myself: 'Perhaps he'll come back this way, and then I'll meet him, accidental like.' "

"Why should I curse you?" Mitka drew his breath with an effort.

"Why! . . . You're strong and I'm weak. The one who loves is always weaker than the one he loves. Love is weakness. A big man always finds some excuse for tormenting a small one. There are always little excuses, master, running about everywhere like little mice! . . . So you've started on that, master!" Evidently he did not believe Mitka's story of his meeting with the hooligan. "It must seem strange to you, for you're not used to it. . . ."

"What are you talking about?" asked Mitka.

"The business on the boulevard."

"You're a fool, Alexander. There are things you can't understand. . . . It was treachery, Alexander, and he had to pay for it. Donka must pay, too . . . he's reckoned too soon on my death. And this writer, too. . . . The most important thing now, Alexander, is to live, to live at any price!" Suddenly he changed the subject and asked how it was that at this late hour Sanka had happened to arrive under the very window from which he had been leaning. He did not notice Sanka's embarrassment, for in a second Sanka had regained his composure and started to explain.

"I WAS in the hospital, master," Sanka informed him gravely. "She asked me to bring her some apples."

"Your wife?" asked Mitka, and he waited, sick with doubt and misgiving, for Sanka's answer.

"Yes, Xenka," Sanka replied reluctantly, and whistled something that sounded like a tune.

"Don't whistle—I can't stand it," said Mitka.

"Are you afraid the whistle is a signal?"

"Don't talk nonsense! Lately you've kept away from me, but I'm fond of you still as I always was. I remembered today how you tied my hands together with the belt . . . you think I didn't understand then, but I understood everything, and was laughing at you. Have you still got your belt?"

"I've lost it," said Sanka sulkily.

They walked on side by side, and their hasty steps betrayed their agitation.

"I was at the doctor's today," confessed Mitka. "He jawed a lot of advice at me."

"That's good," returned Sanka.

"Listen: I had only two—my sister and you. My sister's dead: now I've only you left."

"Xenka's dying, too."

"Do you think so?"

"I know it. My mother used to ask me for apples like that. I brought them to her and she got up, she was so eager for them. Eager for them, do you understand? It's unlucky to touch people like that, they don't belong to us any more."

"Who do they belong to, then?"

"God or the Devil, whichever has a taste for them." Sanka's voice quivered. "The way she let fly at you that time in the bar! One would have thought it was a beast jumping at you. And you sat there so standoffish, master, and didn't turn a hair. . . . (You're a standoffish fellow, master!) Well, I went with the apples to her. . . . She kissed me and cried and pointed at the wall. . . . 'There are always mice squeaking there,' she said. Well, I knocked on the wall and said: 'Don't squeak, little mouse!' "

"She's frightened of mice, is she? Do you remember how Atashez let fly at the mice with a sword once? and he was a brave chap. . . . That happens with a great many people." Mitka had evidently no intention of understanding his friend's distress.

"She asked me to give you back the money you gave her. 'On my deathbed I bid you do it,' she said."

"Oh, it's not worth talking about! I still owe you forty roubles myself."

"Fifty, master! . . . Don't you remember I brought you ten roubles more afterward?"

"Yes, of course! I'd quite forgotten it. I lost your ten-rouble note somewhere."

Sanka started to whistle again, and his walk had begun to drag a little.

"Xenka earned those ten roubles herself . . . she did open work and insertion the whole time. Nowadays they're the fashion, though I don't see anything beautiful in them . . . so have a look, have a look, master, for the ten-rouble note. It's very odd that a ten-rouble note like that should go astray."

Sanka took the offensive, for even at this eleventh hour, when he made his appeal to Mitka's feeling of shame, Mitka had not listened to him. Many other voices were crying at the same time as Sanka's in Mitka's ear, and distracting his attention. Suddenly Sanka flew into a fury.

"I should like you to understand me once and for all, master. The moment has come when we must hide nothing from each other. I've done a great deal for you: I've lain down like a doormat under your feet, and you've trodden on me! Let me have one last talk with you, master, a real talk, a talk to unburden our souls!"

"Later, some time later. . . . I don't like scenes. . . . Alexander, are we both soldiers or aren't we? At the front I struck a man because he cried. . . ."

"I remember, master. Very well, then, I won't. Everything in the world's like that: one would like to, but one can't. The moon runs around the earth (they said so, at any rate, when I went to lectures with Xenka . . . though I can't believe it): it runs around the earth always looking for something. But if it found it, then it would be destroyed. . . . Why is that so, master? Look, the snow's like that, too: it goes on falling and thawing . . . and every time it lies as if it were going to lie forever. I saw a little tree out of my prison window, a dirty, scabby little poplar—one couldn't even have made boot lasts of it . . . but once I guessed what that little tree wanted (it's because we're friends, master, that I'm telling you all this nonsense). Well, you see, it was waving its little wings, flapping them, struggling! but where could it fly to? It couldn't send up any roots into the sky. . . . It couldn't suck food out of space, and yet it felt drawn there. . . . You wouldn't think a common plant could suffer like that!"

"Nonsense!" Mitka interrupted him in a hard, positive voice. "The deeper the roots of a tree drive into the earth, the better it is for it. And it clacks its leaves because its gorged and contented, just as a man clacks his tongue when he's full. Trees and grass and the moon . . . are all gorged and contented. There isn't a sign of suffering anywhere, except in man—and he's built that way." They went on in silence for a full minute. The spring, the real spring, rustled and shed its warm fragrance from every side.

"Do you know what Donka is saying about you?"

"What?" Sanka turned around sharply.

"He says you're a traitor."

"That's a damned shame, master!"

"What's a shame?" Mitka stood still, for Sanka had bent down to tie up his shoelace.

"It's a shame that he's so wicked and spiteful. . . . I threw him out that time, and he shouted out to me: 'You'll pay for this!' It's a shame that a bad man should tell a lie and you repeat it."

"Don't you be afraid! I know you and believe you."

"Do you trust me, master?"

"Your heart's in the right place, Sanka. In any case, what's all this nonsense they talk about the silver spoon? It sounds pretty unlikely. What was it all about?"

"Ah . . . you mean when I ran away? Xenka brought the spoon to the prison, and I made myself a key out of it and got away." He had repeated this fairytale so many times that he already knew it by heart and almost believed it.

"Ah! . . ." drawled Mitka. "You'll go before the thieves' court, Alexander . . . and then we'll get Donka to appear. We'll see then if he can clear himself."

They had arrived outside the house in which Mitka was temporarily living. It was an empty, friendless night, full of puddles and flitting night shadows and frosty sighings of spring. And it was weirdly strange that the same spring should bear in its virgin womb the boundless distance of the blue sky, the sweet, fragrant breath of the birch trees, and the shrill screams of the fighting woodcocks. The face it turned to the city was a different one, and it kept its gifts for others. Mitka looked into the yard. Dolomanova's windows gleamed brightly through the darkness. Sanka waited patiently.

"It's cold, master," he said; he bared his teeth and stamped his feet on the naked asphalt.

"Wait, Alexander. . . . I'll come back immediately," whispered Mitka to him, and hurried to the door.

In such nights a foul stench steams from the cesspools, water splutters from the eaves, and the yard dog barks at the spirits of the homeless dead. Lumps of rain-sodden snow clung to Mitka's feet as he made himself a path to Dolomanova's window. He stroked the dog, who came running out to meet him; dogs were fond of Mitka. He had not even to stand on tiptoe, for the windows are low in the suburbs of the city. Mitka clung fast to the window ledge, looked in, and immediately lowered his eyes. No, it was not that he had caught them unawares, it was the very sight of them that overwhelmed him. He barely had time to retreat from the square of light into the shadow of the currant bushes. Dolomanova came to the window and without hurry drew the curtains across. The garden was plunged in darkness.

His foot struck on a stone and he picked it up, ready to fling it into the ambiguous darkness that now reigned behind the window. Yet the stone slid from his hand, his shame was stronger than his rage. It was all plain now, and before Mitka stepped into the house, he sat for a while on the steps, long enough for them to remove all trace of their deed. Once more he stroked the dog, who, with a soft whine, seemed to demand this toll for his venal silence.

MITKA pushed open the unlocked door without a sound, and slid into the house. It was dark and still in the passage, and through the partition wall Donka's soft laugh reverberated. He stepped quickly into his little room and shut the door. The red glow of the dying embers in the stove shone through the darkness. Throwing off his coat, he stretched himself on his bed and immediately was overcome with exhaustion. He gazed into the coal fire, where blue tongues of flame rose from the ashes and lived again and died, flaring up and merging together in strange shapes, so that Mitka could not take his eyes off them. Between flaming trees and white-hot mountains his drowsy fancies roamed and played, he felt as if trembling fingers had laid themselves gently on his eyelids, and he could not resist them. When he wakened, it seemed to him that midnight was long past, the fiery pictures were extinguished and had changed into an ashen twilight. He felt giddy.

"Donka!" he cried softly, and stretched out his hand to shake the sleeper, for their beds stood side by side. He wanted to hear Donka's voice—to see if he would be afraid at being suddenly . . . reminded.

His hand groped over Donka's rough blanket, but Donka had not yet returned from Dolomanova. Mitka sat on the bed and tried to push the door open with his foot, but it creaked and stuck. Even in the passage there was not a sound to be heard, all was dark. He did not want to sleep, and when he tried to guess the time, he saw a clock face with both hands at two hanging in the air. The events of the day passed through his mind, grotesquely fore-shortened and magnified. In particular his thoughts fixed on Zinka's great belly and on the feline whiskers of The Wax-works King—and then quite by chance he remembered Sanka, waiting for him by the door.

Flinging everything around him to the floor, and knocking against the walls as if the passage had suddenly become too narrow for him, Mitka dashed out into the courtyard. The dog rushed between his legs and leaped whimpering to one side. Leaning against the door and looking up at the moon, which was racing through the foggy clouds, Sanka stood waiting for his master.

"Go away, Alexander . . . what are you standing there for?" Mitka shouted at him while he was still some way off, but Sanka did not reply. "He's offended, I suppose, the fool!" thought Mitka, and, stepping closer, he touched Sanka on the shoulder. "Are you sleeping?"

"No, I'm not asleep, I'm thinking—the old days are gone forever, there's nothing left but the ashes, and a puff of wind would blow them away," answered Sanka in a low voice.

"You're crying!" Mitka looked into his face. "Nonsense, your Xenka 'll get well again. Why, my mother . . ." He tried to lie, but could not. "Everyone . . . I mean when it's in the lungs . . . gets well again quickly. She must go into the country, though, in the spring, and get fresh milk . . . morning and evening, morning and evening!" Mitka was cold, for he had nothing but his shirt on, and he was in a hurry to get back to his bed.

"Xenka 'll die, and that's the end of her! It's a treat to see the way you carry on with all you've got on your shoulders, master, but I've my load of troubles, too, and mine aren't of my own making, either. . . . I want to say a last word to you, master. . . ."

"Go away!" shouted Mitka, shaking with cold, and he looked at the dog, which stood beside them listening to their conversation. "We must get to sleep . . . it's cold! Go away!"

"I haven't anywhere to go," answered Sanka, an expression of anguish on his face, and from his clenched fist he let fall a handful of melting snow. He laughed tonelessly: "Batashiha's living with Tolya now. They're going

to get married." Suddenly he tore himself free from the
post against which he was leaning.

"Kiss me, master! Xenka's dead. . . ."

"What are you saying? . . . When did she die?"

"I've just heard. Kiss me . . . quick, master!"

To get rid of his troublesome friend, Mitka kissed him
hurriedly. They stood opposite each other with their arms
hanging down.

"Kiss me again. On the forehead, here, on this spot,
kiss me! . . ."

Mitka, who had already decided to comply the second
time, suddenly detected a faint tinge of mockery in Sanka's request. He frowned and walked quietly away, but a
shrill cry of warning brought him to a standstill in the
middle of the yard. He looked back. In the open gate
Sanka's silhouette, flooded by the light of the moon,
loomed darkly. His shoulders were jerking.

"And you won't have some kvass? You're only to smell
my kvass to know it's good. Kiss me just once more for
the smell, master!"

"He's drunk," thought Mitka with relief, and turned
to the staircase. "He's had too much, and now has all
sorts of nonsense in his head." He stepped in and closed
the door behind him. The warmth of the house was delightful, if only because it put to flight from his mind
everything that had taken place outside in the cold.
"Devil take it, he'd have stood there till morning, I believe!"

This thought was the last that flitted through his mind.
Through the open door of the room Donka's heavy snoring rolled out into the passage, but it broke off as soon as
Mitka entered. The coals in the little stove were already
extinguished, and on the footstool between the beds
Donka's clock, with the luminous dial, tinkled dully: it
was ten to one. Mitka pulled off his boots and put his
revolver under his pillow, as was his habit; then he undressed, but Donka slept on undisturbed. Lying on his
back, Mitka looked up at the ceiling and listened to
Donka's heavy breathing.

"How did all this happen? . . . It's strange, almost
uncanny! Here we lie, I and my worst enemy, one of us
awake, the other asleep, and both of us looking at the

same thing—what I saw through the window, what he knows with his heart." Visions of adulterous embraces, begotten of the night, rose before Mitka's open eyes clearer than the remembered reality. Masha was sitting, and Donka was lying, his head upon her knees, and carelessly her fingers were playing with his dark, unruly curls, poet's curls. . . . Perhaps he was reading poetry to her, but she was not listening . . . She was looking out through the window, as if she were waiting for Mitka's horrified face to appear there. But why was she smiling so strangely and tenderly? . . .

"There you lie snoring now, tired out by your happiness. How can you snore, you fool, if you're happy?

"And what were you thinking, Masha Dolomanova, as you looked out of the window? Were you thinking of how the ruin of that curly head might help you to your revenge? was that all? or did you fall in love with Donka's poetry and the glow of his wolf's eyes in the snowy dusk? He'll dedicate his last song to you, and the thieves will sing it in prisons and mean streets. And he'll hate you, for you're draining the untamed fire from his wolf's eyes and the world will have no more charm for them. For those who have loved you can find nothing else in life. How many women's fingers have stolen through Donka's curls! Delilah's hand creeps up to Samson's hair, to tear out his strength. . . . You have great strength in you, Masha . . . like the Kudema, when in flood time it swirls and roars in a passionate, inconsolable flood." At this point Mitka's thoughts returned imperceptibly to the turbine with which it was his dream to help the way of all mankind.

Soon he went to sleep and did not dream, although in his drowsy thoughts wild dream fragments danced fitfully. He slept for almost two hours, while outside the night still reigned. A sound awakened him: his revolver had slid from under his bolster and fallen on the floor, but he fancied it was a wish to smoke which had aroused him. He searched in his coat pockets, but found only a box with some crushed cigarettes, and there were none in Donka's jacket, either. It was pitch dark, and only four matches were left in the matchbox.

And then, as he rummaged through Donka's pockets,

he came upon a rectangular piece of metal which roused his curiosity, and he struck the first match. The metal object proved, on closer inspection, to be an old copper likeness of a saint, perhaps a memento of Donka's mother —Saint Nicholas, the protector of all who have strayed from the way, of all those who are lost, even of those who have shed blood. The match burned out, and Mitka looked to see if he could find a piece of newspaper so as to be able to make himself a cigarette. By the light of the second match he examined the papers scattered on the edge of Donka's bed. (Donka was asleep with his face turned to Mitka.) There were letters lying there, and an old dirty note with a few words in a woman's hand. Documents, innumerable documents, even if they were all false. There, too, lay the rough copy of a poem, which imprinted itself on Mitka's memory: ". . . remain pure, step out into the leaden night with me, where the robber's whistle echoes and the red moon of the jailbird gleams." Then in small writing was added: ". . . for the sun has dyed with crimson blood the hour of my birth!" Here the third match burned out. Mitka smiled at the thought that Donka was a dreamer after all, and that dreamers are always liars.

Finally, when the last match but one burned out, he found what he was looking for, a square piece of thin paper. He folded it crossways, sprinkled some tobacco in it, and held it to his lips. It struck him that the paper had a toothed edge, like a receipt, and, in terror of burning an important document, Mitka lit the last match. If he had rolled up the paper from the other edge, nothing would ever have come to light; Donka's secret would have gone up in acrid smoke.

The paper was a ticket of admission to an important government office, which they had forgotten to take from Donka as he went out. The secret was as easy to solve as a child's money box; it was all clear as daylight. Before the match had burned out, Mitka made a note of the number on the permit: a one and two eights. This new proof of Donka's guilt made all further doubt superfluous. "And I've slept side by side with vermin like that," Mitka thought. Then Donka stirred, and Mitka felt a malicious curiosity to hear his voice.

"Listen . . ." He shook the sleeping man. "Have you any matches?"

"In Maruska's room, behind the door . . . a box of them," he murmured expressionlessly.

"I've got clear proof against Sanka now, so go ahead with your charges. Don't waste time! Sorry for waking you up!"

Stretching his arms out wide, he went into Dolomanova's room. . . . In the darkness he nearly swept some clothes off their hooks; he edged to one side and hit his knees against the door. On the little table he found matches and cigarettes.

"Is it you?" asked Dolomanova, and in the darkness her voice seemed to come from some weird and terrifying distance. "Has Mitka come home? . . . Fine out where he was. . . ."

"Yes . . ." answered Mitka, muffling his voice, and in his bare feet stepped soundlessly over the linoleum-covered floor.

MITKA had had no mother of his own, but the other Mother, who had fed him with berries and hardened him with privations, had reared him in the heart of nature, and after his first sufferings, he had been drawn back to his wild home. His father's ludicrous death, his agonizing conversation with Leonty, his two days' wandering through the villages, had all been like red-hot iron laid to his wounds. With his departure from Demyatino, all the threads that bound him to his home had snapped, the Mother had thrust him from her, and the whole world had become indifferent to him. According to Firsov, Mitka had thereby been molded into a citizen of the world, and an ancestor of the men to come, and because of this Mitka, he explained, had learned the folly of his wartime heresies. In any case, Mitka's worst period had begun at that time.

In his utter despair he had seen nothing wrong in establishing himself in Masha's little room, though it meant a capitulation in his struggle to establish personal relations with her. He counted too much on Masha's feeling for him, and his obtuseness had forced her into a protest, her adventure with Donka. (Mitka's criminal activities were flourishing once more, and he had just brought off a memorable coup, the robbery of a private manufacturing concern, which was conducted according to scientific rules.) He had first come to Masha in great agitation, but sober, so that it was clear that he had weighed his decision well previously.

Patches of sun lay on the oilcloth and on the rug, and

in the half-darkness of the room the woollen flowers glowed in riotous profusion. For the first time that spring the sky was free from clouds for two hours. Dolomanova sat in front of the looking glass combing her hair and saw Mitka's reflection before he announced himself; she did not betray any surprise, but for a moment her movements became automatic. Mitka stepped closer and put his turquoise ring onto her finger—it seemed strangely pathetic on Dolomanova's rosy, tapering finger.

"They're looking for you, Mitka," she said simply.

"I know. Are you working on the film today? It's a holiday, you know. . . ."

"What holiday? Oh, of course . . ." She looked at her profile in the hand mirror. "Where are you living now?"

"Nowhere. Often I have to sleep in railway waggons."

"If you like, spend the night with me: you can sleep with Donka. I'll dress now, so go away for a little." She did not mention the ring until he was stepping out of the room. "Have you really given it to me?"

"Yes." Mitka stopped. "It belongs to you, you see. It's only that I've always forgotten to bring it."

To get a night's lodging, as an act of charity from the rich, was no particular humiliation to Mitka: he had his rights, and in his heart he was confident that the last laugh would be his. So from that time he had spent his nights in the little room; the discovery of Donka's guilt followed a week later. The game from now on was played in silence and without quarter. After a long interruption in their conversations, which were fleeting as the sun in the sky that month, they again talked of Rogovo.

"Do you know, I've been to Rogovo. There are strangers living in your house. I was in that little wood where there were the white mushrooms—they were always a bit rotten, do you remember?"

"No, I don't remember." Dolomanova shook her head, and fidgeted uneasily in her chair.

And yet she could hardly have forgotten the happy days of their childhood at Rogovo; it was more likely that she had never forgiven Mitka for abandoning her innocence to Agey's tender mercies. She had called on him, yearningly in her lonely nights, but he had rejected her.

"I am the only one you love," insisted Mitka.

"Love's hardly the word. I love crabs, but I'm crazy about you!"

One day she could restrain herself no longer. "How could you leave me, my darling? You think you've killed your love, but you haven't, you've only crippled it—and I've not even got your tears to comfort me: but you wait, they'll come soon! I'll treat you as my father treated the woodcocks—he went after them in the mating season and shot them when they were singing their love songs. I take after my father, that's why we couldn't live together—I give you fair warning I'll treat you as I treated Agey."

"Don't talk of Agey!" he cried, and his temples flushed. "What price do you expect for yourself, Masha?"

"I want to break you. You've got to suffer, however much you don't want to. You're so arrogant, you trample on people. Look at the way you've treated Sanka! You think yourself God Almighty, but what if you're just nobody?"

"Well, if that's so," said Mitka wincing, "why have you waited for me all these years?"

Even here he voiced his deep assurance that she loved him. He had only to wait and she would call after him, as once she had on the bridge that stormy April day. In his uncertainty he recalled what he had seen that night through the window, but dismissed it as a trick. When he went back to his room, he struck a match to light his cigarette, and a sudden jealousy forced him to look into the face of the sleeper. Donka was sleeping sweetly, his hand laid under his head. On his little finger sat the ring with the turquoise. The stone, with its blue gleam turned inward, seemed to sleep, too, nursed by Donka's warmth. For the first time Mitka realized that his breach with Masha had been something more than a ridiculous little misunderstanding.

Donka laid siege to Masha's heart as vigorously as
Chikelyov had to Zinka's, but the latter had taken an
evacuated fortress while Donka captured his at the height
of its powers. Yet both victories were only of short dura-
tion.

Till now defeat had been unknown to Donka, the celebrated breaker of hearts. He seized and sated himself
with the swiftness of fire and never wept for those he
abandoned, though the abandoned wept for him. He
was a thief of love, who sought for that elusive treasure
"which one only sees in dreams." When Manka the Snowstorm met him first, Donka sank his eyes before her, for
her beauty seemed to mock at his trivial fame. All other
women were incarnated in her, and to conquer her meant
to taste to the last drop the sweet and fatal poison of disillusionment. He almost went out of his mind, and
availed himself of the lover's final privilege; he served her
with doglike devotion and without reward.

Donka triumphed on that evening when, after her conversation with Mitka, Dolomanova had allowed him to
approach within that fatal radius where the force of mutual attraction begins to work. The lovers made haste, as
if their union were a sin that would bring with it an inevitable punishment. Firsov was convinced that in this
month of mutual enchantment the lovers were in reality
at bitter enmity with each other. The writer was once
more a frequent visitor at Dolomanova's; he had taken
to drink: he drank because he was inwardly dissatisfied,
because he wanted to have a grievance, because the pangs

of creation were tormenting him (the scheme of a new novel was taking shape in his mind): he drank, finally, for no reason at all, as only Russians know how to drink, and sat in Dolomanova's room in a corner with his notebook up his sleeve.

In the dark raptures of their love Donka's eyes shone bright with tenderness. He wrote no more poetry; his dream had become one with reality, and in that month his own fate was graceful and felicitous as a poem. For hours long he lay with his head on Masha's lap, and marveled at the peace and the gentle dripping of time.

"Don't be shocked, Firsov!" said Dolomanova, when at some such moment he stepped into the room.

"*Nil admirari deorum est.*" The writer shrugged his shoulders . . . "And that's why the gods are dead. They'll only start living again when they take lodgings in a few men's hearts." And he lamented that his book, into which he had put almost the whole of himself, had astonished no one. After a quarter of an hour he left gloomily, to sit and kill time by his own primus.

This should have been the crowning moment of Donka's life, but he became shy of his happiness when he was alone with Masha. To his awestruck mind Dolomanova was sin itself, which had selected this wondrous and captivating form as its earthly home. Her kisses were like wine whose taste was sour to him; they attracted but did not satisfy him. To hide his terror of the inevitable he assumed the jaunty tone of a street gallant.

"Do you really love me, tell me, now?" he asked, blowing a smoke ring as soft as a maiden's curl. He looked into her face, and her sullen twitching brows still reminded him of the night's capricious tenderness.

"And will you give me a pair of silk stockings?" asked Manka.

"I'll get you a pair of shoes, too," answered Donka, slightly disconverted by her sarcasm, and then once more he sank his gaze into the lustrous darkness of her eyes, as though his fate lay there. "I love you, Manka. . . . I love you. You're quick as a fly and as cunning as God. I don't understand you, but I love you. Your hair is thick as a dreaming wood. The lightning shoots across your face, even when you're asleep. Your eyes see by night what no one else sees even in the sunlight. My reason has been scratched away by your little nails, and I love you because you have no pity for me. . . . You're like gingerbread: it's cloying to eat you every day. You're ruin to anyone you get in your clutches. Yesterday I dreamed they killed me, but even then I still remained yours. You're my joy and my destruction. . . ." He could not find words for his feelings, his teeth gleamed, and his lips twitched convulsively.

"Will you kill me if I'm unfaithful to you?"

"I'll cry . . . but what do you care about other people's tears?"

"Well, what use are they?"

With a jerk she pushed Donka's head from her knees and it slid on to the soft edge of the sofa. "Where was Mitka yesterday?"

"At the cemetery." Donka turned away gloomily; he was ashamed of his tousled hair. "I waited ten minutes for him, but he didn't turn up, so I left. It's driving me wild. My life's as good as wasted, and what's it all for?"

She took his hand. "What are you grumbling about? Do you know how much this ring cost? Do you know the richest treasure a woman can possess? . . . A man like Mitka. Doesn't it look well on your finger? And it's gold. . . ." There was an impatient note in her voice.

"It might be lead, for all I care. Does he visit you at night?"

She did not answer, but looked out through the window, as if Mitka were standing there again, watching.

Every hour brought disaster nearer. Mitka persisted in his ill-boding silence. His days had become drab and dreary like the early spring. Firsov arrived every day with a gloomier face. To make things worse, a ridiculous situation had arisen. Firsov had got half a dozen of Donka's poems published in a small paper, and after a week had made him his first payment, a most encouraging one; and from that time Donka had begun to write rubbishy poems offhand, and succeeded in turning out an average of five a day. He seemed to have completely cut himself adrift from the thieves, and now abandoned himself to his new work with zest; he even composed in trams. He realized quite well his blasphemous resemblance to a certain great poet, and emphasized it. With a huge hat perched on his long hair, and a stick on which was Masha's monogram in silver, he used to go to the editors' offices, and was not ashamed to ask for advances of three roubles. He quickly made himself at home in the vocation of literature.

When they met, Firsov clutched at his head in exasperation, although he had his hat on, but Donka would pull his cigarette case out of his pocket and offer a cigarette.

"Take a look at that, old man." He tapped his finger on the silver lid of the case. "Look, a *troika* tearing along in the snow, and in the *troika* a pair of sweethearts! Not much in that, perhaps, but just look at the coachman's face! . . . It's a murderer driving, and singing songs about his crimes: that's something really Russian! I've just let myself go about it and written a cycle of poems on the subject . . . an onomatopoeic composition in a completely new style. Would you like to have a look at it?"

"It's a perfectly ghastly cigarette case, that of yours," snarled Firsov. "I'll look at the poems some other time."

Donka did not insist, and merely raised his eyebrows indulgently. By that single gesture he expressed the immemorial strife between the poet and the prose writer.

". . . No, my charmer, if you once let men get it into their heads that they're wonderful, they get above themselves and start climbing out of the cage. So Nature just gives them a dig from time to time to remind them . . ."

Firsov was arguing with Zinka, who was waiting impatiently for him to finish, as the last bell that announced her appearance had rung.

"As if I hadn't digs enough without that," said Zinka; smiling; she was shy at Firsov's seeing her in her wide pants.

The conversation took place in the beer hall; the long passage leading to the stage hummed like a shell. It was Saturday, a great day for drinking, and the beer hall was full to overflowing. For the fourth time a bald-headed man, who looked like a marshal of the old regime, announced the name of the singer of "The Songs of Fate." Firsov was surprised to hear that it was Zinka's former name, Balduyeva, and not Chikelyova that was used, but he guessed the reason for it rightly. Zinka had had a miscarriage; Chikelyov's family happiness was hanging by a hair, and he himself was raging like a mortally wounded beast. His official zeal had become almost satanic; even poor Bundyukova, who had weak nerves, gave the chairman of the house committee a very wide berth in case she should get a "telling off." Pyotr Gorbidonich was convinced that they were all laughing at him; in an access of rage he sold to an old clothes dealer the cradle he had put up in his quarters with so many hopes and dreams, and the baby linen followed it. His reappointment to the post of chairman of the house committee did little to soothe him. One day Matvey loudly expressed the opinion that Chikelyov was as stupid as the butchers of Suchum. This insult cut Chikelyov to the heart, although it had by no means been proved yet that all butchers in Suchum were fools. ("I suppose there are night classes going on even among them," pondered Chikelyov with a sore heart.) All the same, Matvey, Zinka's brother, was a serious man, as befitted his high official post. He used always to drive to his office in a car, and never wasted his words.

Chikelyov's uncertainty about the butchers of Suchum tortured him as much as the enigmatic word "Marabu" had done once before. He boiled with rage, and his private friend, The Wax-works King, was the first to suffer for it; he had such a high room rent laid upon him that all the wax in the world would not have sufficed to cover it. But Zinka suffered more than them all.

The end of it all was that one day Zinka got tired of staying up late every night patching Chikelyov's garments, and flung them out of her room. Then she locked Klavdya in and went to the beer hall to get an engagement; she got it, though, of course, on the condition that she was to introduce educational items twice a week. Zinka agreed, and now she sang again, thrilling the working people by the deep tones of her wonderful voice. Pyotr Gorbidonich was at first dumfounded by the new arrangement, but when he had recovered himself, he began to think of revenge. It appeared to him in many marvellous forms: for instance, she might be torn to pieces by wild animals—a certainly unattainable but all the same consoling dream. Soon his rage passed over into mere hatred of any sign of independence on Zinka's part. "This woman has dared to do what she wanted, but I would never have dared. You're a coward, Pyotr Gorbidonich, you've deserved nothing better." (His formula of envy was characteristic, and did not run as it usually does: "Why haven't I what they have?" but: "Why have they what I haven't?" Chikelyov considered himself the paragon of human weakness.)

But even inglorious wounds heal. Zinka sang, Klavdya grew, Matvey carried on in his office, and the Bundyukovs were as busy as ever—being unemployed. Chikelyov, on the other hand, kept thinking how he might vindicate his insulted honor. One evening when Zinka was putting her daughter to sleep, he came into her room and asked if, in consideration of their former relations, she would do him a favor. He wanted her to ask her brother, Matvey, to apologize to him for his remark about the butchers of Suchum, even if it were only in a whisper or even just in his thoughts . . . if he would only look at him with an expression of regret, even if it were scarcely perceptible. In the abundance of his generosity Chikelyov would have been satisfied even with a mere embarrassed smile from Matvey. But Zinka ordered the chairman of the house committee to leave her room.

"Please note that you're playing with fire," said Chikelyov, coughing into his hand. "There's no nonsense about me, and, when anyone crosses me—that's typical —I just gobble him up!"

"Go away, and none of your cheek, or I'll take you by the ear and lead you out," laughed Zinka, and never had she seemed so seductive. "I'm no Manyukin: if I let fly at your chicken snout, it'll hurt."

"You're a cow, please note that!" jeered Chikelyov. "You need a bull, not a man like me. . . ."

So this ridiculous marriage came to an end, and Zinka mourned for her passing youth. The struggle heralded for her the approach of an early middle age. But though she had slipped from Chikelyov's stale embraces, she did not flatter herself that she would find another lover. She felt that she could never quench her thirst for Mitka, even were she to destroy herself. Fortune had never granted her the happiness for which she had longed so ardently. The news about him was vague and scanty; for all she knew he had already been arrested and sentenced for his crimes. She wrote him a clumsy, rambling letter to an improbable address; when she had sent it, she felt as if she had thrown it into a well.

"I don't suppose he even coughed over it," said Bundyukova sympathetically; she was so experienced in affairs of the heart that she herself was now proof against every feeling.

Then Zinka had fetched an old coat out of her box. The holes the moths had eaten had been patched by old Bundyukova herself, who through life had always remained true to the saying: "Put no hindrance in men's path: every stone must fall to the earth and lie in its appointed place." Zinka went back to the beer hall, as Tanya, six months before, had returned to the circus. Everything there was unchanged, only the palm, which had been given such honorable mention in Firsov's novel, was no longer visible. It had faded, and in its place stood a small round table, and on the table a cage, and in the cage a squirrel vainly climbed a wheel. The cage stood on the most conspicuous spot so that everyone, as they drank their beer, could have an uninterrupted view of the squirrel and its vain struggle for freedom.

Zinka poured into her songs all the warmth and passion she had missed in life. Her voice had retained its old power, though now she was accompanied only by a single harmonica player. He was a dry, gloomy man, who looked as if he'd been pickled in vinegar, and often he glanced across at the empty seat on which the singer leaned her head.

"Where's the other one?" asked Nikolka, sitting down at the table.

"He was run over by a bus, poor devil," said pockmarked Alexey, wriggling and bowing, and he ran for the drinks that had been ordered.

"WHAT's the matter with your hand?" asked Mitka, pointing at Nikolka's bandaged finger.

"I crushed my finger. . . . The day before yesterday I was unpacking boxes. For my rule is: 'Don't trust anyone else to do what you can do more quickly yourself.' Other people can take it easy."

"Are you doing a lot of business?" asked Mitka through his teeth.

"Oh, not so bad . . . for a man in a small way like me," said Zavarihin smugly and cautiously as he poured out the beer.

There were three mugs, the third for Firsov, for the writer was drinking away his earnings on *The Adventurers*. Here everyone knew the man who was abused every day in the newspapers, and showed their sympathy for him by the silence simple people have for all who have been humiliated. Everyone who sat at his table was generously treated by Firsov, who "played the demagogue," as spotty Alexey expressed it.

"We're quiet, simple chaps, we've had the pride knocked out of us . . . and we know our places," went on Zavarihin seriously, and Mitka saw that his red fist was firmly clenched. "It's just the way you look at things. I dare say you think: 'He's a dark horse, that Zavarihin,' but it all depends on the way you look at it. To a dark eye everything is dark, but if you have a bright eye, even in prison the sun 'll shine for you. Drink, Mitka, if you're not too grand to drink with a poor beggar like me!"

Mitka did not answer, but turned his eyes to Firsov, who was attacking some stock fish.

"Still immortalizing my crimes?" he said wryly.

"Your exploits, Dmitri Yegorich," answered Firsov hoarsely, and went on munching.

"Well, here I am, alive and kicking! Pinch me and see. If you'd made me more fetching, that's to say put in the frills, I'll be bound they'd have liked it better."

"I've used you as an idea, not as a personality. There aren't more than about seven ideas, but that's enough to go around. They're like masks. . . . Men and states and cities play their part behind them—and only seven of them!"

"Why only seven?" Zavarihin laughed at Firsov's tipsy eloquence.

"Seven? . . . Because six would be too few and eight unforgivably too many. There's only one law in Nature: 'too many or too few'—and we're fools enough to go on trying for a lucky number. We're all of us crazy, masters and men."

"Why do men go on living, then?" asked Alexey in a critical voice.

"Because that's all they're good for!" Firsov made a vague gesture with his hand, and poked at his fish. "And those who understand that die. They die, just as Tatyana Vekshin died—your sister, Mitka, and my unhappy friend."

The three men sat in silent thought at the table in the middle of all the clatter and din; Tanya's name had roused old memories. Just as now, only unknown to each other, a year and a half ago they had sat here in different corners, and it was very hard for them to decide if things had gone better or worse with them then than now. One thing only was clear, that they were sitting here together for the last time, for the end of their curious relationship was already in sight—the end and a new beginning, too. As they sat, their thoughts turned to the old gay days in the beer hall, when Manyukin, the paragon of liars, had still been to the fore.

"The *barin's* gone west at last," said Zavarihin. "Yesterday he was picked up somewhere near the market: he'd

pinched some bread from a woman and taken to his heels
. . . but he slipped and fell and never got up again."

"He was a talented man, but our talent is like Siberian
ore," said Firsov, gazing at the reflection of the electric
light in the green glass of his bottle. "A passing native
begins to dig it up, scrapes at the surface a little, and
then, when he has messed it up, wanders off to some new
untrodden region, whistling. Storm ravages the spot and
wind and snow follow. Yes, the unawakened wastes of
Siberia, that's the root of the matter, gentlemen. He'll
be a happy man who opens it up with powder and knout
and shovel . . . but still more so, if he devotes his love
and his sweat to it. One must work. . . ."

"All nonsense!" exclaimed Zavarihin, but no one listened to him. "It's all nonsense, Fyodor Fyodorich," he
repeated still more obstinately.

Mitka was waiting for someone, as he had waited in
this very place a year and a half ago; he kept turning
around, but the people he was expecting were not yet
ready to appear; they, Donka and Sanka, were standing
together in the bathroom, whispering excitedly together,
and plotting a deed that terrified them both. A sixteen-
candle-power lamp shed a blue carbolic light on Donka's
red cheeks and Sanka's protruding eyes. They had agreed
to the job, but they were still haggling over certain details, and seemed to be trying to overreach each other with
fantastic cunning. Each of them seemed scared lest his
partner should run away and leave him in the lurch.

". . . A real catch. . . . Enough to make one lick
one's fingers," and Donka actually licked his dirty fingertips absent-mindedly. "Sackfuls of gold. . . . Thirty
dozen gold watches . . ."

"Two tumblers full of diamonds!" repeated Sanka, beside himself, and shut his eyes in sheer rapture.

"And one of them, I'm told, is wound around with cotton thread like a reel . . . it's the king of them all, you
see. There's such a fire burning in it that it hurts you to
hold it in your hand . . . one can only take it up with
tongs." And Donka stretched out his quivering palm to
Sanka, as if actually the king of all diamonds lay on it.
His fingers trembled convulsively. Through the open door
came the sobbing of a harmonica, then everything was

still; someone had come to the door and then gone away again. In the bathroom pan water dripped monotonously, and a buzzing sound could be heard in one of the pipes. Unconsciously the thieves played into each other's hands. Suddenly Sanka moved away and leaned against the whitewashed wall, which had been scribbled over with pencils and matches by chance hands.

"You or me?" he asked, but so softly that Donka scarcely caught the whisper.

Each making way for the other, as neither of them wished to go first, they went along the passage to the public room. At this late hour there were fewer people present; Zavarihin had already gone, and Mitka smoked silently in the gloomy society of Firsov.

"We're ready, master," said Sanka, touching Mitka's chair, while Donka made a grimace to indicate that the job must be started immediately. "It's time, master!"

With a calm, indefinable expression, but an unwonted fire in his eyes which his lowered lids could not hide, Mitka rose from his place and signaled to them to go out into the street. But he himself still did not leave.

"Listen, Firsov," he asked in a resounding voice, "is it true that it was you who brought these two together?"

"What two?" Firsov straightened slightly and his brain cleared.

"My sister and that . . . dog. I know what you're going to say, so you can just keep quiet. You and your 'ideas' have done enough mischief already. But don't alarm yourself! I've got over Tatyanka's loss. You're an optimist with your match-making; you might as well try to reconcile a dog and a whip as me and Zavarihin! For let me tell you this: Zavarihin and I are poles apart. Isolation has ruined me, but only half of me. But Zavarihin, for all he's so self-sufficient, won't escape either: his ruin will be more complete than mine. No, I'm no Smurov!"

"But I've just seen you myself giving him money!" the writer retorted. "Was your idea to fatten him up and then give him a knock on the head?" he gibed.

"I'm sorry for your readers, if that's the best you can do! The notes are all numbered and tomorrow the list'll be handed in. Put that in your pipe and smoke it! Now we must get along—by-by!"

Firsov broke into a cold sweat. When he had written about his Smurov, he had never even for a moment conceived of such hatred in his hero; it amazed him, for he did not realize that it had its roots in class feeling. He gazed in astonishment at the gleam in Mitka's eyes and the dull red of his wasted cheeks. Firsov, who had hitherto refused to classify the marvels of creation, was now obliged to admit that the grestest of them all was man.

"Listen, Vekshin, take me with you wherever you're going. I'll tell you something . . . a strange idea has just come into my head. I won't be in your way—I'll be useful to you!"

"We're going to kill a man, if you want to know," Mitka interrupted him, raising his brows, "but a clever man like you won't turn a hair at that!"

"Thieves' court?" Firsov dropped wearily on to his chair. "Donka?"

Mitka told him in a few words the substance of his charges; then, after waiting half a minute, he hurriedly left the beer hall. Firsov ordered another glass and sat on alone. His thoughts chased one another, and when he tried to lay hold of them, they snapped like threads. He sat on till closing time. Then suddenly he jumped up, threw over a chair, and pushed spotty Alexey to one side. Without his cap, and with his coat open, he hurried into the street. The dirty pavement with its film of ice rocked under him; he hurried along the street without knowing where he was going. All that he felt was a longing desire to prevent what had probably already begun. With all his imagination he visualized the whole course of events of which Mitka had spoken.

He ran, thrusting to one side all who came into his way, cursing and shouting inarticulately, and losing his galoshes. A stone wall could not have brought him to a standstill. The omnibuses threatened him with their dim light and their stench of gas. Like marvellous fireflies the rolling monsters raced past him, noisily champing the mud with their curved lips. They seemed eager to chase all living things into their holes and crannies. Firsov saw one of them chasing a small white dog and trying to snap at it with its soft, obscene chops. The road shone in the glare of the electric signs, and through this blinding light the little dog ran on and disappeared, wagging his tail, behind a newspaper kiosk; at the same instant the omnibus flung its double ray, which frothed in the chilly drizzle, right over Firsov's head. Then all was blotted out.

When the writer was picked up out of the mud, a crowd had collected around him, and a burly policeman, bulging with all his capes and coats, scolded him for his lack of care. Firsov wiped away the street dirt from his forehead with his sleeve, poked his finger into his sodden shoes, and exclaimed indignantly:

"Lord! . . . what Asiatics!"

Firsov stepped to one side to escape the gaping crowd, and tidied himself as well as he could. He had not met with any particular injury, but the shoulder onto which he had been flung against the curb was hurting, and there was a big tear in his skin coat. (The writer's skin coat had met with the same fate as the ulster, and had also acquired an extremely indigenous appearance.) Firsov shook himself and turned to the right into a dark street, then to the left, and lost himself in a treacherous cul-de-sac. Suddenly he realized that he was not far from Dolomanova's flat. There was nowhere in particular to go, and the weather was inclement, so he walked meekly into the familiar yard.

He knocked and, when the bolts scraped, suddenly realized why his instinct had led him here. "Is Donka at home?" he asked in a steady voice as soon as the door opened.

"I'm a stranger myself. . . . I really couldn't say," an obliging, unfamiliar voice answered from the darkness. "I come from Rogovo, you know, and . . ."

"Isn't Marya Fyodorovna in bed yet?" Firsov raised his voice angrily.

"The supper's quite cold: I keep warming it up: I'm expecting her any moment. And who are you?" Firsov did not answer this question, which seemed to him stupid, and the other did not dare to repeat it, less from shyness than from servility. The unknown man took off Firsov's coat and one galosh in the darkness. "Give me

THE THIEF 491

the cap, please, and the second galosh. . . . I'll put them on the stove immediately to dry."

"Wha—at?" Firsov began to attend. "Oh, yes, the cap! Well, I've come . . . without a cap . . . yes . . ."

"Ah, forgive me, I understand you: you're hardening your constitution?" the thin voice sniggered. "Tee—hee ——hee!" (He seemed to be coughing.) "They say it's healthy, but, do you know, I don't believe it. I don't believe in God . . . and I don't believe in that, either. Forgive me, if you'll be so good, I don't believe it. My brother, Fyodor Ignatich, was a man of immense strength . . . It was dreadful to look at him when he started to rub himself with snow after his vapor bath for the sake of his health. . . . He got inflammation of the lungs in that way. Very comic: fate's always comic, isn't it?"

"What? . . . inflammation? . . . Yes . . . of course. . . ." Firsov laid his scarf carelessly into the outstretched hand, and knocked absent-mindedly on the door. As no one answered, he took this as permission to enter.

In the half-darkness, which smelled of Antonovsky apples and was dimly illuminated by a shaded lamp, bit by bit all sorts of strange corners and angles and patterns, as well as a blue fragment of a picture under glass, crept into visibility. A lamp stood on the table, and under the lamp lay a book. The light shone on a yellow dust cover, and Firsov guessed that it was *The Adventurers*. He stepped closer on tiptoe, and saw that he had guessed right. (In those days gay, fantastic dust covers were the fashion; they were thought "barbaric.") From under the book the edge of a photograph protruded; it was an enlarged film photograph, and presented Dolomanova asleep. The straight brows of the sleeper, which life had lined, were mysteriously aloof. A curl and its black shadow cut across the pure, virginal forehead. But on her lips, and in the scarcely indicated corners of her mouth, there were marks of secret and indomitable will. "Even in a photograph," thought Firsov, dropping into a small armchair.

He reached out automatically for the book, and, blinking in the cigarette smoke, opened it to the page where the marker lay, and was filled with amazement. A long paragraph devoted to a description of Mitka's character was underlined in pencil in many places. Firsov considered this careful and rather boring paragraph the best passage in his novel. The margin of the page was thickly covered with fine, slanting writing, and various parts of it were scored out or merely blotted out with her finger. Dolomanova had made all these notes in evident excitement. In one place, which had particularly roused her wrath, the word "Lies!" was written over the text, and on the margin she had scribbled the following thoughts: "Mitka is everlasting. He is the best in mankind. He is the disaster that announces great storms. Men will never love him, but how dark the world would be without him! But no, he'll always be there as the wave is always in the sea even when it's calm."

Smiling bitterly, Firsov read a little further, but, hearing steps behind him, put away the book and, looking around, saw an insignificant little person with a gray lock of hair rising from his bald crown. He stood there waiting and smirking sheepishly.

"I'd just like to take a seat here quietly for a bit." He smiled and refused to be daunted by Firsov's unencouraging scowl. "D'you know, I'd rather fancy a little chat with someone. . . . I can't help myself, I feel such a need for it. No one ever speaks to me seriously . . . they all make jokes. I know I'm a comic chap, of course."

"How?" Firsov looked at him distrustfully. "I shouldn't have thought so."

"No, no, it really is the case, tee-hee-hee!" he coughed. "I have . . . how shall I put it nicely, now? . . . a buttery kind of a face. It's always shining, as if I was God knows who . . . and even my eyes are always up to something. They're always running around . . . I can never catch up with them . . . I mean in my thoughts."

"Sit down!" Firsov rubbed his numbed fingers. "Who are you, in Heaven's name?"

"And you?" The man pointed at him with his finger.

"I'm Firsov, a friend of Marya Fyodorovna."

"And I'm Mashechka's uncle. I knew her when she was a child—so high. I've stolen jam with her at my Aunt Pasha's. We're friends from youth. At that time I boarded with her daddy. (We were both of us frightfully strong men: we used to break half-rouble pieces with one finger.

Give me a fifty-kopek piece and I'll show you. . . .
Would you like to? Well, well, I won't force you. . . .
Her daddy, you see, was my brother.) Yes, that's it. Well,
what's one to say? . . . I'm a comic chap! Do you know
my name? Pigr Ivanich. Fyodor Ignatich just called me
Tiger and I myself gave the name a still funnier little
twist. Often when he came home tired from work, I used
to try to cheer him up. For, you know, I'm a useless chap,
a good-for-nothing: but I don't mind."

"Excuse me, have you any occupation? . . ." Firsov
observed this strange creature with sincere interest.

"I've tried everything, but I was always turned down.
I was a billiard marker, a prison editor (you know, for
prison news), an actor (in the old days I took the part of
a Japanese officer in a booth, and I had the whole mob
after me because of it. Yes, and war came then! It was
after that that I began to drink.) You can just imagine
how chaps like me stood it! We sat there in burrows and
waited shivering for the last day. Those who don't work
shan't eat—these words have been directed personally at
me, but it doesn't act as quickly as that, people like us
will live a long time yet."

"Stop talking such nonsense, I don't like it," said Firsov.

"Excuse me. If I'd been in their place I'd have come
out with a law that all useless people should be boiled
down into glue for the good of the useful ones. What do
you think of that? That would make a marvellous glue.
. . . Well, well, I'm only joking. That's merely a facetious
proposal. For some years I've noticed that people find it
very agreeable for a man to humble himself of his own
accord, and I've humbled myself so much that even the
man who humbles me more needn't feel a twinge of conscience. That's me! There's progress for you!"

"Oh, stop making a fool of yourself, you . . . what's
your name?"

"Pigr Ivanich. . . . I'm used to the bread of charity,
and bullying is nothing new to me, either. Do you think
that Mashechka won't bully me? You don't know her!
—she likes to feel important, she's only human. Anyway,
her man's a good-for-nothing fellow, he wouldn't even do
for glue, they'd throw him out after the first boiling. Fyo-

dor Ignatich gave me it in the neck once—it was when his vapor bath was burned down and his daughter ran away; children are as much a burden nowadays as lack of children. I got it in the neck from him and that was that. He died—my little brother—soon after, in the year nineteen . . . and not from hunger, either. Not by no means! I often got him some bread or a hen, and once I wrung a pullet's neck with my own hands—someone else's of course. Animals love me, they come to me of their own accord. I'm a quiet chap, just a doormat!"

"Well, and have you been wringing hens' necks like that ever since?"

"No . . . I've been on the lookout."

"For an honest man? Well, you'll need your lantern."

"No, I've been on the lookout for Mashechka. I looked everywhere, and suddenly I saw her being carried away by ruffians: that was on the pictures. I had a message for her. Pardon the inquiry, but are you on good terms with my niece? I'd like to tell you things, but I'm frightened. We had a young engineer of the name of Vekshin. He was a boy in years, but he had a hard head."

"Well, go on!" Firsov lowered his eyes.

"He went on strike, and Fyodor Ignatich decided to dismiss him, but Mashechka took his part. It's a secret, but I slept behind the plank wall, and I have a very keen ear. (Often someone would shout at night: 'Fetch some kvass, Pigr,' and there I was with the bottle! I sleep like a hare with my eyes open.) Masha pleaded for him, and Fyodor Ignatich gave in. The next morning the boy hit Fyodor Ignatich in the face . . . or rather he didn't hit him, but he took him by his gray hair and shook him a little just to give him a lesson—and yet Fyodor had always rubbed himself with snow for his health. And besides that, he said a lot of wicked things to him . . . about the Czar and a whole lot more. In my opinion all that's just bunkum. A word's like a blue bottle, it buzzes up and down and then it's off and away. But, after all, gray hairs —they should be respected, don't you think? It was a real piece of insubordination, and in wartime, too. Well, the boy was to be arrested the next day, and in the night Masha woke me up. 'Pigr, get up! . . . Wake Vekshin,

I'll wait for him.' She'd never spoken a word to me before, and now she suddenly came to me . . . in the night. Well, my strong point is obedience. And so we went out as quietly as thieves. I called the young fellow, and he gave me, I still remember, a cigarette as a reward. They whispered together, not for long. . . . I hadn't even time to finish smoking my cigarette. We went back and she spoke to me quite strangely. 'Look, Pigr, I've offered to go with him, and he won't have me. Am I just dirt, Pigr?' And she straightened herself and clenched her fists. . . . And she gnashed her teeth, by God! . . . as wild as the very devil. 'No, you're splendid,' I whispered to her, but I cast a glance around me as I said it. We were near the house, and my little brother was sitting on the steps fiddling with a cigarette. 'Let me finish smoking it, Pigr,' and his hands shook as if he'd been shot. 'I've come out to get a breath of air to buck me up. Do you hear? The nightingales are singing.' But how could one talk about nightingales in March, I ask you? Never had my little brother had such a soft voice, and yet he was a man of great strength; he used to rub himself down with snow for his health. The next morning Vekshin was gone, and afterward my niece vanished, too, in a funny way. . . ."

He stopped talking, and his usual expression returned; his flat features glistened, and they had an impudent look; it was only because of the importance of his narrative.

"Why have you gone on looking for her for so long?" asked Firsov, coming to himself.

"I was bored without her . . . and then . . . I have to hang on to somebody. If I'd come to you, you'd have chased me away, I suppose?"

"Yes, like a shot!" Firsov flashed back.

"Yes, and yet you see, all the same, you're well washed, even if you've only one galosh. I always test my acquaintances this way. I say something beastly to them, and then wait. If one of them laughs, then he's beastly himself." He made his hands into a trumpet and put them to his lips. "I've brought Mashechka a little message from her father."

"What sort of a message?" asked Firsov with naïve impudence.

"That sort of a message!" answered Pigr, and, putting his fingers to his nose, jumped to the door. "I only wanted to size you up, Daddy! We all of us know what writers are."

Then Dolomanova came in.

SHE was tired and vexed and despondent, and she barely nodded to Firsov. As soon as she entered the room, a sickly sensation of reality returned to him; at the same time the consciousness that everything was already over filled him with dejection and indifference.

He sat on silently until Dolomanova had finished her supper, which had grown cold. Pigr waited on her.

"Have you made dear old uncle's acquaintance?" she inquired, taking a tiny sip from the red wine Pigr had reverentially offered her. The men bowed silently as if their unpleasant little conversation had never taken place.

Firsov looked at Dolomanova with unconcealed hostility. Mashechka, Manka the Snowstorm, Ageyka's widow, Donka's mistress . . . how quickly she had changed her masks and cast everyone who approached her to the four winds! A whirling wheel, a cyclone, a witch!

"Have you been here long? Have you been entertaining each other? . . . Go away, Firsov! I'm tired, I want to sleep."

But Firsov sat there, as if the armchair held him in its jaws: Masha understood at last the object of his persistence. "Well, let's have your news, and then for God's sake, go! What has Pigr told you? . . . If you knew how tired I was . . ." Firsov sat on unperturbed.

"Donka is paying his debt," he said finally, and waited to see if she would grasp his meaning and betray herself. "For your love and for his poetry."

"I don't understand!" answered Dolomanova coolly, and she took an apple from the table.

"The thieves' court," whispered Firsov sardonically, and he laughed. "It's a man's life, do you understand? I see them struggling in the mud, and Mitka's strength is failing: he is losing his hold on reality: you're the only one who can save him, but there you sit not doing a thing."

"Don't shout, or Pigr will hear. Isn't he perfect? By the way, I hope you've put him down in your notebook. Sorry for the interruption."

"He loves you, as one only loves for the first time. You must understand his pride and silence, for you're the only one who can. You're like two lovers who have lost their way in the desert, and around them nothing but treachery and night . . ."

"Your Smurov may be like that, but Vekshin can hold his tongue. As for Donka, what's to become of him anyway? He's done for."

"But he's innocent. I've seen it all along and I know. They were being played against each other, and now he must pay, though he's nothing left to lose. He can be thrown away like an unwanted card. But just tell me, my charmer, where did Donka get the pass, that infallible proof . . . Well?" He charged her furiously with complicity, but she smiled.

"Try an Antonovsky apple, they're very refreshing in this weather . . . I suppose it's the spring makes you all so excitable, Firsov, and I dare say you've forgotten that you promised your life—oh, and a lot more, too—if I would love you or even be kind to you. In your present mood I shouldn't care to take the risk. I set a certain store by myself. He's not like you, he'll pay up and gladly, too. Lord, but I'm tired, Firsov!"

The duel became hotter, and Dolomanova's features sharpened, as if she were facing a strong wind.

"That time I was with Agey, and he kept asking about frogs, I got an inkling of what was happening, and it was enough to sicken me. Look here, Masha, you knew, admit you knew, they'd kill him that night you were so cruel to me. . . . I knew it too in my heart."

"And yet you came whining for kisses?"

"You were cruel and I couldn't resist you, but don't pretend that that wasn't what you were secretly longing for!" He jumped up excitedly, and neither of them heard a sudden knocking outside. Pigr opened the door and stood a moment gaping in bewilderment at the newcomer, but Firsov heard the tense voice in the other room and knew it was Mitka. His wits deserted him, but suddenly he realized that Fate had offered him a scene of unique interest.

Mitka stood on the threshold, pale and trembling, and swinging his arms oddly by his side. For a moment it looked as if he were going to fall, but he recovered himself and walked toward Dolomanova, who had remained seated.

"Leave me, you, Firsov and Pigr!" said Dolomanova, putting out her cigarette on the arm of her chair.

They did not obey her, but she was not surprised, she had only spoken to relieve the tension. There was a breathless pause, and Firsov had the feeling that every object in the room had torn itself from its place and was trying to force a way for itself through the walls into the void. Pigr wiped the sweat from his streaming brow, but with caution, so as not to miss a word. Suddenly Mitka flung himself at Dolomanova, and Firsov sprang at him to prevent a second crime; but he was mistaken.

"Is my life to count for nothing?" Was this Mitka's cry? Even on the rack Firsov could not have recalled the precise words. It was more vivid than anything in his story, it filled him with regret that his book on Mitka had forestalled life's conclusions—and yet how glad he was, too! It was for his degradation and his sufferings that Mitka demanded his reward, but it was no demand, he had only strength for a last desperate appeal: the words that sprang to his lips were those that all men carry buried in their hearts ready for the moment of supreme trial. Firsov forgot all but the rasp of Mitka's voice as the words were wrenched from him like iron.

Then Dolomanova drew a diamond ring from her finger; Firsov had not noticed it before, but he had seen her fingers moving impatiently, and now he felt that she had long ago rehearsed this moment.

She flung the ring to Mitka, but he missed it and it rolled onto the floor.

"That's for you, Mitka! . . ." she said inexorably.

"Yours was a turquoise, but mine's a diamond. Pick it up, Mitka!"

"Rather interesting this, what?" whispered Pigr into Firsov's ear. He found it so entertaining that he forgot himself, and leaned on Firsov's shoulder.

Firsov flung him off roughly and turned to the door to escape. But he had lost his opportunity, and he started back in pure amazement. For there was a fifth person now in the room, whose presence no one had suspected —Vassily Vassilyevich. Panama the Fat shrugged his shoulders and said excitedly, without addressing himself to anyone in particular: "A nasty business! Tolya has shot himself."

But nobody listened to him, they hardly even saw him or heard him as he stood there, dirty and soaked, with a ragged strip hanging from the knee of his trousers. "He hasn't a face, it's only an omelette," thought Firsov bitterly, and at the same instant an imaginary pencil raced over imaginary paper.

Dolomanova rose and moved to the window, but Mitka knelt on, oblivious, by the empty chair. Suddenly he noticed Panama, and, by a tremendous effort of will, staggered to his feet and faced him. Then they all realized that Mitka was in a state of collapse and gravely ill.

Mitka's illness took an irregular course; the doctors unanimously diagnosed typhus, and mentioned also heart trouble and overexhaustion, and the young doctor from the floor below expatiated at length on the heightened susceptibility to all kinds of virulent microbes of a nervously enfeebled organism. Bundyukova, however, defied all the pundits and insisted that it was "just nerves."

Zinka spent day and night by the sick man's bedside, although he did not recognize her; it filled her heart with joy to sit beside the man she had loved and lost forever. Dolomanova had not opposed the removal of the patient to Zinka's room, and Firsov had taken charge of the actual moving, Pigr also lending his assistance. He had not taken his eyes off Mitka's worn ash-gray face the whole way, but, all the same, he was useful, and hustled on the driver with such resounding oaths that in the end he had been addressed as "your honor." Pyotr Gorbidonich had also run to help when Mitka was carried out unconscious, and had clung lugubriously to the edge of the blanket.

Mitka was laid on his old iron bed, and was conscious neither of where he was nor of what his new imprisonment signified. Zinka warmed the pillow and the bedclothes and forbade her daughter to make a noise when she came in from school, although to Klavdya this was like being forbidden to breathe. She was only a young child, and realizing in her heart the pitiful uncertainty of her mother's life, she spent the whole evening sitting quietly in the corner. Then the night came, long and difficult, and with the morning the smell of medicine ate its way into the walls, and time took its normal course.

In the evenings, when his fever was at its height, Mitka used to open his eyes wide and stare up at the ceiling, though Zinka was obsessed with the fancy that it was his heart he was gazing into; when it was time for her to go out to sing, Bundyukova sat on by his bed, and a week passed in this way. No one knew the cause of Mitka's collapse, though people had connected it with Sanka's sudden disappearance and Donka's strange return four days later. The thieves' court seemed to have missed fire. Thanks to the ready tongue of the ubiquitous Pigr the rumor circulated among the thieves that Donka had rushed in on the fourth day and, with tears in his eyes, had cried again and again to Dolomanova, as he knelt before her: "Marusya, they wanted to kill me. . . ." The next day Donka disappeared from the capital, and not till a year later did he fall into the clutches of the Iron Hand at Harkov.

Vassily Vassilyevich, Panama the Fat, answered all questions with an embarrassed wave of the hand, and tried to exculpate himself by a confused rigmarole. There was not a trace of his old gaiety left in him. "I ran for all I was worth and fell down. . . . I fell and tore my pants," he repeated *ad nauseam*, glancing defiantly at his audience. All the same, Firsov succeeded, by a series of deft questions, in eliciting a more or less accurate account of what had happened, though, of course, there were great gaps that could not be filled in. It was an ugly story, many of whose intricacies were never to be unraveled; all that could be clearly established were the events that followed on Mitka's departure from the beer hall.

Outside in the street he had found Donka and Sanka waiting for him with Vassily Vassilyevich. They probably had all bundled into a taxi, and, on their way to the outlying parts of the city, called at Batashiha's mill to pick up Tolya. He came out to them slightly tipsy, but cheerful and noisy; his wedding with Batashiha had taken place the evening before. (They had not, it appeared, been betrothed in church, as Sanka had predicted, for it was Holy Week.) His convivial guffaws failed to cheer the oppressed spirits of the quartet. (At this point Firsov intro-

duced into his story various picturesque details. Through
the dead, deserted streets the motor raced—a gallant but
battered survivor from prerevolutionary days; in the closed
coupé a small glass vase for flowers still rattled noisily in
its socket. Tolya guffawed and stuck his cigarette butt
into it. The springs creaked and bounced. Outside the
windows the suburbs rose vaguely through the dusk.) A
policeman was standing before a cinema that streamed
with light. The chauffeur went faster than ever, and Tolya
bobbed up and down on the knees of his companions,
laughing uproariously at Panama's spicy stories. Donka
smoked, Sanka leaned back against the cushions with eyes
closed, and Mitka looked out through the window at the
fan-shaped spray that splashed from the puddles. All but
Tolya knew the object of the journey, and therefore all
were quiet. That was how it all happened, as far as it is
possible to tell.

The practical side had been entrusted to Panama; it
was to the traitor whom he was now carrying outside the
city that he had owed his last two arrests. Vassily Vassilyevich was furious and quivered with impatience. On
his orders the car stopped in the middle of a field, and all
except Tolya and Mitka stepped out. Mitka gave some
abrupt orders to Tolya, who seemed to resist, but Mitka
screamed at him, and the others caught the word "cockroach."

Here there is a gap in the story—why did Tolya obey
Mitka? A mere threat of death can, in the circumstances,
have had little weight with him.

Panama had reconnoitered the place of punishment
during the day. It was a claylike field, rough with hoar
frost and the rains of the spring. Here and there snow still
lay in the ditches. Sanka stumbled and Donka held him
fast. Not far away, by the railway lines, they saw the blue
flash of a semaphore, and in the distance, near a little
wood to the right, another light flared up and died down:
there was a row of bushes between the men and the
houses. Here they stopped . . . and it seemed to them
the most natural place in the world for their purposes.
The light of a trader's cottage shone again and winked at
them encouragingly.

This was the moment for Donka to make his escape, if

he had any inkling of the trap; the field was large, the night was dark, and the wind blew toward the chauffeur, who naturally knew nothing of the plot—but in a minute it was too late.

"Go with Tolya," said Vassily Vassilyevich hurriedly, giving Donka a push, and then, losing control of himself, he struck him.

"Stop! . . . Why are you hitting me?" cried Donka wildly, and stared at the hostile semicircle of men, who stood silently with their eyes turned away. It was then that he guessed everything.

"Don't scream or you'll get something else as well," said Panama without his usual delicacy. "What are your last wishes? Wine, cigarettes, chocolate?"

This was left out in Panama's story to Firsov; he hadn't even hinted to him that he had taken a little bag with him containing Donka's last meal.

"I demand leave to speak . . ." cried Donka breathlessly, pushing toward Tolya. "Comrades, you've been deceived. . . . Comrades, can you allow it that there should be injustice between us?"

At this moment Mitka, as it appears, stepped up to Donka and whispered a number in his ear, which, no doubt, made Donka tremble.

"You did it and you must pay for it. The leaders' council has decided. . . ."

"Yes, but it isn't true . . ." stammered the other, gazing like a hunted animal to every side, and measuring the night and the distance with his eyes. (Here we may quote Vassily Vassilyevich's confused account.)

". . . he began to wriggle about and creep around on his belly. 'Give me a flogging,' says he. 'I'll never do it again . . . even though I swear I never did it at all.' His face was the same color as his hair. 'He ought to have a proper hiding,' I thought, 'and then be let off. Look at him just, he's tumbling there like a piece of rotten wood!' But he began to curse and that made me wild. I gave a nod to Tolya to lead him away. He led him away; we waited. There was a shot . . . we waited, but nobody came. I ran to the wood and lit a match. Tolya lay there, and he had a hole in his forehead, that size! and he had a revolver in his hand. . . . There was just one bullet missing and Donka had clean vanished. I went back into the field, there was nobody there. I was in a terrible state, I ran . . . I fell and ran again. . . . Some people brought me back; I told them I was escaping from a thief, and to put the lid on the whole bloody business, I've torn my pants to pieces, as you see."

He said no more, and Firsov had no wish to catch him out in minor falsehoods. There, at the edge of the wood near Moscow, there yawned an abyss from which even his inquisitive soul drew back in horror.

"Supposing it wasn't Donka . . ." interjected Firsov gloomily.

"Nonsense—not possible!" exclaimed Panama, starting back in alarm.

WHILE all this was happening, Sanka had stood in the background without taking any part in the proceedings either by word or deed; it was as if he were not there. When Vassily Vassilyevich, alarmed by the delay, had run into the wood, Mitka looked back involuntarily at Sanka, and in spite of the darkness he saw a sight that surprised him. Sanka was waiting silently, his face covered with his hands, but his whole attitude as he stood there crushed with despair, and even his silence itself, was as eloquent as a cry from his heart. Then Mitka knew that he had only to look in Sanka's face to solve the ghastly riddle of the night.

"Don't touch me, master!" groaned Sanka, and Mitka, enraged at his resistance, peeled his fingers like husks from his face. Suddenly a wild craving for flight swept over Sanka. "Let's run away, master . . . it's all over now! We're even with him!" (for evidently he thought that Donka had been killed).

They ran over the damp, clinging earth, until rainbow rings circled before their eyes. Their hearts beat irregularly and their lungs labored painfully. Then they slowed down and stumbled on over ditches through bogs. They stopped on a rough road, along which the cart ruts wound like glistening black ribbons. Sanka seized Mitka by the sleeve and then let him go.

"How wet you are! . . ."

"It's just a shower: don't be frightened, Sanka, but tell me. Was it . . . you?"

Sanka recoiled as if he had been struck.

"Yes, it was . . . it was!" In his voice there was a ring of pride that now he could strike back at the man whom all these years he had called master. He struck his breast and laughed, laughed with that final shamelessness which neither oppression nor suffering nor death itself can cow. "For a whole month long I've been trying to put an end to you, master. But sometimes I hadn't the strength, sometimes I hadn't the chance."

"Swear," said Mitka, biting his lips.

"I swear to you by the dead man, master!" cried Sanka, and raised his hand to take the oath. "I've warned you time and again, master, and many a time I'd have brought it off if Donka hadn't stopped me." Mitka listened to Sanka's revelations in horror. "Do you know what you were to me? Do you remember how I stole for you? . . . You must remember it all, every kopek. . . ."

"I'm paying it off now," flung in Mitka abruptly.

"I've shed blood for you, I protected you, I served you, I loved you, but you didn't pay any attention. You swore at me and stole from me: you're—a thief! You were the only God I had: even at the front when you were drunk and I tied you up, I adored you, but now I'm through with you and it's not for the first time either—long ago I rebelled against you and wished you dead!" Sanka's whole body shook, he stamped in the mud and panted as he spat out the torrent of his rage. "Why did you bleed me of my last ten roubles, master? Was that your idea of a joke? Well, laugh away, I won't kill you for it. You can do anything with a man who loves you. It was as easy as falling off a log for you: you took my soul, master. I've given up crying for my poor bit of happiness and the cactus, master, but you mustn't play tricks with a heart that loves you, you mustn't rouse the devil in a man who was born for a quiet life. It's the quiet ones who are the devils, and you're simple, master. They've got the better of you, and they'll do it again. Don't believe in people's humbleness!" A cold shudder ran through Sanka and, when it reached his tongue, burst into a shower of burning words. "Lord, it was lucky for you you didn't drink my kvass! When you drink kvass like that you don't get sober in a hurry."

Sanka was romancing, there had been nothing in the

least suspicious about the kvass. When he had called back Mitka with the glass in his hand, he was sure that the master was trying to test his friendship and loyalty. No thought of hatred or betrayal had occurred to him, no shadow of misery or guilt had fallen upon his little bit of happiness—but now he believed in his deadly kvass and exulted in his rebellion.

"Well, do you want to settle up accounts?"

"Accounds—what accounts? Couldn't I fix you up behind a hedge and we'd be quits? I've loved you and I've killed you—and now nothing matters!"

"And yet I don't believe you, Alexander," said Mitka softly.

"You don't believe me? Here, have a sweet! . . ." He fumbled in his pockets, "Here's luck! It's from me. Don't be a coward, but eat it up."

Mitka looked searchingly into the darkness at the spot where he guessed Sanka's eyes to be, and took the sweet from its paper wrapping: the crumpled paper was instantly blown away by the wind into the dirt and darkness. He fingered the sweet and found that it was a thin disc of chocolate.

"All right, I'll eat it," said Mitka, bringing the sweet to his lips.

"Don't, it won't agree with you!" tittered Sanka, sitting down on the ground.

Mitka threw away the chocolate angrily and walked to the car (Sanka was amazed that in spite of their passionate conversation, Mitka had not forgotten in which direction the car was). The chauffeur was sleeping or pretending to sleep, and awoke with suspicious alacrity. The car began to throb and, leaping forward, plunged into the darkness and the night.

"Then it was you who gave the show away in the Pirman affair? And now you thought you could use Donka to blacken me, did you?"

Sanka said nothing. "Is your wife dead?"

The car climbed up a hill, clinging desperately to the moist earth with racing wheels.

"It's all over now, Dmitri Yegorich."

And so it went on till the streets began. Then they left the car and walked on together for a time.

"Master," Sanka patted Mitka gravely on the shoulder, "the sweet had nothing inside it, it was quite an ordinary one. I once brought Xenka the same kind to the hospital."

"Well?"

"It's odd how frightened you've become, master. One's only got to lift a finger and you take to your heels. You don't trust people, you think they're all rogues." He paused a moment. "This weather . . . is really like spring."

Mitka stood still and then said: "My advice to you is: get out! Get out and don't let me hear of you again. I'll blot out from my mind everything that ever happened between us, and for both our sakes we must never meet again. . . ."

Then he went away and, leaving Sanka at the crossroads, made his way to Dolomanova. The nearer he got to the house, the quicker he walked, and by the time he reached her door, he was almost running.

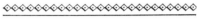

ZINKA gazed at Mitka's haggard brow, and searched in vain for her darling and her joy. Chikelyov hovered around inconspicuously, spinning his everlasting webs of fancy. The ingenious clockwork of life functioned as before.

One day Mitka opened his eyes and recognized Zinka; his face was quite bloodless. He gazed out for a moment from the depths of his unconsciousness and sank back into it again, for it was there that he found healing and peace.

Zinka's tenderness was uniform and comforting as the warmth of a radiator. Now all she felt for him was a mother's love. Firsov, who ran in twice to see her, exclaimed that her sleepless nights had made her more beautiful; there was an almost virginal softness and gentleness in her words and glances and movements—but he secretly noted she had begun to grow old.

"It's strange, Fyodor Fyodorich," she said, as she pulled at a branch of hothouse lilac that Firsov had brought her, "when we got to know each other first, I used to feel as if my soul were sealed up, and I couldn't break the seal. But now all the doors are wide open as on a holiday . . . there's a little wind blowing, and everything's lovely."

"That's the spring," sighed the writer, absorbed in his thoughts. The pavement was already dry on the sunny sides of the streets, and the young sun frolicked shyly among the tender clouds. But the moist earth was still black and cold, and there was a breath of dampness and decay, while through the night the bleak, wet wind swept across the roofs. When Firsov went away, Zinka made herself some tea and sat down to sew for the night. The doctors announced the approach of the crisis, yet no one came to share in her unpaid task. Only Chikelyov lay awake in the night and suffered, for he was in love.

When, through the chink in the door, Chikelyov announced the arrival of Dolomanova, he did so in such stentorian tones that Zinka started to her feet. It was in the middle of the night. Dolomanova came alone, without any escort, and Zinka led her to Mitka and offered her tea and jam. She asked no questions, for everything was clear without them. They sat placably the whole night, but more than once Dolomanova's inward agitation betrayed itself.

"Do you dye your hair?" she asked, playing with her teaspoon as if she longed to fling it at Zinka.

"I haven't washed it for a long time," explained Zinka simply, and refrained from saying that Mitka's illness had been the reason.

"If you go about without washing your hair, you'll find Mitka won't go on loving you," said her visitor bluntly.

"He doesn't love me . . . and never has. You're the only one he loves. I always see you together in my dreams."

"In dreams? . . . A great deal happens in dreams . . ." murmured Dolomanova skeptically, and stared at Zinka's nose, which was swollen: she had a cold. "You're stupid, Zinka."

"Stupid people are happy," smiled Zinka, "so I can't be so supid after all. But you're small, and so your heart's too near your head; that's why you are spiteful." (It needed Zinka to make a dwarf of Dolomanova.) "Spiteful people are strong. If they haven't enough happiness of their own, they grab at other people's and they're never satisfied—but if I had just a scrap of your happiness I'd be in heaven."

The night wore on and Mitka raved and tossed in his bed. The same nightmare always haunted his brain: a belfry he was trying to push through a window. "It won't go in, it'll break in two . . ." he whispered with parched lips, but then it all vanished, only to rise again and to press against the window of his consciousness again and again until his brain reeled.

"Perhaps he should be given some water," said Dolomanova, rising anxiously.

"No. . . . I'll just moisten his lips with a cloth," Zinka answered calmly, and stepped behind the screen. "He has flung the sheet on the floor," she said, sitting down at the table.

Suddenly Mitka screamed; both women got up, but the scream broke off abruptly.

"He's screaming!" said Dolomanova in alarm.

"He's having a bad dream . . . it's like that every night."

"What are you cutting out there?" asked Dolomanova after a short silence.

"A little dress for the child."

"But you've cut it too short."

"I'm going to put a border at the bottom."

Often the pauses in their conversation lasted half an hour. The clock ticked, the scissors clicked. Slowly the night dragged on.

"Why have you come, Marya Fyodorovna?"

"Are you jealous?"

"I could only be jealous of a woman I liked."

"Am I so disagreeable?"

"Your face is all right . . ." Zinka could not control herself any longer. "But you're a bad woman."

"That's because I know a great deal about Mitka, though I haven't lived with him."

"If you knew about him, you'd love him."

"When you get to know all about him, you'll stop loving him. I've not come to turn you against him—you're welcome to him, the trash!" The teaspoon twitched, as if it had come alive in her lean fingers. "He's got about as much heart as my spoon. You're an optimist if you think you're going to get much of a thrill out of it."

"Well, he's got some sort of a heart, even if it's made of steel, and you've got none. You're dried up and tormented for want of one, and you'll never be satisfied. Why do you stand there insulting a sick man? Go away and let him alone! Trash indeed!" Zinka leaned over the table and pressed Dolomanova's hand. "That night . . . the only night we had together that mattered . . . he had no idea. . . . You know what I mean."

"Yes, he's as hard as steel! A wheel will go on buzzing round in a machine till it snaps to smithereens—but you've got to meet pride with pride, Zinka. You think of him as a whipped puppy and love him, but Mitka's just a thief. You won't wash his sins away with tears. You've seen, I suppose, how they've been going on at him in the newspapers? A man like that needs to be kept under."

"Well, he's down all right. Look at him! What more do you want?" cried Zinka contemptuously. "Even children don't hit another child when he's down. . . ."

The night flowed on. Mitka tossed from side to side in his bed, and behind the door Chikelyov paced restlessly. When Zinka went into the kitchen to warm up some tea, she met him there nailing up the latest regulation of the house committee to the wall.

"How are things going?" he asked, and, throwing everything away, he ran to meet her.

"He's very feverish and miserable."

"What about giving him a drop of port wine," he whispered, and turned the water tap obligingly. "Port wine is very beneficial to sufferers. Last year, for instance . . ."

"Turn the tap off, Pyotr Gorbidonich," said Zinka listlessly.

"Oh, well, it was only a suggestion. I don't insist on it, of course. I only wanted to show a little attention. I'll even swear it . . . (although in general, please note, I'm against the taking of oaths) . . . I only make myself disagreeable so that people shan't eat me up: in reality I'm quiet and peaceable. I'm even willing to believe that he doesn't steal for any ordinary reason, and that there must be some secret hidden here as large as life. . . ."

"I don't understand what you're talking about. . . ."

"I'm suffering terribly. I'm quite alone now . . . I haven't got anyone to fight with even. I'm growing old, but I've still got my feelings. I admit I'm no devil, I don't even look like one . . . my hair's going gray and there's not much of it either—but we've the same tastes. The only difference between me and a demon is that he can fly. . . ."

He did his best to hold her interest, but she had already pushed past him. However, she shut the door again immediately and stood waiting outside. Dolomanova was moaning and sobbing and calling on Mitka with an inexpressible tenderness unknown to Zinka. A minute later Zinka opened the door again, but again from a feeling of delicacy refrained from entering.

"Everything will pass, believe me, Zinaida Petrovna . . ." stammered Chikelyov. He hung around her pathetically in his shirt sleeves. "It's all happened before, and after, too . . . but we pretend it is something new. . . . Sleep, that's the best thing against a sea of troubles. But I'll always be the same, everlastingly and unchangeably . . . everything suits my face—the soldier's tunic, the peasant's smock, jacket, and morning coat. I repeat —I'm unchangeable as the Almighty above . . . who, of course, does not exist, but is merely an invention of bourgeois dreamers. That's our life: we're the foundation stones. Rage against us as much as you like: the earth can support the weight of mankind. I'm unalterable because I can turn myself inside out, and there I am again like a new pin, and without a twinge of conscience! . . . Go and sin, Chikelyov will forgive everything and even find justifications for you himself! . . ."

Zinka went into the kitchen and listened meekly to Chickelyov's theories, his attempts and struggles to tackle life and get the better of it. The water for the tea had long been boiling. Suddenly she jumped up and ran out into the passage.

Dolomanova's skin coat was there no longer. Her visitor had gone away without saying good-by. Mitka lay there as before; his lifeless eyes, round as apples, were staring without consciousness at the ceiling. The crisis had passed.

MITKA's convalescence had begun, but the snow still swirled in the streets. Zinka had grown sad and heart-sick, for she felt the day approaching when she would lose him forever. A strange meekness and resignation had come over Mitka. He could walk about now, but he looked on men and things with incomprehensible surprise. He often played with Klavdya; she was the only human being with whom he talked, but what they talked about Zinka never managed to hear, for both of them were always mysteriously silent if a third person came into the room. Usually, though, they made bridges of blocks, and towed under them a little tin steamer from which the paint was peeling—a venerable toy which Chikelyov had given Klavdya when he was her "daddy."

One day Zinka's brother, Matvey, arrived. He and Mitka sat in a corner and had a long talk together, and Zinka felt out of it once more. She had expected quarreling and raised voices, but it ended in hearty handshakes on both sides.

"Well, that's good! That's splendid!" declared Matvey as he went away, rubbing his hands with satisfaction.

"Zinka," said Mitka a minute afterward, "your brother's an odd chap, but he's right . . . he's right, Zinka. But the point of it all is that I'm right, too. . . ."

During the last few days Mitka was quiet and strange; he sat the whole time by the window watching the drifting snow and looking across the roofs at a tiny blue patch of sky.

One day when Zinka returned from market, Mitka was

not to be found, and none of the other tenants could tell her where he had gone. She searched for a note, but he had left none, and so she sat down and cried—yet not wildly or desperately, for in her heart she had been prepared for everything. She ran out into the street in the twilight. In Dolomanova's doorway drunken old Pigr tried to block her path, but she swept past him like a wild beast robbed of her young.

Dolomanova had visitors, and there was a feeling of tension in the room. Someone was strumming a guitar and singing, and there was a smell of almond peel. When she saw Zinka, Dolomanova stepped out with her into the passage.

"Is he with you?" began Zinka excitedly. "You're welcome to him, only tell me   . . . is he alive?"

"Mitka isn't with me, I've got guests here. Won't you come in? I'm having a little celebration. Pigr has arrived with the news that my father cursed me before he died. What do you say to that?" She closed her eyes for a second. "I'm going to tell it to the guests in a minute: they don't know it yet. . . . Pigr, you don't know Zinka. You must make her acquaintance, she's a wonderful creature!"

"Pigr the first . . ." he began with a smirk, but Zinka had already rushed away.

She lit no light in her room till late in the evening. Suddenly in feverish haste she dragged out the top drawer of the chest of drawers, where she hid her money; six out of seventeen roubles were missing. The thief had not even left a note, and that showed that he intended to remain alive. Rejoiced at her loss, Zinka sat with closed eyes on the edge of the bed, struggling to prolong the last hour of the tempest in her soul. When it was time she dressed and went off to her work.

Nobody knew anything of Mitka's fate. No one saw him calling on Puchov ("I'm not saying good-by to you, Primus! I'll come again! In five years I'll come again. . . ." And with a last glance at Puchov's modest stock of iron oddments he left the workshop). No one met him at the station when he took his ticket for his long journey. His carriage was old and rickety, but warm with human breath and thick tobacco smoke. All who lay and sat there felt themselves united by their wayward, wandering destinies. When evening shrouded the window, the train started to move; past the window raced the twilight powdered with lights, then came fields and then a lilac-tinted, snow-swept stream, and then villages, and then night.

On an upper berth, in the din and the stifling air, Mitka drowsed, his boots under his head. It was the first time since his illness that he had slept so soundly. Through his dreams the phantoms of reality persisted, he saw the carriage and the people and the unending night behind the rattling window—but all as if it were far away. Nearby Nikolai Zavarihin sat on a berth and, with his legs dangling down, played a harmonica. Mitka opened his eyes, and from the opposite corner streamed the simple strains of the harmonica above the roar of the train.

His short sleep had freshened Mitka and made a new man of him, and slowly the weariness and satiety fell from his soul. He pulled on his boots and stepped onto the open platform between the carriages. The strong winter air clasped him about, and he had to cover his mouth with his hand to breathe more easily. All along the line snowy expanses stretched, sparkling with jets of ice in the track of the wind. The night dragged on. Mitka saw his own shadow in the great band of light that raced along with him, and his heart became glad. The shadow raced along beside the wheels, and leaped lightly across everything in its path, the bald summits of the snowdrifts, the piles of sleepers, and the hedge of switchman's cottage. As an answer to his own question Mitka said: "It isn't enough, still not nearly enough," and went back to his carriage.

Below him voices were speaking. "The forests are being cut down, and the *mouzhiks* are taking fright; there'll be less and less earth, when the tree roots are gone. Soon there'll only be enough earth to fill a nutshell when the last stump has rotted in the ground. . . ." Then another began: "Still, one must fall in with the spirit of the time." Was there any end to the chatter of *mouzhiks* in their long journey through the night!—Mitka was lulled to sleep by the murmur of the talk. The whole of the next day he lay in his berth, with an aching pain still in his heart—the wheels rolled on and on, steely and untiring.

A guild of carpenters, who were sitting below, treated him to sausage and tea from a sooty teapot. The little woods and bushes were beautiful in the evening light as they rushed past the window; and beautiful, too, was the roar of the train through the misty vacancy.

In the chill of morning, when the carriage was filled with loud peasant snoring, Mitka forced his way to the door, past hanging arms and legs. The train was approaching a country halt. The platform was empty except for a *mouzhik* with a lantern. Immediately behind the station building a thin, freshly planted wood began. Mitka jumped from the train while it was still in motion, and fell stumbling on his hands on the crackling, crushed snow. He got up and, stepping quickly, passed the platform. Soon he was in the wood, walking along a narrow snow-blown path, which lost itself in the dim yellow glow of the sunrise. The somber sky escorted him on his way through the wide plain of unknown fields. He covered a great distance on foot. The road took him up a hill, and then flung him down into a valley to lead him up again half an hour later to a wide, bare, snow-clad plateau. Here he stopped and looked around, as strangers from far away look when they are confronted by vast spaces. Birds twittered over his head. Mitka tore up a note he found in his pocket, stretched out his arm, and opened his fingers. There was a puff of wind and the scraps of paper rustled as the gusty spring wind carried them away.

Yes, it was spring, and the winds of March flowed over the ruffled snow. In this season of bad roads and flood and foul weather Mitka met with only two things he remembered—a spring in a wood (like an ageless heart that had beat for a thousand years), and a *mouzhik*.

"Hi, where are you from?" the *mouzhik* called out from far off, and stared at Mitka's new boots.

"I'm a stranger in these parts," Mitka shouted back, and wondered at the sound of the long-begotten phrase. Then he began to climb down the hill, breathless with the wind, and skidding on the frozen snow.

The rest—how Mitka came to the wood cutters and was first beaten and then kindly received; how he worked in their guild and surfeited on the food he earned with the heavy labor of tree felling; how he toughened and went into a factory and studied (the great days of study had come into the land), and how he won again the name he had lost—all that is outside the scope of this story.

He stepped into the forest, a new-born creature, and recognized his home. Tossing its mane like an untamed horse, which seeks its rider through the world, the sun rose over Russia.

LEONID LEONOV was born in 1899 in a suburb of Moscow. He was educated there in the culture of the old intelligentsia to which his self-educated father, a radical journalist and a poet, aspired to belong. In 1910, when his father was exiled to distant Archangel, the young Leonov accompanied him, and lived there until the period of the First World War. At the age of fifteen Leonov began publishing verse in his father's Archangel newspaper. His experience was expanded, subsequently, while he worked on a Red Army newspaper in the Crimea during the Civil War. His novella, *The End of a Petty Man*, and his first full-length novel, *The Badgers*, appeared in 1924, and was followed by *The Thief* in 1927.

THIS BOOK is set in Electra, a Linotype face designed by W. A. Dwiggins (1880–1956), who was responsible for so much that is good in contemporary book design. Electra cannot be classified as either modern or old-style. It is not based on any historical model, nor does it echo a particular period or style. It avoids the extreme contrast between thick and thin elements which marks most modern faces, and attempts to give a feeling of fluidity, power, and speed. This book was composed, printed, and bound by The Colonial Press Inc., Clinton, Massachusetts. The paper was manufactured by S. D. Warren Company, Boston. Cover design by DICK BOLAND.

Vintage Books